Praise for *Room for Love*

"Room for Love *is a delightful read for any woman searching for that proverbial room of one's own. With writing that glitters like the NYC skyline itself, it's a smart and sexy urban romp that'll have everyone calling Meyer the downtown Candace Bushnell."*

—Erin Torneo, coauthor of *The Bridal Wave: A Survival Guide to the Everyone-I-Know-Is-Getting-Married Years*

"Readers will be rooting for Jacquie as she bravely navigates the turbulent territories of love and real estate in NYC."

—Melissa Clark, author of *Swimming Upstream, Slowly*

"A funny and sexy debut with a delightful heroine and clever premise. Gives 'room for rent' a whole new meaning."

—Karen Mack, author of *Literacy and Longing in L.A.*

Room for Lo♥e

Room for Lo♥e

andrea meyer

st. martin's griffin ⚏ new york

This is a work of fiction. All of the characters, organizations, and events portrayed in this novel are either products of the author's imagination or are used fictitiously.

www.stmartins.com

Design by Ruth Lee-Mui

Library of Congress Cataloging-in-Publication Data

Meyer, Andrea.
    Room for love / Andrea Meyer.—1st ed.
        p. cm.
    ISBN-13: 978-0-312-37078-7
    ISBN-10: 0-312-37078-4
    1. New York (N.Y.)—Fiction. 2. Chick lit. I. Title.

PS3613.E898R66 2007
813'.6—dc22

                                                            2007017430

10 9 8 7 6 5 4 3

Acknowledgments

First and foremost, I would like to thank my amazing agent, Jennifer Gates, at Zachary, Shuster, Harmsworth Literary Agency—without whom this book would literally not exist—for having the vision to imagine this story and having faith in me and my ability to tell it. Thank you to my editors, Jennifer Weis and Hilary Rubin, at St. Martin's Press for your astute readings and Stefanie Lindskog for facilitating the publishing process.

I could not have done it without Hamida Bosmajian, Julie Merson, Kerry Eielson, Rachel Sussman, Kathleen Fleury, Victoria Rowan, and the talented writers of TK who read pages and chapters and drafts and never let anything slide.

I am forever indebted to La Muse Writers' and Artists' Retreat, the Writers Room, Aquiloni, and Sympathy for the Kettle for providing me with a quiet place to write; Faye Penn for assigning me the article that became the book; Ryan Smith for helping me sort out legal mumbo jumbo; K. J. Bowen for sharing the smoldering details; Shari Smiley for taking an interest in the book's future; the American Red Cross and that one hunky Thirteenth Street fireman who was willing to talk to me for the info; Mark Payne for making me look good; Jason Greenblum for making me look even better; and Liz Swados for once saying, "I want you to become a writer."

Heaps of deep gratitude to Grant Shaffer, Andy Bailey, Colin Weil, Lisa Rosman, Shane Evans, Christy Frantz, Kim Sandler, Kenny McCarthy, my furry friends Fred and Leon, the indieWIRE crew—Erin Torneo, Jacque Lynn Schiller, Brian Brooks, Eugene Hernandez, Anthony Kaufman, and Taylor Deupree—and all the ex-boyfriends, yoga teachers, East Village characters (canine and human), and Craig's List boys whose humor, insight, and assorted forays into my life inspired and spiced up these pages.

Deepest thanks to Courtney Gant, LJ Krizner, Dana Segal, Mae McCaw, Melissa McClure, Carolynn Carreño, Susan Shapiro, Debbie Stone, Leslie Oliver, Deborah Wakshull, Sara Berrisford, Kathryn Saffro, Maura Hurley, John Fanning, Eduard Espinos, the women of my NY book group, Haig Bosmajian, and the wonderful Herschorn family, for all kinds of kindness, advice, and support.

Most of all I want to thank my sister, Katya Meyer, for having the brilliant idea that became this book and for being my cheerleader even as I wrote a sister character much brattier than you are in real life; my wonderfully supportive parents, Miriam and Michael Meyer, for encouraging me never to stop learning and for giving so much; my grandparents, Helen and Wolf Herschorn, for your boundless love and inspiration; Jack and Maggie for the entertainment and unconditional cuddles; and so much love and appreciation to Harlan Bosmajian, my incredibly attentive, open-hearted, giving, sweet, gorgeous, perfect divine romantic partner, for gently kicking my butt (and getting me a Writers Room membership), for reading (and improving) draft after draft (even forty-eight hours before our wedding), and, above all, for loving me and making me smile even when I was at my most insane.

For Katya, who gave me the idea
that began my story, and
Harlan, who gave me
my happy ending

32-year-old woman seeks roommate for gorgeous, sunny, East Village one-bedroom. Ideal candidate: 30-something male. Considerate, honest, laid-back. Smart, funny, creative, financially stable, good in bed. Roommate must display a passion for movies, books, and food, must be able to handle his booze and ready for a serious relationship. Good with hands a plus. No vegetarians, commitment-phobes, or Republicans need reply. Dog lovers only. Above all, must make said 32-year-old female's heart race—wildly. Anyone fitting this description, call Jacquie. ASAP.

1

Hey. It's me. Would you *please* let me know if you're coming tonight?" I hang up with a clank and eye the corner of my computer screen. It's five o'clock. "Fuck!" I say more loudly than I'd intended, and everyone in the room audibly stops working and turns their head in my direction. "What?" I ask.

Steve, my perpetually tanned and smiling Zen Buddha boss who's sitting Indian-style in his Ikea desk chair that isn't big enough to accommodate this position, and Samantha, my blond Barbie-doll coworker who stopped blowing bubbles in her chocolate milk with a straw during my little outburst, return to their work. Then, as the atmosphere is gradually restored to its earlier, calmer state, Chester, our sweetly spastic intern, a gangly NYU film student with pubescent tufts of peach fuzz on his face and

Ronald McDonald hair, trips and drops the wooden crate of videotapes he's carrying around for no apparent reason. A collection of mediocre independent films that no one will ever see crashes to the ground, skidding and scattering all over the oddly shaped loft space we call our office, some cracking, others zipping across the scuffed yellow floorboards.

The place erupts, as Steve and I jump to help Chester pick up the tapes. Meeting me eye-to-eye over a saccharine tale of lesbian lawyers in love (shot on digital video for under fifty thousand dollars), Chester takes the opportunity to say, "What's *your* problem today, potty mouth?"

"I'm your boss. A little respect, please."

"Yeah, whatever. It's gotta be that dick."

"It's five o'clock and I still have no idea if he's coming to my birthday party."

At this point, Sam and Steve, apparently eavesdropping, plus Spencer, chiming in from the conference room at the other end of the office, join Chester in the familiar refrain: "Dump him!"

"Do it. Like Malkovich dumped Pfeiffer in *Dangerous Liaisons*, man," Chester says. "Brutal, final, balls in the nutcracker."

"Really, Jacquie," Sam says dryly, not even glancing up from her expertly shaped red nails, which she began filing while the rest of us were wrangling videotapes. "There's no point in prolonging the drama."

I'm used to this kind of treatment. Rolls right off me. And I'm sure as hell not giving in to their shameless peer pressure. This time, I revert to my oft-employed sixteen-year-old Valley Girl voice and reply, "Whatever, you guys!" before strutting out of the room, stomping my four-inch boot heels as I go. In the hallway, I slide down the wall, landing my butt on my heels and wishing I had a cigarette. A hand emerges through the cracked door, handing me one—and a lighter.

"Thanks, Chester."

I pull smoke into my starving lungs. I don't smoke, except

when I'm drunk or stressed out, and this moment would qualify as the latter. I stretch my legs across the narrow hall, settling in to consider my lot in life. It's not just that we're shipping the current issue of the magazine to the printer tomorrow with an alarming amount of work still undone. More urgent, I'm turning thirty-two today and I'm barely able to pay my rent (I mean mortgage; I'm not used to the change in status) *and* I'm still putting up with men who can't be bothered to attend my birthday party.

On any other birthday, I might have told myself not to worry—even thirty didn't faze me. I felt energetic, ambitious, full of hope, and I was in a serious relationship—but this one is momentous. When I was a kid in Los Angeles doing MASH charts with my friends—employing a precise science to determine if we would live in a Mansion, Apartment, Shack, or House and every other piece of information pertaining to our perfect future—everyone was praying to live in a mansion in Malibu, marry Rob Lowe, work as a movie star, drive a Porsche, and have three kids by the time they were twenty-five. Everyone except me. Even then, I knew I wanted more time to play solo and announced boldly that I would tie the proverbial knot at thirty-two. It seemed like a grown-up age, when my screen-diva career would be thriving and I'd be ready to stop dabbling with the Brat Pack and walk down the aisle with a lawyer or a surgeon or a truly talented hot actor—like Tom Cruise, for example—and settle down with him in the palatial estate in Malibu I had *earned*. I didn't even care when my friends protested that thirty-two was way too old to land a cute husband.

Somehow, through the years, when relationships ended and I'd feel that particular panic start to bite, something in the far reaches of my mind would soothe me, cooing, "It's all right, honey child, you're not even thirty-two yet!" Thirty-two became crystallized in my mind as the age when I was supposed to start acting like a responsible adult.

And here I am. Not only do I not have any husband prospects (or a mansion on the beach), I don't even have a proper boyfriend. In my mind, this birthday is the clock striking twelve and if I don't get my act together by midnight, I'll turn into a big, fat, pumpkin-faced loser who's doomed to sit alone in an attic wearing rags, stitching the hemline on some evil supermodel's Monique Lhuillier wedding gown, and picking ashes out of my hair. For me, being thirty-two and single means watching ring fingers (instead of people) walk down the street. It means scanning the wedding pages in *The New York Times* every Sunday, looking at nothing but the photos and the brides' ages, feeling validated by the ones who are older than me and humiliated by the ones lucky enough to find true love at a tender, young age.

"Look at this chick," I announced at brunch last Sunday with my best friend, Courtney, and my sister, Alicia. "Marrying her high school sweetheart. How quaint can you get? Here I am, well into my thirties, fifteen years of dating under my belt, and I haven't met a single guy I'd marry."

"You're just fine," said Courtney, whose advice I regard with some reverence, since she and her husband, Brad, are the only happily married people I know. "You're on your own unique path. Imagine if you'd married Philippe, for example." Philippe is my impossibly beautiful and adoring French ex-boyfriend, with whom I shacked up in a minuscule garret overlooking Paris for two years after college. When I decided to go to grad school in New York rather than continue to hustle for gigs teaching English to bored housewives and lecherous businessmen in France without working papers, he proposed.

"Marry you?" I'd responded incredulously. "I don't even know if I like you anymore." It was my cruelest moment, the memory of which still makes me wince. True, I'd been having doubts about him and France and my life choices in general, but I can't remember anymore why I felt compelled to brutally break the heart of the only man I ever considered worthy of my love. My usual pop-psychology explanation is I wasn't ready: I was too young to make that kind of commitment, so I convinced myself there was something wrong with him.

"I'm sure you could have been very happy with Philippe," Courtney went on. "But you never would have moved to New York or become a journalist." I could have lived with this assessment, but she went on. "You would have been married for, wow, seven, eight years to a darling French doctor and you'd probably have beautiful, bilingual kids. Maybe by now they'd be in school and you'd be writing a memoir about your life as an American mom in Paris, maybe in an office overlooking the sea at Philippe's family home in the South. But you wouldn't"—she bit her lip in concentration—"be so independent. You wouldn't be the strong, career-driven, New York woman that we all adore." I stared blankly at my friend, whom I wanted to throttle.

Alicia reached over and pried the Styles section out of my fist. "This couple?" she asked, indicating the smiling blond faces that had piqued my jealousy. "Look at him." We did: smarmy frat boy turned smarmy investment banker with a crooked smirk on his face. "They'll be divorced by the time she's thirty. He'll be sleeping with some bimbo he met at a conference in Miami. She'll take him for everything he's worth, driving him to drink and rehab and remorse. By the time he comes back begging, she'll have found herself, sunk his millions into a successful catering business, and started having sex with her twenty-two-year-old personal trainer named Ed."

We reassessed the photo.

"I sure am glad I didn't marry *my* high school boyfriend," I said.

"He's gay," said Alicia.

"Oh yeah." We returned our attention to our six-dollar chai lattes.

Even if I'm not regretful about my life so far, I do know it's time to give up the hopeless cases that always seems to provoke my passion, say adios to the ubiquitous commitment-phobes, and meet The Goddamn Guy already. When I say The Guy, I mean the one whose name I would tattoo across my tummy. I've had boyfriends, loads and loads of boyfriends. In fact, I calculated that I've spent ten solid years of my life in serious relationships—or some combination of serious relationships and tempestuous affairs that felt awfully serious at the time. All those years in and out of love, and it occurred to me the other day with a sharp gasp that there wasn't one man among them that I considered tummy-tattoo-worthy. I fall in love the way most people tumble into bed after an excruciating day: immediately, giddy with anticipation, semiconscious, every exhausted muscle releasing into fluffy relief. My frequent romps, as passionate and consuming as they can be, tend to burn bright and fizzle fast, and I'm way too smart to get a tattoo while my head is still spinning. My longer-lasting relationships, on the other hand, have been with guys like Philippe, who loved me but never inspired the kind of certainty in me that would justify putting a sharp needle to my soft, unsullied flesh, not to mention indelibly branding me his babe.

I'm currently doing the dance with Jake, a twenty-nine-year-old artist I met at a Halloween party thrown by the specialty division of a movie studio. He was there courtesy of his roommate, the assistant to the VP of publicity, dressed as the sexiest Bamm-Bamm Rubble ever, with his messy coffee-colored hair gelled into a hyperactive mane and a tight, furry, leopard-skin outfit that showed off sinewy thighs and toned biceps. He was flying on ecstasy. I was a devil in a skimpy red dress and fishnets, soaring as high as he was on the endless stream of multicolored martinis that kept arriving on cocktail waitresses' trays. After two minutes of enthusiastic chitchat, he said, "Do you want to make out?"

"Okay," I said.

And we did.

With all that vodka and ecstasy coursing through our veins, how could it be anything but bliss? By the time we were groping each other on my couch, I was enamored—of his unruly hair, his soft kisses, the way he gazed at me with intense, celery-green eyes and said, "God, I like you," so lovingly I almost believed it wasn't the ecstasy talking. We had sex on my kitchen floor, my head banging against my refrigerator as October rolled into November— and I was a goner. The next morning, while I was popping aspirin to relieve my bruised skull, he told me, "Damn, you're gorgeous," and "I'm obsessed with your body," and "I like you, but I'm not ready for a relationship." I chose not to listen to that last part, because I liked the first bit and because I wanted to keep having sex with him.

My wise little sister tells me that men are simple creatures. When they say something, they mean it. Like "I have to eat something right now" means feed the guy or he is going to break something. "I don't know how to be faithful" means the dickhead is about to sleep with his slutty ex-girlfriend who's been skulking about lately. And "I'm not ready for a relationship" really does mean "I'm not ready for a relationship."

Even before my postcoital first date with Jake, the warning signs were in place: the premature gush of passion, the fact that he didn't call for five days, forcing me to call and hang up on his voice mail twelve times (dialing *67 so my number wouldn't show up on his Caller ID) before he finally picked up, enthused and genuinely surprised that so much time had passed. He wanted to see me that night, which he did (his friend's band's gig, cheap burritos, sex in the cab on the way back to his place) and continued to do, but the rules had been established.

We spent one weekend lying around his apartment eating takeout and watching bad movies on cable and finally dragged ourselves to the grocery store on Sunday afternoon, because Jake had a sudden impulse to make spaghetti Bolognese. On the way there, I made a remark about how much I love it when a man cooks for me and he made one back about how I'd better find a boyfriend who cooks, then. I didn't respond. Instead, I went silent and his words sat in my gut festering like a bad oyster. Picking up a package of ground beef, Jake said, "You all right?" I nodded. But I'm like a kid when it comes to hiding my emotions. In the pasta aisle, he nudged my shoulder affectionately with his chin and asked, "Hey, what's up?"

I swallowed hard and pulled my eyes away from a box of multi-colored bow ties to look at him. "If this relationship isn't going anywhere . . ." I forced myself to look in his eyes. "Then what are we doing?"

He grinned and said, "Having fun, right? I mean, I'm having fun!" He said it with this big exclamation point at the end, as if there was nothing wrong with the sentiment, and then threw a couple of items into the cart. "Oops, forgot the parmesan." He planted a peck on my cheek and bounced off to find a hunk of cheese, as I stared into jars of marinara sauce with tears blurring my vision. But I can't quite bring myself to leave. That night, as he was kneeling over me, inching his way toward orgasm in the windowless Brooklyn cave he calls a bedroom, I stared up at him: his clenched jaw (framed lovingly by my feet), loose curls just barely grazing his broad shoulders, the tattoo that circles his left arm rhythmically tensing and untensing, impossibly slim hips, golden hair creeping down his tanned, hard stomach, which was glistening ever so lightly with sweat, and I thought, *You're a god. I will never be able to leave you.*

Tonight Jake has a meeting with a gallery owner who supposedly likes his bizarre paintings, and I should be supportive of his burgeoning artistic career, but the idea of going home solo on my thirty-second birthday makes me sick to my stomach.

I spy a beer can someone's left in the hallway and shake it to see if by chance it's still full, cold, and fizzy before ashing into it. I balance my cigarette on the top of the can and reach my body forward over my legs, letting my chest collapse onto my kneecaps. I close my eyes and take a few deep breaths, holding on to the bottom of my boots, gently nudging away anxious thoughts the way my yoga teacher advises. Then I lift my head from my knees, straighten my back up against the wall vertebra by vertebra, and breathe deeply in and out, before taking another hit of the cigarette.

Talking to Jake about his financial and professional woes helps take my mind off my own. The big news is I just bought an apartment. I never would have thought that I could afford it, but then my old yoga teacher, Tara, announced that she was moving to Vermont to open a studio and selling her magical mini-loft on East Eleventh Street between Avenues A and B, just as I was getting booted from my apartment. As one of those ethereal yoginis, Tara was determined to install "a loving soul" in her "space" rather than "gouging a stranger for a price dictated by an inflated real estate market. Om shanti" and sold it for substantially lower than the amount she would have gotten if she'd listed it with a Realtor. I'd been to Tara's for tea and, as corny as it might sound, it felt immediately like home. Sunlight spilled through four enormous, south-facing windows onto rough, slightly slanted hardwood floors. She had redone the kitchen, with a new stainless steel dishwasher and fridge and glass-fronted birch cabinets. The bedroom was spacious for the East Village—big enough to fit a queen-size bed and a dresser and still run and jump around a bit—and had a walk-in closet and two small, east-facing windows that filled the room with light in the morning. When I went to scrutinize the place before buying, a pigeon was warming two tiny eggs in the nest she had built outside on the sill and her eyes met mine without fear. I took it as a good omen. I knew I could transform this space into my personal room of one's own, that paragon of peace and self-examination that I had yearned for since first reading Virginia Woolf in college.

I thought I had found it once before. Days after my arrival in New York eight years ago, I landed an absurdly cheap railroad flat on East Tenth Street with hammered tin ceilings and charmingly warped floors. A friend of a friend was moving to an island in the

Caribbean and didn't want to give the place up, just in case she ever chose to relinquish tropical paradise for urban squalor. It was a great deal, but I always knew I could be booted if the landlord found out about me. A modicum of fear lived in the far reaches of my mind, a miniature tiger I could sense every time he sharpened his paranoid fangs on the inside of my skull. When my fears became reality, however, I was caught unawares. I was in the shower, actually, and heard pounding so loud I thought maybe my building was burning down. With the shower still running, I wrapped a towel around myself and made watery footprints to the door, only to find a burly marshal standing there. He forced the door open and said, "Put on some clothes, miss. You're being evicted."

I scrambled around still wearing a towel, trying to determine my next step. I threw my computer, underwear, DVDs of *Manhattan*, *Women on the Verge of a Nervous Breakdown*, *La Dolce Vita*, and the complete second season of *Sex and the City* into a bag, while calling Courtney, who said I could stay with her, and then dialed a lawyer I once slept with who informed me that the marshal wouldn't leave without me, so I had better go without a fight.

"Put on some clothes, miss," the marshal said again. I snarled and threw my toothbrush, condoms, and teddy bear into the bag.

In the movie version of my life, I won't have to change a thing.

That's when my stellar housing karma kicked in again: The very next day, Tara sent an e-mail around saying she was looking for someone to buy her place. My parents said it sounded like a good opportunity and agreed to loan me the $25,000 I needed for a down payment and co-sign to ensure my loan and co-op approval. And after crashing at Courtney and Brad's for a few weeks, I finally moved in three months ago. Between the mortgage, maintenance, taxes, and the lifetime repayment plan I set up with my parents, I pay about $1,400 a month. This is minimal by Manhattan standards, especially considering the amount of space I get for it, but hefty for a single, financially challenged editor of a struggling film magazine, especially one who has spent the last eight years subletting for $450 a month. Which reminds me. I drop my cigarette into the beer can, toss it into a nearby trash can, and hoist myself up off the floor.

Once reinstalled at my desk, I e-mail Clancy, an acquaintance who used to assign me movie blurbs at a trendy New York listings site, who just got a job at a new glossy women's mag, *Luscious*, editing articles about the hot new venereal disease and the most effective sexual position for firming the buttocks. Film might be my passion, but I'm more than willing to write about cellulite-reducing sneakers and celebrities' must-have beauty products if it enables me to pay my bills. I have been pitching Claney on average seven story ideas a week since she got the job, but so far nothing has stuck. I make my message quick and to the point.

Hey lady, any news on my last batch of story ideas? Can't wait to hear what you think! xx, Jacquie.

Then I Instant Message my sister about more pressing matters: **Jake is making me insane.**

I hear the "You've Got an Instant Message" jangle and Alicia's deceptively innocent-looking moniker, AliCat22, appears. **don't mention his name,** she writes. **makes me want 2 kick him *really* hard in the face.** Nice.

Ever since we were kids, I've had the impression that my little sister physically feels my pain. I remember being in the doctor's office with her when I was about seven and Alicia almost three. We were both on the examining table and the doctor informed us that I needed a shot. I was terrified, but held out my trembling arm like a brave little trooper. As the needle punctured my skin, I whimpered a bit, but it was Alicia whose face quivered before crumpling into tears. It's the stuff of family legend (and it was pretty damn adorable), but here is something to ponder: If she actually, physically, feels my pain, then isn't her drive to alleviate it a selfish act?

Alicia wants to rid me of the affliction that calls itself Jake and tells me so on a daily basis. But she doesn't really know Jake. Sure, he wears a perpetual Billy Idol snarl on his lips. Sure, he occasionally makes me cry. But he does have his good qualities. Alicia doesn't know, for example, that when we're alone he actually smiles sometimes. And it feels good to be the person capable of making an unsmiling man smile. One word of praise from me, and he goes from looking like a small-town scam artist—lips a-pout, eyes darting as if he's up to something—to resembling the dynamic front man for a boy band. Alicia also doesn't know that Jake sleeps holding on to me so tightly that I have to pry his hands off me to go to the bathroom at night. She doesn't know what I know about Jake: He is so unsure of himself that sometimes he lashes out at people more confident and grounded than he is, people like Alicia, an L.A.-born smart-ass, who scares the hell out of guys much tougher than Jake. I know that I shouldn't excuse Jake's behavior just because I understand it, but I do anyway. Because I do understand it. And because he's so cute I don't really want to live without him, or at least not until the weather warms up.

Jake's just getting me through winter, I write back.

jacquie, it's march

It feels like winter. It's two degrees out.

any excuse, get rid of the loser already. he's a drag a bimbo not smart enough 4 u an idiot illiterate MO-RON. looooze him

I'm not sure how to respond to this. I notice I'm inspecting a handful of my dark, wavy hair for split ends and biting off each one I locate, and flick myself with a rubber band around my wrist. It stings. My cognitive-behavioral ex-therapist taught me this trick to break my bad habits—like a well-conditioned little Pavlovian doggy. It occurs to me that I should flick myself every time I think about Jake.

He's not illiterate, I write after doodling a pretty-girl face with long lashes and collagen-injected lips on my notebook. **He**

e-mails, with some more or less forgivable spelling errors. And
he has a book. I got it for him. I picture the untouched copy of
On the Road still sitting on the arm of the couch where Jake was
lounging when I gave it to him and add, He won't read it.

can't meet mr. right if you're still sleeping with mr. retarded, she writes.

"Jacquie?" Steve's voice interrupts our scintillating correspondence. "Will I be able to look at the rest of the text by tonight?"

"I think so," I say, shuddering at our habit of leaving so many
details until the last minute. "Copy editor's dropping the last couple articles off before the end of the day. Do you want to give
them a read tonight and I'll go through them first thing in the
morning?"

"Sounds good."

I'm the managing editor of a small, cheeky New York film
magazine called *Flicks*. With a staff of five (plus Chester), we all
pretty much do everything—and too much of it. Steve gives final
approval on all text and art, but since he is also the one raising
money for our survival, he is too busy to get involved with details.
Samantha oversees photography and helps Steve with ad sales.
Trevor is our design god. And Spencer and I assign and edit
text. Everyone contributes articles, but because we're all swamped
and cannot afford the army of freelancers we would need to fill
our pages, Spencer and I end up writing most of the magazine as
well. Sweet Chester tackles everything the rest of us don't have
time for, and I get the honor of dealing with the remaining
muck—i.e., fact-checking, making sure we're on schedule, and
staying on top of the writers (who have slipped through Spencer's
fingers), photographers (who have slipped through Samantha's),
advertisers (who have slipped through Steve's), the printer, the
copy editor, and Trevor. It's a tough job, as they say, but somebody's got to do it. And because I absolutely, positively love it,
that person is me.

The May issue of the magazine—theme: "May Day, May Day:

Do Movies Just Suck?"—is shipping to the printer tomorrow, which means that all the art and articles have to be as close to print-perfect as possible.

"Hey, Sam?" I glance over my shoulder at the desk behind me. "Have you finished reading the text?"

"Yes I have," she says, interrupting the hushed conversation she's having on the phone. "I've been through it twice now. What about you, Mademoiselle Managing Editor? Gotten much work done *aujourd'hui*?" The way she peppers her sentences with Franglais makes the hair on my arms stand up in protest. Sam puts down the phone, wheels her chair swiftly over to me, and presses her lips together in what is supposed to resemble a polite smile, before aiming a crisp stack of marked-up computer print-outs at my throat and wheeling back to her desk.

She picks up the phone and launches back into her hushed tones. At five feet tall, my twenty-seven-year-old coworker is a flawless, fairy-tale creature with azure eyes, a miniature Victoria's Secret–model figure, and straight blond hair that falls to her waist. I'd envy her if she didn't have a smug sense of superiority to match her looks. Samantha has one other object of envy: the ridiculously low price she pays to share a dream duplex in Chelsea with a handsome filmmaker-slash-trust-fund-baby, who hit it big when Sony Pictures Classics bought his independent thriller after a protracted Toronto Film Festival bidding war. His parents bought him the multilevel two-bedroom as a film school graduation present—and he charges Sam next to nothing to rent the spare bedroom. In New York, nobody has enough space, and everyone obsesses about real estate and dreams about pulling off that kind of coup.

The article on top of the pile is Spencer's interview with the semi-talented squirt the press at the Sundance Film Festival just declared "The Next Big Thing." His directorial debut is hitting screens in two months, and Spencer's exploring the who-gives-a-shit? angle. Halfway through his second paragraph, in which he compares the experience of watching the film to eating rubbery eggs that have been sitting on the counter at Denny's attracting flies for an hour, I hear AliCat22 summoning me.

seeing another apt today

Thank the LORD ALMIGHTY, I type back.

Alicia's apartment search is not going fast enough. My sister moved to New York from L.A. a month and a half ago, following a midlife crisis at age twenty-eight. She announced that producing commercials was a useless occupation that no longer fed her soul; quit her job; moved out of her cozy bungalow in Venice; dumped her cat with our parents (like a restless teenage mom who isn't ready to be saddled with a squawking kid); and came to New York to crash on half of her big sister's brand-new bed in her big sister's brand-new apartment. I love my sister, but after six weeks of tunneling through her mess to reach my closet and sleeping with a pillow on my head to block out her endless inter-time-zone chattering and late-night TV addiction, I asked her (very nicely) to please find a room of *her* own, and she has been searching ever since.

hate hate hate, can't bear 2 c another $1400 hole

You'll find something, they're not all that bad.

yesterday saw 4 places, one on the scariest blk in Bklyn, Bed Stuy I think? rm the size of yer toilet, guy wanted $1000! he wuz cute tho ☺

Princess has yet to find a place in which she would deign to rest her more-than-a-little-demanding bones. However, her search is yielding unexpected perks: She met an Italian chef who invited her for a home-cooked meal; a wily jack-of-all-trades and the self-proclaimed mayor of Williamsburg, who promised to introduce her to the best bars in "the 'Burg" (as those in the know call the hip Brooklyn 'hood); and an actor so good-looking she became frazzled just breathing the same air as him. They fondled each other in front of his TV set and decided it would be best if she didn't move in.

going out w/the actor tomorrow. nervous. might throw up.

Stop puking and find an apt please.

chill

Hey, are you at my place?

ya

Will you bundle up the newspapers and dump them in the recycle bin? Trash goes tomorrow.

sorry, out the door. late for spinning

"Hey, Jacquie?" I turn around to face Samantha. Still gabbing on the phone and examining her nails, she doesn't even look up. "Have you gotten the Cate Blanchett piece in yet?" Samantha sometimes surprises me. She can sit there looking emphatically blond, gossiping with her friends all day long, and at the same time search photo archives online for just the right glamour shot of some British starlet, then out of the blue throw out something like, "Have you gotten the Cate Blanchett piece in yet?" I completely forgot that my cover story is running late and the copy editor saw it for the first time only this morning.

"Where the hell is Stella?" I ask no one in particular. "She was supposed to bring that and a couple of other pieces over by six-thirty. It's six-thirty."

Alicia IM's again: i have a story idea 4 u, how looking for an apt's a good way 2 meet guys. 3 more called today, one sounded cute. u shld try it

I dial Stella, the copy editor's, number, and type: I'm not looking for an apartment.

so fake it

Stella picks up and I say, "Hey, where are you?"

"In front of the building in two minutes," she says. "Come let me in."

I check my e-mail again. A message from Clancy says, Sorry babe. Ideas won't fly. V. picky here. Editorial mtg tomorrow a.m. if you want to try again.

I groan and leave my seat in a huff to buzz Stella into the

building and wait by the elevator so she can physically deposit the precious folder of text into my hands. When the elevator arrives, Courtney gets out as well. My best friend since college, who's taking me out for pre-fête dinner, is in classically Courtney party attire—that is an outfit that only Courtney can get away with: a flowing red skirt she nabbed for next to nothing at a Catherine Malandrino sample sale, a thrift-shop tight yellow shirt with a bright, multicolored flower pattern all over it, unbuttoned to reveal a lacy peach bra, red patent-leather boots, a big pink plastic flower in her hair, and a short fake-fur coat from H&M that I covet. It is the kind of outfit a classroom full of sixteen-year-olds would regard with great admiration, which is only one reason she's the most popular teacher at the ritzy Brooklyn private school where she teaches art. A guy walking down the hall lets his eyes wander from the top of her silky, black bob to the pointy toes of her boots, until she catches him staring and turns the color of sliced watermelon before dropping her eyes anxiously to her cherry-red fingernails.

"Love the flower," I tell her. She grins a toothy grin that turns her eyes into green slivers and kisses both my cheeks. We walk back into the office.

"Hey, Jacquie?"

I look back at her over my shoulder. "I brought the champagne," she says.

What champagne? I think as she pulls a Veuve Clicquot bottle out of her bag.

And on cue everyone starts singing. I spin around to see the staff beaming around a big, pink birthday cake with my name and seven candles on it. Courtney hugs me and says, "Happy birthday, old lady. You look stellar for your age." Courtney is exactly five months younger than me, and has been reminding me of that fact since she and the rest of my freshman-year dorm floor kidnapped me on my eighteenth birthday and made me drink upside-down margarita shots and sing Prince songs in a fountain until I passed out in the arms of the arrogant frat boy I obsessed about for the rest of the semester.

We hold up plastic cups of bubbly, and Steve makes the toast. "Here's to Jacquie's annual twenty-seventh birthday! Last year's was a blast and the one before that, but I have a feeling that this will be your best twenty-seventh birthday yet." While we're indulging in our first cocktail of the day and shoveling gooey chocolate cake into our faces, Jake finally calls.

"You coming?" I say, trying not to sound too anxious.

"I'm gonna try. It depends on this guy, you know? We're meeting at the gallery at eight and if he wants to get drinks after, I gotta go, you know? This could be major, you know?"

"Yeah, I know," I say, biting off a split end, snapping my rubber band, and willing myself not to say anything needy. "I've got a cuter date anyway."

"Use a condom."

"Jake, I hate it when you say that shit."

"I'm kidding. Jesus Christ."

"You're really funny. I'm grabbing food with Courtney before the bar."

"Give her a big sloppy one for me."

I cringe again.

"Please try to come. It's my birthday." I catch Courtney's pitying glance out of the corner of my eye, turn my back to her, and whisper into the phone, "I really want you there."

"Okay, okay, I'll be there, but it might be late." For a minute, my heart chokes me as it tries to jump out of my mouth. Then, as quickly as it arose, my elation passes. Why should the news that the guy I'm sleeping with is coming to my birthday party elicit such palpable joy? I worry for a minute that I am heading for emotional devastation—"But I told you I wasn't ready for a relationship," he will say—but suppress the thought.

"All right, I'll see you later." I hang up and look over at Courtney, who's doing a spacey hippie dance, eyes closed, hands undulating like slow-motion butterflies above her head. It occurs to me that she might be stoned. Suddenly she drops her arms, faces me, and says, "Happy birthday lovely lovely lovely lovely—"

"Jacquie!" Samantha interrupts, before I find out just how many *lovely*s I deserve. "Courtney! *S'il vous plaît*, listen up. I have an announcement to make." Sam's cheeks are flushed with champagne and her smile is so wide it might crack her champagne-flushed cheeks. Chester has put on a Madonna CD and is dancing on Spencer's desk and Spencer is yelling at him to get down. Stella is showing Steve the last few articles for the issue.

"You guys!" Sam shouts. "Chester! Be quiet!"

Down from Spencer's desk, our disobedient intern saunters over and asks me if I want another piece of cake. I mime barfing violently and point at Sam. "Chester, please listen," she scolds, as if he were six. Then she marches over to the stereo on a mission and shuts it off with a petite stomp of her designer Pumas. "Listen. Everybody!"

We all stand at attention. "So guess what?" She pauses theatrically and we take the opportunity to fill our glasses again. Chester bumps my desk and spills my champagne. I jump up and we both grab paper towels to wipe it up.

"Sorry," he says to Sam, hands full of wet napkin.

"Out with it, Samantha," Spencer suggests.

"Okay, fine. You know Charlie? My . . . my, uh . . ." She claws the air with her middle and forefingers to form quotation marks. "Roommate?"

"You mean your roommate Charlie with the long lashes and luscious lips?" Steve asks. We all chuckle.

"Yes," beams Sam. "Charlie with the Paul Newman baby blues and James Dean *je ne sais quoi*, Charlie with the darling petite *chambre de bonne* that he charged me suspiciously little for all these months." She pauses for emphasis. "Well, we're in love!"

The room goes silent. "That's right," she continues, bouncing up and down, as if she is about to make an attempt at springing up to punch a hole in the ceiling with her head. "*C'est vrai!* Gorgeous, sweet, *wonderful* Charlie, who hasn't charged me a cent since *I moved into his room a month ago*, asked me to marry him! *This summer!* Charlie *loves me*. He gave me this!" She turns around and fumbles in her pocket for a second before turning dramatically to display a diamond on the ring finger of her left hand that must be at least two carats, surrounded by baby sapphires. It is huge. Beaming but solemn, she adds, "It's the ring his grandfather gave his grandmother."

I plunk down in my chair, stunned. Everyone else flocks around Samantha to congratulate her and check out the rock. Another bottle of champagne pops.

"This is so *Goodbye Girl!*" Chester swoons. "Roommates doing the wild thing with roommates." Sam giggles in giddy response.

I stare at my disorganized desk and sip the warm champagne they brought for my birthday from a plastic cup. Only Courtney refrains from the ooing and aahing to hang back and place a comforting hand on my back. This is so unfair. Sam doesn't have boyfriends; she doesn't date so much as collect admirers who swarm around her as she flicks them away like so many insects. And now she answers a random ad for a room in *The Village Voice*, and she's engaged? I suddenly feel competitive.

"Don't take it too hard," Courtney says. "He'll realize how annoying she is eventually and call the whole thing off." It's not like Courtney to make a joke at someone else's expense, so I force a smile at her attempt to cheer me up.

Someone turns the music back on, and everybody starts dancing around the office to "Everybody." Courtney forgets about me and resumes her hippie dance. My desk is a mess, and I feel like I have to get out of here fast.

I hear the IM sound from my computer. Apparently AliCat has time for one last comment, but not enough to take the trash out. The screen says:

I'm not looking for an apartment.

so fake it

And then the latest: honestly it's a good way to meet guys,
easy 2 screen 4 losers, u c their gross kitchen, sweaty socks,
pix of chix. one hottsy wuz in his boxers. NICE PECS

Yeah, I think, *that is a great idea for a story.* I sit up straight
in my seat and, typing so hard that my fingertips throb, e-mail
Clancy a pitch, subject heading: "Catch!"

Hey Clancy, I write. I just came up with a GREAT story idea!
It's about looking for a roommate as a great new way to meet
guys. My sister's apartment hunting right now and she's got a
date EVERY NIGHT! This system is better than the Internet, because a guy's home doesn't lie. You get right in there, see if
he's a neat freak or a slob, check out his books, his music, find
out if he waters his plants, slings jockstraps on the living room
floor or has pictures of his mother—or some chick—on his
nightstand. You cut right through the crap, get to know who
this guy really is. You're allowed to ask him anything you want,
because he thinks you're going to be living together. It's more
immediate and intensive than Internet dating, the personals,
trolling the bars . . . It's an untapped market. The dating
scheme of the moment. What do you think? Talk soon! Jacquie.

Pretty damn satisfied with myself, I hit Send and check my Instant Messages one last time.

Alicia's last remark reads, dude, write an article and pretend
ur looking for a room to rent. i have a feeling. u'll meet your
husband.

Looking for roomies!!! Two small bdrms avail in basement of sweeeet artist loft/gallery/ workshop/recording studio/party space on the southside of Williamsburg, Brooklyn, the best neighberhood in Nueva York! (The Burg ROCKS) Share livingroom, kitchen, ect. with artist/musician/party promoter/ mellow dude. Guys, girls, your all welcome. Get ready to chill out, hang. Know what I'm sayin? Mnth2mnth OK. Call me. JAKE

2

*O*n our way to the bar where we're celebrating, Courtney and I stop by my apartment to do a ritual she devised for my birthday. Courtney is big on rituals—and astrology and homeopathy and green, leafy vegetables and howling at the full moon. When we reach the top of my four flights of stairs and walk through the front door—after dumping our coats on the floor, since I don't own a coat rack and the closet is still packed with floor-to-ceiling cardboard boxes, even though I have been here for three months—Court goes into the kitchen to assemble the necessary paraphernalia and I run for the loo. We had too much sake and beer with our excessive sushi dinner. When I hit the light switch, the bulb over the medicine cabinet sparks, like it does every time the woman downstairs turns on her blow-dryer or vacuum cleaner, and makes me scream. I have to remember to do something about that. I close the medicine cabinet, which Alicia left open, toss her sweats and bra into the hamper, and scoop up the pile of makeup that is strewn on the counter and shove it into a drawer, trying not to get overwhelmed by the sight of the two neglected gallons of pink paint, brushes, rollers, and drop cloths glaring accusingly at me from the corner of the room.

As much as I love my apartment, becoming a home owner as a single girl has its drawbacks. In addition to the bathroom, which needs a paint job (Court and I did the living room when I first moved in), there are floors to refinish and shelves to build or buy to house my millions of books that are still in boxes. Also, I had a brainstorm that the kitchen needed an unusual backsplash over the counter and bought a ton of metallic mosaic tiles I fell in love with at a going-out-of-business sale, and now they are sitting dejected on my kitchen floor along with more cardboard boxes. I don't have curtains on my bedroom window yet, so in the meantime I duct-taped a towel to the molding above it. An annoying living room window will not stay shut. There is a lot of renovating and personalizing left to do, and not only are my credit cards maxed out, but I'm irritated with the strapping, selfless, handy boyfriend I don't have who would be dying to build me shelves and hang my pictures and fix my window and hold my hand on daily Kmart runs.

Each time I'm sweating my way back from Bed Bath & Beyond with bags full of shower curtain, stepladder, ironing board, and plunger-type stuff, I curse the guy I haven't met yet who should be helping me lug it all. The other day I was at the hardware store on First Avenue, which I love because the guys who work there are so helpful and the owner has a big, friendly white mutt named Buster (after Buster Keaton) who lounges by the door. When I first moved to the neighborhood eight years ago, I was a disaster; I didn't even own a hammer. After I had borrowed about sixteen basic household tools from the grumpy British bald guy who lived next door to me, he directed me to the hardware store, where the owner, a handsome Irishman in his sixties with a twinkle in his eye, set me up with everything I'd ever need in a toolbox: hammer, nails, screwdriver, screws, adjustable wrench, putty knife, spackle, awl, pliers, tape measure, utility knife, and paintbrushes, all neatly arranged in a bright red box, plus a plunger, turpentine, and baby wipes, which he said always seem to come in handy. I ran around, eyes aflame, bouncing on my toes, squealing for joy with each step I took toward being a functional adult with my own apartment. Sweet Mr. Connelly must have thought I was a lunatic, but he acted like I was the nicest girl in the world.

So, the other day I was in there getting a box of nails to hang pictures and the two buckets of Rosé Sorbet paint that will eventually coat the bathroom walls, and I just about lost it. A cranky old man bumped into me, causing me to lurch forward and drop the box of nails, and they scattered everywhere. I was so flustered and tired already and there were so many nails spread so far, I burst into tears. Mr. Connelly's cute son who runs the place since his dad died about six months ago—broad shoulders, strawberry-blond hair, lumberjack attire, the Connelly twinkle—rushed over to sweep them up.

"Don't worry, it's not a big deal," he said. "Hey, sit down here—" He patted an upside-down milk crate on the floor by the register. "I'll go get you another box." He smiled at me and his pale, freckled cheeks turned geranium pink.

"Okay," I croaked. When he came back, I whined to him about how it wasn't right that I had to fix up my whole apartment by myself; that my sister was staying with me, but she has the eeriest ability to be running late for an apartment visit or a Pilates class every time I ask her to unpack a box or buy toilet paper. And that I'm dating a guy who is useless: He prides himself on being a good handyman, but in his current I'm-not-your-boyfriend phase he likes to remind me on a regular basis that he should not have to do boyfriend duty. I realized I was getting a bit too personal and stood up.

"My girlfriend's bad about that stuff, too," the cute hardware-store guy said, his cheeks turning pink again. I'd seen him in the shop with a girl a bunch of times, one of those naturally pretty hippie waifs who wears size-2 Urban Outfitters and no makeup. "You can leave the stuff here and I'll drop it off at your place when I get off," he said.

"No, that's really nice of you, but I'll be all right," I told him, touched by the offer.

Before leaving, I turned back.

"Hey, I've been meaning to tell you. I was so sorry to hear about your dad," I said, my cheeks warming at the unexpected intimacy, which I wasn't sure was appropriate. "I guess I haven't seen you much since then, but I wanted to say something."

"It was awful," he said. "Caught us all by surprise."

"I really liked him," I said. "So much." He smiled, but looked sad.

"Well, I'd better go," I said, backing right into Buster. "Excuse me, sweetness," I said, petting the dog and waving awkwardly to his owner at the same time.

I walked out onto First Avenue, bulging bags and paint cans banging against my shins, wondering why everyone in the world is nicer to me than my boyfriend. It's clear to me that Jake is not the guy who will someday move into my new apartment and wonder with me if it would be fun to squeeze a crib into our small bedroom or more logical to sell the place and buy more space in Brooklyn or Queens. Sometimes I worry that I jinxed myself by buying an apartment before I had someone to share it with. Then I try to convince myself that I've laid the foundation, you know: "If you clean it up, paint it, and make it cozy, he will come," *Field of Dreams*-style. This space could accommodate a couple, I tell myself, and it will. I'm not doomed to live alone forever. It just feels that way sometimes.

Checking out my uniform—jeans, black tank top, hoodie, and boots—in the full-length mirror on the back of the bathroom door, I announce to Courtney, "I'm putting on a party dress." She sprints for my closet. Courtney lives for the opportunity to go through my clothes, either to help me choose an outfit or threaten to burn one. Last year for spring cleaning, we made a pot of stinky tea Courtney swears is a wonder cleanser for toxic livers like mine, and she watched me try on every item of clothing I owned. She made me get rid of everything gray or brown ("You have pale skin and freckles. Neutral colors wash out your natural beauty and light"), unfashionable ("It reminds me of third-season *90210*"), or inappropriate ("You're a woman in your thirties and that getup shows six inches of thigh and three of midriff"). She also completely reorganized my closet and drawers, without my asking. She's a Virgo—and a goddess.

"Something low cut," I shout from the bathroom, where I'm scrutinizing the lines beginning to appear under my eyes. When I was in my teens, my skin was as smooth as heavy cream with a smattering of faint freckles across it and in the sun it would pinken, crackle, and peel. People used to say with my light skin and dark tangle of hair, I could be an Irish barmaid or, on good days, an Italian model. Beige crescents have always cradled my eyes, my beauty bête noire since I was old enough to grasp the concept of physical imperfection. When I first discovered my mother's makeup at eight or nine, I smeared creamy white eye shadow over my dark circles and was transfixed by the transformation. Nowadays, I no longer burn in the sun and my dermatologist says I'm a perfect candidate for chemical peels. I run a finger over the wiggly creases that have settled permanently under my eyes, in spite of heavy lotion day and night, and wonder if guys in their twenties still find me attractive. I remember with relief that Jake is twenty-nine.

"There's no saving my face," I call out to Courtney. "I at least need my boobs to look good."

Courtney bursts breathlessly in without knocking, holding two dresses. I grab a purple Diane von Furstenberg number with a swooping neckline and ruching down both sides, and squeeze myself into it. I study myself in the mirror, grab handfuls of my tummy fat, and decide I look like a pastier Sophia Loren on steroids.

"The red one," I yell into the living room, where Courtney is lighting incense and digging through drawers for candles. As she flings the dress at me, the phone rings. I check Caller ID and instinctively roll my eyes: my mom.

"Hey, I can't talk," I tell her. "I'm late to my party." I struggle to get the polka-dotted fabric over my womanly hips, but it's so tight it actually hides most of my bulges.

"I just called to wish you a happy birthday, dear," she says. She already sent a card saying to buy myself a spring outfit on her.

"Thanks," I say, walking down the short hallway into the living room to show Court the dress. She gives it the thumbs-up. "And thanks so much for the gift."

"Is that *boy* coming to your party?" my mom asks. She sounds like she's referring to a disease that could make my ears fall off.

"Jake? Yes, he's coming," I say, puckering my lips at my reflection in the living room window.

"You know, Jacquie, what they say: Can't find Mr. Right—"

"Yeah, yeah, Mr. Retarded," I say, making the hand sign for "chatterbox" at Courtney.

"What?" my mom asks.

"Nothing."

"Let me put your father on," she says, handing over the phone.

"Daddy!" I say, sitting down on my desk chair to savor the one conversation I'll probably have with my dad for the next three months.

"Happy birthday, baby," he says.

"Thanks, thanks so much. What are you guys doing tonight?"

"Your mother's making dinner and I have blue books to grade."

"On what?"

"It's for my first-year survey course on Western political thought. They will be awful."

"It'll be a long night," I say.

He laughs. "Yes."

"Look, I really have to go. I'm so sorry, but we're late for this party, and I'm the guest of honor. Can we talk soon?"

"Yes, baby," he says. "Have fun."

Courtney has dimmed the lights—they're all on dimmers, one of my apartment's many attributes—and lit three candles that are neatly placed on a tray on the floor. One of them she apparently brought with her from home, because it's covered in glitter, animal stickers, and magazine pictures of happy things she hopes will come into my life: babies, kittens, sunny beaches, yachts, kisses shared by a pretty girl and a tall, hunky guy. I already have one similar candle creation à la Courtney by my bed and another on the edge of the bath. She makes them with her students. Courtney kneels with a pad of paper and a pen in her hands. "All right, beautiful thirty-two-year-old Aries woman, make three wishes."

I sit cross-legged in front of her. "Okay. I want to find a really well-paid writing gig. . . ."

"Say it in the present tense," she says.

I kick myself for forgetting the first rule of creative visualization. "Okay, I *am finding* a freelance writing job that I love that will supplement my income so I'm not killing myself to pay my bills every month."

"Keep it positive, Jacq," Courtney corrects me. "And be as specific as possible. You're more likely to get what you want if you can define it."

"Sorry, right. Okay, I am finding a regular writing gig for a high-paying, glossy magazine, that I love doing and that will provide me with enough extra income to keep me living the lifestyle that I'm accustomed to." I smile, all proud, and concentrate on my next wish. "Okay, I'm finishing fixing up my apartment."

"Specific," Courtney says.

"I am painting the bathroom and putting up the kitchen tiles and refinishing the floors and buying curtains and hiring some-

one to build shelves." I pause to figure out if I've forgotten anything. "And I'm getting rid of Alicia." Courtney laughs. "Seriously,
I'm transforming this apartment into my vision of the beautiful,
peaceful home I know it can become, one that can be my sanctu-
ary in the big, noisy city and where maybe I can even settle down
and build a life with someone."

"One more."

I blush, struggling to find the right words. "I am marrying and   **29**
having babies with a man who is totally gorgeous, with beautiful
lips and eyes and broad shoulders and a thin waist, who's really
smart, brilliantly witty, who appreciates Godard, but maybe secretly likes Truffaut better, oh and who worships Wong Kar-Wai
and Bergman and Fellini as much as I do, but I guess it would be
okay if he had different taste, like he's a big Bresson or Kubrick or
Tarkovsky freak, I mean it would give us something to talk about,
but he has to like Almodóvar films and David Lynch films and he
absolutely has to like *Moulin Rouge*! And, oh, I'd love it if he's
lived abroad—no, wait, he's from another country! Italy or France
or Brazil or Australia, maybe, so he's got family there and a house
in, like, Positano or the Cap d'Antibes, where we can spend summers, and who loves dogs, God, who has a dog. I guess he should
have money; hell, I am describing my perfect guy, after all!"

"Okay, slow down, love. That's great, good details. But is it really necessary to be with someone with a passion for French
movies? Think hard and list the qualities that are actually most
important in your perfect divine romantic partner. That's who
you're looking for, after all. For example, I think it's time you
found someone attentive. I think that's an important one for you,
and openhearted. I've seen you with too many self-involved men
whose hearts are closed."

"Right." I close my eyes, take a deep breath, and start again.
"Okay, I'm meeting and falling in love with a man who is attentive
and openhearted." I think about Jake and all that's been missing in
our relationship. "A man who is giving and sweet—sweet is so

underrated—intelligent, financially stable, confident, firmly established in an interesting, creative career, who has, um, good taste in movies and books. God, I know it's superficial, but I need to be really attracted to a guy. Without chemistry, it'll never work."

"That's all right, you can say that if it's something that matters to you. Don't be embarrassed, just verbalize the qualities that you really need in the man you love."

"Okay, who's handsome, sexy, honest, loving, considerate, and who loves me as much as I love him." I pause to think. "God, at this point, he has to be able to build bookshelves and lug shit, so handy, and thoughtful, I guess, and who loves dogs and makes me laugh and who's a hot, smokin' babe that I want to eat every time I see him."

"Don't forget ready for a relationship," she says, nodding.

"Yeah, the most important thing: ready for a relationship, excited about a relationship—with me, of course."

"Now write that down," she says. I do my best.

"Okay," Courtney says. "I'm going to burn your wishes, to put them out into the universe." I love Courtney.

We stare into the middle candle for several minutes, until I feel entranced by the flame. Then she breaks the spell by pulling the piece of paper with my wishes inscribed on it out of my hands and letting the flame gobble it up.

Thanks to all that positive thinking, Courtney and I are running forty minutes late to my own party. I take a last look in the mirror, pile all thirteen tons of my mop on top of my head, stick it up there with a barrette, add red, red lipstick and a spritz of perfume, throw on a puffy red jacket that matches my lips, and waltz out the door. Luckily, my friends are gathering right around the corner at my favorite bar on Avenue C, which boasts forty-two different kinds of beer and a mojito famous for making patrons do things they wish they hadn't.

On the way down the stairs, Courtney says, "So, Jake's coming, finally?"

"Yeah, kind of late, though. He has his meeting with that gallery guy."

"You know, Jacquie, it wouldn't kill you to go out on a date with someone else from time to time."

We walk outside into the frosty night. The multigenerational posse of men who spend their lives hanging out in front of the garage next door to my building are sitting in a row of lawn chairs, bundled in matching Windbreakers. They stop chattering in Spanish and nod in silent recognition as we pass. I nod back. Beyond them, at the end of the block, JESUS SAVES burns red and periwinkle neon against the black sky. Dry leaves rustle on the cold pavement, as the wind whips them into the air, and swirl wildly above all our heads. We all stare upward.

"Courtney," I say, snapping out of it, "whatever you might think of Jake, I am seeing someone right now and I'm not just going to start going out with other people. I'm going to let it play out and then we'll see. I might be a slut, but I'm pathologically faithful."

She walks silently beside me. I can feel her frown without even looking at her. We both watch a woman with fluorescent pink hair in a leopard skin coat and combat boots pushing a stroller, until my gaze is drawn to a yellow Lab wearing tiny red booties on his paws who's tied up to a parking meter outside a deli. "Hey, baby, nice footwear," I say, reaching out my hand to pet him. He gives me his paw to shake instead, then licks my palm passionately.

"Plus, I don't date," I tell Courtney.

"You're always saying that, but it's not really true, is it? You and Jake go on dates."

"That's not dating. That's getting food with someone I'm having sex with. I do that, I mean, I have to eat."

As Courtney shakes her head, I say, "I just don't go out with guys I don't know. I meet someone and either we have sex and fall instantly into a relationship—fling, affair, whatever—or we don't. I mean, you want to sleep with someone or you don't, so why force yourself to make dinner-table conversation with a guy if you don't feel an immediate, barely controllable urge to jump on him?"

"Well, apparently that routine doesn't work very well," Courtney says. "You end up with these men who don't treat you well and wasting time that could be spent meeting someone great."

I stop in my tracks right in front of the bar and turn to face her. "Look, Court, I know what I do. I've been doing it since I was, like, fifteen. I just don't know how to stop." Mid-rant, I wave and make kissy lips at a passing poodle in a shearling coat, then continue, "You know, sometimes I actually pray that I'll meet someone and let myself slowly get to know him and it will slowly dawn on me that this sweet, attentive, generous, intelligent, *openhearted* person is actually The Guy, because he is so damn wonderful and sweet and the rest of it, and then we'll live happily ever." I'm well aware that I'm raising my voice now, but I don't care and the whistling wind seems to be whipping up my volume.

"But the thing is, Court, after I'm done praying, I usually do something like tequila shots and hook up with some cute blond boy and run around grinning for weeks or months or whatever until he commits some unforgivable crime that makes me realize he's a dick, but by then I'm already hooked, 'cause he's cute and I like sleeping with him, not to mention the pure drama of it all. Courtney, where would I be without the crying and screaming and showing up at your place in the middle of the night to sob on your shoulder?"

"Oh, honey," she says, defeated. "Let's go get you a drink."

The first person we see inside is Alicia, who's holding her long, straight black hair in her fist while pounding tequila with her friend Claire. Alicia scrunches up her dark eyes and lets out a whoop, slamming the empty shot glass onto the bar, then bites a wedge of lime and grimaces before throwing one arm around Claire's shoulder and the other around me. I hug them and in return get the requisite "happy birthdays" and free drinks, mixed by my bartending friend Johnny, a naughty Irishman who gets a thrill out of turning my brain into mush.

"Happy birthday, gorgeous! Love the polka dots," he calls from the other end of the bar. "Next one's on me." I pull myself onto the bar to give him a smooch.

By midnight, forty of my friends and acquaintances have taken over the place, one group playing a game of advanced quarters at a big table in the back. I haven't turned into a pumpkin, but I have marinated my brain in mojito, which makes the conversation I'm having with Stefan, a onetime boyfriend who's trying to persuade me to go home with him, almost bearable. Jake still hasn't arrived. Courtney keeps looking at her watch, throwing menacing looks at Alicia, and making ever-so-subtle comments like, "I'll strangle him," under her breath.

My lanky gay boyfriend, Jeremy, dances in, wearing an off-white puffy jacket and matching ski cap, high from a successful first date.

"Well, where is he if it was so great?" I ask him.

"He had drinks plans after dinner, but it was magical, really. We're going out again this weekend."

Jeremy's always getting his heart busted by some guy he's supposedly going out with again this weekend, so I'm skeptical. Gay Boyfriend and I met at the dog run. I don't technically have a dog, but I do have dog envy that drives me to hang out at the dog run and flirt with other people's. I used to fantasize about meeting a handsome dog owner and knocking out the desire for canine and desire for canine-loving beau with one stone. Unfortunately, the only person I ever fell in love with there was Jeremy.

One blissfully balmy summer night, Jeremy's Chihuahua got spooked by the unsavory advances of an enormous Rottweiler named Ralph and ran away so fast that he slipped right out of his tiny collar. Jeremy was chasing him through the park, shouting, "Napoleon!" when the little guy came to an abrupt halt at the sight of Larry, the mini-mutt I was babysitting while his mom (my neighbor) was out of town. It was homosexual puppy love at first sight for Napoleon and Larry.

While they sniffed each other's butt, barked gleefully at big dogs, and got their leashes adorably tangled, I was busy falling for Napoleon's dad. He was tall and masculine, with a smile that reminded me of Robert Redford circa *Butch Cassidy and the Sundance Kid*.

"He has a little dog?" my sister said when I called her later. "He either has a girlfriend or he's gay."

I wasn't aware of that rule—or maybe I was in denial. I could have noticed he was a little too well-dressed and -behaved when we met in the park, but who stops to ask if someone's gay when you just don't want him to be? As the sky drained of its color and we chatted as if we'd always been friends, I envisioned myself on a deserted beach, barefoot in a simple yet striking white dress—like Katharine Hepburn in *Philadelphia Story*, only sexier and shorter and sleeveless—clutching Jeremy's hand before a female justice of the peace, our three scrappy kids—boy, girl, boy—with dirt on their faces climbing tangled trees in the sprawling backyard of our charming Catskills cottage, one of the boys tumbling from a branch, scraping his chin, crying for Daddy. I guess my intentions became clear, because Jeremy interrupted my reverie with a non sequitur: "My ex-boyfriend used to work at a bar on a beach in Spain." I was like, "Come again?" We had not been talking about Spain or bars or beaches. The only relevance was a sexual preference that Jeremy apparently thought he needed to insert, however gracelessly, into the conversation. I was crushed.

"Where's Boytoy?" Jeremy asks, referring to Jake.

"In the shithouse," I slur.

"No blowjobs for a week."

Courtney takes the opportunity to cut in. "Would you miss his birthday, Jacq? I don't think so." She kisses Jeremy before running off to supervise the quarters game.

"Oh, baby, you need a drink." Jeremy orders me another, after taking his cell phone out of his pocket, looking at it puzzled, and putting it back. I shake my head. Jeremy is a victim of what I call compulsive ob-cell-sive disorder, an affliction that causes poor souls like Jeremy to constantly hear their cell phones ringing when in fact they are not. A bus screeches to a halt and he thinks it's his phone. A baby cries, gunfire roars from a TV set, the Beatles sing "Magical Mystery Tour" on the radio—and Jeremy fumbles frantically for his cell, which is silently snoozing in his pocket.

"Looks like you could get Stefan in the sack," Jeremy says, checking his silent cell again and sadly putting it back in his pocket. Stefan, the chiseled, still-struggling actor who once trampled my heart, throws a practiced come-hither look my way from the back of the bar, his scruffy bangs falling seductively over penetrating brown eyes.

"You think so?" I ask. "He just told me my tits look terrific."

"Isn't that what you were going for in that dress? He's looking good."

"I can't go back there. Our breakup landed me in therapy for two years." Jeremy puts his arm around me in commiseration. "You know, Jake had this really important meeting tonight with a gallery owner. They probably had to have drinks afterwards or something," I tell him. "Maybe it's a good sign?"

"Did he say he was coming?"

"Well, he was going to try, but it wasn't definite," I say.

"Pardon me while I cringe," says my sister, appearing from out of nowhere, a phantom invoked by any reference to my bad boytoy.

Courtney is on her heels. "Stop making excuses for him," she says. "He should be here."

As I slam the rest of my drink, wincing as the lime juice burns the back of my throat on the way down, my phone rings: Boytoy dialing up from the shithouse.

"Hey," he says in the I'm-so-tired-I-can-barely-move-let-alone-get-on-a-subway tone I recognize as the one he uses every time he flakes. "I just woke up."

"I didn't know you were sleeping," I say, pushing my way to the front of the bar to escape the indignant glares of my friends.

"Yeah, I stopped at home to drop off my stuff and passed out in front of *Seinfeld*," he says. He's missing my birthday for reruns.

Courtney, Alicia, and Jeremy circle like vultures. I know if I talk loud enough to alert my protective posse to this turn of events, my relationship with Jake will be in peril. There's always someone trying to guilt me into breaking up with the assholes in my life. As if I didn't know they were bad for me without my loved ones' disapproval. Don't they know that I choose the drama? That I thrive on it? That I wouldn't know what to do with a life empty of senseless acts of self-destruction?

"Jake, can I call you back in two secs?"

"I'm going to sleep, Jacquie."

"It would take you, like, half an hour to get here. Less in a cab." I lower my voice and press my forehead against the front door of the bar, just in case the birds of prey are near enough to sense my defenselessness and come in for the kill. "I'll pay for it."

"I can't do it. I'm sorry," he says. "Look, can I take you out for dinner tomorrow night? For your birthday?"

"Yeah, that sounds good."

"Hey, sorry," he says.

Tears well up in my eyes. "You're always apologizing these days."

"Yeah, I know. But I am sorry. I'll call you tomorrow."

When I swing around, Courtney, Alicia, and Jeremy are standing shoulder-to-shoulder an inch from me, forming a barrier between me and the crowd of people I'd like to escape into. They're an angry mob, eyes blaring, out for blood. I compose myself. "He's taking me out to dinner tomorrow night."

They become a sort of Greek chorus hurling modern-day moral code at me—or hurling something, anyway. It goes a bit like this:

Courtney: "Tell me you broke up with the jerk."

Alicia: "Loser."

Jeremy: "Inconsiderate turd."

Alicia: "Let's hire someone to break his kneecaps."

Courtney: "Burn down his house."

Jeremy: "Cut off his balls."

Alicia: "He'll never have sex again."

Courtney (giggling): "He'll talk like a twelve-year-old girl."

Alicia (eyes gleaming): "He'll be in so much pain."

They all pause to savor the thought of it.

Jeremy: "A boytoy has only one purpose in life."

Courtney: "To make you happy."

Alicia: "When he stops?"

Jeremy: "Unplug him."

Alicia: "Cut off his cajones."

Jeremy: "What was it this time?"

Courtney: "Taking a nap?"

Alicia (sarcasm): "Making a masterpiece?"

Jeremy: "Washing his hair?"

Alicia: "Clearly something much more important than . . ."

"HIS GIRLFRIEND'S BIRTHDAY!" shout all three evil preachers masquerading as my friends.

"I'm not his girlfriend!" I shout back. "Not really. He's not ready for a relationship."

"Duh," says my mean gay boyfriend. "If he's not ready for a relationship with a goddess like you, he doesn't deserve you," he adds, swooping me into his arms and nuzzling my neck. It makes me horny.

7

Just then Samantha strolls over to say goodbye.

"Jake didn't make it? *Quelle* surprise," she says, kissing both my cheeks. The four of us watch as she cinematically flings her long, blond locks over one shoulder and glides out into the night, as if the sidewalk was a stage and she a diva making her entrance, her engagement ring glistening as it catches rays off a streetlight.

"I gotta go. I'm not feeling so hot," I say, surveying the bar and deciding that my friends will live if I don't say good night. I grab my purse and a shopping bag bulging with the books, smelly candles, flowers, and sexy underwear my friends gave me, avoiding the eyes of the scary threesome studying me with concerned looks, and run out of the bar.

The icy air braces me, sobering me up ever so slightly. I lean against the wall, throw back my head, and close my eyes. The world spins and I open them again quickly, taking a couple of deep breaths before beginning my walk up Avenue C. I stumble left onto Ninth Street and let my fingers run along the chain-link fence bordering the community garden on the corner. The cold feels good on my fingertips. Jagged aluminum pinwheels in a variety of colors adorn the top of the fence. Most are rusted from years of weather. Some are twirling frenetically. Gazing up, I feel a gush of affection for my strange little neighborhood. One of the primitive sculptures looks like a gigantic sunflower with pointed, razor-sharp petals that would not feel so good if they fell on my head. I move swiftly away from the fence and spot a stack of terra-cotta flowerpots in perfect condition on top of a trash can, some of them painted in bold shades, probably by a local artist who got bored with them. I could use those, I think, wrapping my arms around them. I hear music in the distance as I cart my treasure down the sidewalk piled high with garbage bags just beginning to stink.

When I climb into bed, the world is still spinning so badly I can't close my eyes. I guzzle a glass of water and take two aspirin, but it doesn't help. After staring at the ceiling for a few minutes, I get up and stick my fingers down my throat. Up come the contents of at least seven mojitos (I lost count), a jug of sake, and some sushi. Tuna, I think. My eyes water and sting and my mouth tastes like vomit. I brush my teeth again, get back into bed, and vow never, ever to drink again—or at least not more than two (or three) cocktails in one night.

I close my eyes and imagine Jake spooning me, his arm tightly wrapped around me, his hand between my breasts, my hand clutching his.

"Fuck him!" I say aloud and try to come up with another guy to insert into my bedtime fantasy. Johnny Depp? That guy from yoga I'm pretty sure is straight? (He smiled at me when I stumbled out of Ardha Chandrasana pose and onto his mat.) The Italian barista at the café on the corner of First and Tenth with the hazel-nut eyes and perennially pursed lips?

Ever since I was old enough to envy the girls making out with dreamy-looking men in the moonlight on *The Love Boat* and *Happy Days*, I've lulled myself to sleep with fairy tale love stories I make up in my head. They go something like this: On a perfectly glorious sunny day, I am strolling alone down an East Village street (in Central Park, through SoHo), dressed in something flattering in red (pink, yellow), maybe with polka dots. This guy—say, Cute Café Boy—is walking his golden retriever (mutt, beagle), sort of running, laughing, playing tug-of-war, not looking where he's going, and he crashes right into me. He looks up, stunned, apologetic—"I'm sorry, are you okay?" His voice is raspy, masculine, full of emotion. When I look into his electric-blue (brown, green) eyes, the attraction is instant and mutual. I assure him that I'm fine, I forgive him; the bump and bruises won't be so bad that I can't cover them with makeup. He laughs and invites me for coffee (brunch, dinner) to make up for it. We get lattés-to-go and sit on a bench in the park. Conversation gushes like a waterfall onto slippery, wet rocks below. Coffee becomes drinks become dinner, and then we're back at my place. The sex is a revelation. His dog mopes in the corner, neglected, and then licks my feet, making us laugh till our sides hurt. We stay in bed for days. He calls his boss (agent, partner) to say he's coming down with the flu, and by the end of the week, we announce our engagement. I'm pregnant. We're thrilled and planning the wedding at his family's sprawling villa on the Amalfi Coast.

I am an Aries woman, and we, the most relentlessly wide-eyed, trusting, and optimistic sign of the zodiac, are not known for great patience. I for one want it all and I want it now. (My ex-therapist confirmed the diagnosis, although she failed to recognize the astrological correlation.) I don't want to wait for the whole getting-to-know-you thing. I want Harlequin Romance Man to emerge from the mists on his towering black steed and carry me off into a fiery sunset. I want *Romeo and Juliet* (without the death part). I want insta-bliss: love, babies, lifelong commitment—at first friggin' sight. Unfortunately, I have yet to meet the guy who is willing to comply.

So, Cute Café Boy's strong, protective arms are wrapped around me, his hand fondling a boob. Not even this soothing vision is capable of getting me off to sleep. Handsome Café Boy keeps morphing into stupid Jake. I keep changing positions. Café Boy can barely keep up. I grab the phone.

"Jake?" He's totally asleep. "Wake up. I need to talk to you. You awake?"

"Now I am."

"Please come over," I say in my most irresistible voice. "I can't fall asleep."

"Goddammit, Jacquie!" The force of his outburst blows me into sudden sobriety. "I told you I'm fucking sleeping! I'm so sick of this shit."

I don't know how to respond to his unexpected fury. Every other time I've called him in the middle of the night he's at least indulged me with conversation.

"Fuck! I'm so sick of this 'you always disappoint me' shit and you expecting me to act like the good boyfriend on your birthday and making me feel all guilty if I don't. I'm not your fucking boyfriend. I've told you a million times. I like you and I'm cool hanging out or whatever, but I told you: *I can't do this*. Every time we have this fucking conversation we end up staying together, you know? I never wanted to have to not see you anymore, 'cause I like you, but you're driving me crazy. I can't handle you crying and that sad voice. Fuck! I have enough things to worry about without you being mad at me all the time."

It's the most words I've ever heard him string together. I'm in shock.

"You there?" he asks.

"Yeah."

"You okay?"

"Uh-huh."

"Can I call you tomorrow?"

"I don't think so."

"Okay."

Silence.

"Hey," he says. "Call me when you feel okay talking to me."

"Okay," I say. And I hang up. And cry. And cry and cry and cry and cry. I'm lying in my bed, naked and squeezing my teddy bear, Chubby Joe, the same one I've squeezed at times like these ever since my "Secret Santa" in my freshman dorm, a skinny guy named Joe, gave him to me.

I know Jake's right that this pseudo-relationship has gone on too long. And yet more than anything I wish he were here with me. I want Jake to comfort me about getting hurt by Jake. I feel completely distraught that I won't see him anymore, stunned that I won't sleep with him again, furious with him for saying I was driving him crazy and with myself for not breaking up with him before he broke up with me. I was supposed to break up with him first. My pillow is drenched. Chubby Joe is soggy (and pissed). My abs hurt from heaving. Maybe I'll look skinnier in the morning.

I close my eyes and imagine myself walking down Prince Street in SoHo. It's late at night, long shadows falling across the cobblestoned streets, lights eerily illuminating the empty storefronts. And suddenly the cute Italian guy who works at the café on my corner appears staring into the window of a furniture shop. It's funny to see him outside the neighborhood, and we both smile shyly as our eyes meet. He asks me if I'd like to get a drink

with him. Later that night, he winds up with his arms wrapped tightly around my waist, his hand nestled lovingly between my breasts, and I finally drift off to sleep.

Filmmaker seeks female flatmate. Big, sunny room in 2-bd SoHo lft on Grand (Mercer/Greene). Own bath. Shared kitchen w/ new stainless appliances. Lovely. Quiet. Loaded with light. Flat so bright, I must wear shades & a visor inside. I work from home, travel often. Easy to live w/, highly intelligent, sparkling sense of humor. Seek same. Call Graham

3

When my alarm shrieks in my ear the next morning, I leap out of bed and stand trembling, naked, my toes gripping the cold, wood floor, trying to figure out if the evil sound is coming from outside or inside my skull. I'm wondering if someone might have launched a car alarm through my bedroom window when reality clanks me hard around the head and I grab the offending clock to turn it off. The ensuing silence soothes me until the sensation that someone used my head as a bowling ball takes its place. I groan and drag myself into the bathroom to find pain relief.

Without getting dressed, I creep into the kitchen to put water on for green tea, rip off the end of the stale baguette on top of the fridge, and sit down at my desk to check e-mail. There's nothing good except a belated e-card from Brad, Courtney's husband, apologetic about missing my party. I am relieved that he stayed away, because I hate it when he witnesses my shame. Brad and I have been close since college, and he plays the protective big brother I never had. Unfortunately, all his friends are either married professors, twenty-something musicians who smoke too much pot, or residents of Seattle, his hometown. I have had drunken escapades with many of them and we don't mention most of their names anymore. I tell Brad that I

wish technology would advance to the point where he could clone himself. He tells me I'd make Brad-clone love me and dump him, because he's a nice, normal guy and I only fall for dickheads. He's probably right.

Brad teaches music composition at NYU and plays in a band. An amazing thing happened a few months back: He self-produced a solo album of ballads that he'd written through the years, and it took off like a rocket. There's this one song, "Still in It," about him just kind of watching Courtney piddling around the kitchen and making coffee and watering a plant. He describes how she gasps when the cat jumps onto the counter and glances at him, embarrassed, and it makes him fall in love all over again, even though they've spent every minute together for the last twelve years. It's not corny at all. It has a rock 'n' roll beat and avoids love-song clichés. I'm not exactly objective, but the song brings tears to my eyes every time and I feel honored to know the guy who wrote it. Some DJ in Portland heard it and next thing, it was being played in dorm rooms nationwide and turning up on celebrity playlists and Brad was being compared to Jeff Buckley and the Coldplay singer who knocked up Gwyneth Paltrow, and we were like, "Our little Brad?" He got a record deal, took a sabbatical, and tomorrow he starts a tour of the whole friggin' planet (or at least the North American part). Needless to say, with all the organizing, rehearsing, and stressing out, he doesn't have much time to attend the birthday parties of mere mortals like me. The e-card's a funny one, with a monkey playing "Happy Birthday" on the banjo. It sticks its big, pink tongue out at the end.

When my kettle squeals, my sister, whom I hadn't noticed sacked out on the couch, bolts upright. She's wearing her bra and underwear and is wrapped up in one of the curtains that are eventually supposed to adorn my living room windows.

"Jesus Christ, you scared the shit out of me," I say, pulling myself out of my chair and into the kitchen, shoving a heap of Alicia's clothes on the floor with my foot as I go.

"You're always naked," she says. "It's kind of gross."

"I was hammered when I got home last night."

She grunts and goes back to sleep. It will be nice when my sister finds a place to sleep that is not in my apartment.

A half an hour later, I walk very slowly out my door, past the woman who sits on a white, padded stool on my block advocating Bible studies, and notice tiny green buds just beginning to peek through the tips of the branches on a skinny tree behind her. In spite of my throbbing head, I feel relieved. There is still a chill in the air, but at least spring is on its way. Summer is my favorite season, but there is nothing I love more than the sudden burst of color as flowers pop out of frozen, scraggly trees in New York City after months of cold. Okay, the one thing I love more is running around in a skimpy dress and flip-flops on a balmy, New York summer night that will never cool down.

I'm not a regular morning caffeinator, but today I need a boost, so I stop at my favorite corner café. The adorable barista smiles when he sees me and I stiffen, afraid he'll sense that I imagined him doing naughty things to me last night.

"Ciao bella," he says, still clinging to a slight Italian accent, even though his family moved from Sicily when he was fourteen.

"Not bella today," I say.

"You're the best thing I've seen this morning." That makes me feel a little better.

"Thank you," I say. "But my head is pounding and my stomach is queasy. Think a latté and a croissant might help?"

"Let's give it a try."

I watch his arm muscles bulge in all the right places as he twists the espresso into the machine and foams the milk. "So, what did you do last night?" he asks.

"It was my birthday. I drank too much."

"Happy birthday!" he says, reaching into the pastry display to pull out a cookie. "For you."

"Thank you."

"Please smile. I can't make it through the day without seeing you smile once."

I grimace at him and he flashes his lovely white teeth in response. He doesn't let me pay for my coffee and croissant. Creeping up St. Mark's Place, I try to pick up my pace, knowing I have a magazine to ship. The sun is shining much too brightly. I wonder if sunglasses stop working at some point—mine don't seem to be doing their job today. This particular block is never calm; even before the rows of dirty T-shirt and hat shops open, there's a certain noise and griminess to it. A pile of dejected Gap underwear is lying on top of a Dumpster—the ones that say, "I love you, I love you, I love you . . ." in different fonts and sizes and the ones covered in red hearts on a navy background. Some poor kid whose girlfriend dumped him must have trashed them last night. A band of skinny boys in tight, leather pants, who are probably crawling out of their K-holes, shiver around greasy slices of pizza on the corner. A homeless guy is sprawled facedown on the curb, covered in a kid's sleeping bag with cartoon bunnies and pink flowers on it. I take in the detritus of the night before, barely able to muster a smile when a bouncy girl with a shaved head skips by with a waddling corgi on one leash and a dappled dachshund on the other. They're wearing matching orange parkas.

"Hey, precious," I manage. They grin up at me in unison. Their mommy throws knives at me out of her eyes before continuing to bounce. Mean people should not be allowed to have dogs.

Impinging on my space, a cell phone rings. The lounge lizard walking in front of me still decked out in last night's purple, shimmering three-piece suit yanks out his phone, at the same time as the annoying girl behind me screeches into her phone, "Where are you?"

"I'm on St. Mark's?" says the lounge lizard. I'm surrounded.

"Where on St. Mark's?" says the girl behind me.

"I'm on St. Mark's," says the guy, louder now.

"No. *Where* on St. Mark's," the girl screams.

"Oh, *where* on St. Mark's!" the guy screams back.

I stop in my tracks, causing Annoying Girl to bump into me. I turn around to face a teenage toothpick sporting a checkered minidress under fake white fur, and a bleached-out hairdo two feet high. "He's right there," I say, pointing at her buddy prancing three paces in front of us.

As I continue walking, she shouts, "Oh! My! God!"

"That's, like, so fucking weird," says the lounge lizard. Completely forgotten by the whole freak reunion, I walk more quickly until their shrieks fade out of earshot. It occurs to me that at least I'm not thinking about Jake. Then I see a couple making out at a bus stop and tears fill my eyes. "He's not my fucking boyfriend," I growl at myself.

When I duck into the deli next to my office, the cashier, who must be about twenty, is showing a sonogram picture of his baby to a guy standing next to me at the counter.

"Tres meses!" he says, beaming. His sweetness makes me weepy again.

Sam is the only one in the office when I get there and she's chattering on the phone. "I'm thinking of going with lilac," she says, turning toward me. Her mouth literally falls open when she sees me. I wonder if she might drool on the back of her chair, before recalling that she doesn't do normal-human-being things like drool. *"Au contraire.* You look outstanding in lilac," she says. "Hey, can I call you back?" She hangs up and says, "You were so drunk last night, I thought for sure you wouldn't be here until noon."

"We've got a magazine to put to bed," I say, dumping my stuff by my chair but not removing my sunglasses.

"How are you?" she asks.

"Thirty-two and still standing," I tell her.

"That's a start," she says.

"I brought doughnuts," I say, placing a box of Krispy Kremes on the drafting table in the middle of the room and selecting a glazed one for myself. "I need them to soak up whatever poison is still in me." I eat half of it in one bite, as Samantha jumps out of her seat and grabs two doughnuts for herself. My petite co-worker has the metabolism of a professional basketball player.

"Hey, have you proofed the text yet?" she asks. "I just read your Cate Blanchett piece. *C'est magnifique.*"

"Thanks. Yeah, doing that right now."

I take the pile of articles from her and sit back down at my desk to read them for what feels like the eighteenth time. The pounding in my head has dulled to a mere thud. After getting halfway through the first page, I feel myself drawn to the phone. I want to call him so badly it hurts, but I won't. First of all, he'd still be sleeping—he rarely gets up before two. Second, I have to break myself of the habit. I snap the rubber band on my wrist and focus on the sting as I try to dream up a way out of my funk. I could eat another doughnut and think about how no one will ever love me again if I get fat. I could go outside and pet puppies, but that would mean moving. I cruise around Friendster for a while, inviting everyone with a picture of a dog to be my friend. For some reason, a black Lab called Bert I've befriended, who loves "barking, playing demolish my squeaky toy, and smelling other dogs' weewees," reminds me of my chat with Alicia yesterday, the one that invoked strangers' sweaty socks, admirable pectoral muscles, and the fringe benefits of hunting for a roommate. I pick up the phone.

Clancy, one editor who gets to work on time, answers on the first ring.

"I was just about to call you," she says even before I announce myself. The wonders of Caller ID. "You're a genius."

"Really?"

"Just had an editorial meeting. Doing a whole section for July on alternative ways to meet men. Your story could fit in nicely."

"Cool," I say and hold my breath.

"But you'd have to do it," she says.

"Do what?"

"Test it. Look for a room. Make the necessary phone calls. Hit the pavement."

"But I'm not looking for an apartment," I say, feeling like I've had this conversation before.

"Jacquie, you're a reporter. It's research."

"Hmm," I say. Why does everyone want to make a dishonest woman of me? When I even slightly rumpled the truth as a child, my mom would see it all over my nervous little face and punish me. I learned my lesson. I don't want to lie to anyone. I just want to write a good story and make a few extra bucks. "I'm not a very good liar," I tell Clancy.

"You're not lying. You're going undercover," she says. "Now get to work. A thousand words. You've got six weeks. Two dollars a word. I'll put a contract in the mail." Two dollars a word? That's two thousand dollars! That's what I make at my job in a month, working ten, eleven hours a day. Jesus Christ. I spring out of my chair, sprint into the hallway, and scream at the top of my lungs, all the while jumping around like a spaz. A FedEx guy leaving the graphic design firm down the hall smiles at me and shakes his head.

I return from my episode with my heart racing, convinced that I'm utterly incapable of facing "10 Awesomest Flicks to Watch While Taking Bong Hits," which is next on my pile of articles to proofread this morning.

"Hey, Sam, where is everyone?" I ask.

"Steve is at a breakfast meeting with an investor, Chester has class until eleven, and Spencer and Trevor are MIA. Apparently. Steve called and said you're in charge, get to work, he's counting on you. Maybe you should think twice before planning your next birthday party on the night before we ship." Sam is a self-righteous twit. *N'est-ce pas?*

Everyone's momentary absence buys me some time to slack off, and if there was ever a morning when I needed to slack off, it's today. I type "craigslist.org" into my browser. "New York. Housing. Rooms/shared." Boom. About a million listings come up. I click on them one by one, at first uncertain what I'm looking for. Most ads are thoughtful enough to include a neighborhood in the heading, so I click on apartments in downtown Manhattan—the Village, SoHo, NoLita, the Lower East Side. I figure if I actually have to visit these apartments, I should stick as close to home as possible. It occurs to me that I should also focus my energies on apartments with outrageously high rents. I'm not going to have to come up with the money because I'm not really renting the place, but the piece is about meeting guys I'd like to date, so I should look at apartments likely to be inhabited by guys I'd want to date—i.e., financially sound ones. God knows I don't need another struggling, unsuccessful new boyfriend. Done with boytoys! Done with commitment-phobes! Done with poor, starving jerkoffs who won't be able to provide for me and my future children! Tribeca lofts appeal to me, as do charming brownstones in the West Village and cozy, sun-filled floor-throughs with gardens in Cobble Hill. On the first few pages of ads, the most promising apartments are inhabited by women or groups of twenty-something guys. It takes me fifteen minutes of solid browsing to find something interesting enough to investigate: a filmmaker renting a room in his 2,500-square-foot loft in SoHo. He's asking $2,200, which sure qualifies as a lot for half an apartment.

I glance surreptitiously around the office. Sam is engrossed in a shopping site, apparently browsing for lilac bridesmaid gowns. I roll my eyes and get up to nonchalantly put on a mix of songs from Chester's favorite sound tracks and saunter casually back to my desk as Modern English belts out the opening lines of "Melt with You" (featured in *Valley Girl* and *50 First Dates*, both on my list of top-ten chick flicks ever, and the little-known indie *Cherish*, which I also dig). I dial Graham's number. A sleepy voice answers. It has a British accent. I picture a tawny-haired Englishman, his aristocratic good looks buried in a sage-green flannel pillowcase as he reluctantly holds a phone in one hand and wipes sleep from his crinkly blue eyes with the other.

"Hello, Graham?"

"Mmmm."

"Sorry to wake you."

"Never mind, I should have been up ages ago. Thanks for reminding me."

"My name's Jacquie. I'm calling about the room."

"Pity, my sweet, I rented it last night."

"Oh."

"No sadness, please, Jacquie, not this early in the morning. You haven't even seen the place. Chin up, love, you might have hated it."

"But it's supposed to be beautiful and sunny and loaded with new appliances."

"All lies."

"Ah, just luring pretty young things down to your lair?"

"She's a smart one."

My groin reacts on cue to flattery in an English accent. I'm so easy. I envision the two of us, Graham (played by Hugh Grant), wearing a gray Cambridge sweatshirt with a hood, sitting across from me at my corner café reading the Arts & Leisure section of the *Times*, blowing me a kiss when our eyes meet.

"You wouldn't believe how many of them came down here dolled up and ready to bed me if only I'd had the audacity to ask," he says.

"But you didn't, of course, because you're a gentleman."

"You'd better believe it, baby."

"What kind of movies do you make?"

"I'm editing my second documentary right now, about an incredible blues musician I met on the subway. He used to be quite famous, really, but he's been homeless and battling schizophrenia for the last eight years. Still plays in the subway, a tremendous talent. It's, shall we say, a labor of love."

"How does a documentary filmmaker afford to live in a forty-five-hundred-dollar loft in SoHo, pray tell?"

"That's very personal, isn't it, missy?"

"Independently wealthy, are we?"

"Look at the time. I'd better begin my day!"

"All right, I promise, no more impertinent questions."

Steve walks into the office chattering loudly on his cell phone. He waves at me. I wave the pile of text back at him.

"I have to go to, too, Graham. Good luck with your new roommate."

"And you, Jacquie. I hope you find yourself a marvelous flat."

I hang up with my heart banging against my rib cage and run out into the hallway again, an instant replay of my earlier explosion. I laugh out loud, amazed at this thing that I've discovered. I want to kiss my sister, and I wonder what excuse I can invent to call Graham back and try to get him to ask me out. He sounds like a scoundrel, but all the good ones are, aren't they? Then again, there must be hundreds of Grahams out there. This is New York City, after all. The number of eligible bachelors looking for roommates has to be limitless. I should have come up with this plan ages ago. I almost shriek for joy, but this time I control myself. Okay, so I'll have to be a sneak and a snake for a couple of weeks, but look on the bright side: What if I actually do meet someone I like in the process? Now *that* would make a good story.

"Where the hell is Jacquie?" I hear Steve shout from the other room.

"Here, Steve! Here I am," I say, running back into the office, where he's rifling through a pile of text looking for the Cate Blanchett piece that he hasn't read yet. I grab it off my desk and hand it to him before positioning myself in front of my computer again. I glance at the time on my screen, smiling so hard that my face feels like it might break, and realize that I haven't thought about Jake in over half an hour.

"Fuck Jake," I say, feeling like Graham has completely cured me of him.

fuck jake, says the Instant Message I get at that very instant from my sister. I love how she can read my mind.

Precisely what I was thinking, I write back. You'll be happy to hear we broke up.

you broke up with him, right?

Sort of. Mutual really. I feel my face getting hot at my fib, but I guess it's kind of true. I mean I was planning to break up with him eventually, anyway. Guess what! I type, changing the subject. I got an assignment from Luscious—1000 words on searching for men in the apt ads!

good idea. how'd you come up with it?

I know, I know. THANK YOU, BRILLIANT HERMANA, I write.

And then I give in to the irresistible pull of Craig's List. Here's what I learn right away: Unlike computer dating, the people who place apartment ads don't necessarily list any personal information, so some research is required. My first step is to send out a dozen "Who lives in this apartment?" e-mails. I get responses like, I am a German woman, a sculptor and I'm a bartender and a musician; Tommy's in film school; there's Sammy and Zab (Zab?); Curt's moving out, you're in his room. It's dope! You should tooooooootally come see the place!! Come over now, man, have a beer!!!!

I jot down a couple of phone numbers: John, a musician in the East Village; Steven, a thirty-four-year-old doctor with a duplex in the West Village; and a thirty-seven-year-old with a newly renovated two-bedroom in Tribeca. One ad intrigues me:

> Looking for a roommate to share spacious, bright, immaculately decorated E. Village 2-bedroom that's bursting with charm. 1800 square foot roof garden is stunning. $1500. Call Chad.

I shoot off an e-mail: Who would I be living with? A few minutes later I receive the following: You'd be in one room, my boyfriend Jurgen and I in the other. Best, Chad. I should have known. Straight men do not call their apartments "stunning" or "bursting with charm," and their homes most certainly aren't "immaculately decorated." Most straight guys—metrosexuals excepted—scratch their balls, look at their dank, laundry-strewn pad with its navy-blue futon, entertainment center purchased at Kmart, and stack of video games and porn in the corner, and call it "cool, dude." I become obsessed with meeting a man with an eighteen-hundred-square-foot roof garden.

Truth be told, I'm having a hard time focusing on work. How can I be expected to care about Sam's exposé on Suzy Q. Starlet or Spencer's review of the movie he calls "the best thing to emerge from Spain since sangria" when some guy I don't know is out there waiting to become my new boyfriend, and all I have to do is show up at his door. I grab a handful of hair, scrutinize my split ends, and bite them off one by one. I flick my wrist with the rubber band and watch a pale welt appear.

Suddenly the office turns chaotic and, contrary to my nature, I am forced to forget about boys for a minute. (Men, I mentally correct myself. "Until you start calling them 'men,' you will continue to meet unformed, noncommittal boys," says Courtney.) Chaos: Steve's arguing loudly with an advertiser. I'm on the phone with the copy editor debating the finer points of parentheses. Sam's running between the two of us, demanding final decisions about which pictures go where. Trevor's frantically inputting changes that the rest of us are throwing his way. Then it's lunchtime and we're ordering burritos from the taco stand around the corner. Chester's blasting the Pet Shop Boys and shaking his hips like the wily gopher in *Caddyshack* when he should be proofreading, while Trevor's brand-new Jack Russell puppy named Maximus runs laps around the office, barking incessantly. Then it's eight o'clock and we've pulled it off. I'm checking the most recent version that Trevor printed out to see if we missed any copy mistakes, and it looks good. With Maximus snoring softly in my lap and another issue of the magazine in the can, I suddenly feel high on it all, as if everything is going to turn out fine.

> EV rock star looking to shack up: Rm avail in the grooviest digs on Ave B. Live with a bass player, cool cat, nice guy, can put you on the phone with the man vacating to nest with his main squeeze. He'll vouch for me—I won't even have to pay him ☺. A girl might be nice this time, but I'm not picky. Call John.

4

There's an illness that afflicts New York couples: They're living happily in some shoebox apartment in Manhattan, and life is groovy. Then they get married—and start to feel queasy. Suddenly shoebox makes them claustrophobic. Delusional thoughts and paranoia set in. They could swear that the city has become noisier, dirtier, more urban somehow, way too noisy and dirty and urban for their liking anyway. Suddenly, their skin is crawling and they're sure they will die if forced to spend another second of their put-upon lives in this horrible place called Manhattan.

Next thing you know, they move to Brooklyn.

I'm not making this up. It has happened to every single person I've ever known who got married while cohabitating in New York. After dating since junior year in college, Court and Brad finally got hitched six years ago and, naturally, they mutually agreed (probably the day he proposed) to give up their mind-blowing East Village one-bedroom— and its marble mantelpiece, massive skylight sending sunshine over a funky, sunken living room, windy staircase leading to their *own private roof garden*—to move to Park Slope. I almost lost my oat-bran flakes when they broke the news to me. I was writing freelance movie reviews for a free newspaper at the time and waiting tables at a dive to cover my student loans and credit-card debt, so I couldn't afford to take over their lease. At only a thousand dollars a month, it was a steal, but still out of reach for me. Instead, they gave notice, the landlord did minor renovations to justify jacking up the rent to twenty-two hundred, and some trust-fund deadbeat with a drum set moved in. I fantasized about dating him for a minute, just so I still could visit the apartment, but he smelled like b.o. and his drumming sucked. My best friends moved into a perfectly pretty two-bedroom located on a quaint, tree-lined street in the Slope, where baby strollers outnumber dogs four to one. Worst of all, it's a forty-five-minute subway ride from me.

When the *Flicks* crew—bouncing off walls following a frenzied day—heads out for a drink after work, as we do every time we wrap an issue, I decline. I promised Brad I would come over and hang out with him and Courtney while he packs. So Steve et al. saunter off to our usual dinner and beer spot a few blocks west of our office, which has crayons on the tables and a great bacon cheeseburger, and I take a ten-minute stroll up to West Fourth Street to hop the F train to Brooklyn.

I open the door with my own key while Courtney is ordering dinner. She is about to hang up when she hears me banging in and shouts from the kitchen, "We're ordering Thai. Steamed dumplings, veggie pad thai, lemongrass shrimp, and green chicken curry. Want anything else?"

"Sounds like you hit it," I say, slinging my bag onto the mushy green couch on which I've spent many nights. "Sorry,

Chaz," I say, as it lands on the cat's head. "Didn't see you there." I throw myself down next to him and nuzzle his white furriness. He kneads the cushions and purrs, gazing at me lovingly with big, blue eyes. "I love you madly, fat man," I tell him.

"I had to order. Kitchen closes at nine-thirty," Courtney says. I shake my head in disgust—only in family-happy Park Slope do restaurants shut down before anyone over age five has even digested lunch. She wanders into the living room, holding a Ziploc bag bursting with every vitamin and herbal remedy ever made, which she must be packing for Brad, and a Corona. She points at the beer. I nod and go into the kitchen to grab one.

"Brad, want a beer?" I yell.

"Uh," he grunts from the front bedroom, which they use as an office. This means yes. He's checking e-mail in green sweats and no shirt, with a red bandana wrapped around his bushy blond head. "Nice look, homey. Move over." I scoot him over and squeeze onto his chair with him. "I want to show you something." I type in the address for Craig's List and go to the roommates-wanted page.

"Check this out. Court, come here. I'm writing a piece for *Luscious*! Two thousand bucks!"

"You go," says Brad.

Court ambles in, nibbling a handful of wasabi peas, and throws her arms around my neck.

"I'm so proud of you, sweet," she says. "What's it about?"

"I'll show you," I say.

Court perches herself on the windowsill behind us and plays with Brad's ringlets with her free hand, while I click on the people I highlighted at work, telling them about the story assignment as I go.

"Let's call someone," Courtney says and grabs the cordless phone. I give her the number for thirty-four-year-old Steven, the doctor with the duplex in the West Village.

"Hello, is Steven there?" she asks, sitting on the floor. "Hi, I'm calling about the room you're renting. Can you tell me a little about it? Uh-huh. Oh, I see, that's not really something I'm interested in. Thanks anyway." She hangs up. "He's gay."

"How could you tell from a two-second conversation?" Brad asks.

"You just can."

"Oh, right, her infallible intuition strikes again."

"Shut up, you guys," I say, clicking on the next one. "Thomas, pricey two-bedroom in Tribeca."

Courtney calls him and babbles for a couple of minutes. I keep clicking on apartments that Brad yays or nays. We glance at Courtney, who's rubbing Chaz's tummy and still listening to this guy ramble on.

"So, tomorrow's the big day, huh?" I say, still scrunched up next to him on the chair, my right thigh hanging over his left.

"Uh-huh," he says.

"Where you going first?"

"Northampton."

"That should be fun. College girls can't get enough of you. You be careful, though. They'll be all over you." I laugh, but he doesn't say anything.

"Nervous?" I ask.

"Nervous as hell."

"You're going to be great, Brad. Your record's amazing."

"It'll be hard to be away from you guys, to be away from Court."

"I know, but you'll talk every day, and I'm sure she'll come see you whenever she can."

"I know." He pauses, still looking at the screen and not at me. "You know, the only time we've been apart was when you guys went backpacking after college. It's been like ten years since we've spent a single night apart."

"Brad, that's pathetic. It's about time."

He elbows me in the side.

"Shithead!" I elbow him back. We're giggling and bruising each other's ribs, when Courtney kicks each of us hard from her spot on the floor and Chaz flees. We look guiltily at each other like scolded children and Brad sneaks out of the room to go gawk at his luggage. I do wonder how Court puts up with our juvenile behavior sometimes. We bring it out in each other, and it must kill her to have to play mommy with her husband and best friend all the time.

"Are you baked?" I shout after him. He doesn't answer. Courtney kicks me again. Brad puts his head in the door, makes a pig nose at me with his thumb, and runs out of the room again. I click on John the East Village rock star.

I look at Courtney as she says, "Well, I'm not really sure if I'm giving up my current apartment yet. I'll be in touch as soon as I know anything, all right? Remember that life offers us many lessons if we allow ourselves to be open to them, especially in times of grief and uncertainty. You're so welcome." She hangs up. "Poor guy. He was telling me about this breakup he went through, his girlfriend sued him for everything they ever bought together and he can't afford a lawyer and he's had the flu for three weeks, but I'm certain it's his body giving in to his emotional distress. It was totally depressing."

"Jesus Christ. Okay, how about this guy? John, a musician, he calls himself a 'cool cat,' who lives in 'the grooviest digs on Avenue B.' He sounds cool."

"No way," Brad shouts from the other room. "No more starving artists. You want to meet men who are worth going out with, not guys like Jake."

"You're a musician, Brad," Courtney says.

"I'm a professor," he replies, appearing in the doorway. "With a hobby that has suddenly become more lucrative than I'd imagined. There is little chance that your friend there will have the same luck. Odds are against him. And he probably doesn't have much of a backup plan."

"You're right, you're right."

"Hey, Brad, don't forget to stick a copy of your itinerary on the fridge, okay?" Court says. Brad wanders off to find one. "And leave me contact info for that guitar guy. I'm gonna have to pay him while you're gone."

"Shit, I forgot," he says.

"And pack your blue coat. It will still be cold up north. And tea-tree oil in case your skin thing acts up," she adds, getting up to check on the state of his suitcase. "I guess I can always send you anything you forget," she says, before smoochy noises set in. I click on John the musician again. The doorbell rings, giving me just enough time to jot down his number and run for the door. Their buzzer is broken, so I have to run down two flights of stairs to the front door of the building to let the delivery guy in. "I'll get it!" I shout on my way out.

We sit at the dining room table, happy family that we are, quieted by anxiety about what the next few months will bring us, and shove noodles into our faces together for what we know will be the last time for several months. No one mentions that fact.

"Well, I guess I'll go then," I say once I'm stuffed. "You guys should have a little bit of time alone together on your last night."

"Oh, you know we have no fun when you're not around," Brad says.

Courtney looks at him with sad eyes. "I'm kidding!" he says. She doesn't smile. "Baby, you're the light of my life," he says, grabbing her around the waist and kissing her neck, softening her a bit. I feel like she's going to cry any second, not because his teasing bothers her but because he's going to be gone for such a long time.

"I'm out of here," I say, putting on my coat. Court starts clearing the table. "Be careful, Brad. It's a wild world out there."

"Hard to get by just upon a smile," he says.

"Winter, spring, summer, or fall, all you've got to do is call and I'll be there."

61

"Thanks," he says and hugs me. We're not really phone friends, so I know I'm unlikely to talk to him for months and I will miss him. "While I'm gone, no hooking up with any of those hunky musician types, right?" he says, still squeezing me.

"Jesus Christ!" I say and pull away from him. "You know, it's easy for you perfect happy loving couples to give people like me advice. How do you know that this hunky musician isn't the love of my life? How will I know if I don't meet him? I mean, not all of us have the luxury of meeting our soul mate when we're fucking nineteen." Court comes back into the room and stands at the kitchen door, watching me.

"Jacquie, it's cool," Brad says. "Do whatever you want. I just want you to find someone who's worthy of you, that's all, and your odds will only improve when you start diving into a certain kind of pond."

"Yeah, I know," I say. "I'm sorry. I guess I'm just still a little raw about Jake. And I'm sad that you're going." Saying it makes my eyes well up. He hugs me again.

"Okay, now I'm out of here. Court, I'll call you tomorrow. Brad, check in sometime. Break a leg. All that crap." And with that, I'm out the door.

Once I hit the street, I'm on a rampage. Courtney and Brad just love giving me romantic advice. Oh poor single Jacquie who's always messing things up for herself, let's offer her all the wisdom that we've gathered through our vast amounts of experience. Ha! Neither of them has ever gone on a date in their lives, or not since they were seventeen or something—and making out at keg parties doesn't count. Brad and Courtney have never really been single. They have never experienced trolling bars full of losers or hooking up with losers at New York film-industry parties or being set up with losers by well-meaning friends. Who the hell are they to give me advice? Feeling deliciously rebellious, I pull out my cell with such vigor that I slip on a frozen puddle on Court's corner and almost eat it. Where the hell is springtime anyway? One minute it's warm, the next minute the streets are frozen. *All those pretty little green buds are going to freeze to death*, I think as I dial the number for John. The musician who didn't have the good sense to get a Ph.D.

Turns out John is a twenty-four-year-old bass player who bartends for cash. (Living in New York, I've found this to be a common professional combination.) He cracks me up. After twenty minutes on the phone—I talk to him all the way to the subway and then hang around the entrance talking some more—I know his life story. I know he grew up in Portland, went to college in Santa Cruz, majored in environmental studies, and played with a successful local band that landed—and lost—a record deal his senior year. He moved to New York to start a new group and is currently auditioning musicians and playing with random bands at the Mercury Lounge and the Knitting Factory. He smokes pot daily (can't get through a conversation with his mother without it), worships Pink Floyd, is suffering from post–California-surf withdrawal, and broke up with his college girlfriend only a couple of months back, when she decided she couldn't handle the schizophrenic energy of New York and moved back to Santa Cruz. He doesn't seem to care which coast she's on. "My music is my number-one priority right now. Know what I mean?"

When I hang up, I feel with some certainty that if I take twenty-four-year-old bass-player-slash-bartender John up on his offer to check out his apartment tonight—the fact that it's almost midnight doesn't faze him—he will be the kind of scruffy blond boy who makes me go wobbly in the knees. That he'll offer me a beer or a joint or both. That the conversation will pop. That the apartment will be a hole. That the sex will be spectacular. But I also know I shouldn't. He's young and he's clearly commitment phobic. I need serious guys for this piece, not to mention serious guys in my life—or one anyway.

Plus, John is an Aries. I'm an Aries, and I'm not supposed to go out with them, mainly because my dad is an Aries and it's common knowledge that we spend our whole lives trying to make our dad (or someone just like him) fall in love with us, which is enough to make anyone insane. Jake's an Aries. He makes me insane. Stefan's an Aries. *He* made me insane. My college boyfriend who left me for a girl who once posed for a Gap underwear ad, but still showed up in my room late at night just to make sure I remained insane—Aries. The guy I lost my virginity to when I was sixteen was an Aries. I have distinct memories of him: He wanted to wallpaper his room with my picture. He would go weeks without calling, forcing me to spend my days willing the phone to ring and my nights calling and hanging up on him (subliminally remind-him-of-my-existence kind of thing). He once told me he was "like, in love" with me and I treasured those words for, like, ever. The morning after we had sex for the first time—My First Time—he left at four A.M. to go surfing. We stopped seeing each other when I punched him in the stomach one night because he was dancing with another girl. (This behavior might qualify as insane.) The list of Aries men who have contributed to the decline of my mental health goes on and on.

Aries guys are driven, confident, full of childlike wonder. That's why I want to devour them on sight. But they're also stubborn, infantile, and don't know how to let go. You'd think that fire and fire would make a great match. Try two deranged rams, swirling horns locked, loving every minute of frantic, sweaty combat, until one of the two lies bleeding. I wish I had a T-shirt that said, CUTE ARIES BOYS GO HOME. Nobody told me they would turn me into a possessed, love-sick lunatic when they were teaching me other important facts of life. As the eloquent expression goes, I had to learn it the hard way.

When I get off the F train at First Avenue at 12:38 I'm pretty sure I'm going to John's place, in defiance of all my good reasons not to. Once I get something stuck in my head, no matter how absurd or unhealthy, I know I'm going through with it. What's the harm, really? It's only a block out of my way. I soak up my eclectic neighborhood, passing by a bouncing Caribbean restaurant, a rinky-dink radio station with two twenty-something guys in headsets inside nodding furiously to the tunes they so cleverly programmed, a yoga-studio-slash-Buddhist-sanctuary-slash-vegan-eatery, a fluorescent-lit joint specializing in pizza and pasta and gyros and shish kabob and barbecue and chicken. Outside a crowded bar, people hover, smoking cigarettes. The bouncer hushes them. "Yo, think of the neighbors! Please!" he says. I pass a Vietnamese take-out joint, a twenty-four-hour Laundromat, an appliance emporium, an all-night café where attractive people lining the windows check their e-mail and cruise MySpace. A girl walks by with a bouncy schnauzer who grins up at me, tongue hanging out of his mouth. "Hey, monkey," I tell him before crossing the street and walking over to Avenue A, which is buzzing, like it does every night of the week.

The East Village, my home, is heaven for NYU students, recent college grads, and twenty-four-year-old musicians bent on making it. There must be an average of three bars per block, probably a third of which feature live music. Among the bars you can find the dingiest dive next to the swankiest lounge next to the friendliest neighborhood joint. My mother doesn't understand my affection for this dirty, ugly, noisy former slum that's virtually teeming with teenage degenerates covered in piercings and tattoos. She can't fathom what a woman in her thirties would still be doing in such a place. I figure as long as I'm single, this is where I belong. I can go out alone and always find a sympathetic soul with a booming personality and juicy past to chat with over a pint, and I rarely have to leave my twelve-block radius. Living in the hoppingest part of town, everyone comes to me. While I might someday outgrow the all-night buzz of the East Village, I tell my mom that I am devoted to these grimy streets and the tenement buildings growing out of them and swear I'll have my kids here and grow old here, even struggling up flights of battered, rickety stairs with a cane if I have to. But I'm probably full of shit.

I find myself walking east on Sixth Street straight past Avenue A (which would lead me home) toward Avenue B. "I don't care what Brad thinks," I say aloud. "'No hooking up with hunky musicians.' Easy for you to say, Mr. Getting-laid-on-a-regular-basis-since-you-were-twelve. I'm having sex and you can't stop me." I march past a hip, dimly lit Asian bistro and a skanky eatery with hipsters and hoodlums hanging out the windows and wind up standing in front of the deli on the corner of Avenue B across the street from John's building. I crane my neck to look up at the fourth floor, where he lives, hoping to catch a glimpse of him. I see an attractive guy with messy blond hair holding a beer. *If he looks my way, I'll go up*, I think before realizing that the skinny silhouette could belong to just about any guy on the block, any stoned, twenty-four-year-old, beer-swigging, bass-playing hottie in the goddamn East Village.

Brad is right: I don't need to meet that guy anymore, not at this point in my life. I am writing a story about how to meet the right kind of man, the kind who could potentially wind up my husband, not another hot young thing to drag into my bed. I march quickly up Avenue B and don't look back. Then I start running, toward home, fast and furious. I work up a sweat flying up the four flights of stairs to my apartment and grab a pad of Post-its once inside the door. I peel one off and write:

**No guys under 30.
NO ARIES.**

I stick it to my fridge door.

Proud of myself, I throw on sweats and get to work sanding a bench I found on the sidewalk the other day. I'm painting it tangerine and pasting a photo collage on top, thinking it will make an unusual coffee table. It's only when I've smoothed out the first leg that I realize that my apartment is a horror story. The fourteen outfits that Alicia tried on before settling on whatever she wore for her date with the actor are strewn all over the living room floor, my blanket lies in a heap in the doorway to my bedroom— guess Princess took a nap?—and the boxes of books stacked from floor to ceiling behind the couch fill me with renewed irritation. The temperature has dropped again, so I get up and try to shut the stupid broken window, but give up as always. I stomp into the bathroom, where it looks like bad guys have turned the place up- side down searching for clues. In the kitchen, half a can of tomato soup sits congealing in a pot on the stove. Dirty dishes clog the sink. I make a mental note to strangle my sister as I toss the gelat- inous red mess down the drain and put Beethoven on the stereo, hoping some sonata therapy will cool my anger.

After lighting a candle, I return to my project, slowly sanding, and breathing in the unmistakable scent of Votivo red currant. My apartment has good energy, despite my sister's Tasmanian devilish cleaning habits. Courtney's sage-smudging worked. The memory of her puttering from corner to corner shaking smoke at my walls makes me chuckle. She'd shake shake shake while telling me to think about what I want to invite into my life (love, peace, a coat rack) and what I want to purge from it (loneliness, fear, the stench of sage). Sometimes her methods strike me as mad, but they actu- ally seem to work. The apartment feels cleansed and peaceful. We did make space for abundance, self-discipline, and a healthy rela- tionship to enter my life. Once the bench is prepped for a first coat of paint, I trash the dust I've created and make my way to bed, doing my best to ignore the disorder around me. But when Alicia stumbles in and crawls under the covers at three A.M., giggly and reeking of scotch, I kick her.

> Recently divorced 40-year-old man seeks
> a nice young woman to share roomy UES 2
> bd. The room is large. I'm a nice guy, easy
> to live with. Give me a chance! What have
> you got to lose? My name's Stanley.

5

Over the weekend, psyched about beginning my research in earnest, I send Alicia off to brunch and plant
myself at my desk, which is tucked into a little nook of my
living room with a window to my right. I live on a quiet
block, but it is one of the first warm days of the year and
I'm easily distracted by kids playing in the garden I can see
below and pigeons' springtime mating coos. I force myself
to stay glued to my chair—except for one break when I allow myself to paint my new coffee table—and spend the
day scouring Craig's List.

My only experience with computer dating was a quick
trip through one of the more popular sites after a friend of
a friend went out with an average of two guys a day for six
months and eventually met her husband. I figured what
the hell, bookmarked a few cuties, and developed a crush

on a guy named BabarBoy from Brooklyn. As big a crush as you can develop for a flattering headshot and a series of pithy yet sincere answers to some banal questions. The second time I checked the site, BabarBoy had mysteriously vanished from that particular cyberzone. I figured that's the kind of luck I have with online dating and never went back. When everyone was first in their Friendster and then MySpace phase, I went out on five disastrous dates with guys who had seemed perfectly normal in their profiles, and carried on a passionate six-week correspondence with a writer on a retreat in Locarno. I was in a frenzy over possibly meeting The Guy until he returned to New York and we had coffee, and I learned he had bad skin, bad table manners, and no personality off the page. I was so embarrassed by the whole affair, I ran home and deleted every word of our gushing cyber-romance.

Looking for love in the real estate section, though, makes me feel the way big-time computer daters must feel: like the possibilities are endless if only you put in the time and chalk up the numbers. I have the funny impression of shopping for a boyfriend, feeling these men out the way you might finger plums at a farm stand: metaphorically admiring their purple sheen, squeezing them to test their firmness, sniffing for sweetness, eventually buying and taking a bite—or not. I decide I should have rules of conduct, so I write them down, excited to put words on a page.

Rule #1: During the initial phone conversation with a potential "roommate," tell him immediately that I'm not necessarily looking for an apartment. I'm just seeing what's out there, because my current living situation is precarious and I might have to move fast. Nothing is definite—yet. This provides an escape route since clearly I'm not really moving in with the guy. Clever Courtney did this during her test calls the other night, and it worked remarkably well, leaving no one feeling dumped or duped.

The biggest hurdle with this whole project is my complete inability to tell a lie. I don't know if it's a belief in the beauty of truth or fear of being caught, but regardless, anything more than a little white lie ("My breakup with Jake was mutual"; "I'll be there in thirty seconds, just walking out the door"; "I'm almost done with my Matt Dillon piece, Steve, just doing final tweaks") sets my voice wavering, my cheeks burning in shame. I realize pretty quickly that this scheme will require me to overcome this phobia. I have to pretend I'm not sitting in a beautiful new apartment in the East Village chatting on the brand-new portable phone I just plugged into my brand-new, flawlessly painted eggshell-white wall, but that I really want to move into the spare room in some guy's charming duplex in Chelsea. After the first few awkward calls and some initial guilt pangs, I come to an important decision: It's time to swallow my scruples and commit myself to going on a Man Hunt (the cheesy *Flashdance* song has been playing in my head for days). Which means becoming an expert at telling untruths, and fast.

"I should find out if I have to move by next week," I say to Clarence, a thirty-three-year-old guy who works in marketing and has an alluring South African accent. "Can I come look at the place this afternoon, just in case?"

He lives only a few blocks away, so I tell him I'll be there in half an hour and rip open my closet.

Rule #2: Wear something cute. Sexy is essential. Whether or not the guy knows I'm trolling for eligible bachelors, I am, so looking good is key. I'm not much of a makeup person, but for apartment visits, I wear lipstick, mascara, a spritz of the Tiffany perfume my mom gave me for Christmas (she'd be happy to know she's contributing to my quest for both a suitable mate and a higher income bracket). When I walk through that door, the guy has to think, *Wow, I hope she doesn't want to live here, because I want to marry this woman, and it wouldn't really be appropriate to stick the mother of my children in the spare bedroom.*

When Clarence opens the front door to his apartment, I know I've chosen the right outfit. His jaw drops and he literally stutters, "H-h-hello," and proceeds to address my chest instead of my face as he forms the words, "Come in. Please. Yeah, come on in, um, Jacquie." I say a silent, *Woo-hoo!* and make a mental note to go with sheer clothing whenever possible.

Now, Clarence is a good-looking guy. He's got that hip East Village thing going on. Beige cords hanging off his hips. Sweater he's been wearing since college, judging from the threadbare state of the elbows. Greasy bedhead I find inexplicably attractive. And, as I mentioned, he has an accent that could send you straight to heaven. But Clarence's apartment is not a place where human beings should be allowed to enter, let alone live. Inert in the doorway, my eyes scan the place: There's lots of brown. Shabby beige futon. Shit-colored armchair with foam popping through ripped vinyl. Faux wood paneling on the walls. Piles of junk—crumpled newspapers, toppled paint buckets, empty beer bottles, broken Styrofoam, forgotten milk cartons, orange peels so hard they could be sold as guitar picks, a G.I. Joe doll, an unwashed cereal bowl with a trail of ants marching through it—on every grimy surface. It's *Animal House* the morning after the toga party, except here there's a shower in the kitchen, a stall the size of a coffin right there next to the spaghetti sauce–splattered fridge, with a once-clear, now grim, waterstained curtain hanging over the side facing me, duct tape running along the rim of the base, and a bottle of Head & Shoulders perched precariously on one moldy wall. I can't believe he pays $2,400 for this pit. That's New York City in the twenty-first century. I don't have much time to take it all in, though, as my senses are instantly scrambled by the stench: garbage, baked garbage, bags of rotting eggs, takeout, coffee grinds, bong refuse, festering for days, if not weeks. It smells like the streets of New York on garbage day, mid-August. If it's not a smell you're familiar with, be thankful. It's what I imagine that dead body, on, like, day four, smells like. It hits my nostrils like a fist, and I wonder if there's vermin hanging out in his trash.

In Clarence's case, there's no need for Rule #3: Scrutinize the guy's bathroom, kitchen, and bookshelves ASAP. I won't bother with Clarence's. Mess can be dealt with, wardrobe can be up-graded, fashion faux pas tossed while he's asleep, but a guy who doesn't mind inhaling filth all day is a guy who doesn't mind in-haling filth all day. This time I don't poke around to see if his plants are dead or alive (or if he has any). I don't check out the photos of his mom, dad, and college buddies, or notice a whole wall devoted to some big-breasted redhead. On this particular visit, I don't get the chance to peek into the cupboards or glean the invaluable insight into a man's taste, intellect, and psyche that one can glean from a glance at his library.

I reluctantly cross the threshold into his apartment, breathing very slowly through my mouth.

"Wanna sit down?" he asks, still addressing my chest.

"I don't have a lot of time," I say, resisting the urge to pull my shirt up over my nose. "Can I see the room?"

Safely settled in the empty box this guy wants me to move into, where the odor is a bit less pungent, I relax. "So, this is it?" I say, glancing around. "There's nothing in it!"

"Yeah, my roommate left fast, took it all." He looks down at his feet. "You know, the guitarist from the Strokes lives downstairs."

"Neat," I say, assuming the apartment downstairs is a smidge larger, cleaner, more fragrant. "You like the Strokes?"

"Oh, yeah. It's cool that we have so many cool people living in the neighborhood."

"I agree," I say, wandering out of the bedroom and into the mildew-infested bathroom, just a toilet stall with a rusty medicine cabinet on one wall, a cracked sink, on its edge a thumbnail-size sliver of soap the color of dishwater—Irish Spring, I presume—with blackened grooves running through it, and a shaky, particle-board cabinet on the floor, I imagine full of cleaning products and condoms.

"What did you say you do again?" Clarence asks, making conversation.

"I'm a writer and editor at a film magazine, *Flicks*."

"That sounds so cool," he says, his eyes lighting up. "I wish I liked my job better. God, you have an amazing smile."

"Thanks. Thanks so much," I say. "Look, Clarence, I kind of have to go. I'll call you?"

"Yeah, that sounds great," he says, leading me back to the door.

I hold on to the wall outside of his building for support and fill my lungs with deep, nourishing breaths of fresh, clean New York City exhaust before hurrying back to my place. On my way home, I spot the cute hardware-store boy and his girlfriend walking Buster through the park. They're holding hands and strolling silently, no need for words I guess after all these years. I experience a sharp pang of envy.

When I reach my place, Alicia is IMing friends on my computer and gabbing loudly on the phone at the same time.

"So, he stands up and starts showing me judo moves," she's telling a friend, "you know, standing behind me, positioning my arms and hips, and I was like, he's really cute! Then he goes, 'Do you want some wine?' and I was like, 'I could use a glass.' I couldn't believe how cozy we were getting so fast—"

"Jesus fucking Christ!" I explode in the middle of her darling house-hunting tale.

"Okay, okay," she says, jumping out of my chair. "My sister's home. Can I call you back?" She hangs up. "I'm just here for a minute. I'm sorry! I'm going to look at an apartment and going to the gym. I'll be out of your way in, like, half an hour. I'm gonna take a really short nap. I got no sleep last night, that guy was too cute, I had to drink, I . . ."

"Alicia, I can't deal with this anymore." I look around. There's a pile of laundry on the floor, random items of clothing sprawled on my kitchen counter, a bowl of tuna that's turning brown, an open mayonnaise jar. "Look at this shit!"

Something dislodges in my brain and I start picking up magazines, bras, tank tops and throwing them for emphasis, shoving the stuff on the counter. "This is my apartment! Of course I let you stay here because you're my sister, but honestly, show some respect. I can't live this way! I need it to be neat so I can think straight! You don't pick up your shit, you sit there IMing all day, what the hell are you doing with yourself? You can't just sit around doing nothing."

She starts running around picking clothes up and folding them. "I'm sorry. I'm sorry, really. I'm gonna do laundry right now. Want me to do yours?"

"I don't know," I say. "Jesus Christ, Alicia, what is up with you? You're not working, you're not really looking for a place to live. Why would you? You've got mine and it's a free bed and phone and Internet and food and company. Shit, you're twenty-eight years old and you're doing nothing but hanging around these guys who are, like, twelve and live in Williamsburg and play the drums."

I'm pacing now, gesticulating wildly with one of Alicia's hot-pink flip flops, which has taken up lodging on my kitchen counter. "God, you've got this perfect life in L.A. and now you're over here dumping your shit all over my apartment. I just—I need to get out of here. Would you please clean up? Would you try to find an apartment?"

My coat is still on, so I just turn around and exit the way I entered, and head for the corner café. I let a glass of white wine poured by my favorite Italian calm my nerves and pull my notebook out of my purse. An ad placed by someone named Peter sounds appealing. I dial his number on my cell. Peter tells me he lives in a "cozy [read: minuscule] two-bedroom in Little Italy" and spends his days reporting for *The New York Times*. He's thirty-two, scratchy voiced, funny, and flirtatious. He says there's someone interested in the room, but he isn't sure if it's going to work out and he's leaving the country tomorrow to spend two weeks on a boat off the southern coast of Turkey and write about it—hello, the guy's perfect—so if I want to see the place, it has to be now.

I'm still wearing the see-through shirt that caught Clarence's eye, but I reapply lipstick, slam the last of my Pinot Grigio, and jump into a cab.

My cab pulls up to the corner of Elizabeth and Spring in No-Lita, brakes screeching to a halt in front of a bland beige building with a rust-colored door. This is a nice neighborhood, expensive with new, overpriced boutiques and trendy bars popping up every day to replace the old ones that are forced to close their doors, victims of the ever-increasing rents. I'm undaunted by the appearance of the building, aware that hidden treasures often lurk behind unsightly facades. I buzz and climb a dingy, poorly lit staircase with two-tone walls that are peeling and crumbling. The top half was once off-white but has been weathered into a rough shade of grime, and the forest-green bottom half looks as if a feral cat comes out every night after the inhabitants' bedtime to claw at it rabidly. I've learned not to judge an apartment by its stairway, any more than the edifice's exterior: At least downtown, nine out of ten hallways feature scuff marks, stairs beaten by decades of overuse, and cheesy, misguided paint jobs by management too tight-fisted to do it right.

Standing on the landing of the third floor is a tall, hot teacher's-pet type with short, dirty blond hair wearing faded jeans, an untucked, light blue Oxford shirt, thick tortoise-shell glasses, and a big smile. He's unfairly good-looking.

"Hey, thanks for rushing over," he says.

"I'm excited to see the place," I respond, taking his outstretched hand firmly in mine. In spite of strike one (Clarence), I realize that Alicia was right: This idea is ingenious. A man's apartment is a reflection of him—his passions, his temperament, his compulsions, his soul—and I am about to invade Peter's.

I wag my hips as I enter an apartment that is as cozy as he described it. Honey-colored wood floors, exposed brick, exotic rugs, eclectic furniture, a fireplace, funky, multicultural knick-knacks cluttering every surface, and a tiny, old-fashioned corner kitchen, someplace Annie Hall might live. Bookcases packed with books: quality novels, biographies, political nonfiction, art monographs—not a testosterone-fueled action adventure or Atkins manifesto in sight. As I scan the shelves, I can't believe my luck. It's only my second apartment, and I've stumbled upon a smart, attractive, straight guy with great taste. God, what if this is it? What if I meet the man of my dreams on my first day on assignment? That would make a perfect ending to my story.

My heartbeat quickens and I apply Rule #4: If I find him attractive and his apartment acceptable, skip banalities and get personal fast.

"What makes a guy hold on to a porcelain bunny with a missing ear that's probably been around since 1978?" I ask him as he stands fidgeting in the kitchen, which is separated from the living room by a sturdy bar topped with wood the color of caramel.

"My grandmother gave me that when I was six. Haven't been able to let it go, I guess. It reminds me of her," he says as I finger the spine of a weathered copy of *Anna Karenina*. I've held on to everything my grandmother ever gave me, too. We spent a lot of time together when I was growing up and were incredibly close; I became ill for a week when she died three years ago. I'm not ready to tell Peter about my grandmother, though, as cute as he is.

"I read a lot," Peter says. "Can't bring myself to throw books out, either. A bit of a head case, right? Hey, do you want something to drink? A beer? Tea?"

What I want is to throw this cute, sensitive head case onto the couch and get to work making a blond, brainy kid with a thing for literature and clutter, but instead I accept a Corona and ask to see the room. First we visit his: chunky, wood-framed, fluffy-white-comforter-covered bed that almost fills the room. No other furniture except an elaborately carved Asian armoire and a small chest of drawers. I run my finger suggestively along its edge. One wall is completely covered with framed black-and-white photographs.

"You take these?"

"Most of them," he says. "I dabble."

I study the photos taken in places as diverse as Bangkok, Beirut, and Botswana, Paris, Puerto Rico, and the Poconos. He likes shooting children and old people, the two human sub-groups I've always found most appealing. He notices details. His compositions are unexpected. He's talented, understated, a pack rat like me.

"What's your sign?" I ask.

"Aries."

I move to the window and look out onto Elizabeth Street, momentarily dismayed, but hopeful that some other aspect of his chart will make him a suitable candidate for my heart. Once we start dating, I'll get his time and place of birth and pass them on to Courtney to sort it all out. Peter stands next to me. His left hip touches my right, making me tingle.

"See that window?" He indicates a dimly lit rectangle in the building across the street. "There's this couple that lives there. I can see them sometimes in that chair, you know." He lets out an embarrassed laugh. My cheeks flush. This is an extremely good first date.

"Let's look at your room," he says, a clear attempt to flee his bedroom before suffocating under the sexual tension.

The second bedroom is the size of my closet. You could barely fit a full-size bed if you didn't have any other furniture, but it has a hefty closet. He tells me that the girl who lived there previously was clever with space and put up shelves to the ceiling right over the bed, but she unfortunately took them with her. He indicates where her creation used to be, stretching his arm up high, his shirt rising to expose a tanned six-pack. I gasp quietly, and he turns toward me.

"So, someone else is interested in the room?" I squeak.

He says the other potential roommate is supposed to let him know by tomorrow. He'll call and leave me a message before he takes off. I start to feel bad about lying to him, recognizing what a terrible way this is to start a relationship. I say I'm not sure if I'm moving yet, that my situation is up in the air, I'll let him know as soon as my plans solidify. We exchange e-mail addresses.

We make our way back to the living room, and I sit on the couch. He plops down next to me and absentmindedly turns on the TV and we stare at scantily clad women taking turns scaling a building. When the doorbell rings, he buzzes without asking who's there.

A couple of minutes later, a girl saunters into the room and kisses him on the mouth. His sister? She's Asian. And skinny. And striking, with poofy, red lips and skin like vanilla Häagen-Dazs. Could she be one of those girls who kisses male friends ambiguously on the lips whether or not she's sleeping with them? I hold my breath.

"Jacquie, this is my girlfriend, Stacy. Jacquie's looking at the room."

I smile weakly up at her from the couch, which suddenly feels very low to the floor. "Nice to meet you," I croak, feeling like a dwarf all alone on a planet populated by tall, pretty people.

We make polite conversation for ten minutes and watch TV, while I groan inwardly and display an expression that says, *Chipper! Relaxed! Enthusiastic would-be roommate!* After all, this enchanting, good-looking guy—and his equally enchanting, good-looking girlfriend—thinks I want to move into this apartment. I gnaw my left thumbnail and snap my rubber band. Ouch.

"Guess you'll miss Peter when he's in Turkey," I say lamely.

"I'm going with him," Stacy says perkily. "I'm psyched!"

"Yeah, cool, lucky."

That clinches it. I stand up, drop my empty beer bottle onto the coffee table with a clink, and announce that I have to leave. What's the point? I'm completely depressed and feel an urgent need to get out of the joint and call Jeremy to meet me for a stiff drink in the East Village, my turf, where I feel confident and protected.

"Well, Peter, I don't think I'm interested in the room after all," I announce.

He looks up at me, perfectly baffled, while Stacy continues to smile beatifically. Of course Peter is perplexed. If there's anything I have learned in my thirty-two years on the planet, it's that people generally believe what you tell them. If they own a liquor store and you tell them you're organizing a fund-raiser for the American Cancer Society next week—like my best friend in high school once did—and you're going to be ordering fourteen cases of wine and sixteen of beer and would like to check prices, they believe you. And when you add, incidentally, "I think I'll take a bottle of that cheap white wine-in-a-box on the shelf behind you right now," they hand it over, even if you're seventeen and wearing a private-girls'-school uniform.

And if you tell a guy you want to rent a room in his apartment and actually go over to look at it, it never occurs to him that you might have ulterior motives. Why would it?

I stop by my apartment, which Alicia has miraculously straightened and momentarily evacuated, and check my messages.

"Hey, Jacquie, John here, remember me? Room for rent, Avenue B. I know you're not looking for a place to live anymore, but I wondered if you wanted to come by—"

I erase it midmessage.

"Hi, my name's Herbert. You left me a message about my room for rent. You wanted to know more about me. I am fifty-six, never married. I live with my six cats (Greg, Peter, Bobby, Marsha, Jan, and Cindy) two parakeets (Mike and Carol), iguana named Alice, and tarantula called Sam the Butcher—"

Delete.

"Hi, Jacquie. It's Matt with the apartment in SoHo. Hey, can you come by Tuesday instead of Wednesday? That would be sweet. Let me know."

"Hi, this is Denise. My boyfriend, Rufus, told me you called about our extra room?"

Delete.

"Hey, Franz here." Sexy accent. "You called about the apartment. Me and my girlfriend would love you—"

I punch the Delete button with my fist, causing my answering machine to topple off its perch. "Sorry!" I tell it before placing it nicely back in its spot.

"Every guy in New York has a girlfriend," I bitch to Jeremy over drinks at a onetime dive on Avenue A that now charges eleven dollars for a Cosmopolitan but Jeremy likes anyway because they let Napoleon sit on his bar stool with him. "I'm getting totally pessimistic about this whole endeavor."

"What did that one guy say?" he asks, while Napoleon, decked out in a leopard-skin hoodie, compulsively licks his wrist. "The investment banker in Tribeca who raved about skinny-dipping in Ibiza."

" 'She's over sometimes, but I wouldn't worry about it if I were you.' "

"That guy doesn't have a girlfriend," he says, ripping Napoleon off his arm and feeding him from the bowl of pretzels on the bar. "He wants you to know he won't jump on you when you walk through the door. Here's what I think: If they don't live together, he's fair game."

"Maybe you're right."

"Of course I'm right," he says, leaning over to check his phone, which is sitting silently on the bar, and scooting back in his stool, disappointed. "Any mildly attached guy who's still living alone sees you, he's dumping her. Or at least having an affair."

"You say the sweetest things. You know, if you'd fall in love with me, I wouldn't have to go through this insanity."

"Are you kidding? This is the best thing that's ever happened to you. You'll meet a guy so hot, next year every hipster in New York will be"—he makes quotation marks in the air with his fingers—" 'looking for a roommate.' It'll be the new trend in dating. You'll be famous and go on *Oprah*, as if having a hot new boyfriend and an article in the women's rag du jour weren't enough."

"I like that."

"What's rule number five again?"

"Rule number five: The date's the prize. Do what it takes, whatever it takes, to nab the date."

"You're such a vixen. You'll definitely get a date soon."

I wonder silently why no one has asked me out yet, but wipe the thought from my mind.

"Whatever happened to that guy you went out with on my birthday?" I ask.

"Never called."

We bow our heads. Napoleon gets nervous and barks twice. "It's all right, Nappie, Daddy's got it all under control." Addressing me again, Jeremy says, "I called him and left a really cute message and then when he didn't call back, I left another totally nonchalant one, and then yesterday, I left one saying, 'Look, if you want to go out for a drink sometime, let's do it. If not, please call and let me know. I had a really good time the other night and I think you did, too. I just want to know one way or the other.'" As I shudder, he goes on, "I am so sick of these people being dishonest with me. I don't really care what happens. He was way too built for me anyway—I don't like a guy with too many muscles—but just be straight up, you know?"

"My sister would kick your ass for leaving three messages. She says you should never, ever leave a message. If you absolutely have to call him or you'll die, use *67 so your number comes up 'unknown,' and hang up if you get voice mail."

"Oh yeah, I'm sure that's what you do," he says, checking his phone again.

"Yeah, every time. I'm a disaster, I call so incessantly someone should lock me up, but I never leave a trace."

By the time we leave the bar, Jeremy has decided what I'll wear when I go on *Oprah* and how I'll slyly plug him as the hottest new fashion designer in New York. "I think what first made my perfect new boyfriend fall in love with me was the stunning dress I was wearing, designed by my sickeningly talented friend, Jeremy Frye. I have a picture of it right here. Isn't it gorgeous?" (He makes me rehearse it fourteen times.) The bartender has bought us a round and given Napoleon a ratty old shoelace to chew on, making life-long devotees of all three of us. And I have decided to change the rules slightly. For one, I decide that it is essential to find out if a guy has a girlfriend before I set foot in his pad.

"Is there anything else I should know about you? Like do you maybe have a girlfriend who sleeps over all the time?" I ask Jörg, a Norwegian designer with a "snazzy" loft in the West Thirties, whom I call the next day.

"Not all the time," he answers enigmatically. *Screw him*, I think. I'm not about to drag myself to the West Thirties for a guy who won't tell a strange woman if he has a girlfriend or not.

"My sweetheart lives in Virginia," says a thirty-six-year-old vet named Jeffrey. "She comes up on weekends and plans to move here next fall. That's why I'm only advertising the place as a six-month sublet. It could be longer, depending on her plans."

"Gloria lives here, too," says Thierry, a Belgian massage thera-pist with a duplex near Gramercy Park. "It will be wonderful if you ladies will like each other."

Getting the dirt up front saves me a lot of time and dashed hopes.

I also decide to start calling older guys. Some men in their late thirties and early to mid-forties are very attractive: George Clooney, Viggo Mortensen, and Brad Pitt, for example. And I relax the location rules. Okay, so I don't particularly want to live on the Upper East Side, but I could conceivably date a guy who lives there, provided that I can persuade him to move downtown once he falls in love with me. Then again, maybe I'll meet a guy with an old-school, vine-covered manse with four bathrooms, three fire-places, original Schieles and Chagalls, a panoramic view of the park, a doorman named Sid who will become my new confidant, a car (or two), and so much cash that I could take cabs everywhere and never even notice I live in New York's stuffiest neighborhood. What that guy would be doing looking for a roommate I can't fathom, but that's not important. Maybe he's lonely. Maybe his cushy upbringing left him chronically craving attention, or his cat just died and he needs company but isn't quite ready for another furry friend. Whatever. Point is, I decide to expand my parameters and therefore call Stanley, a recently divorced forty-year-old who lives on the Upper East Side.

Stanley and I have a nice conversation. It isn't witty or flirtatious or deep, just nice. He tells me about his house in New Jersey, which his wife, Kelly, got in the divorce. He gushes about his two daughters, Kelsey and Kai, with whom he goes to amusement parks and baseball games on alternate weekends. He tells me about his Central Park soccer team and his real estate law practice that he hopes will really thrive now that he's living in the city full-time. Stanley is a genuinely nice guy, so I give him a chance. Just in case, I ask Alicia to accompany me.

"The Upper East Side? Are you smoking crack?" she asks. But she comes along anyway.

Stanley's apartment is located above an Irish pub on what must be the noisiest block of Lexington Avenue. This clearly isn't my guy with the race car, the bulging bank account, and the dead kitty. There isn't a vine or a doorman in sight. I'm ready to blow off the whole meeting but know I'd feel terrible later and plod on. *He just moved to the city,* I tell myself, *he can't be blamed for a questionable first location.* Alicia's face registers disdain. But I haven't gotten asked out on any dates yet, so, knowing that I need to inject some juice into my article, I buzz.

We have to walk up four flights of stairs to get to the apartment—Alicia groaning all the way—and the guy standing at the door when we finally get there looks exactly like a recently divorced forty-year-old should. He's sporting a graying version of

Adam Sandler's haircut in *The Wedding Singer* and a faded, baby-blue Lacoste shirt and acid-wash jeans. He asks us if we want "a soda." His nondescript bachelor pad looks like it belongs to a nice, forty-year-old guy who just lost his shirt—and most of his other possessions—in a grueling divorce: cramped, almost empty (besides the mess of cardboard boxes clogging the hallway), in desperate need of a woman's touch. We sit down on his exhausted, checkered futon, which probably used to live in his suburban basement. When my sister excuses herself to go to the bathroom, he looks so nervous about having to carry on a one-on-one conversation with me, I feel sorry for him. I smile dumbly as he babbles on about his partner at the law firm.

"It's a weird partnership," he says. "Sometimes we don't get along. He yells and slams doors, but when we're making money and things are smooth sailing, we click literally like hand in glove."

"Gee, I know how that goes," says Alicia, appearing suddenly at my side. "My gloves make such a huge racket when I put my hands in them, it *literally* breaks my eardrums."

I give her a look that says, Lay off this poor guy, cupcake.

"I guess you and your partner click just like a couple of LEGOs most of the time," she says to Stanley. "Just like ice falling into a glass. So, what you're saying, Stanley, is you used to get along swell, but lately you're just like cats and dogs. Literally."

Stanley stares at her with his lips slack and lightly parted, his tongue protruding just a smidgen. Then he starts to laugh, a light chuckle, and shakes his head from side to side. Stanley isn't a bad guy. I tell him I'll call him as soon as I know more about my living situation. His face droops, the ends of his eyebrows turning down. He looks so sad, for a minute I consider moving in with him.

"Really, I'll call you this week."

Leaving Stanley's place, I tell Alicia I'll never look at another apartment above Twenty-third Street again and vow to myself to always trust my gut. It is infallible. It knew Philippe was not the guy I was going to end up with, even as my heart went pitter-pat and my head shouted *Marriage material!* It sent me to bed with Jake, which is where we were destined to spend a season even if it did eventually lead to turmoil. And it knew that Stanley was a Nice Guy *but*. That's what we used to call guys like Stanley. Stepping out into the warm day, I say out loud, "Go with your gut. God!" No sparks means no sparks. Compromise is forbidden. If it feels like a bowl of cream of wheat and it smells like a bowl of cream of wheat, it's going to taste like a bowl of cream of wheat.

My sister leaves me at Fifty-ninth and Lexington to meet a good-looking cameraman, whom she met apartment hunting, for a walk in Central Park. He wants to take pictures of the blossoming trees.

"How come you meet cool guys and I meet Stanley?" I ask.

"Because I don't give a shit," she says, disappearing into the subway station.

Then I do the logical thing and call Jake. Just to check in, see how he's doing, and wish him a belated happy birthday. I missed it since I wasn't speaking to him. I have a hunch it was selfish of me to cut off all contact with him just because he bruised my ego. He doesn't have many true friends in New York (he only moved here eight months ago), and he's grown to value my friendship, and I've decided I'm willing to overlook my hurt feelings to maintain contact with him. He says he's grateful and sounds like he means it.

An hour later, we're having sex in my bathtub. Afterward, while eating Chinese takeout in bed in the middle of the afternoon, I tell him about my scheme. He thinks it's "awesome." I'm pleased.

"Well, we're not going out anymore, right?" he asks. "I mean, we did break up, right?"

"Yeah," I say. "Of course. I mean, don't you want to?"

"Yeah, yeah, I do," he says. He doesn't speak for a minute. "It wasn't working out. Shit, Jacquie, you can be such a pain in the ass, but I was happy you called." Pregnant pause. "I missed you."

"It's only been a week."

I'm touched by his confession and even wonder if there might be hope for us. Then he gets up, quite suddenly announcing that he has to go, and leaves, only after advising me to "have fun bonking those apartment dudes." I get out of bed and scribble "Trust Your Gut" on the Post-it barely clinging to my fridge. Then I call Courtney.

86

"Hey, I just saw Jake. He was really sweet, then he was a jerk. I don't know, why do I stay hung up on these guys?"

"Jacq," she interrupts, "you used to stay in going-nowhere relationships for three, four years. Now you're starting to get out in three, four months. That is an improvement. It's progress. Don't regress now. Jake isn't *the one*."

"Right," I say, scribbling, "No More Jake!" on my Post-it. "Hey, Court? How come no one's asking me out?"

"Hmm, I don't know."

"Me neither. I'm wearing tight clothes, flirting like a sorority girl on Quaaludes."

"Well, you tell them you're not moving in, right?"

"Um."

"I don't think they're going to ask you out on a date if they think you're moving in. That would be inappropriate."

On Monday, before I even go to work, I call Clarence and tell him I'm not interested in his apartment.

"Well, maybe we can have a beer in the neighborhood sometime." I'm literally jumping up and down as I tell him I'll check in as soon as I have some free time. Then I call Stanley and say I don't actually have to leave my apartment. He asks me out to lunch, and I tell him I have a boyfriend. Dishonesty is coming a lot more easily these days.

I'm smiling so hard that my lips feel like they might leap off my face as I hop on my bike to go to work. I curse myself like I do every time I ride for being too vain to wear a helmet and concentrate on dodging traffic and trying not to die. I ride hard and fast for a few blocks of Ninth Street, taking in the New York City tapestry of serious-looking suits brushing up against deli delivery guys rushing past anxious young nannies chasing toddlers. Holding my breath as I zip down Seventh Avenue in a speedy bike messenger's wake, which requires the focus and faith of a zealot, I laugh out loud.

It's working, it's working!

Now, if I could only meet someone I like.

The next few weeks yield more meetings with strange men than the rest of my life put together. It's a relatively dead period at work between issues, Alicia's in an apartment-hunting frenzy, Courtney's in Boston playing groupie, and T-shirt weather has finally arrived, so I just go for it. Here's what I come up with:

Bachelor #1: Matt the model lives in a loft in SoHo. It's sparsely, but smartly, decorated. Couch is expensive, fire-engine red, facing a nice flat-screen TV. Bookshelves are blue milk cartons stacked sideways on top of one another, shoved up against a brick wall, mostly filled with Matt's portfolios, fashion magazines, and framed photographs of his Midwestern family and childhood pets. The enormous coffee table was probably from Ikea once, but Matt has pasted hundreds of fashion shots (many featuring his flawless mug) all over it (presumably when stoned). Lamps—he likes lamps—are a funky assortment of designer and flea market. One wall of the living room has floor-to-ceiling windows facing west that display a string of roof gardens rosy against the sunset sky. Matt's model roommate took off on a world tour beginning in Japan, which Matt tells me is standard practice. Matt also did a stint in Asia—they loved him for his handsome six feet two inches and shoulder-length, butter-blond hair—where he bunked with four other male models in a Tokyo dump, spent his days flashing his pretty teeth for casting agents and climbing the StairMaster, and killed brain cells all night at clubs where house music pounded and giggling teenage girls flocked. After Japan, he hit Paris, Munich, and, finally, London, where he landed a major contract with a major designer and moved to New York to pour way too much rent into two thousand square feet on Spring Street. As far as I can tell, there are only three books in Matt's apartment: a coffee table book full of famous people and their pets, *Giving Good Orgasm: The Man's Guide to Tantric Pleasure* (I'm completely serious), and *Flowers for Algernon*, which I find adorable. It's a book I haven't read since elementary school, and imagining cute Matt poring over it makes me want to run my hands through his silky sheath of hair. Matt is handsome as a god and dumb as meatloaf, and we make tentative plans to have drinks next week. I assume we'll both blow off the date and wish I knew someone ditzy and pretty enough to set up with him.

Bachelor #2: Timothy, a thirty-something account exec at a major ad agency, lives in a two-bedroom that spans an entire floor of a brownstone in the West Village, my favorite neighborhood in Manhattan. In the cluster of blocks he described in his ad as "absurdly quaint," cobblestoned streets are adorned by gingko trees and ivy-covered brick buildings fronted by pristine shady stoops. Unlike my 'hood, where the street signs read 1, 2, 3, A, B, or C, here the picturesque, winding roads are called Horatio, Leroy, Morton, and other names of boys in whose faces I would have laughed if they'd asked me to dance in fifth grade, or named for the posher set: Christopher, Jane, Charles, Cornelia. I saunter, nose to the windowpanes of shops that must be obligated to adhere to a cuteness code: There's one devoted entirely to cupcakes, another to rubber stamps, innumerable to lovely, overpriced pottery and picture frames by local artists. The coffee shops all smell like freshly baked pie. As I turn to walk up the steps to Timothy's, I smile at a young woman wearing a Pomeranian puppy in a Burberry backpack strolling with another chic mom whose Baby-Björn holds a human child.

Timothy's cozy brownstone smells faintly of cinnamon, and not so much as a single stray sock litters the floor. Houseplants, scented candles, and glass jars filled with seashells are placed just so. Original paintings by unknown artists inspired by Monet and etchings reminiscent of Matisse hang tastefully on cream-colored walls. Pottery Barn perfection suggests an ex-girlfriend with good, if a tad conventional, taste or a flirtation with a salesgirl at Crate & Barrel. His books range from five whole shelves of travel guides to a Martha Stewart cookbook, everything ever published by *The Onion*, and, amusingly, *He's Just Not That Into You*.

Timothy has classically handsome features, hazel eyes, and yummy Abercrombie & Fitch physique and attire, and I learn that he played lacrosse at prep school and was president of his fraternity at Berkeley. He is, in short, the guy I've secretly fantasized about marrying all my life. The *It Happened One Night*–style banter between us gets my adrenaline pumping: I'm pulling clever responses to his rapid-fire queries out of one sleeve after the other, and he's hurling equally strong ammunition back at me. At one point he drops to the floor and gives me ten push-ups, to prove how dedicated he is to healing the environment. A minute later, his hilarious impression of his slave-driving boss has me clutching my sides.

"You know, I'm not sure I really need to move," I tell him, hoping he'll ask me out, but he doesn't. I wait an hour after leaving his place to call and inform him that I've learned that I'm definitely staying put, and his response is, "Fantastic news. You know, they say moving is the third most traumatic life experience after a death in the family and divorce."

I take a real risk then and say, "Maybe we can get coffee sometime."

His response: "Maybe."

Why is it that those guys in their untucked button-downs over well-worn khakis never seem interested in me? Why is it that those boys with their good bone structure and blindingly white teeth who play beach volleyball and summer in East Hampton never want to be my boyfriend? Sure, in college one of those V-shaped boys on the crew team usually wanted to suck face with me bleary-eyed at a frat party or even suck face with me bleary-eyed at two or three frat parties in a row—but it never went any further. When that guy with his country club stock and pack of hard-partying best friends stopped sucking my face, it was usually to date a blond tennis player named Kimberly. While I had tortured sex with a deranged would-be poet.

Nameless bachelors #3, 4, 5, and 6 live, respectively, in a generic Greenwich Village two-bedroom, of the cheap parquet floors and faux granite countertop variety, a minimalist NoHo duplex, a Chelsea six-story walk-up, and a Lower East Side hovel. Even though there's not an original morsel of dialogue or a face that tempts me to drop my knickers among them (and I decline the two invitations I receive), the quick succession of visits fires me up, makes me feel on a roll, like I'm conquering the world, conquering the male race, conquering my fear, my solitude, and my fear of solitude all at once.

Bachelor #7 is German, his name is Claus, and he lives in one of the most stunning apartments I've seen in all my years in New York. Claus is an interior designer and it shows. His space was probably raw when he moved in, but in the fourteen years he's been there, he has transformed it into a bohemian paradise. He boasts about having redone the kitchen—all shiny chrome and white terrazzo—with his own hands, tiled the enormous master bath lime green, built floor-to-ceiling bookshelves (I make a mental note to find someone to build mine first thing tomorrow), and dragged most of the eclectic mix of furniture in from the street or cheap stoop sales, with a couple of nicer items acquired during a series of trips to India and Tibet. Big, bushy ficuses and ferns stretch toward a skylight that invites sun to shine upon Claus's exotic treasures. I feel as if I'm inside a jewel box, and I don't really want to leave. Claus is attractive despite an early Flock of Seagulls 'do and a pair of groovy, chrome sunglasses that he wears indoors.

I make what I consider a valiant attempt to apply Rule #4

("Skip banalities and get personal fast"): "You seem to have a real love of beautiful things."

"Doesn't everyone?" he asks. "Here's the room."

Through French doors shaded by a luscious purple curtain lies what Claus has dubbed "The Animal Room." A zebra-skin rug snuggles up to the floorboards while a leopard-print bedspread luxuriates on a king-size mattress on the floor. A floating cabinet with glass doors is filled with statuettes of lions and tigers and bears (oh my!), and a random assortment of animal paintings covers most of the wall space.

"I love animals," I swoon.

"This is fortunate," Claus responds. "The room is very bright." Sure enough, sunlight streams through the window.

"Do you want it?" he asks. Very direct, those Germans.

I launch into my usual spiel: "Well, I'm not really sure if I'm moving out yet. I'm just looking around a bit, getting a feel for what's out there."

"Why don't you know?"

"Oh, it's an issue with my landlord. I may have to leave at the end of the month, but it's not clear yet."

"Didn't you pay a security deposit?"

Where exactly is he going with this? "Uh, yeah, I think so."

"Well, you can use that for your last month's rent, so you would not leave until the end of next month at very latest."

"Um, I hadn't thought about that."

"That is very strange if you're in discussion with your land-lord."

"Right." I suddenly feel like he's backing me into a corner, the lion tamer swinging his whip. I jump up and put on my jacket. "Well, I'll let you know what happens, okay?"

"It sounds to me like you won't be moving in here, Jacquie. I am looking for someone for the beginning of next month. We spoke of that on the phone."

"God, yeah, you're right, Claus. I don't know what I was thinking."

"This is a waste of my time."

"I guess. God, sorry. I should run."

An odd little smirk flickers across his face and I'm convinced that he's figured the whole thing out.

"You're a journalist, right?" he asks.

"Film journalist," I say. "I write about movies."

His face clouds over with confusion as I fairly sprint out the door, waving, and kicking myself for not thinking through my process more thoroughly. I escape into a cab mercifully emptying itself of a passenger right in front of Claus's building and call Courtney and Alicia to set up an emergency meeting for tomorrow morning.

"All right," says Courtney, removing a skimpy, dirt-brown towel from her naked body and plopping it down onto the slick, white-tiled bench in the steam room of the Russian & Turkish Baths on Tenth Street around the corner from my pad. "Let's get started."

Wednesday morning is Ladies' Day at the baths, so that's when we go, Alicia, myself, and Courtney if she can get away from work. We meet there at nine; sweat, scrub one another's backs, shower, and shoot the breeze for two hours; and if we still have time, have an early lunch. My coworkers understand that I don't come in until noon on selected Wednesdays (I love my job). Courtney called in sick this morning, probably for the first time in her life, because I told her I needed her.

"Hey, do you guys mind if I put lemongrass and eucalyptus oil in the steam?" she asks. "It's great for opening your pores and sinuses."

"Sure," I say. Alicia nods in agreement, her eyes closed, head resting against a steamy window.

The bony blonde sitting next to me gets up and leaves the steam room. Without opening her eyes, Alicia says, "That girl needs a cheeseburger."

"Okay, that's enough already," I say. "Court, please sit down. This is a desperate situation."

"Okay, how long have you been looking for an apartment?" Courtney asks me, settling onto the wet tiles.

"Just started this week. Third one I've seen."

"Good. And why do you have to move out?"

"Well, it's not definite, but my landlord, the jerk, is trying to kick me out. My lease is up and he can, like, quadruple the rent if he boots me." I close my mouth and inhale deep breaths of lemongrass-eucalyptus steam. I start coughing and Courtney pounds my back.

"You could try, 'His mother had a stroke and he wants her to move in so he can take care of her,' " Alicia suggests. "I once heard of that happening."

"That's too huge a lie," I say. "I'd never be able to pull it off. The other story is kind of what happened to me in my old place. At least the guy was a jerk and not some lovable lunk who worships his mother."

"It's really hot. Let's get out of here," says Alicia. We follow her into the only cool room in the place, where white subway tiles line an icy dipping pool and women of all ages, colors, and body shapes lounge naked, putting mud on their faces and henna in their hair, exfoliating one another's backs, chattering in a symphony of Russian, French, and English of every possible descent. We put our towels on an empty seat before plopping our naked butts down. Courtney gets the award for best products today for a new citrus wonder scrub from Bliss and a hydrating mask her ayurvedic guru made himself.

"Where were we? Oh yeah, my cruel, heartless landlord can up the rent if he hurls me onto the street. Woe is me, blahdiddy-blah."

"You know, Jacquie, I can always tell when one of my kids is fibbing if he can't hold eye contact with me. You're all over this place."

I look right into her eyes. "Can you believe this guy? He wants to throw me—little old me!—out onto the streets!"

Alicia jumps in, "Well, this city protects its tenants pretty stringently. I can't imagine he'll be able to actually remove you from the premises for at least six months."

I think for a second before responding with a self-satisfied a-ha. "You have no idea. I've been fighting this guy for months. We've been to court twice and apparently he has a case. It looked like things had calmed down, but now they haven't been returning my calls or cashing my checks, and I feel as though the ax is about to fall. That's why I'm starting to look. I may need something as early as the first of the month."

Courtney nods, impressed, and Alicia laughs and says, "Nice to know my sweet, honest *hermana* is capable of lying through her teeth. You should be in advertising."

"Shut up! This is about having an article in a national women's magazine, not to mention potentially finding the man of my dreams. It's huge! It's worth twisting the truth just a little, isn't it?" I take in their disbelieving expressions and scoop stinky facial mask into my hand.

"Whatever," I say.

"Remind me to give you some cover-up for that," Alicia says.

"Jesus Christ," I say, suddenly self-conscious about the zit on my forehead.

"I'm sorry! It's staring at me, even through all the sweat and freckles. I can't focus on what you're saying." She walks over to her makeup bag resting on top of a pile of five more tiny dirt-brown towels, pulls out her M.A.C. concealer, hands it to me, and mimes gently patting it on the eruption big enough to be a second head. "Pat lightly, like this."

"So, did you like that German guy?" Courtney asks.

"Yeah, kind of," I say. "His apartment is amazing, you can tell he's very attentive and caring with the things he loves. Who am I kidding? He's a drip, just has a nice pad. At least he doesn't have a girlfriend. But I gotta say it is so cool to be meeting all these guys. When there are so many possibilities, there's less risk of obsessing about any one of them. It's awesome. Anyone for the dry sauna?" We walk into the hottest room of all and lie down on wooden benches.

"Alicia, how's your hunt going?" Courtney asks.

"I found a place."

"What?" I can't believe she hasn't told me.

"I'm moving to Williamsburg. Remember that one photographer guy I liked? He found another roommate, but it fell through. He needs someone right away."

"I thought you said he was too sexy to move in with."

"I don't care. I don't want to go out with anyone. I'm happier when I'm single."

"You know what I worry about?"

"That that pimple will slowly expand until it's eaten your entire face?"

"You're evil. I'm annoyed that my thirties are no different from my twenties." I get up and yank on the cord hanging from the ceiling and ice-cold water rains down on my head. "I'm still dating idiots and I don't see any reason to believe that will change. Honestly, I haven't dated a nice guy since Philippe. I swear it's karma for treating him like shite."

"I told you," Alicia says. "You're gonna meet your perfect man through this apartment thing."

"Hmm, that would be nice."

"Speaking of perfect, how's Brad?" asks Alicia. "And when is he gonna knock you up?"

Courtney rolls mutely over onto her stomach and I ask, "How's the tour going?" refusing to give in to the baby babble. I know she stopped taking the pill, but I dread the day she tells me she's pregnant. What the hell am I going to do when Courtney has a kid?

"The tour is going fabulously," she says, sitting up and clutching her towel, eyes glowing. "The shows have been mostly selling out, getting great reviews. I can hardly believe that after twelve years with this man, I have wound up married to a rock star! It was astounding watching him move around in that world, as if he belonged there, as if it had never existed without him, really, and I was watching quietly from the sidelines—" She lowers her head and smiles. "His muse. I felt so proud and in love with him, it was ridiculous." We remain quiet, taking a moment to feel the heat and contemplate the miracle of true love.

If words like arroz con pollo, mole poblano, chilaquiles, carne asada, quesadilla, enchilada, and flan make your mouth water, this is the place for you. I'm a chef and I need a roommate for my very big loft in Williamsburg. You have a room for you, we share a small bathroom. Big, light kitchen often smells of fresh tortillas. I will cook for you. $900. Call Javier.

6

After an insane day juggling three stories that I'm writing myself with loads of text coming in from freelancers, followed by the screening of an extremely bloody Japanese horror film, it's nice to come home to a spotlessly clean apartment. Alicia's bags are packed and stacked neatly by the front door. I snoop around the bedroom and bathroom and notice that she's gone so far as to scrub the bathroom sink, maybe for the first time in her life, and straighten the makeup drawer. I wonder if she hired someone. I have a message from Javier, the guy who's compulsively left me messages all week reminding me of our rendezvous. I'd forgotten anyway and only have time to wash my face, wriggle into a miniskirt, and race to his apartment in the still-sketchy part of Williamsburg that lies beneath the BQE—the Brooklyn-Queens Expressway—in all its vrooming, honking, exhaust-spewing glory. Javier's head appears from a window three flights up. "Catch the key!" he shouts, and tosses down a yellow and green tube sock with his keys balled up inside, a common New York trick. Javier is an intense Mexican guy with black eyes that bore into mine when he speaks. A chef doing time at a trendy pan-Latino joint in his neighborhood until he's raised enough money to open his own place, he whips up a gooey, garlicky shrimp quesadilla. We gobble it up with Dos Equis after Dos Equis in his cavernous, sparsely furnished loft as he rants about the system in his country and the system in mine. I poke around when he's cutting the lime for our next round and uncover mountains of books by his unmade bed: cookbooks, *The Communist Manifesto*, film scripts, software instructional manuals, so much varied reading material, I assume he doesn't sleep. A silk kimono hangs from his bedroom door, and below it on the floor are mud-caked hiking boots. The man is a mess of conflicting or perhaps complementary passions. Shoving a beer bottle in my direction, Javier grabs my hand, nearly yanking my arm off, and drags me up four flights of thick, concrete stairs, until I'm staring dumbfounded off a beautifully decked, two-thousand-square-foot roof that doesn't seem to belong on top of this rundown building.

Gazing out at the sparkling lights of downtown Manhattan, Javier says, "I admit that my apartment is large but loud and not beautiful. I stay here for the deck." He spins suddenly, runs his fingers stiffly through bristles of black hair that stick straight up toward the pinpricks of light in the sky, and says, "Let's do something, let's do something, you and me, Jacquie, what should we do?" I don't know if he means have a cocktail, throw eggs onto the highway, or start a revolution, so I let him continue. I'm enormously entertained. He leans over the thin railing, sways dramatically to look over his shoulder and straight at me with his big, black eyes, and says, "There are not many Americans you can discuss these complex ideas with, Jacquie. Let's watch a movie." With that we scramble downstairs as quickly as we scrambled up them and he sticks in the video of *Weekend*, the enigmatic classic by French cinematic giant Jean-Luc Godard, not exactly first-date fare, but I go with it. I adore the film, even if I don't entirely understand it. When I begin to nod off from too much beer, cheese, and intellectual stimulation, Javier nudges me softly. "Jacquie, are you going to move into my apartment?"

"No, I'm not really looking for an apartment."

"I didn't think so," he says. "Will you have dinner with me tomorrow?"

"I'd love to," I say, woozily lifting myself off the couch.

I call Alicia on my cell the minute my feet hit the sidewalk in front of Javier's building. "A date," I sing onto her voice mail. "Oh my God, I'm going on a date with an apartment guy! Intense. Mexican. Oh my God, it's working."

When I get home the next day from an interview with Cameron Diaz, who's slumming it on Broadway in a comedy by a buzzed-about Irish playwright, Alicia is in front of the building, loading her luggage into a cab.

"I've run up and down the stairs a million times. Wish you were here to help," she says.

"You could have waited until I got home," I say.

"Whatever," she says. "Well, gotta go." She gives me an awkward hug and climbs into the back of the cab. I watch it roll to the end of the block and turn left onto Avenue A. Alone again, I climb the stairs slowly to prepare for my date.

I meet Javier at a Gallician restaurant around the corner from my apartment, where tapas are served with potent sangria on barrels spread out on the sawdust-covered floor. Javier is glaring intently at *The Village Voice* when I arrive.

"Hey!" I announce, sitting on the stool next to him. He doesn't budge. "Javier? You there?"

He snaps out of his rapt state and looks at my face. "Oh, you are much better. What I'm reading here is such shit. I hate critics,

I think critics are the lowest-level people of the earth. They can't make their own art, so they tear apart other people's. Here is a review of a film of Pedro Almodóvar, a man I regard with the greatest esteem, and the mindless masturbation this cockroach applies to his work—" He stops suddenly and takes a sip of water. "Jacqueline, you are not a film critic, are you?"

"Not exactly. I'm a writer, and film is my area of expertise. Let's call me a film writer."

Javier starts laughing, I think for the first time since I've met him. His laughter bubbles up warmly and softens his angular face.

"That would have been bad," he says and continues laughing. He kisses both my cheeks.

"Can we order?" I suggest. "I'm starving."

"I love a woman who eats," he says. We order a pitcher of the white sangria and an array of tapas—chorizo, Spanish tortilla, tomato salad, garlic shrimp, olives, and chunks of Manchego. He feeds me pulpo gallego—boiled octopus sprinkled bright with red pepper—with his fingers, studies my face, and says, "Jacquie, what does a film writer do?"

"Well," I say, popping a green olive into my mouth, "I interview actors and directors. I write articles about industry trends. For the magazine, I cover DVD releases and obscure new releases I'm excited about. I admit some of those are basically mini movie reviews, but I try to personalize them as much as possible."

"Does this satisfy you?"

"Does it satisfy me? Well, I like it a lot," I say. "I get to meet directors and actors I respect and write stories about them that I hope are entertaining. It's a form of writing I'm comfortable with and I think I have a knack for interviewing. Plus, I get invited to parties and film festivals and see movies for free."

Javier swirls his glass of sangria, seeming to study a slice of orange very intently. "I don't think you challenge yourself."

"Sure I do," I say, defensive. Then: "What's so important about being challenged anyway? Everyone's always like, 'Oh, it's only really satisfying if you have to work for it,' but that's such b.s. I love what I do. I'm making a living as a writer in New York City! And writing about my greatest passion. How many people can say they earn a living doing what they love? I meet amazing people— I've interviewed Quentin Tarantino and Faye Dunaway and Benicio Del Toro and Nicole Kidman. God, I've interviewed JLo! Who would impress you? Um, I've interviewed Steven Soderbergh and your own country's pride and joy, Gael García Bernal, and the director Alfonso Cuarón. That's cool, isn't it? Sometimes I walk down the street thinking, *Is this really my life? I am so lucky*. And it's not an easy job. I have to juggle a million details as an editor. There are looming deadlines, cranky writers, two-faced publicists, disjointed stories I have the job of piecing together. Sure, the writing itself isn't the hardest thing in the world. Sure, I practically write these stories in my sleep, but I love it. I fucking love it."

He looks at me with either admiration or pity in his eyes. "Jacquie, I like very much spending time with you," he says. "Tell me about your youth."

I tell my story the way I always tell it, the ten-minute stand-up-routine version I've been perfecting all my life: the Southern California upbringing in a town where kids grow up too fast, exposed to drugs, celebrity, and the kind of wealth that inevitably leads to envy and an unnatural sense of entitlement. My well-practiced illustrations include sneaking out of my bedroom window to dance at nightclubs with men in makeup and women in nothing but leather teddies and high heels; flattering bouncers into overlooking my pathetic homemade fake ID; going home with pretty boys in their twenties—construction workers or struggling actors by day, clubbers by night; making a pit stop at a four-star-hotel parking lot to buy cocaine from a valet instructed to sell to anyone who knew the elaborate password, then stopping the car around the corner with a girlfriend to howl with elation at how racy and sophisticated our teenage lives were.

As I'm about to launch into Chapter 2—my first two aimless

years of drinking relentlessly and coasting academically at a notorious party college—Javier stops me. " I can see you've told this story many times. It is humorous and carefree," he says. "But I wonder about a girl so nice as you, fifteen years old, dancing at night with men who want to touch a young girl. What was it you wanted?"

"I wanted love," I say.

"You thought you would find it there?"

102

"I went to parties with guys my own age, too, kissed a lot of them, but the club guys impressed me. They were so beautiful. I think they wanted to be discovered the way people want to be discovered in L.A. They looked like *GQ* models, they posed and spoke like people in a movie. I think at that age I was looking for the kind of love you see in the movies *Valley Girl* and *Sixteen Candles*, so I pursued those guys with a vengeance, fell down bruised when they left me, and cried afterward for days and went over and over the details with my friends on the phone, wrote frantic, gut-wrenching notes to them in class about how my life was over, how I'd never love again. But of course it was just histrionics. I always got up, dusted myself off, moved on to the next guy, the next one, who would surely be the true love of my life."

"You are a young soul," he says.

"I think you're right. That's not a good thing, is it?"

"It's not a bad thing. You are innocent. I love the innocence in you. You are still looking for love in wrong ways. It's very moving." He touches my cheek, and I want to cry. When Javier presses his chapped lips to mine, I let him. We might not have the kind of chemistry that goes snap, crackle, pop, but I really like talking to him. Javier seems to be an actual prospect, someone interesting and smart who I may learn to like eventually. This idea excites me and I kiss him back, even resting my hand on the back of his neck, pulling him toward me, throwing my leg over his. Luckily he's consumed as much garlic as I have or it could be embarrassing.

Javier walks me home. We kiss some more at my front door, and I'm impressed with myself for leaving him there all by himself.

By the time I've bounced fairly giddily up the four flights, he has left me a message thanking me for a nice time and asking me out again, which gives me a jolt, almost instantly turning my mild interest in him into panic. What if he's a stalker? Or, even worse, a loser? I wish Alicia were home so we could tear him apart. No one is quite as adept as my sister when it comes to analyzing someone's shortcomings. I decide to go the healthier route and call Courtney.

"Jacquie, for once in your life will you give a nice guy a chance?" she says, when I tell her I don't know if I like him. "Calling a woman to thank her for a date is called good manners, which might be something you are unaccustomed to."

"Yeah, I guess. But I didn't want to have sex with him. Usually if I like a guy, I do."

"Sometimes attraction creeps up on you. You said he was good-looking, right? There's nothing wrong with waiting until the third or fourth date, when you have a stronger feeling about whether you actually like him or not. I like this. I'd like to see you go with this, take things slowly for a change. Consider it an experiment."

I promise her I'll go out with him again and the idea actually doesn't sound completely distasteful. "Hey, how's Brad?"

"He's doing great. Got a rave review in some Canadian paper. He's gonna send it to me."

"Ever heard of the Internet?"

"I want to have it, to put on the refrigerator. My hubby's famous!"

"Do you think he has groupies?"

"Some girl came up to him after the show yesterday and told him she wanted to have his baby."

"He told her there was someone much prettier already on the job, right?"

"Something like that. Hey, Jacq, I have to go. I'm exhausted."

"Yeah, I have work to do myself. Deadlines up the wazoo. Talk soon?"

"Yeah, okay," she says.

I hang up and Javier calls again. Does the guy have no shame? I remember what Courtney said and agree to have dinner with him on Friday night. I must admit the normalness of it all is nice, even if he doesn't give me goose bumps. A man took me out to a pleasant dinner, paid, called to thank me, and then asked me out again—the same night. It occurs to me that this is a proper grown-up dating experience. No games, no giddy stupidity, no deferring to blinding lust or hormones. It could be nice. He asks me where I'd like to go and I suggest an expensive sushi place in NoHo I've been wanting to try.

Thursday afternoon, I get a call from my neighbor whose dog, Larry, I take care of when she goes out of town. She unexpectedly needs to go upstate to visit her brother who fell out of a tree and broke his leg. I love having Larry over and tell her I'll take him for as long as she wants. After a boring postwork-cocktail dealie celebrating a new Manhattan film festival (as if we don't have too many already), where the bar is so dark I can't see the bland floating hors d'oeuvres I shovel into my mouth, I let myself into Larry's mom's apartment and watch him go berserk. Larry is a little white mutt with the cutest face on the planet, and we love each other in a deep, primal way. I throw myself on the floor and let him climb all over me and lick my face. I hug him and squeeze him and kiss him back.

"Guess what, baby! You're sleeping over at my house tonight!"

He goes berserk again. I swear he understands everything I say. We trot upstairs to my place, where I put on George Michael (Larry's favorite) and dance around, while Larry barks at me and runs in circles and rubs his face with his paws and other things he does that are so cute I could scream. I do, and he barks in response. Then we climb into bed and I read, while he burrows tunnels in my blanket.

"You are my little monkey!" I tell him. "I love you madly! You are the cutest little monkey I ever did see." He cocks his head and looks at me like I'm insane. Then he goes back to burrowing tunnels in the covers.

For Date #2, I lose my usual jeans and put on a skirt and heels for Javier. I figure if I'm going on proper dates, I should dress the part. Javier arrives at the restaurant a few minutes after I do and hands me a white rose. I resist my impulse to think, *Cheesy!* and instead say, "That is so sweet," and lean in for a kiss. His lips are soft. He's moisturized them since last time. Sober, there's not much electricity, but I tell myself it could come with time and tell my gut to shut the hell up.

While reveling in mountains of sashimi, a seared tuna and seaweed salad, and perfectly steamed shrimp shumai, I decide that Javier is a combative person. That's okay with me; I can argue with the best of them. We fight about movies and the mayor and the relative merits of raw salmon (yuck) and tuna (so heavenly it's worth risking mercury poisoning). Then, in the middle of a story about an ancient, hunchbacked neighbor of his, he grumbles that the guy has a dog he often fantasizes about poisoning in his sleep. My mouth goes dry.

"Well, it's interesting that you should mention that, because I'm dogsitting at the moment and need to stop by my place to take the little guy out after dinner. I was hoping you wouldn't mind getting a drink in my 'hood, someplace where we can take the dog."

He looks pained, but says, "Sure, why not?"

"I can't go out with anyone Larry doesn't like, so we'd better get this out of the way."

"Okay."

It's odd for Javier to come over to my apartment on only the second date. And it's odd that it's odd, because my usual protocol is to bring a guy home ASAP and from there launch into relationship mode without stopping for breath. But here's this guy I've had dinner with twice, whom I find physically attractive, but still haven't slept with. Unheard of. I don't know him very well, so there's a certain nervousness in inviting him up, even if it's just to grab the dog. I run ahead of him, babbling anxiously about an edgy gangster film I just saw that's coming out next month. When I fling my door open, Larry erupts as if he's been raiding the amphetamine supply in my absence, and I dive to the floor to check in.

"Hello, my baby, baby, baby, look at my silly little boy!" As Larry jumps all over me, I glance up at the nonplussed Javier, who has yet to cross the threshold. "This is Larry! Isn't he the cutest thing ever? Oh my God, are you the cutest little baby face I ever did see!"

Javier clearly does not consider Larry the cutest little baby face he ever did see. He pushes past our frenetic love fest and sits on a bar stool at my kitchen counter and doesn't really look around my apartment; he just sits there and pouts. When I turn on a light and ask if he wants a beer or a glass of water, he shakes his head and flips through a Victoria's Secret catalog. With no other real option, I grab Larry's leash and a plastic bag for poop and say, "Well, should we go then?"

"Sure," Javier says, with about as much enthusiasm as he might muster if I'd offered him a shot of warm cough syrup. As we walk Larry wordlessly, I feel self-conscious pointing out how adorable Larry is when he tries to hump an uptight standard poodle or what a good boy he is for taking a shit, which I subsequently pick up with the plastic bag and carry awkwardly until we reach a garbage can on the corner. Larry is as amused as I am when a pit bull strolls by with a banana in her mouth. Javier is not amused at all.

"Should we get a drink?" I ask, when we reach my bar. Javier shrugs. Because I'm fairly dying for a cocktail at this point, I take this as a yes. The limp mood is broken by the jollity of the place. Johnny scolds me for staying away for so long and tosses a dog biscuit onto the floor for Larry, which the finicky mutt regards with indifference. I pick it up off the floor, assuming he'll change his mind later when he's enviously sniffing our pretzels and beer and wishing he had something of his own to chew on. All the regulars hug me and pet Larry and nod suspiciously at Javier, who's now wearing a petulant scowl that I'd regard with suspicion if I hadn't brought him here.

We order pints of amber beer and sit at a table in back. I catch Javier visibly wincing as I pull Larry up onto the bench next to me. The clever little fella climbs right over me and into grumpy Javier's lap. I chuckle. He does his best to awkwardly pet him. "Are you all right?" I finally ask.

"I don't know."

"What do you mean?"

"I don't know. I don't feel right about this dog thing."

"This dog thing."

"When I think about going out with a woman, I don't imagine bringing along a little dog and cleaning up after him. Now I have the feeling that this is an evening out with a dog."

"Well, it doesn't have to be. He's perfectly happy to just sit here. We don't have to pay any attention to him."

"But you seem to love him very much, and as I said, it is now like an evening out with a dog for me. I wanted to be with you, to look at you and speak to you and start to know you more as a person."

"Well, I had to take him out. He had to pee, and I thought it might actually be fun. I guess it could have been if you weren't clinging to some notion of what a date is supposed to look like. Hell, seeing me interact with Larry probably tells you more about me than hours of conversation, let alone seeing my apartment, my local bar. Some people might consider that pretty intimate for a second date. Guess it depends how you choose to look at it."

"Perhaps," he mutters.

"Anyway, sorry I put you through such hell. Didn't mean to."

When I get home, I add, "Dog People Only" to the Post-it on my fridge, and, needless to say, never speak to Javier again. Larry wouldn't allow it. And so grumpy Javier remains my first and only attempt at proper dating.

I check my messages:

"Hi, Jacquie. My name's Samuel. I'm returning your call about my two-bedroom in Gramercy. It is very spacious and nice. I have a key to the park, which, I'm sure you realize, is quite an honor. Call me if you'd like to take a look. . . ."

I jot down his number, while a husky male voice says, "Hey, my name's Anthony. Got a call from someone named Jacquie about the room I'm renting in my apartment. Sorry it's taken so long to get back to you. I'm on this shoot in Pittsburgh that keeps getting longer. If you're still looking, let me know and we can set something up for when I get back."

"Hey, beautiful woman, it's Court. Call me, I feel like we haven't talked in days. Have we? Kind of spacey at the moment. Anyway, call me."

I pick up the phone to call her back as the last message explodes into my darkened apartment: "Hey, gorgeous!" Jeremy. "How are you? Why isn't your frickin' cell phone on, pray tell? All I do these days is sit in a candlelit room, looking through old photos of you and me, thinking about the old days. Here's one of us trying on goofy hats together, and remember that crazy pillow fight we had? Oh, and I love this one of us torturing a stray cat with a fork. Anyways, bellissima, I hope you are good. Met your charming prince yet? Remember you promised I get to be a bridesmaid! Call me. I was such a bad boy last night! Brunch this weekend?" He makes kissy noises.

I dial Jeremy's cell and he answers, "What's up, lezzy?"

"Just making out with my girlfriend."

"Yum, giving up the man hunt?"

"No, just taking tastes from everybody's plate."

"Ah, my little omnivore, guess all this sex hasn't left much time for anything else. Certainly not your, ahem, friends."

"Not exactly sex; I've just been meeting guys for the story and working like crazy. Not much time for friends or yoga or girl day at the baths, but it feels good to work this hard. It's going really well. Steve has been all gushy about how great the magazine looks and how it's all because of me blah blah and the *Luscious* story is coming along. Life is good."

"It's because you broke up with that bad boytoy of yours."

"You're probably right. I feel unbelievably sane. I haven't freaked out once since we broke up."

"Speaking of freaking out . . ." Jeremy's voice goes suddenly somber.

"Oh, baby, what?"

And he proceeds to tell me about his latest obsession with the latest jerk he met at a club and bedded, and the guy vanished in the middle of the night without even asking for his phone number. "I'm devastated. I really like him. We had a really good conversation."

"About what?"

"I have no idea. I was hammered," he says. "What's your point?"

Saturday I take a break from my editing frenzy—we're shipping the June issue to the printer this week—to check out the two-bedroom overlooking Gramercy Park that belongs to Samuel, a would-be comedian who earns a living doing freelance accounting. Samuel's is the rare neighborhood below Midtown that feels like it belongs uptown—manicured, civilized, calm, quiet, and all grown-up. Well-kept high-rises with uniformed doormen tower over tree-lined streets and lush, gated parks, the jewel being the one for which the neighborhood was named, an exclusive, shady green city block, which requires a key for entry. Only residents of the buildings immediately facing the park are eligible for a much-coveted key, which they have to rent at $350 a year (and pay a steep thousand to replace if they dare lose it).

Something about this neighborhood—maybe all the shade, maybe the preponderance of strollers—slows me down. After a leisurely stroll, I arrive at Samuel's door, immediately disappointed by him physically. He's short and stocky with, incongruously, a diamond stud in his left nostril, and one of his eyes never looks straight at me, but I'm too exhausted by this whole process to come up with an excuse to leave. He shows me around, pointing out prosaic details like the brand-new gas stove, the pull-down ironing board, and the hundreds of immaculate *National Geographic*s he's been collecting since 1987. While he's in his closet searching for an ashtray he made in his pottery class that I've "just got to see," I peek in the drawer of his nightstand and find a stuffed kitten, handcuffs, a matchbook from the Vavavoom Room, which I assume is a strip joint based on the busty babe on its cover, and a signed headshot of Britney Spears.

"Hey," he says while we're examining an enormous fern his mother gave him for his first apartment that he's kept alive with a diet of Miracle-Gro, affection, and Aretha Franklin songs. "I bet you're a very nurturing person, too, with those big, womanly thighs of yours." I'm aghast.

"What does your eye thing say about you?" I ask.

"Jean-Paul Sartre had eyes like mine," he says. "They say it's a sign of genius."

"The word *genius* is so overused," I say, about to bolt when the front door swings open and in jaunts a grungy angel in baggy jeans and a backward baseball cap.

"Jacquie, Hunter, my roommate who's moving out."

"Yo. You'd sure be an improvement over me. Sammy, my man, you go. You guys want a beer?" I say yes and from that point on don't say another word to Samuel, who eventually skulks off to his room to do his taxes or something, leaving Hunter and me alone.

"So, where are you moving?"

"I found this space way the hell out in Red Hook. It's out of this world. It's far and there's no subway out there, but I ride my bike everywhere anyway. The place is raw. It's huge. I can play my music as loud as I want and paint and build walls. I can't tell you how psyched I am to get creative with my living space. Oh, wow, let me show you this picture."

He pulls out a book about lofts with shreds of Post-its stuck to selected pages. Every time he reaches one of the shots he's marked, he jumps a little and says, "Check that out! Man, love it." When he smiles, a dimple appears in his left cheek. He has all sorts of plans: painting the ceiling orange, building walls with Plexiglas windows so the light can pass from one room to the next, organizing weekly artist salons so his friends can come by to read or display their work, play music, talk about what's going on in the world. He keeps grabbing the top of his scruffy, chocolate-brown hair with his fist for emphasis. His enthusiasm is infectious.

"How did you wind up with this grump?" I ask.

"Oh, him? Harmless. Just answered an ad, you know how it goes. I knew it was temporary. You gonna live here?"

"I don't think so," I say, feeling deceitful. "He and I don't really get along. I'd like to find a space like yours."

"Well, you'll have to come to the salon! Hey, what are you doing right now? Want to grab some food?"

We eat at a cheap Mexican joint I like about a block from my place. The proximity makes me feel guilty about lying to Hunter. I take a deep breath. "You know, Hunter, I have to tell you something." He looks at me, big eyes suddenly concerned. "I'm not really looking for an apartment."

"What do you mean?"

"I'm writing an article for a magazine about meeting guys by pretending to look for a roommate," I laugh. "You know, a dating scheme."

He lets that sink in. "That's fucked up. You've, like, been going to all these places, telling people you want to live there, wasting their time, and you're not even looking for an apartment?"

"Well," I stutter, ready to defend myself. Then I realize that he's right. "Yeah, I guess."

"Wow. You and I met, like you've been meeting all these other guys, and a bunch of them ask you out, including me. I guess that's the point."

"No, it's not really like that. I haven't met that many, I mean, I haven't gone out with very many, only the ones I liked."

"Jesus Christ, isn't there enough duplicity in the world? You're playing right into it. You know, I spend my whole life trying to create something honest. I try to surround myself with people who have those values. And I thought you were cool."

"Jesus, aren't you overreacting? I wouldn't have told you if I didn't like you and feel bad about lying to you."

"Whoa, I feel really special now."

I feel like crying. It doesn't help when he stands up, reaches deep into his pocket, pulls out some bills, throws them onto the table, and says, "I gotta get out of here." I bite off a split end, flick myself with my rubber band, and start whimpering like a spoiled starlet whose Jimmy Choos got swiped from the edge of the dance floor.

Then I do what I usually do when I feel like shit: call Jake.

"Can I come over?"

"What, like right now?"

"I'm in a terrible mood."

"Okay, see you in a few." I jump in a cab. When I get there, the place is hopping. Jake moved to New York just under a year ago from Boulder, where he was snowboarding and running a successful bar. He came here to focus on his art and, I suspect, to create something as popular and thriving as his bar, but with an artsy, urban bent. He's run up against a host of unforeseen challenges, namely a city full of equally talented, energetic young people who are equally eager to make art and friends and a big, loud, dazzling splash that forces everyone in New York to stand up, mouth agape, and listen.

I give Jake the kudos he deserves for trying. He moved into an enormous, unfinished warehouse space on the south side of

Williamsburg, a largely Hispanic neighborhood that's only recently begun to catch up to the more gentrified part of the 'Burg, which is already booming with the swanky bars, shops, and eateries that have transformed "Billburg" into a bastion of youthful appeal to rival the East Village. Jake single-handedly knocked down and threw up walls, wired and decorated and demolished to create a trippy, multifunctional space that goes like this: You enter into an art gallery with fire-extinguisher-red walls covered with large-format paintings by Jake that do a sort of disturbingly annoyingly confusingly abstract Bacon-meets-Pollack thing. Tear your eyes away from the dizzying display to pass behind a black curtain thumbtacked over an opening in the back wall, and you enter the equally red living room, a cavelike space in which the only furniture is a thrashed black futon facing a big-screen TV, a turntable and accoutrements in the corner, and a chunky plywood bar dividing the entertainment area from the kitchen. Not a soft or pretty flourish in sight. It is painfully obvious that no women live here and the girlfriends don't last long enough to make a mark. The kitchen, however, looks remarkably like any other kitchen. There's a microwave, fully stocked fridge, cupboards, toaster oven, stove, coffeemaker. Besides the front of the gallery, there are no windows.

When you move through the next thumbtacked black curtain, you enter Jake's studio and workshop, the lab where Maestro makes art. His tiny bedroom—loft bed, dresser, white shag carpet, that's it—lies beyond, where those daring to enter remain high on the fumes emanating from Maestro's laboratory. There's a plunging cement staircase to the left of the bedroom that leads to a basement, in which there are two eight-by-eight cells that Jake rents out to like-minded souls, an office housing his impressive computer setup, and an honest-to-God functional recording studio that Jake also buffed out with his own pretty little two hands. It's got a drum set, a range of guitars and keyboards, and all the

113

gadgetry that pro studios offer, including two large bongs and a wet bar. It looks very professional to these untrained eyes, anyway. I try not to go downstairs very often. If the upstairs is a virtual dungeon, the subterranean recesses are the netherworld, from which I fear no one returns with their faculties intact.

When I arrive, Jake's latest roommate—they come and go like the tides—a Jim Morrison look-alike with no personality, is spinning records. Two other guys I always confuse, wearing matching hairdos and short-sleeved T-shirts over long-sleeved ones, are doing coke on the kitchen counter, and Jake is standing over a pot of boiling pasta. I mix myself a vodka tonic, let the alcohol pull me out of my funk, and move my hips to Jake's roommate's groovy tunes, trying to regale the crowd with tales of real-estate-ad dating. Unfortunately, the snorters are almost as offended by my antics as Hunter was; they pronounce the process of judging men by their homesteads "harsh, dude" and keep snorting. Jake's roommate, who takes himself very seriously as a DJ but serves Cosmos and Mojitos to swooning, fishnet-clad gamines on the Lower East Side for cash, loses his headphones just long enough to catch the Javier and Larry episode and return to his musical bubble. Jake, perched quietly on a bar stool hurriedly shoveling spaghetti into his face the whole time, finishes his meal, pushes his unruly bangs out of his face, and turns to me nonchalantly.

"I'm going to bed. You can come if you want."

"Gee, an invitation I can't refuse," I say to my public before making a dramatic exit on the heels of my little grinch. I know how pathetic I must seem trotting off after him, but I also know how shattered Jake would be if I didn't. His tough-guy routine is only an act, and I can tell he wants nothing more than to cuddle up with me right now.

I take off my clothes and shiver my way into his freezing bed. He flips off the light and aims a space heater at me.

"That better?"

"It will be."

He strips down and climbs over me, and I wrap myself around his icy body, warming us both.

"How's it going, mister?"

"All right."

"Anything ever happen with that gallery owner?"

"Nah." He's quiet for a minute. "Nothing ever happens with those guys, at least not for me. I'm not sure what I should do, maybe open another bar. It's something I know I'm good at, which is cool, but the bureaucracy in New York might kill me. I looked into it and the permits alone can take months."

"You'll figure it out. I have complete faith in you."

"You're the only one. It sucks to turn thirty with nothing to show for it. Last year, everything was, like, great, and I move out here to, like, get my art thing going, and I feel like I have nothing all over again. People aren't buying my work, I don't know anyone, the money's running out."

In the shadow, I can see the outline of his pretty face, which he turns to me. His eyes look so sad. I squeeze him tighter.

"I was just thinking," he says.

"That you have no one else in your life that you can talk to about this stuff?"

He laughs. "No, that's not what I was thinking. But I guess it could have been." He pulls me in closer. "You're amazing, but I can't do this."

"I know, I know."

"You're gonna find it, Jacq."

"Leave me alone."

"You want it. That's what matters. You're gonna knock on some guy's door who's looking for a roommate and he's gonna open it and not believe how lucky he got to have this beautiful girl standing there, and you're gonna see his face and just know. I'll probably be kicking myself, but I'm just too selfish to put anyone ahead of me right now. You know I'm right."

"Yeah, I do." He turns toward me and we kiss. I figure this

will be the last time we have sex. As we hold on to each other, my tears drip down my face and onto his chest and neck. He licks them off my eyes and cheeks. I think, *They're all wrong about you. You're not a bad guy. You're just not ready to love me as much as you already do.*

34-year-old documentary filmmaker seeks female roommate fast! My former partner in crime skipped town with two months' rent in his grubby fist and i'm more than a bit desperate. What can I say? I'm tall, dark, handsome, not-too-dumb, not-too-self-involved or irresponsible. Oh, wait, I'm looking for a roommate, not the love of my life. Hell, if you think you might be the love of my life, you can call, too. The room's $1300. It's bright and big, and I think I have fairly decent taste and housekeeping habits—for a guy. Place is in Billburg. Give me a call. Name's Anthony.

7

Sunday morning after my night with Jake, I drag myself to yoga. There was a time not so long ago when I went to class four, five times a week. Now I'm lucky if I make it three times a month. Between work, the man-hunt-slash-research for my story, and a general laziness that has some-how crept in, physical activity has dropped significantly among my priorities. This morning, though, my body is begging for nourishment.

I barely make it to a class taught by my favorite teacher, Gwin, a forty-something rocker with long, red hair and the hardest yoga body in town. Ten minutes in, and my body is screaming at me. The simplest downward-facing dog feels like medieval torture, and I have to suffer through an hour and forty-five minutes, pushing my body through a seemingly endless series of poses. I guzzle water. I rest a lot in child's pose. I vow to go at least two times a week for the rest of my life. Clearing my mind has always been my biggest yoga challenge, and today my head is cluttered with Jake withdrawal, cheesy attempts to keep myself positive, various possible endings for my piece.

When we're finally relaxing in the prostrate position fittingly called "corpse pose" at the end of the class, Gwin starts talking about clarity. She says that when we are silent and look within, we find that in fact we already know everything we need to know. "Call it intuition, call it your gut, but it is true that we already have all the information, knowledge, and wisdom we need inside ourselves. When you leave class today, rather than letting the world crowd in on your mind, you might think about using a simple mantra to bring yourself back to the sense of calm you're feeling right now, to tap in to your internal wisdom," she says. "I was thinking about it this morning and came up with something simple and quite beautiful for us all to repeat to ourselves when our minds are racing around like they so often do in this city. It's 'sut nam.' Think 'sut' when you breathe in and 'nam' when you breathe out. It's a mantra that's used in kundalini yoga and it means, 'Truth is my identity.'"

That's just great. Even my yoga teacher is mocking my lying ass.

Gwin ends the class by telling us to put our hands together in front of our hearts and take a moment to think of something for which we are thankful. I think of my wonderful, soothing apartment.

As I'm walking home, I try to think "sut" when I inhale and "nam" when I exhale. I make a valiant effort to ignore the distracting thoughts performing an avant-garde opera in my brain, the scruffy mutt who sniffs my shoes when I tie my laces on a stoop, the white buds bursting from the trees in the park, so pretty that they make my heart race, the drunk, presumably homeless man I've been passing for years, who's shouting at no one in particular, "You don't know nothing about love! You ain't never gonna know nothing about love! All you know is having sex and counting your money." But trying to focus on my breath is useless in the face of so many things to see, smell, touch, especially now that spring is bringing color back into the landscape. I run my fingers along the side of the building on my corner as I pass, watch a woman laughing to herself about some private treasured memory, drink in the fading sounds of the homeless guy's angry lament, squeeze the smooth, moist trunk of a scraggly tree.

God, I'm bad at yoga, I tell myself. *God, I need yoga.*

I feel desperation growing in me like a pair of chubby twins squirming restlessly in my belly. Vague anxiety about my future, both professional and romantic, has been simmering for a while and now feels like it has hit the boiling point. Sure, I experience a pang of loneliness and fear every time I kiss a boy goodbye for the last time, but this time the panic is exacerbated by my article and the onslaught of wrong men I've been meeting.

For years I've done what for me felt like the normal thing: meet guys, sleep with guys, fall in love (lust, infatuation) with them, drive them crazy, get driven crazy, dump them, get dumped. College was a series of back-to-back relationships with brief periods of sluttiness in between. Then, in the real world, there were longer relationships broken up by shorter, intenser ones—and the inevitable periods of sluttiness in between. I've never gone without sex or affection for long. So, why do I feel antsy and desperate, like if this scheme doesn't work, I'm going to be doomed to spend the rest of my life living in misery in a one-bedroom apartment full of greedy, smelly cats?

Courtney insists that human beings want to fall in love. By nature, we do not want to be alone, so sooner or later we all pair off. It was reassuring the first time she said it to me. But I was also twenty-four years old and bopping around arrogantly dumping near-perfect guys because of some minor flaw (leaves used dental floss in the shower, loves me too much), under the assumption that there were more near-perfect guys where they came from. But now it's almost a decade later and I still haven't met anyone as great as the boyfriend I dumped at twenty-four, and I have begun to doubt the wisdom of her words.

But this article is messing with me. Even as I run around saying it's just for fun and two dollars a word, even as I craft witty sentences proclaiming that it doesn't matter if the scheme leads to love or not, I know that it *could.* I mean, why couldn't I walk through the door of an apartment that happens to belong to the love of my life? My sister suggested that I'd meet my husband this way, and part of me hopes that and wants that and believes that the only reason I'm still single is that I didn't come up with this plan earlier.

I reach home with a sigh. I wish I had a pet that would wake up from its nap at the sound of my key in the lock and cock its head adorably before running over to demand some affection. If I weren't so broke and unsettled, I'd adopt a dog tomorrow. I wonder if Larry's mom would let him come play, but can't even muster the energy it would take to walk down one short flight of stairs to find out, and if they weren't home, I might not survive the disappointment. I've been avoiding finishing my roommate-hunting piece because I don't have a satisfactory ending. Right now it basically makes the odds sound about as strong as they are for Internet dating: You can meet some nice guys, but it's hard to find the real thing—or at least I haven't found it yet.

I sit down at my computer and write, "In three weeks of hunting for men through the real estate ads, I've made forty-nine phone calls, sent thirty-eight e-mails, seen the insides of thirteen guys' apartments, and gone on three bona fide dates. I've turned down five additional invitations and developed an unfortunate crush on a guy who wouldn't pay attention to me even if I tap-danced naked on his Pottery Barn coffee table. Which adds up to a lively love life but no real love. Now let's look at Samantha." What about Samantha? How does her experience relate to my article? She randomly met Charlie when she answered his ad in the paper and rented his spare room because it was clean and affordable and because Charlie seemed like a trustworthy, reliable potential roommate. They also both worked in the film industry and had mutual acquaintances and similar interests, backgrounds, and tastes. It was a natural connection. But what if she hadn't moved in? What if they'd had that initial interview and she'd decided not to take the room? What if she had a cold that day and didn't look her pretty, perky self, or he was in a bad mood because his latest film got turned down by the Venice Film Festival? They might have slipped quietly out of each other's lives, rather than fallen in love. Maybe my hypothesis is full of holes and this scheme is no better than Match-friggin'-dot-com. Or maybe it's not the looking at someone's apartment that makes a match, but the living together, the accumulating of daily, shared experiences. I write all this down, simultaneously having an epiphany: Finding love is completely random.

Samantha just happened to move into the home of the man she would eventually marry, while Courtney met the love of her life bleary-eyed in an eight A.M. German literature class. I'll probably bang foreheads with the man crazy enough to ask for my hand while we're reaching for the same watermelon at the corner deli. There is just no way to figure out the mystery of who and when and why, even if you are knocking on three doors a day, and there is certainly no way to force it. *Goddammit*, I think, getting up out of my chair to take a trip to the refrigerator. I have no idea what I'm looking for, I'm not even hungry, but I'm frustrated with the piece. I don't have any idea if this roommate thing works. It did for Samantha and Charlie, but maybe in their case it was a fluke. Or maybe it was destiny, for God's sake. I grab a peach yogurt, slam the fridge, pull a spoon out of a drawer, and go back to my desk to stare at my screen.

"What's my point?" I scream. "What the hell is my point?" I put down my snack, spring out of my chair, and start doing jumping jacks, then drop to the floor and do twenty curls. I'm just starting to break a sweat when the phone rings.

"Hey, it's Anthony," says a husky voice on the other end. I search the file cabinet in my brain for an Anthony. "I left you a message a couple weeks ago. I was out of town so you couldn't come see my apartment. Well, I'm back, finally, and still haven't found anyone. You still looking?"

The thought of seeing any more apartments instantly makes my temples throb, but I go into autodrive. "Actually I am still looking," I hear myself say.

"Cool, what's your day like?"

"I'm working, but I can find the time. Where do you live again?"

"Williamsburg, just off of Bedford."

I'd rather let Larry lick the soles of my feet until I die of excess tickling than haul my ass back to Williamsburg, but I feel like I have to keep up the search.

"Look," he says. "I'm totally open today. Any time that's good for you."

"Okay," I say, summoning the energy to get back on the subway. "I can be there in around an hour."

"Sounds perfect. Gives me time to throw my mess under the bed."

Bedford Avenue is just one stop from mine on the L train, which crosses the East River under water and deposits me in about five minutes, even though I've entered a whole new borough. It's a sunny Sunday, so the hipsters are out in full force, selling their old leather jackets and last season's iPods on street corners, hunching over steaming paper cups of strong coffee, laughing loudly at one another's witticisms.

There's a palpable buzz to the neighborhood that I've always loved (and fortunately I'm a whole subway stop from Jake's place, so there are no immediate visual references to make my heart ache). I suspect that this is what the East Village was like before I lived there, truly bohemian, with creativity coursing through every conversation and a layer of grit that all the expensive boutiques on the block can't quite mask. A pair of old men playing checkers on a stoop says hi as I turn onto a quiet street.

Anthony's building resembles a storage facility, a two-story gray box positioned indifferently behind a heavy iron gate. He told me to buzz when I got to the gate and he would come unlock it for me, but I arrive as one of the other tenants is about to re-attach the heavy chain holding it together. He lets me in and points me to Anthony's door on the second floor. I knock.

The door swings open, and standing in front of me is my ideal man. I mean, if I was going to describe my ideal man, this is what he would look like: He is about six feet tall, broad shoulders under a chalky blue T-shirt that leads down to a narrow waist in worn 501s that are slipping off his hips. He has dark hair falling across eyes the color of a late-night sky surrounded by lashes so long that they should belong to a woman, Marlon Brando's nose, a wide mouth, and a square jaw covered by what looks like a week's stubble. He looks as taken aback by my appearance as I am by his. He blinks hard a couple of times and shifts from one foot to the other. Then clears his throat.

"Jacquie?"

"Yeah. I'm Jacquie."

He steps back, pushing the door open wider with his back so I can move past him. I can feel the heat from his chest as I edge past him—I'm that close and he's that hot. I look down at the floor, wide pine slats that have been getting nicked and scuffed for a good half a century, feeling my cheeks warm under his regard. When I look up at him, he blinks again and raises his face to point across the room with his chin. I follow it with my eyes to a beige, L-shaped couch taking up the corner of a sprawling living room that's piled high with clutter. There are boxes of magazines, stacks of film and photography books, wilted plants that have taken up residence on top of the stacks, camera equipment, videotapes, a laundry basket overflowing with whites and a couple of colored items I fight the urge to remove, a beach cruiser leaning against an armoire that looks Indonesian, a wobbly desk with an old-school tangerine Mac in the middle of it, surrounded by more piles. Almost every inch of wall is covered with photographs, some black-and-white, some saturated in color, and sketchy paintings of nudes with no frames that remind me of early Toulouse-Lautrec charcoals, which are among my favorite works of art. More framed photos are stacked on the floor. I feel like I've entered a Bertolucci film from the seventies and any minute a throng of intense, cigarette-smoking intellectuals will enter stage right arguing about Marxism, the merits of *Star Wars*, and who was doing lines off of whose breasts at Studio 54 last night. It's too much to take in, so I sit on the couch and gaze up at bits and pieces.

"I just got back from a shoot," Anthony says, picking up a duffel bag off the couch and putting it on the floor. "I'm sorry it's such a mess."

"Don't worry about it," I say. "It's a great place."

"Yeah, I lucked out, moved to Williamsburg with the first wave, back when you could afford to live in big spaces like this. Should have bought back then I guess," he says.

I open my mouth to tell him that I just bought a place in the East Village, but remember that I'm supposed to be looking for a room and close it again. He picks up the laundry basket off a chair and tucks it into a corner behind the armoire. "Hey, do you want a beer? I kind of feel like one."

"Sure," I say nervously. He jogs to the kitchen, which is open like mine, with a concrete-topped island and pots and pans hanging from the ceiling above it. He's wearing no shoes and filthy white socks with a hole in one toe and when he pads across the floor, his feet slip out from under him and he almost eats it. I giggle when he looks back at me through his lashes, embarrassed by his momentary loss of suavity. He bends down behind the refrigerator door and then his head pops up again. I can't believe how beautiful he is. He smiles for the first time when he catches me looking at him, revealing sparkly, slightly crooked teeth. One of the front ones is chipped. He opens the two Rolling Rocks and, holding them both in one hand, grabs a bag of tortilla chips and a jar of salsa from the counter. He seems more comfortable with something to do. After depositing the goods, he opens the armoire and turns on *Abbey Road*, probably my favorite album of all time. I can't speak.

He sits down in the corner of the couch and leans in with his beer. I pick mine up and hold it in his direction.

"Here's to finding the perfect roommate," he says.

"To finding the perfect roommate," I repeat, and we click beer bottles.

"What's your sign?" I ask, immediately wishing I could take it back.

"Do you believe in that shit?" he asks.

"Not really," I say. "But I like it. And if it can help me find someone I can live with, I'll take it."

"I'm a Leo," he says. "Headstrong, intelligent, passionate, a born leader." I relax into his couch cushions, relieved that he's not an Aries. He doesn't ask for my sign.

"What do you do?" Anthony asks.

"I edit *Flicks* magazine, so I interview actors, directors, and watch way too many movies."

"Most excellent," he says, *Bill and Ted* style. "I'm a filmmaker myself, docs. Right now I'm working on this TV show about these three college students trying to figure out what they're doing with their lives. It's so compelling, really digging deep to get at the truth beneath the surface details of these lives that, you know, superficially could belong to anyone."

"So, it's reality TV?"

"Well, yeah, but not the lame kind."

"I guess I still think of reality TV as anorexic girls in bikinis eating slugs for a million dollars or eccentric urban dwellers ready to kill each other to be named the next big designer, filmmaker, chef, cover girl."

"That's how it became popular, a bunch of attractive people living in an apartment together, a surprising mix of strangers trapped on an island and forced to do outrageous tasks. That's the hook—the competition, the allure and humor of its banality—but it's become so much more. At its best I believe reality programming can be like the old-school doc guys, cinema vérité, Pennebaker, the Maysles, you know, turning a camera on and letting the truth unspool. Great stuff. Great stuff."

It sounds good to me. And the way his lips look while he's spouting it is even better. I can't take my eyes off them. Quite suddenly, Anthony stops talking and puts his bottle down on the table. I watch him as he leans back on the couch and stretches his legs out to rest his feet on the coffee table, and imagine that he reaches over, takes my face in his hands, and kisses me. Heat rushes into my cheeks as I picture him drawing me on top of him, my leg wrapped around his thigh, pulling him against me, one of his hands on the ass of my jeans, the other lost in my hair. He pushes himself back up to the edge of the couch, looks into my eyes, and clears his throat. I put my beer down next to his on the table and blink nervously, imagining us seated together on a nighttime beach, the splash of the waves crashing onto the hard, cold sand for our entertainment, his strong arms wrapped around me, my face hidden in the neck of his warm, wool sweater. He leans toward me, his face very serious, and I think, *My God, he's actually going to kiss me.*

But just then the sound of a key in the door alerts us to spring apart, and Anthony jumps off the couch as if caught doing something forbidden. A gangly blond guy walks in with a young, fat bulldog at his feet. The puppy spots Anthony and gallops across the room to passionately rub up against his leg.

"This is Lucy," he says, getting down in her face to kiss it. "My little angel."

He has a dog.

"How's my angel?" Anthony asks Lucy, as the little fatty rolls over onto her back so he can rub her tummy, her back leg kicking furiously. "My little Lucy belle! Lucy, this is Jacquie." I rub her tummy along with him and she gratefully moans and barks a couple of times before rolling onto her feet, awkwardly hoisting herself onto the couch, and squirming around on Anthony. "This is Barrett," he says, indicating the lanky guy, "the man who's been taking care of my home and my baby in my absence."

"Hey, man," says Barrett.

"You hanging around tonight?" Anthony asks.

"No, heading to Clarissa's."

"Cool, say hola."

"No prob," Barrett says. He waves at us and heads for the door.

The magic interrupted, we return awkwardly to the chitchat. I'm preoccupied as Anthony tells me about his show, which is currently focusing on a woman from rural Pennsylvania who got married just out of high school and is now back in college trying to figure out if she should major in psychology or law. I keep wondering how to break it to him that I'm not really looking for a room; I really like him and wish I could tell him the truth. Anthony tells me how the point of his show is to invade every nook and cranny of the students' lives, following them around almost 24/7. His subject's marriage is on the rocks and her seven-year-old has been acting out and wetting his bed ever since she went back to school. She's begun taking yoga classes to calm her constant rage. I laugh out loud as I remember that I began the day at yoga, breathing in on "sut" and out on "nam," a constant reminder that truth is my identity. I'm such a hypocrite.

"Reality TV really is the wave of the future," he says. "It's documentary for the masses. Beyond the dating and top-model muck at the bottom of the barrel, you know, like you were talking about, I think it will become a serious art form, as long as it remains truthful. I mean, what is more powerful than the truth?

Where it crosses a line into exploitation is where it's no longer truthful."

Jesus Christ, I think, *how many times can one person use the word truth in one conversation?*

"Hey, do you want to stay for dinner?" Anthony asks suddenly, hopping up from the couch. "We could order in, Thai, burritos."

"Sure," I say, and the doorbell rings.

"What the hell?" Anthony says, walking toward the buzzer.

"It's Brit," a female voice says over the intercom.

"Oh man, I completely forgot someone else is coming to see the room," Anthony says. "Don't go, okay? We'll order some food when she leaves."

Anthony runs out the front door to let her in and a minute later returns with a very tall, thin blonde with creamy skin.

"Hi," I say, standing up.

"Jacquie, this is Brit. She's looking at the room." *I bet she is,* I think, meeting her big, gray eyes, which are staring at me with a look that says, "You're attractive in that big-boobed, bohemian smart-girl kind of way, but no match for my Scandinavian perfection." Or maybe I'm being paranoid. She brushes her choppy bangs out of her lovely face and crosses the room to shake my hand. It's a weak handshake and she looks demurely down afterward, as if ashamed of interrupting whatever was going on between Anthony and me before she got there. She looks like she might in fact be the sweetest girl in the world, which could be worse.

"All right, let's do it," Anthony says and leads Brit into his spare bedroom, which I have yet to see. I sit back down on the couch and look around the place. I notice dirty dishes on the kitchen counter. In the next room, Anthony and his new best friend are giggling, while I sit alone on the couch gnawing on my thumbnail. I snap my rubber band and savor its sting.

When they come back into the room, Brit is smiling smugly. She looks directly at me and blushes. I wonder if she grabbed his crotch in the bedroom or something to ensure her chances of landing the room—or the guy. Come to think of it, Anthony has a smug smirk on his face, too.

"This is the kitchen," he says with a sweeping arm gesture. "Your basic, um, Williamsburg kitchen." He reaches up to tug on a chain hanging from the kitchen ceiling that turns on a peeling, red light fixture and accidentally bumps Brit's chin with his elbow. She moans in sex-kittenish fashion and puts her thin, pale hand to her face.

129

"I'm so sorry," Anthony says tenderly, taking her face in his hands. "Are you all right?"

"I'm fine, fine, really," she says, in a voice that suggests she comes from Norway, Sweden, one of those countries that produces a disproportionate number of sickeningly beautiful women. But she doesn't sound fine. She sounds to me like she's begging for comfort from the guy who's supposed to be my new boyfriend.

"Anthony," she chirps as they pull reluctantly away from each other. "I really am very interested in the room."

Something snaps as I sit there on Anthony's well-worn couch watching my handsome would-be boyfriend and his exotic supermodel-slash-potential-paramour standing so cozily close to each other not ten feet away. My mind is flooded with images of Anthony and Brit kissing in a field before a kindly old minister surrounded by masses of loved ones as strains of Mendelssohn erupt into the fresh country air. I imagine the two of them, breathtaking in designer casual wear, pushing newborn twin boys in a stroller down Bedford Avenue. I imagine Brit, golden hair flowing down her shapely back, straddling Anthony on this very couch, sweat glistening on her flawlessly tanned, heart-shaped behind, which is moving rhythmically above him. In my mind, Anthony gazes up into Brit's cloudy eyes, mesmerized by her throaty, Swedish-accented moans. As her thrusts pick up speed and his groans grow more passionate, my own fantasies lie whimpering near death in a dank corner somewhere. I almost shout, "No!"

And then it hits me. I know exactly what I have to do to stop this deafening fantasy from becoming reality. I know how to save my article, to create the perfect ending, to keep my romantic day-dreams alive.

I push myself up off the couch and turn boldly to face them.

"You know what, Anthony? I think I actually will take the room," I hear myself say. My gut says, *What the hell are you doing, Jacquie? Shouldn't you think this through?*

But Anthony is so wonderful, I just can't have some Scandinavian Bond girl named Brit moving into his apartment.

A genuine, warm grin appears on his face, and Anthony turns away from Brit's beautiful blondness to say, "That is so great, Jacquie. I am really excited." He walks out from under the kitchen lamp and back into the living room and, without looking back at Brit, says, "Sorry, but she was here first, after all."

As Brit meekly gathers her purse and smiles angelically at us before slipping out the door, Anthony grins and bounds across the rug toward me, like a bouncing baby bulldog himself, and, unexpectedly, gives me a hug so strong that I'm afraid he might crack one of my ribs.

Beautiful, good-size 1BR in the East Village.
I have to vacate unexpectedly and need
to find a subletter ASAP. It's on a great
block, full of light and air, has an awesome
kitchen with stainless appliances, washer/
dryer, cable TV, DSL, amazing shower, fully
furnished with great, eclectic stuff, everything you can dream of in a home. I love
my apartment. Whoever gets this place
scores!!! Call Jacquie

8

"You did what?" Courtney shouts so loudly that I have to
pull my cell phone away from my ear. I'm on the sidewalk in front of my office, late for work, but I have a feeling
I shouldn't take this particular conversation inside.

"I don't know what came over me," I say, knowing very
well how insane it must sound. It even sounds insane to me,
and I'm the one doing it. But it also feels right, and that's the
part I'm having a hard time conveying to Courtney.

"I'm concerned about you, Jacquie. Let's take a moment
to think about this," she says. "You can't just move in with
some guy when you just bought your own apartment."

"I know, I know it's a little weird," I say. I stop pacing at
the front door of the building and close my eyes and run
my hand over my face, as if washing it in sunshine, and start

pacing again. "Sure, I was a bit reckless. But this is exactly what my story needs. It wasn't coming together."

"Jacquie, you weren't really looking for an apartment, remember?" she says. "You were just faking it. You have an apartment. That's why your interviewing other people who really did end up with their roommate."

"Yeah, well, I wasn't finding the right ending for my piece," I say.

"You're a writer," Court says. "You'll figure it out."

"Well, you know, I haven't been able to so far, and then this came up and it made sense."

"I just think you're taking it too far," she says. "The lying, the deception. Think about this guy."

"Well, that's the thing, Court, he's kind of amazing," I finally confess. "We had a real connection. I feel like something could happen with us and now maybe it will. Imagine what a great ending that would be for the story!"

"What ending? That you totally lie to this guy you like and move into his apartment, even though you have your own, just to see if you can seduce him?"

"Court, you're being a little melodramatic. Why couldn't something happen organically between us?" I stop pacing and say, "Let's imagine he winds up being the love of my life, that he's the guy I'm going to have babies with—would it really be so bad then?"

Courtney doesn't answer for a second. I pet a passing beagle on the head. When his owner, a stout woman in a lemon-yellow sweat suit, pulls him away, he stands up on his hind legs and reaches out to me as if begging me to save him from his miserable existence.

"Court, are you there?"

"Yeah, I'm here, I'm just thinking," she says. "Jacquie, this is bad. If this does lead to something, you're lying to him, which is not a good way to start a relationship. And how do you even know if you like the guy?"

"He's awesome, Courtney. He's a producer-director-doc guy.

We know a million people just like him, only less gorgeous and smart and sweet. He lives in a great loft. He has goodness in his eyes. He has a friggin' bulldog!"

"Okay, all good things. I am glad he has a job," she says. "But even if he is the man of your life, you're still moving in with him and you have your own place. It's absurd. What are you going to do with your apartment?"

"I'll get Alicia to move in."

"Okay," she says, in a tone that suggests a vague suspicion that perhaps I've retained a modicum of my sanity.

"So, it will almost be like I still have my own place. I'll just be sleeping at his, but eventually I'll explain everything to him and we'll figure it out."

"Then why don't you just tell him now?"

"I wanted to the other day, but chickened out. I have a bad feeling about it. I think he'll freak out that I lied to him in the first place, well, not really lied but withheld the truth. He has this thing about the truth, you know, honesty," I tell her. "And I need to at least move in and live there for a while before I mess things up, I mean for the sake of the story. But God, Court, wouldn't it be amazing if we got together, you know, like Sam and Charlie? It would be like destiny or something."

"No, it wouldn't, Jacquie. You're manufacturing this."

"You know what, Courtney? Not all of us were lucky enough to meet Mister Perfect when we were nineteen fucking years old. Most of us have to put up with Mister Wrong drooling on us or dumping us and still hope that someday something will work out, and once in a while that might mean taking a stupid, ridiculous risk. I like this guy, I did what I did, and I don't want to have to defend myself to you," I tell her, raising my voice quite a lot. People walking past stare at me and I glare back. "Please don't ruin this for me, okay? I have to go to work."

I hang up and walk huffily into the building, dialing Jeremy's number as I go.

"I am thrilled for you, gorgeous," he says breathily when I tell him the news, with Napoleon yapping enthusiastically in the background. "It's the most romantic thing I've ever heard."

I arrive in the office feeling reassured. When I got home from Anthony's, I stayed up fretting for most of the night, picking at my hair, decimating my cuticles (a habit I gave up after college graduation, or so I thought), zapping my poor, inflamed wrist. I kept wondering if I was doing the wrong thing and then wondering if there is such thing as the wrong thing or the right thing, for that matter, and if my dishonesty in this case would automatically classify this as the wrong thing. But what if it's for the sake of my art? My career? What if it's for the sake of love? Does that make a difference? I lay awake, my eyes stinging, my head aching, for hours, but then woke this morning feeling optimistic. I even decided that maybe moving in with Anthony was exactly what I needed. I'm doing what my article proposes: getting into someone's home as a means to find love, peeking behind the closet doors, seeing what my romantic prospect looks like first thing in the morning before he puts on his polite, public face, getting a megadose of him and figuring out if he is somebody with whom I could share my life. And, most important, the experience will lend legitimacy to my article.

Everyone in the office seems a little lethargic. Sam is gazing at wedding gowns online. She did what I'm doing: moved in with a guy and then got to know him as intimately and intensively as you do when you live with someone. They built a strong foundation for their relationship because they got the chance to hang out beyond the awkward realm of dating, kicking around in pajamas, eating cereal, flossing their teeth. I guess the difference is that she actually needed a place to live, but that's negligible.

"Hey, you guys," I say, plunking myself down at my desk. Chester grunts. There's an enormous pile of mail on my desk. I start opening envelopes and trashing most of their contents while sending Alicia an Instant Message.

Hey, don't suppose you want to move into my place? I write.

u made me get out, she responds.

Well, I'd actually want you to live there without me. I met this guy Anthony through the apartment story, he's really cute, big loft in Williamsburg. I'm thinking of crashing at his place for a while. I need someone to pay my rent.

crashing at his place?

Fine, moving in with him.

When she doesn't immediately respond, I add, He's INCRED-IBLE and he thought I was looking for a room and I'M DOING IT FOR THE STORY, WHICH IS REALLY FUCKING IMPORTANT TO ME AND I DON'T CARE WHAT YOU ALL THINK! IT'S JUST WHAT I'M DOING.

chill, she writes. ur loca. glad u met a dude but can't afford ur rent, mine is *cheap.*

I hadn't thought about that. I'd offer to kick in, except that rent at Anthony's will be almost as much as my mortgage. There's no way I can afford both.

It's not that expensive, I write. Come on, you love my apart-ment.

can't, no cash, no job, my place is cool, come see it. later

My mind races hard and fast until it arrives at the most obvious destination: Craig's List. I laugh out loud at the irony and Sam glares at me for disturbing her sacred bridal-gown research. I have a thought and jot it down: "When he opened the door to his pleasantly cluttered Brooklyn apartment and looked down at me with piercing blue eyes, the first thought that popped into my mind was, 'I love you.'" I'm aware as I write it that it sounds corny, but it's true—and very *Luscious*—and I am relieved that the end of my piece is in sight. When I got home last night, before I started flipping out, I started writing notes for the perfect happy ending to my story. I saw a handful of apartments, met a lot of frogs, and then came face-to-face with a prince in an expansive, if disorderly, loft in Brooklyn that I am now going to call home—and at some point (before my piece hits the stands), if anything does happen between Anthony and me (and I will do my damnedest to ensure that it does), I will fall to my knees, confess to his highness that in fact I entered his kingdom under false pretenses and I will kiss his knuckles and beg him to pardon me and love me anyway. I know my editor, Clancy, is going to be ecstatic.

On Craig's List, I type in my cell number and file an ad. In about thirty seconds I get a call from a woman named Serena who needs a place immediately. She broke up with her fiancé three days ago and has since been wincing as he slams doors, "accidentally" breaks her dishes, and talks loudly into the phone about what a bitch she is. She produces commercials for some hotshot director, travels constantly, and says she basically needs a place to sleep and store her belongings when she's in town. She doesn't mind that there are still boxes lying around and that I'll be leaving some of my stuff there. We make an appointment for her to come over after work to see the place.

"It's great," Serena says, about six inches through the front door. "It's perfect." The petite china doll of a girl with bleached blond hair and gray rings under her pale blue eyes looks so drained that I open a bottle of white wine, hand her a glass, and watch her disappear into my couch.

"I just wasn't ready," she tells me. "I love Rory, but getting married terrifies me. We weren't going to do it right away, but I felt like I had to put the whole process on hold."

"Had you started planning the wedding?"

"Not really. Every time we'd talk about it, I'd have a panic attack. I'm sure I'm classic therapy fodder. I'm in this great relationship and flip out as the marriage approaches, clearly because my dad died last year and I haven't really processed it yet. Rory stuck a card for some shrink up on the medicine cabinet this morning. Jerk."

"I don't think you sound that unusual," I tell her. "Marriage is a big deal."

"Tell me about it," she says, downing the rest of her wine. "I can't believe this is all happening. God, I didn't mean to tell you my life story. It's just been so hard. You know, I told him I thought we should wait awhile, maybe start talking about a wedding in a year or so, but Rory lost it. Really freaked me out, screaming and yelling, shoving stuff around. Then he went from apeshit to penitent and sat there crying for, like, four hours straight. I didn't think that was possible. When I brought all this up, I didn't think we'd break up, I just wanted to postpone the wedding date, but maybe it's better this way."

After finishing off the bottle of wine, I trade a set of keys to my apartment for a month's mortgage and maintenance and a security deposit. I tell Serena I'll be stopping by every week or so for my mail, which doesn't bother her. She seems so despondent, I give her a hug and wish her luck over the next few days until she can come back with her things. I think I might have a panic attack of my own as I shut the door behind her. What the hell am I doing? What will I tell my parents? Am I really letting some woman I just met move into my beloved apartment? It wouldn't be the first time—I always sublet my place when I go out of town, it's the only way I can afford a vacation—but this time I'm not planning to return anytime soon. I've lived here barely four months, and I'm handing my beautiful home over to some girl who seems perfectly nice but who shouldn't be living here. I should. I walk through my apartment. It's as pretty and unfinished as ever: the bag of tiles still sitting on the kitchen floor next to the untouched buckets of paint, the pile of curtains I've been meaning to hang still in a heap, the little orange table I never turned into a masterpiece. There's still a towel duct-taped over my bedroom window and fourteen boxes of books piled against the living room wall. *There were so many ways I wanted to improve this place,* I think wistfully. I guess that's all on hold for now. I pull a suitcase out of my closet and begin to fill it.

By the time I move into Anthony's, I'm less freaked out. Alicia helps me pack and lug, bitching all the way. We're each hauling an enormous suitcase that's impossible to carry down my four flights of stairs, so we drag them. They thump as they hit each stair on the way down, and the *thump thump thump thump* gets all the dogs in the building barking and howling. My neighbors must be happy to see me go. As we're climbing into a cab on the corner of Eleventh and Avenue A, my phone rings. Of all people, it's Jake.

"Hey, stranger," I say and tell the driver where to go.

"What up?" he asks.

"Funny you should ask. I actually . . ." Telling Jake makes my situation seem even more surreal. "I met somebody. I'm, um, moving in with him."

"You high?"

"No, just moving in with this guy," I say.

"He's moving in with you?" he asks.

"No, I'm moving in with him."

"But you have the spankin' pad," he says.

"It's complicated," I say, feeling defensiveness rising out of my belly. "God, Jake, it's for the article. I'm moving in with a guy I met through the apartment thing. It's, you know, research."

"Oh," he says. "I guess you don't want to go to an art opening tonight then."

"No," I laugh. " I can't."

"Well, I have a piece in this group show in Chelsea," he says. "If you get a chance, check it out. I'll e-mail you the info."

"Sounds great," I say.

"You should come see the show," Jake says. "It's kind of a cool group of people and I was thinking about you and you and me and stuff when I did the painting, you know? I don't know, you might dig it."

"I'll definitely go when I have a chance," I say.

"Where you moving?"

"Williamsburg."

He laughs a Beavis and Butthead laugh. "You get sick of your dude, you know there's a place you can come hide."

"Thanks for the offer," I say and hang up. I watch the buildings of my neighborhood float by the cab window, feeling in my
bones how much I will miss them. I see the cute café guy walking
to work as we stop at a light and our eyes meet for a second. How
strange that I will no longer flirt with that guy every day of my life.
I look over at my sister, who's staring equally intently out her window. Beyond her I catch a glimpse of the Bible-studies lady rushing past the colorful fruit and flower stand fronting a crowded
deli, clearly headed for my corner. She's wearing a navy skirt suit
and black boots as always and holding an umbrella over her bundled head, even though it's seventy degrees with hazy sunshine,
no chance of showers.

As we drive over the Williamsburg Bridge, the skyscrapers of
Manhattan loom behind me like a guilty secret. I twist around in
my seat and watch the city where I've lived for the last eight years
recede into the distance. I've considered moving to Brooklyn before, to a cheaper, bigger space in one of the quaint, brownstone-
lined regions you have to cross a bridge or tunnel to get to, but I
was never quite able to tear myself away from the downtown bustle. I wondered if I would lose my drive and inspiration if I left the
city. I wondered if the trip back and forth would become daunting
and I would hole myself up in some cozy flat with spacious
rooms and a shady stoop, spend my days lazing about reading the
paper and watching *Friends* reruns and never go out again. But
here I am, in the back of a cab that's transporting my clothes,
computer, and beauty products into a dirty, practically treeless
barrio on the Brooklyn side of the bridge. We pull up to Anthony's
building, to the bland block of concrete that from the outside
could be a warehouse—or a prison. I hand the cabdriver ten
bucks and he helps me hoist my two monster suitcases and random plastic bags bursting with my belongings out of the trunk.

Anthony already gave me a key, so Alicia and I let ourselves in.
He's sitting on the couch watching an old movie starring Bette
Davis and looks up at us, startled. He's wearing old gray sweats

with a white button-down shirt hanging out. He's as cute as I remembered, I notice with some relief. The place is still in a state of disarray, although he's straightened some of the piles.

"You're here," he says, flipping off the tube and jumping up. He sounds pleased and smiles at both of us shyly. He has a dimple.

"You live in the 'Burg, too?" he asks Alicia.

"Yup, on the gnarly side of the tracks," she says.

140

"We should all hang out sometime, get brunch at Diner or something."

"Sounds like a plan, man," she says, throwing an approving glance my way before fleeing, probably for fear that I'll recruit her to help me unpack.

I feel as if I'm sleepwalking as Anthony shows me the cluttered room that's now mine, chattering along the way about his former roommate, a neuroscientist he'd known since college who didn't mind burrowing through years of accumulated junk to find his bed. My new home is about twelve by twelve with a big window. About half of the room is stuffed almost to the ceiling with books, boxes of tapes, another bike, a surfboard, a sled, Rollerblades, a skateboard, scuba equipment, a beer bong, an electric guitar. The section of the room housing the full-size bed is otherwise empty.

"I've started clearing some of the junk out," he says. "But we've got our work cut out for us." He puts the surfboard into the crowded hall closet as I move boxes of books into the living room, stacking them on top of the stacks. I almost bump into Anthony hauling a Nerf basketball hoop over his head. I back up to let him pass, blush and look away. Suddenly it hits me like a brick to my skull that I'm going to live in this small, cramped room in Brooklyn. I am going to have a roommate. I am going to have to take the subway to work every morning. I am doing all of this why? Is it really for the sake of the article? Or is it because of this guy?

"Hey, Anthony, do you want a cup of tea?" I ask him.

"What I want is a drink," he says, making a move for the kitchen. After rummaging around for a minute, he shouts out, "Beer's not gonna cut it for a cleaning spree. Out of vodka, but I've got a bottle of Patron. Shots, anyone?"

"Who am I to say no to good tequila?" I shout back from inside the closet where I'm cramming an enormous stuffed elephant I found under the bed. Next thing I know we're doing shots, blaring Led Zeppelin, and playing strip Boggle. I guess having a masters in English has at least one advantage—I'm kicking his butt, which is covered in nothing but red boxers, while I remain relatively clothed. Knowing he's about to lose his last scrap of an outfit, he tells me he's "sick of this lame-ass game."

"Were you really gonna make me tea?" he asks.

"Yeah, I was," I say. "We'd be a lot soberer if I had."

"I don't think I have any tea," he says.

"I brought it with me. Moroccan mint tea, mint *green* tea, chamomile, lemon-ginger, apricot black tea, honey vanilla rooibos, Egyptian licorice tea, which is way better than it sounds, raspberry leaf tea for, uh, women's issues."

"You're a regular tea store."

"A tea junkie."

"A tea-mophiliac."

"That's retarded," I say, cracking up.

"Did you call me retarded?" he asks, with a loopy smile on his face.

"Uh-huh," I say, sucking on a slice of lime and closing my eyes 'cause it's so sour.

"Nobody calls me retarded in my own home. There's no way you can live with me now," he says, looking very stern.

"Too late, bud," I say and throw the lime rind at his face. It hits his right cheek. "You're stuck with me."

"You are way too hot to be my roommate," he says, getting up off the couch to play the air guitar in his underwear. I bob my head along with him and he picks up the lime rind that I threw at him and throws it back at me. It hits me on the forehead and I open my mouth widely as if offended by the nerve of him.

"Oh my God," I say, jumping to my feet. "I have to sleep in that room! What are we thinking? We have to clean it!" I run into the room with such drunken gusto that I bang my forehead against the door and it starts throbbing with pain.

"Ow," I say, putting my hand to my head and feeling really stupid.

"Are you all right?" Anthony asks, rushing into the dark where I'm sitting on my new bed, cradling my aching head. I nod as he pushes my hair out of my face to get a good look at my wound, sending a jolt of electricity right through me. I guess he felt it, too, because he looks suddenly discombobulated and very sweet. He kisses my forehead where I bumped it, pauses for a moment, and then kisses me very gently on the lips. It is both audacious and the most normal thing in the world. Getting hammered and making out with some hot guy I just met? This is what I do. I'm good at it. The fact that I've been trying to stop and the fact that Anthony is my new roommate are both inconsequential next to his extraordinary looks and soft lips. I am much too drunk to care and much too susceptible to cuteness to resist. Not to mention that this is the most perfect ending I could have imagined for my *Luscious* piece. It is completely natural and expected when Anthony pulls me on top of him and we spend the next ten minutes kissing each other, his messy spare bedroom spinning wildly around us as if it has never seen a kiss before. We are giddy, weightless, floating, as if pumped full of helium (and tequila), inches above the hard, bare mattress.

"I can't believe you're my roommate," he says. We both laugh, softly at first, until we're clutching our stomachs like teenagers who just took our first hit of pot, tears streaming down our cheeks, gasping for breath. Finally he stands up and pulls me onto my feet.

On our way into his room, he turns to me and slurs, "Don't

worry, no funny business." We fool around for another hour, grinding away at each other in our underwear like virgins in naive agreement not to go all the way. It's only in the morning that Anthony dips into the pack of condoms tucked neatly into the drawer in his nightstand, purrs, and slowly makes his way out of his clothes and into mine. I almost stop him, telling myself I have no excuse anymore for moving so quickly. But then lust trumps reason, as usual, and I bury my face in a pillow and let him have his way with me. Afterward, we fall lazily back to sleep until ten, when I wake again with a shock. "Shit, I'm supposed to be at work!"

"Don't go," he says. "Please! You can't leave me. I'm tired and hung over and so, so crazy about you. I can't let you go yet."

I grin at him. "I really want to, but we're shipping the issue tomorrow. It's like the craziest day of the month."

"Pleeeeease," he pleads, his hands clutched together in front of his heart. He's kneeling on his bed and he has a hard-on.

I call Steve and tell him I have the stomach flu and can't make it in.

"Shit," he says while I hold my breath. "Okay, I'll have Sam and Spencer get on the text. You feel better. I really need you tomorrow."

"Thanks, Steve," I say, "sorry," and pounce on the gorgeous guy grinning at me from the bed.

Through my woozy post-tequila haze, I feel a pang of guilt about the elaborate deception I've constructed with Anthony and our fragile new romance at its center. I want to tell him the truth right now, but how would I explain now that I've actually moved in? I've pushed things too far for any explanation to make sense. He would hate me. That guy Hunter got so pissed off at me when I confessed to him the real object of my quest and I hadn't done anything as bad as really moving into *his* apartment.

"You know, Jacquie, I was thinking, now that you're moving into *my* bed," he says, grinning, "we could turn the spare room into an office. We could both use one."

"Isn't this all a little fast?" I ask him, suddenly uneasy. "I mean, wouldn't it be better if I moved into the other room and we got to know each other a little bit and sort of waited to see what happens?"

"Shhh," he says, mashing his body against mine. I can feel his warm breath on my lips as he speaks. "Didn't I tell you how crazy I am about you?" I nod. "This is going to be fine. *We're* going to be fine. There's no such thing as too fast. We met, we dug each other, and here we are. Not to mention that it was like fucking fate or something. I mean, you came here looking for a roommate and we wound up, like, madly in love!"

I make an attempt to smile at him, even though I feel like a jerk.

"So are you gonna help me turn the spare room into an office or what?" he says.

I nod obediently as words run typewritten through my head: Not only do I have a gorgeous new boyfriend, but I have landed myself a spacious two-bedroom apartment in one of the hottest neighborhoods in town. Two bedrooms mean one for us, another for my clothes and my computer. What other dating strategy can yield that kind of unexpected perk?

I envision two desks placed side by side and nervously bite off a split end, anticipating the sting even before I hook the rubber band with my finger. I picture my desk at home, Serena perched on my gray swivel chair. Lying on his back next to me, Anthony takes my hand in his and squeezes it tightly. Who is this guy? He grins as if to say, "Stop worrying, angel, it'll all be fine."

Besides sleeping off our hangovers and rolling around his bed, we spend the day wandering around Anthony's neighborhood in cowboy hats and dark sunglasses, dodging the hoards of disheveled twenty-somethings with no apparent jobs who populate Williamsburg. Anthony thinks I'm nuts for talking to every dog that makes the move on Lucy as if we were old friends, but says it's nice that I have an affinity for the world's dumber creatures.

"They're not dumb," I tell him. "They're completely loving and trusting and their whole world is tied up in whoever is loving them right now. I think I must have been a dog in a past life." Anthony shakes his head as if I'm nuts again, but wraps his arms around me and kisses my forehead.

"Hey, what if someone offered you a million dollars to get on the subway back to Manhattan and never see me again? What would you do?" he asks me as we're meandering slowly back to his place. His eyes are so pretty. "I mean, maybe I'll be nothing to you, or maybe I'll be the guy you grow old with. But it's hard to know now, isn't it? A million dollars."

"Tough call. What would you do?"

"Take the million bucks for sure," he says. "You're pretty cute, but I could make a lot of great films for a million bucks. Or at least a couple." He laughs and covers my face in kisses.

When I wake up from our second nap of the day, long after the sun has fallen out of the sky, I hear Anthony on the phone and walk sleepily into the living room, where he is leaning on the kitchen counter, ordering sushi. I'm wearing nothing but a pair of his socks and boxers and suddenly have the urge to do the splits. I'm close but not quite there, so I hold on to the back of the couch and try, however inelegantly, to slide into my imperfect version of the agonizing pose. He glances over at me and says into the phone, to whoever is taking his order, "I have the sexiest girlfriend in the world." Unlike Jake, this guy has no problem assuming the role of boyfriend. This is a man who digs me and wants the whole world to know it.

"Think about how much cash people flush renting two apartments," Anthony says, gesticulating with a veggie vermicelli roll wrapped in a lettuce leaf that's between his thumb and forefinger. "In New York, it's financial suicide." He swallows the last bite, kisses me hard on the mouth, and grins at his sister, who shakes her head.

We're at Anthony's favorite Korean restaurant on First Avenue, a sleek, dimly lit cube with creative cocktails and the best bulgogi in town, which is located a mere Frisbee toss from my apartment, which he doesn't know exists, having dinner with his sister, Suzanne, and brother-in-law, Bill. His big sister is a public relations maven in a gray suit who, with her petite, lightly freckled facial features and blond bob pulled back with a purple paisley silk scarf, looks like the heroine on a Harlequin Romance cover, perhaps the prim schoolteacher who's about to rock some handsome tycoon's world. Her lean husband has come straight from the gym and is sporting jeans and a navy fleece jacket over a Knicks shirt. "Me and Jacquie are the new urban couple, saving money, time, and a ton of needless agony arguing about whose house is closer or how many sleepovers before you get your own toothbrush," Anthony says. "And hey, if we get sick of each other, we do rock, scissors, paper to find out who moves to the spare room." He chuckles, throwing an arm around me.

"All right, all right, you can drop the pitch. We get your point," says Suzanne, finishing off her third beer. "Guess who I bumped into at Fairway the other day? Ben Carroll's mom."

"Scrawny three-pack-a-day-Ben Ben?" Anthony asks.

"Not anymore," she says. "Apparently a couple of years ago he met this woman, fell madly in love, got her pregnant in five minutes, and they moved to, guess where—Bali, one of *my* favorite places. I guess his wife makes jewelry and had always wanted to go there, so they sold Ben's apartment and skedaddled, and now they run a successful import-export business and he's a dive master and she sells her jewelry for a fortune in Beverly Hills, SoHo, and Barcelona, and they have two kids. But the most impressive thing is this house they bought over there, this *gorgeous*, thatched, indoor-outdoor Balinese affair they expanded into an enormous compound with a big modern kitchen and a wooden staircase that winds down to a riverbed. It's fabulous. Just can't afford that kind of space over here. His mom showed me pictures, she carries them around alongside the photos of the kids, who are adorable."

"Sounds lame," Anthony says. "Wasn't Ben gonna be some big political journalist or something? He just dumped all that to do what? Import tiki dolls and incense? Big whoop. His wife must have a real nice tight leash on him."

"It sounds pretty great to me," I say. "Dropping everything and moving to some beautiful spot and doing what it takes to get by. I've always kind of fantasized about that when the city has gotten oppressive. I figure I could write anywhere. Anthony, you could make movies anywhere, too; I'm sure there'd be something interesting to document in Bali, or wherever. I respect people who just go for it, you know, team up and go out and conquer the world together. It's bold and romantic."

"Well, apparently that's what Ben and his wife did," Suzanne says.

"Ben, Ben, Ben. I liked it better when we were talking about me," Anthony says with a cocky grin.

"Well, you might not have the balls to move to Bali, but you sure do like to take your life in your hands," Suzanne says.

"Oh here we go, Hawaii and the mountain bike," says Bill.

Suzanne nods and says, "Don't remind me. It was a bloody mess. He flailed over the handlebars at some outrageous speed, he was probably riding with no hands, knowing my brother. That's how he chipped his tooth," she tells me. Anthony grins, proudly displaying his battle scar. "My brother lives for danger, and besides the occasional bump or bruise, he is good at everything he does, you will learn, and even worse, he never, well rarely, gloats about it." My chest swells with pride as we all serve ourselves another round of food.

"In any case, Jacquie, " Suzanne says, "if he's going to shack up again, you seem like a good person to do it with."

"Thanks," I say, glad I've made a good impression. Shack up again, huh?

"It's true what you were saying, Tony," Bill says. "I know unhappy couples who have stayed together for years just because they can't afford another apartment in the city. It would be their financial ruin. You two just might be the archetypal New York couple."

"Fate brought Jacquie to my door," Anthony says, provoking guilt so strong I start coughing on it. "I am aware that sounds hokey, but how else can you explain it? Babe, are you all right?" I'm coughing uncontrollably, holding a napkin over my mouth with one hand and waving away their offers of help with the other. As Anthony bangs my back, I guzzle a glass of water and my fit slows to a chain of sporadic hacks.

"God, sorry, something went down the wrong way," I say.

We make our way up First Avenue past a crowd of "Olé olé olé olé!"–chanting NYU students. When we've almost reached Suzanne and Bill's car—they are one of the few New York couples I've met who have a garage in their Upper West Side building and actually drive in the city—Suzanne links arms with me and tries to get personal. "So, I feel it's my womanly duty to warn you that my baby brother, how do I put it, really likes long-term relationships," she says.

"That's a good thing, isn't it?"

"Well, yes," she says, drunkenly bumping her hip into a parking meter. "But in his case, I'd call it serial monogamy." *Better than serial killer,* I think. "It's like a sickness," she says. "He's with woman after woman for years at a time, but then somehow when it comes to taking the plunge, he always seems to find an excuse to get out. One girl started applying marriage pressure and he suddenly needed to focus more on his work. I have a sneaky suspicion the next one got knocked up. They started fighting all the time and one day she was gone. We all really liked that one, Natalie. Oh, and there was this one girl a few years back who wanted him to move in with her and bam, he realized he wasn't really in love with her after all."

"Well, he and I have already moved in together," I say. "Maybe it's different this time."

Suzanne halts at her black BMW SUV. "That's what his last girlfriend said." It occurs to me that maybe she's saying all this because she's loyal to the ex. Maybe she's trying to get them back together.

"I guess you really liked his ex-girlfriend, Natalie."

"She was all right. I like you better already," she says, swaying. The boys arrive and everyone hugs. As they're settling in to the car, Suzanne waves me over to her window and rolls it down. "Hey, I didn't mean to worry you. You're sweet and I can tell my brother likes you. Who knows? Maybe he's growing up. You're right, you did get him to move in with you. It's a start!" When they drive off, I walk slowly over to Anthony and he wraps his arms around me. As we come out of our embrace, we practically bump into Serena, my subletter, who's stepping out of the health-food store next door to my favorite café, where I've been buying my groceries for years. I open my mouth but no sound comes out.

"No way! Serena?!" This is Anthony talking. I'm baffled.

"Anthony!" she exclaims, and they hug each other.

"Wow, Jacquie, Serena and I haven't seen each other since, God, is it actually since film school?" he says. "Serena, this is my girlfriend, Jacquie."

As she says, "Oh, Jacquie and I actually . . ." I take a step behind Anthony and perform the universal hand signal for slitting my own throat.

"Um," she says, "I think we've seen each other around, haven't we?"

"Yeah, you look really familiar," I say, finally letting out my breath, which I've been holding since her brutal appearance.

I have to tell Anthony, I just have to, I think as they reminisce about the years that have passed since they went to film school together at NYU. I can barely hear their chitchat over the racket in my skull. No one in downtown New York has more than two degrees of separation from anyone else, if you ask the right questions. Anthony is bound to find out that I lied to him. He's bound to find out that I have my own place and showed up at his door because I was researching an article. He's bound to find out that the girl who starred in the first short he ever made is sleeping in my bed because I lied to him so that I could sleep in his. He'll hate me. I smile at their conversation when it's appropriate.

"You're doing a show with Will?" Serena asks. Will is Anthony's editor. "He's so talented." New York is a frighteningly small town.

"The best," he says. "I can't tell you how many times he's saved my ass."

"Well, if you ever want to get into commercials, you should send me your reel."

"I'll get you one anyway. I'd love to hear what you think." They exchange cards, I say goodbye without looking at Serena's eyes, and then finally we're alone again.

"You all right?" he asks.

"Tired, really tired," I tell him. "It's hard to meet so many of your people all in one night. I feel like I'm taking Anthony 101 and cramming for the final."

"All right then, let's get you home to bed," he says, thrusting his arm into the street to hail a cab.

Misery loves company. I need a roommate. No, I'm not clinically depressed. My
girlfriend moved out and left me with a big
1 BR in Gramercy I can't afford on my own.
Sm office can fit a bed. Don't worry, there's
space for two. 24hr drmn, great vus, cable
modem. Call if interested (or if you want to
help me drown my sorrows at bar downstairs. Grt bloodies). Rory

9

told my parents we'd come over for dinner when I get
back from my shoot," Anthony says, lounging on the
couch, picking up a piece of tuna sashimi with his fingers.
He pulls the bright red flesh apart with his other hand,
puts one half in his mouth, and gesticulates with the other.
"Take a trip to the 'burbs for a night. That cool?"

"That is so gross," I tell him, amused.

"What?"

"Picking up fish with your fingers."

"Does that gross you out?" he says, waggling the fish at
me. Lucy lifts her head up out of dreamland and sniffs it,
and Anthony pushes her away with his elbow. He plops the
stinky pink morsel into his mouth and wiggles his fishy
fingers as he scoots over to me on the couch.

"Eeeuw!" I yelp as he pins me down and tickles me

with his rank, sticky fingers. I'm the most ticklish person on the planet and laugh so hard I'm afraid I might choke. Lucy lifts her head, shakes her droopy jowls at us, and goes back to sleep. Once I calm down, Anthony kisses me. We're just getting into it when the phone rings. We ignore it. He takes off his shirt and flings it toward an armchair, but it doesn't quite make it and lands on the plate of half-eaten sushi. I giggle and run my fingers along his lovely bare chest. His cell phone rings.

152

"My mom or my sister. They're the only ones who call both lines," he says before wrapping his arms tightly around me and kissing me again, more passionately this time. Suddenly the TV comes alive, with Elizabeth Taylor squawking at Richard Burton about what a pussy he is. We paused *Who's Afraid of Virginia Woolf?* when the delivery guy buzzed and forgot to turn it back on. "Jesus Christ, it's the attack of the technology!" Anthony says and grabs the remote off the coffee table to turn off the TV. His cell rings again and, before it's even stopped, mine joins its irritating jangle.

"Oh my God!" I scream, and Anthony grins at me while jumping off the couch.

"Come here, baby, let's go hide from the world." He holds out his hands. I reach up and he pulls me off the couch and into the air. As I land on my feet, a brutal buzz from the kitchen announces that our clothes are dry. Lucy barks at it three times before going back into her coma and a car alarm screeches outside. We laugh our way into the bedroom, where I leap onto the bed and Anthony takes his clothes off, ranting about the noisy city and how someday he's going to live in a little cabin by a lake where the only sounds you ever hear are the loons calling out to each other and the rain batting against the roof. I watch him pull off one sock at a time, in awe of his beauty.

"You are the cutest thing I've ever seen," I tell him.

"I am not cute. I am a handsome and dashing man."

"That's what I meant."

He grins slyly and pounces on me.

I wake up a few hours later and drag myself into the bathroom to pee and brush my teeth. One shelf in the medicine cabinet is all mine. I also get one in the vanity underneath the sink, and there's a basket full of my makeup and assorted products on the deep windowsill. When I first moved in, there was some negotiating of space to deal with. Apparently Anthony's former roommate didn't have much in the way of toiletries, probably because Anthony's share engulfed the entire bathroom. I made fun of his ten different hair products and the pretty little wrapped soaps and bath beads he'd probably gotten as gifts for college graduation. Or maybe one of the exes left them. When I asked where they had come from, he suspiciously said he didn't remember. The bottles and boxes and tubes and tubs he was willing to part with filled two plastic grocery bags, which we hauled outside to spread their contents on top of the four garbage cans lining the side of the building. By the time we came home from dinner an hour and a half later, everything was gone, except for an unopened jar of bright blue hair goo that he must have bought in 1987. You've gotta love New York. By the next morning, even the blue goo was gone, most likely pinched by a homeless person who would try to sell it on Bedford or some kid bent on bringing Mohawks back into style.

I turn my face slightly, push out my lips, and make a sexy face at myself in the mirror. It's strange having a boyfriend. For a love junkie like myself, it's been a while. Of course there was Jake, but that didn't really count. With Anthony, I'm amazed at how smooth the transition has been from singledom to being half a couple. I've been living here for almost a month and, besides the medicine cabinet incident, it's been easy. I've been working my buns off at the magazine—we're shipping the issue in a few days, so the office has become chaotic again—and Anthony is in preproduction on a show about three kids recently released from juvenile detention centers and figuring out how to function in society again, so he's working long hours. During the week, we tend to just catch a glimpse of each other before bed. I've met a couple of his friends, but he hasn't met mine. I'm nervous about his first encounter with Courtney, considering her opposition to my move. Things have been a tiny bit icy between us. I should probably ask her to tea or plan a trip to the baths, but she's spent quite a few weekends out of town with Brad and my weekdays have been packed.

I'm planning to turn my text in to Clancy tomorrow, so, while I'm awake, I boot up my computer for a final read-through. I've spent the last week refining the piece and doing a little reporting to flesh it out. I ran an ad on Craig's List asking if anyone had ever dated someone they met through an apartment ad and got a few responses. One guy married a girl who had once been his roommate and spoke so sweetly about how they slowly fell in love watching the news together in the morning and chatting late at night when they'd bump into each other in the kitchen, both fumbling around drunkenly for a snack. Another guy told me about a friend of his who met so many girls in the course of interviewing potential roommates that he kept inviting them over even after he'd found one. He said the guy had never had more sex in his life. I also interviewed Sam about how she and Charlie had gradually realized that they had a real connection beyond a shared electricity bill. She said it took a while to figure out that she wasn't blushing out of embarrassment when she walked in on him in the bathroom and he scrambled to cover himself with a towel, but because she wanted to sit down on the edge of the tub and watch while he dried himself off.

The piece has gotten good and it couldn't have a more perfect ending—meeting Anthony, of course. "I haven't figured out yet how to tell Anthony that I own a beautiful one-bedroom apartment and that I'm subletting it to his friend," it says. "Maybe on our wedding day I'll reveal my secret and he'll recognize that my deceptiveness was in the name of a good cause—love—and all will be forgiven."

I hear the door creak behind me and turn as Anthony creeps in, looking at me with sleepy eyes. "Whatcha doing, pretty?" he says, as I click swiftly on another document that covers the article on my screen. He kisses me on the head. "I gotta go back to bed."

"I'll be right in," I say, gnawing a hangnail and wondering if I should ask Clancy if I can run the piece under a pseudonym, then zap my wrist as I decide it wouldn't be a good career move and realize once again that I'm going to have to tell him about the piece before publication. Even if Anthony doesn't read chick rags, it's too likely that someone—his mom, his sister, a friend with a secret passion for fashion don'ts—will see it. I tiptoe back into the bedroom and look down at his peaceful face on the pillow, his hair pointing limply at the thick wooden headboard above him.

Baby, I have to tell you something, I think, wishing I could confess telepathically without having to open my mouth. The phantom words in my head are enough to make my heart flutter. "Baby," I whisper. He doesn't stir. "Baby?" I say a bit louder. He continues breathing as lightly as a puppy. *Not tonight*, I think, *I won't bother him with it tonight.* Instead, I turn off the living room light, crawl under the covers next to him, and wrap my cold body around his warm sleeping one.

A few days later, Anthony is packing to go to Chicago for a shoot that could last as long as a month. I get teary when I leave for work and he's throwing sneakers, sweatshirts, tapes, and his digital camera at a duffel bag on the floor.

"Nice technique," I tell him.

He grins. "I'm gonna miss you, too."

After work, I go by my place in the East Village to pick up the mail. I haven't been there once since I moved out. Serena and I have spoken a couple of times and she didn't ask why I acted strangely toward her in front of Anthony, just said she's always thought he was cool and thinks we make a cute couple. She left today to shoot a commercial in Miami, so it's probably a good idea for me to stop by and empty the mailbox. The neighborhood hasn't changed in the weeks since I left. The man who runs the photocopy shop on my old block calls out my name as I pass. The scraggly mobile bike-repair guy has hauled his mountain of greasy parts out onto the corner of Tenth and A, like he does every year when the weather warms up. I take a detour through Tompkins Square Park, hoping I'll bump into Jeremy, and sure enough, he's sitting in the small dog section of the dog run with Napoleon in his lap. When the furry munchkin sees me, he starts moving his butt around ecstatically. I let myself in and sit down beside them on the bench. Napoleon jumps into my lap, grins up at me, and scampers back onto Jeremy's. I give my gay boyfriend the kind of hug usually bestowed on someone who's been away at war. I feel emotional being in the neighborhood where I'm used to bumping into my friends often. I guess I miss it more than I realized. Or maybe it's PMS.

"I haven't seen you here in a while," I say.

"I haven't been in here much," he says. "And when I see you coming, I hide behind a tree."

"Very funny." I watch a Scottish terrier and a pug in a pink leather jacket running in circles around each other. "You dating anyone?" I ask Jeremy.

"Oh, didn't you hear? I'm getting married," he says, sarcasm oozing from his perfectly nonexistent pores, insinuating that I've been so out of touch, he's met someone, fallen in love, and become engaged since we last spoke.

"I get to be a bridesmaid, right? I mean, you are the bride, right?"

"Easy, girlfriend." We link arms and Napoleon growls at me. He's possessive of his daddy and doesn't like it when others get too close. "Napster, you be nice to Auntie Jacquie even if she *has* been hiding her new boyfriend from us. It's been, what? Two months? When do we get to meet him?"

"Oh, soon, he's just really busy right now. He's doing a shoot in Chicago, God, he'll be gone for a month, I'm going to miss him. We don't go out much. It's embarrassing, really. There are weekends when we literally don't leave the house. I don't know, we just get so into each other, I guess we don't want to dilute it with other people's company or something. I'm sure it will pass."

"Honeymoon, schmoneymoon. You're probably ashamed of me. 'Oh, Jeremy, he's not really my *friend* per se. He's more like a stalker.'"

I laugh, put my arm around him, and lean my head on his shoulder. "Oh, you're right. I'm busted," I say.

"Met any of his friends?"

"Um . . ." Guilt. "Not many. His sister, we ran into one of his friends in the neighborhood and had brunch with him, one night we went out with some of his work friends, but barely, really." Jeremy looks down at his hands. I can't tell if he's hurt or just admiring his manicure.

"Can you tell I've been working out?" he asks, thrusting out his chest. "You can't really see it under my coat, but I am so ripped." I touch his waist and feel his ribs. "Be honest, have you found any flaws in the man? Any warts on his baby-soft booty?"

"He's perfect. He's gorgeous and smart. We have a lot in common—the movie stuff, books, and he has a dog! It's all very easy. We moved in together after five minutes, and we get along amazingly. I absolutely recommend finding a boy and just going for it."

"Oh, come on, there must be something about the guy that drives you batty. You can tell me."

"Well," I say. Six little dogs are playing tag around the perimeter of the small dog run. I follow them with my eyes, seriously considering his question. "He eats raw fish with his fingers." Jeremy widens his eyes as if we've stumbled upon some devastating evidence.

"He's not very domestic. He doesn't cook, he's a slob."

"So pick up after him."

"I have no desire to be a live-in housekeeper." The pug is trying to hump the Scottie at our feet. The Scottie seems willing to give it a go. A bunch of other dogs gather round to watch: puppy porn in the dog run.

"Okay, this is bad," I say and pause, afraid to go on. "Sometimes he does things like, um, use 'real' when he means 'really.' I'm actually not sure he's ever used an actual adverb in his life."

Jeremy shudders and says, "I can't let you have sex with this man." We have a drinking game where we take a sip every time a celebrity or the president makes a grammatical error. We wind up wasted.

"He doesn't really have the 'I/me' thing down either," I add. "But I swear it's not that bad. And he's so cute I barely notice. It must be true love, right?"

Jeremy hides his head in his hands, aghast.

"There is one more thing," I say.

"No holding out."

"Okay fine, apparently he's a serial monogamist."

"Big deal, so are you."

"Yeah, but it might mean he's a commitment-phobe."

"Big deal, so are you."

I widen my eyes in an expression of mock shock.

"Know anything about the exes?" he asks.

"One left not so long ago. According to his sister, she was bugging him about moving into his place or something, so he hit the road."

"You've got one up on her already," he says.

"I know! And his sister told me out loud that she likes me better."

"She came right out and told you she didn't like the bitch?"

"I think she said 'witch.' I know it rhymed with 'itch' anyway."

On the way to my place, I pass the bike-repair guy again. Now he's leaning up against his cart in the middle of the street, taking a nap in the sun. He shakes awake and grins at me, his ratty beard blowing in the wind. He changed a flat tire for me once. It was flat again a week later. But we're still friends. I wave and move up the street to where the Bible lady, elegant in a snazzy navy skirt suit and hat, is saying, "Sign up for Bible studies." Next to her sits a shopping cart covered with a blanket, and I wonder for the first time where she goes at night. It never occurred to me she might be homeless. Her voice is so clear and resonant, I've always thought she could have a career doing voice-overs. As always, the Yorkie who lives two buildings down from me yaps wildly from his window as I pass.

"Hey, sweet thing," I call up to him.

When I open my mailbox, it's packed full, but at least half is trash, which I dump into the recycle box in the hallway. I look around the building, feeling vaguely as if I don't belong there. I know every inch of wall and floor, but at the same time don't recognize it. It's like when I get home from a long trip and it takes me a second to remember which key opens the door. I make my way slowly up the stairs and turn the top lock. The door doesn't open. I panic, paranoid for a second that Serena has had the lock changed, but then realize she's fastened the bolt that I never use.

Inside, there are unopened boxes and duffel bags stacked up against the kitchen counter. Serena hasn't done a lot of unpacking. My bedroom looks like a tornado hit it, with clothes strewn frantically over the bed and floor, reminiscent of the Alicia period. An open suitcase leans against my dresser with sundresses and sweaters spilling out. The pictures that I had up on the wall—my parents, Alicia and me, a group of college friends, Larry licking my face—are in a stack on top of the dresser. I guess she wouldn't want them hanging over the bed.

On a pad of paper by the answering machine I notice a message from Planned Parenthood asking me to donate and one from my mom, who must have called my place by accident. I hit the button to hear the outgoing message and it's Serena's voice saying to speak at the beep and instructing people to reach me on my cell. I guess I won't have any messages here the next time I come by to snoop. I open the fridge, which is sparsely stocked with blueberry yogurt, a carton of eggs, milk, a box of strawberry-frosted Pop-Tarts, a head of lettuce, a jar of pickles, and Chinese food containers. I open one and take a bite of cold chow mein with my fingers before putting it back. It's good. I take the box out again, grab a fork out of the silverware drawer, and carry it to the couch and turn on the TV. I channel surf for a while and go back into the kitchen to toss the empty Chinese food box. There's a bag on the floor full of paper towels, toilet paper, grout, and screws. I'm wondering what Serena plans to do with the stuff when I notice a guy's jean jacket on the back of the stool at the counter. It's very worn and has lamb's wool on the inside. I walk around to the other side of the counter and touch the soft, faded denim. When I lift a sleeve to my nose, it smells warm and male, like leather and grass. Is Serena already seeing someone new? I look around for other signs of a man's presence. She's probably getting ex-sex. Hell, she was with Rory for three years and they're supposed to go cold turkey? I pull the jacket off the back of the stool and put it on before moving stealthily into the bedroom to look at myself in the full-length mirror. I pull it tightly around me, feeling like a teenager wearing a guy's jacket against the cold for the first time. When I'm putting it back on the stool, I notice that my broken window is shut. I run over to it, unlock it, and open and close it a few times. Sure enough, it's fixed. Right on, Rory.

As I'm leaving, Alicia calls. She sounds depressed, says she's had a low-grade headache for days.

"Do you think it's a tumor?" she asks.

"No, but you're definitely sick in the head."

I invite her over for dinner and movies since I've got the place to myself. "You can sleep over if you want. I'll probably be lonely."

When I arrive back in Brooklyn, Alicia is sitting on the curb in front of Anthony's apartment, waiting for me and looking glum. "Guess you were anxious to get over here?"

"Yeah. I brought food." She holds up a plastic bag that smells like rice, beans, salsa, and the rest of the trappings of a Mexican feast.

"That's so unlike you. Hope you got a lot, Courtney's coming, too."

She nods and hoists herself off the sidewalk to give me a stiff hug.

"Here, I got you keys," I tell her, tossing them to her.

"Thanks."

"You know what? I'm gonna run to the deli on the corner for ice cream and beer," I say. "Do you need anything?"

"A cat scan, a job, and a rich boyfriend," she says.

"I'll see what I can do."

When I get back, Alicia has become a mushroom growing out of the couch. "We don't even have cable at my place," she says. "I think I'm gonna buy a cheap DVD player. I'm going crazy."

"Well, Anthony's gone for a month. You can stay here."

"I'm over my apartment. Why did I want to live with a guy again?" she asks. "I need a roommate with feet that don't stink and a subscription to *Lucky* magazine."

We eat our burritos in front of *Days of Being Wild*, directed by one of my favorite directors, Wong Kar-Wai. Court arrives during a scene where Maggie Cheung and her boyfriend, played by Leslie Cheung, are lying in bed. I move a stack of Anthony's tapes to make space for Court on the couch. In the movie, Maggie says, "How am I going to tell my dad about us?" And Leslie, her boyfriend, goes, "What about us?" Court sits on the edge of the couch and says, "Can you believe this jerk?" Maggie starts putting on her clothes. She asks Leslie if he wants to marry her and he says, "No." Maggie storms out, saying she never wants to see him again. Something about the scene bothers me, makes my stomach tighten, as if the movie is trying to tell me something I already know, but I don't know what.

"That's so typical," my sister says, holding up half a burrito that we saved for Court, who touches it with the tip of her finger to see if it's hot and takes a bite.

"What?" I ask, trying to snap out of my momentary panic.

"Dude's a dick," my sister says. When I stare at her blankly, she gestures at the TV set with her napkin. "You know, unable to commit, like most guys."

"Not only guys," I say. "What about you."

"Uh, me?" Alicia says. "What about *you*, Miss Only Dates Twelve-Year-Olds with Intimacy Issues?"

"Excuse me?"

"Oh come on, you know what I'm talking about. It's easy to 'commit' to emotionally unavailable men. You seem like this total relationship junkie, but you don't really have to give shit, because those guys will never let you get too close. You get to feel all in love and poor me, I'm such a victim, but it's total bullshit. Deep down you know as well as they do that it's not gonna last."

"Excuse me, Dr. Phil, if you didn't notice, I'm living with someone."

"Someone you met four minutes ago. Let's have this conversation next month."

"I can't even believe this is coming from a girl who goes out with a different guy every night of the week!" I say, shaking my head at her. I pick up a couple of dishes and take them into the kitchen. "Court, would you rewind the movie a little? I want to watch it." She picks up the remote with a smirk on her face. I know she's eating this up.

"What's up with you, Alicia?" Courtney asks, changing the subject. "I haven't seen you in such a long time."

"Life sucks. I sleep so much, I'm always tired; I need to find something to do."

"I wondered how you could just leave L.A., with your house, your job, your cat. I can't believe you gave him to Mom," I say, getting back onto the couch and rubbing Lucy's tummy with my foot. She gets excited and climbs onto the couch, smooshing her fat butt between Alicia and me.

"Don't even talk to me about him. It kills me, but I wasn't happy there. My job sucked. I had no life."

"Are you okay for money?" Courtney asks her.

"I can probably last about six more months on my savings and subletting my bungalow in L.A., as long as I don't spend a lot."

Courtney puts her arm around Alicia. "I worry about you. Are you all right?"

It's as if the sudden tenderness flicked a switch that makes Alicia's polished veneer crack. Her voice wavers as she says, "I don't know what I'm doing with my life anymore. It seems kind of worthless. I don't like what I was doing before, I don't want to work in advertising," she whimpers, "but I don't really think I'm good at anything else."

"You know," I say, touching her leg—we don't touch much in my family. "I don't know if I told you about when I first finished grad school. I felt kind of the same. I kept getting jobs I didn't like and then started working as a personal assistant to this amazing director. She once seated me down and said, 'I think you should do volunteer work.' I was like, 'I don't think so,' but she insisted, said it would be a way out of myself and my rut, a way to start doing something concrete and productive for someone else. The next week I started delivering lunch to men with AIDS, just giving food to people who couldn't get it themselves, and she was right. I felt better, I stopped freaking out, and I actually started writing. I got my first gig a couple of months later. I can't say it was because of the food deliveries, but I do know my head cleared up a lot. Maybe you could walk dogs at a shelter or something, I don't know, do something for someone besides yourself. I don't mean to lecture you, but I know all about staring at your navel and starting to think everything that matters in the world is inside it."

"Yeah," she says glumly. I think she's taking it in even though she's staring with great concentration at Leslie Cheung's lanky body doing a slow, dreamy rumba around his room in his undershirt. Court and I watch the rest of the movie, while Alicia falls asleep with her body curled around Lucy, who has never looked more content. As I'm throwing a blanket over them, the door bursts open and Anthony walks in.

"Oh my God, hi, baby," I say, jumping off the couch. "What are you doing here?"

"We got held up," he says, "and had to push our flight till tomorrow."

"Wow, that's great."

Courtney holds out her hand toward him. "It's incredible that we haven't met yet. Courtney," she says, grabbing her jacket and putting it on.

"Can't say we socialize much with anyone besides each other," he says, glancing at me lasciviously. I nudge Alicia with my foot and she stirs. Anthony plops down on the couch, turns off the DVD player, and flips through channels until he settles on a basketball game and relaxes into a comfortable slouch with his feet on the coffee table.

"Hey, lady, Anthony's home," I say.

Alicia moans and slowly sits up. Lucy wakes up, too, and smiles up at her dad. Alicia sleepily puts on her shoes and jacket.

"So, your husband is Brad Garner," Anthony says to Courtney. "That's amazing."

"Yeah, he's on tour. He's doing really well," she says. When no one responds, Court says, "It's hard on me, being without him, not feeling that daily connection between us that's always let us both know that we're strong. I miss him a lot."

"Yeah, must be tough when your man's on the road to rock stardom," he says, staring at the screen.

"Well, we should be going," Courtney says. "It's late. Come

on, Alicia, I'll walk you home and grab a cab." I hug them both and start clearing the take-out containers off the coffee table in front of Anthony and rinsing off our plates. Anthony is still staring at the game.

"Your friend seems a little hippy-dippy," he says, flicking off the TV.

"I guess she is a little," I say, placing beer bottles in a recycling bag and wiping off the countertop. "One of the many things I love about her."

I look around the living room to see if I've missed anything and stand by the couch.

"I'm so glad your flight got messed up," I say. "You're working so much."

"This is my life, baby, when I'm on a project," he says, clicking off the TV and heading into the bedroom.

"It sucks."

"I miss you, too, you know," he says.

"What time do you leave tomorrow?"

"Five."

"Jeez, you're getting no sleep."

"I'll sleep on the plane. Hey, can you take those videos back to the place for me? I keep forgetting and they're like three weeks late."

"Jesus Christ, three weeks?" I ask. "How do you forget to return videos for three weeks?"

"I know, I know, I forgot," he says. "Won't do it again, Mom."

I turn away from him to go brush my teeth. When I go back into the bedroom, I think he's sleeping.

"I didn't mean to bark at you," he says quietly.

I burrow into the side of him, nestling my face into his armpit. He turns toward me, so his hip bones knock gently against mine. I drape my leg over his torso, as always astonished at how well our bodies fit together.

"I love you, Jacquie."

"You do?" I ask incredulously, pushing myself up on my elbow and looking down at his serene, chiseled face.

"Mmmm."

I squeeze him as tightly as I can, but I'm unable to respond and fall asleep quickly while he strokes my hair.

The impatient crowd on the platform at the Bedford Avenue subway station is particularly annoying this morning. We have an editorial meeting at ten, it's nine-thirty and I'm not in the mood to push and shove and glare my way into a seat on the train. It's been over a week since I turned in my article to Clancy and I haven't heard from her, and I'm feeling grumpy, anxious, and unwilling to deal with the Williamsburg brigade. The hipsters with jobs are out in full force, preening, pontificating loudly enough to make sure everyone can overhear last night's exploits, proudly displaying their well-worn copies of Jane Austen, Joan Didion, and Jonathan Safran Foer. *I'm too old for this neighborhood*, I find myself thinking, and force my way onto the train with my fists.

I arrive late to the meeting and announce my apologies all around. They have moved beyond this month's issue and are discussing canning one of the magazine's sections—a monthly gossip column in which an L.A. freelancer slams Hollywood and everyone in it—and replacing it with a new tech column, which would give Chester a chance to show his expertise and cheekily expound the virtues and flaws of whatever new gadgets, technologies, and Web sites turn up. Sounds like a yawn to me, but Chester's a good writer and Steve wants to prove we have our finger on the cultural pulse. He also thinks we should remind our readers that Hollywood is not our beat. Before we make our way back to our desks, Steve stops me.

"You okay?" he asks.

"Yeah, great, maybe a little distracted, but I've got a ton of editing to do today, it'll keep me focused."

I go back to my desk and call Luke Benton's personal publicist first thing. The It Boy of the moment has uncharacteristically starred in a low-budget indie, *Bad Rap*, in which he plays a recently released convict doing his best to assimilate, and he's really good. It's the feature-film version of Anthony's reality show, I make a mental note to point out to him. I've done everything but go to Benton's publicist's house and personally offer to give him a blowjob, and they're still hemming and hawing over whether he can be our August cover boy. Our publication is small and under-funded, but everyone in the independent film business likes—and reads—it. The publicist's flamboyantly blasé assistant says he's in a meeting. I don't leave my name, although I'm sure she knows my voice by now. I call Smith, another publicist who is handling the New York press for the film, a bitchy gay man I've been playing this game with for years, and beg a bit more. I tell him that if he gets me Luke, I'll walk his dog, Foofy, while he's at the Cannes Film Fes-tival. I know I'm safe, because Smith's live-in boyfriend, Pierre, doesn't fly and is afraid to leave his angel for more than three hours. Foofy's a Pomeranian who's adorable, but yappy—and old and half blind. I RSVP to a month's worth of screenings and cock-tail parties and feel satisfied that my social calendar is full enough for me to weather Anthony's absence.

Checking my e-mail while I'm on with Smith, the first mes-sage that appears in my box is from Clancy. I hold my breath and make myself ignore it until I'm off the phone. "Later, doll. Thanks sooooo much for pulling for me," I tell Smith, hang up, say an-other petite prayer, and click on Clancy's e-mail.

Hey you. LOVE YOUR PIECE. Putting contract through, call to discuss next assignment. Elated, I pick up the phone.

"Hey, Clancy, got your e-mail."

"Yeah, loved it. Text is off to the printer."

"Great. I'm so excited."

"Any ideas for another piece?"

"I was thinking about something for your Takes Two to Tango section: 'How to Spot a Commitment-phobe.' "

"Nice. A list? An essay? A reported piece?"

"I guess a kind of list: 'Ten Ways to Spot a Commitment-phobe'? I'll interview heartbroken friends, of course, but can you get me the number for some kind of shrink-slash-relationship-expert?"

"I'll e-mail you Joanne Love's info. She's the best. Eight hundred words. Can you get it to me by the fifteenth? That's two weeks."

"Sure, no problem." I hang up and do a little dance in my seat. Looks like I have proven myself to *Luscious* magazine. On my computer, I write:

1. He buys CDs you already have.

Anthony bought the new Beck the other day even though I have it. I got sullen and whiny, because I thought it meant we wouldn't be living together for long, and he said I was crazy, he just wanted to take it on his trip to listen to on the plane, and when I said I could have burned it for him, he changed his story and said he forgot I had it. I still think he got it just in case we break up.

2. He doesn't make an effort to meet your friends.

No big deal in our case—I mean it's only been a month, for God's sake, or a little over, but whatever. Now, Jake is a guy who couldn't care less about my friends. Isn't there some movie where the guy keeps the girl all alone to himself in their apartment and then in the end you learn he's not a real boyfriend at all but one her imagination has cooked up and she's actually insane? If it's not a movie, it should be.

3. Beware of serial monogamy.

I guess it's been on my mind lately. Let's see, I'd better define the term.

A serial monogamist is a man (or woman, but for
these purposes let's focus on the male version) who
goes from long-term relationship to long-term relationship, but never quite reaches "I do." Relationships
are a compulsion to this person, a security blanket
that cannot be provided by flings or one-night stands,
but they also have a shelf life usually determined by
the love object's ability to ride happily along without
pressing for proof of long-term commitment. Serial
monogamy is an insidious type of commitment phobia,
because the perpetrator seems like the perfect
boyfriend—loving, present, more than ready to spend
weekends together, introduce you to his family, and
tell you he loves you. Beware the man who opens himself up too quickly.

Wow, I didn't even realize how insidious some of Anthony's
behavior seems until I came up with this story idea. He told me
he loved me after less than a month, which must indicate some
kind of mental imbalance, right? I mean, I feel like I love him, but
to say it so easily means he's said it before and often and clearly
doesn't need to take a relationship very seriously to define it as
real.

4. He tells you he loves you too soon.

I remind myself that I'm only writing an article. It's not like
Anthony's enthusiasm for monogamy is a sure sign that our relationship is nothing but a breakup in the making. There are loads
of things worse than buying a Beck CD or saying he loves me.
Maybe he does love me and just couldn't keep it to himself anymore. Maybe he wants to listen to music that reminds him of me
while he's out of town, which is actually incredibly romantic!
True commitment-phobes do terrible things. I'm suddenly re-

minded of that movie *Once Around*, where Holly Hunter is having sex with her boyfriend and bugging him about getting hitched and he tells her point-blank that he will never marry her. That's a good one. Come to think of it, the guy in *Days of Being Wild* did the exact same thing.

> 5. If he says he will never marry you, that's a very good sign he never will. I've always said men are simple creatures. When they say it, they mean it.

Hmm, what else?

> 6. Sleeping with someone else right before the wedding would be a pretty good indicator.

When Andie MacDowell has sex with Hugh Grant while engaged to that old Scottish guy in *Four Weddings and a Funeral*, you know her marriage is doomed. There's this Spanish flick *Lovers* where a good Catholic boy who's engaged to a good Catholic girl sleeps with Victoria Abril and she puts a string of love beads up his butt during sex, and he goes so crazy with desire to please her that when she asks him to kill his fiancée, he does it. That guy has a serious problem with commitment.

> 7. It's probably not a good sign if your boyfriend plots to kills you.

I crack myself up.

> 8. Flirting with every other woman on the planet could also be a warning sign.

Check out *Alfie* or Truffaut's *The Man Who Loved Women*. Or maybe it's less fish-in-the-sea syndrome and more about restlessness, feeling an uncontrollable urge to move on to the next thing, like in *Carnal Knowledge* and *Five Easy Pieces.*

What is it about Jack Nicholson that cries out, "Cast me as a scumbag who is incapable of loving just one woman"? Same with *Witches of Eastwick, Something's Gotta Give.* That's a whole article in itself.

I e-mail Clancy and say that the piece might be more interesting if I relate each of my commitment-phobia red flags to a movie. It's my area of expertise and it will be more original than most articles on the topic. She e-mails me back to say to go for it and send her a draft as soon as possible. She's not entirely sure it will work, but would love to see what I come up with. She adds that I should probably include some expert testimony anyway, to give it credibility. She suggests having the expert analyze the afflicted fictional characters, thinks that would be a funny twist. I'm so fired up, I don't hear Steve the first time he asks me whether I've heard back from Luke's publicist.

"Sorry, got caught up in an e-mail. I'll try him again right now."

Seeking our dream house! We own our beautiful (but small) Chelsea duplex with 2 tiny bedrooms and are starting to think about trading up for a larger space with an extra bedroom. Outdoor space a must. Family-friendly locations (Brooklyn Heights, Cobble Hill, Park Slope) preferable. Spacious closets, washer/dryer, dishwasher, good water pressure a must. NO WALK-UPS s.v.p. If you have any leads, sellers, brokers, please contact Samantha toute de suite! Merci beaucoup!

10

I've had a hard time sleeping ever since Anthony left town. It's been almost three weeks and I'm experiencing my worst insomnia since a brief bout of postcollegiate existential angst that zapped my early twenties. He tends to call me when he gets home, which was around eleven o'clock the first week, but lately it has been closer to two. He and his crew are following Mikey, a delinquent seventeen-year-old with a racy nightlife, so almost every night they're at parties or clubs in the sketchier parts of Chicago. Then they're up at dawn, when this obsessive-compulsive girl, Delores, who is doing a better job of getting her life back on track than Mikey, goes jogging with her Shetland sheepdog Maggie Belle before school. On certain days she swims or practices tae kwon do in her front yard. Anthony's favorite moment was when Delores slept in by mistake and threw a temper tantrum when she finally got up. I guess she actually picked up and threw the dog (she was fine) and then cried hysterically at her rash behavior. Her mood swings are making for great television.

The late-night calls are tough. He's so amped after work, his energy seeps through the phone, leaving me rolling around and sighing a lot after we hang up. Sometimes I drag Lucy onto the bed with me, but her snoring and grunting don't help. Tonight he called especially pumped up because Mikey was hanging around outside a convenience store where his friends loiter every night, drinking forty-ounce beers out of paper bags and doing skateboard tricks, and apparently one of Mikey's friends had sold some kind of bogus white powder to this other kid for the price of cocaine and the duped guy turned up fuming. There was a huge brawl, with racial slurs blurted and blades pulled, like something out of *The Warriors*. The cops showed and Mikey's friend got hauled in, but fortunately for Mikey, he escaped over the flimsy fence at the back of the parking lot. He's on probation now and it could have been a big deal. Anthony was understandably excited about the footage he got: the action, the cuffs, the bad "your momma" jokes. When it heated up, Anthony called his second camera guy to rush over to the police station, while Anthony chased Mikey all the way home, where he was sweating and swearing and vowing to kill those guys if they ever messed with him again. Mikey doesn't sound like a guy who's too cognizant or concerned about the risks if he gets caught committing a crime again.

How the hell am I supposed to sleep after all this excitement? I throw my arm around Anthony's pillow and do my best to picture him lying beside me with his arms around my waist. Instead, I keep hearing sirens wail and imagining Mikey panting his way down some Chicago back alley with Anthony on his tail. "Uuuh!" I say. I've got enough on my mind without this nonsense cluttering it up. Steve is applying pressure to put Kevin Smith on the cover of the magazine instead of my boy Luke. The overhyped indie icon has a movie coming up, the issue wraps in a couple of weeks, and it's deadly not to have a cover story in place, but his bearded mug has graced our cover twice in the last three years and my gut tells me that Luke is going to come through for us. *Whoa*, I think, in a moment of revelation and sit up in bed to appreciate it: *Stefan, my actor ex-boyfriend, went to school with Luke Benton! He knows him!* They're not best friends, but they meet for coffee to grumble about the business when he's in town. Why didn't I think of this before? I drag myself out of bed and find my cell. It's two A.M., but Stefan picks up.

"I will call Lucas," he says when I ask. "Right now. It's early in L.A."

Completely awake now, I go into the living room and plunk down on the couch. Lucy smiles up at me, happy to have company. I flip on the tube and walk around in my underwear picking up old newspapers and magazines that have been accumulating since before I got here and make a pile to keep and a pile to trash. Under the Sunday *Times* from six weeks ago, I find a videotape that's been rented ever since. *Jesus Christ, he can be a flake,* I think. The phone rings.

"Luke will do the story," Stefan says, very serious. "His people never told him they were considering it."

"No way. They told us they passed on our request to him weeks ago."

"Yes, he will call his publicist now and you will hear back from him in the morning."

"Stefan, I love you. You're the best."

"Do you want to come over?"

"Tempting, Stef, but I'm living with someone."

"I didn't know."

"It's pretty recent," I say and pause for a moment, waiting for him to ask for details, but he doesn't. It always was all about Stefan. "Good night, Stefan. You're a god."

"Good night, Fluffy," he says. He always called me Fluffy, with a maniacal grin on his face and a little shake of the head. Hard to believe I used to love this lunatic.

When I sleepwalk into the office the next day, Steve hugs me. Warmhearted as he is, Steve never hugs me. He never hugs anyone. "I don't know how you did it," he says, "but you did it. Smith called this morning. I guess Benton's publicist called him in the middle of the night frantic because Luke is dying to be on our cover and he didn't know if we still wanted him. Apparently he told his publicist"—Steve lowers his voice to mimic Luke's famous drawl—"'*Flicks* is my audience, man. It's where I want to be. Especially when it comes to this movie, this little miracle that means all the world to me.' Jacquie, you're the best."

Before I can respond with false humility, Sam interrupts. "Uh, well, I've got some news, too."

Now what? She probably won the lottery.

Her face glows as she announces, bouncing up and down, "I'm, uh . . . prego! *Enceinte!* Yup, bun in the oven!" Total silence surrounds us. "It was a mistake, *obviously*, but we are so excited. It's only been a month, so we're not really supposed to tell anyone, but the thing is we decided to get married before I start to show too much, just to preserve the natural order of things—and because my mom insisted!" She throws her head back hysterically. "So we're doing it right away, two weeks from Saturday, in this little restaurant in our new neighborhood. Everything's changed. *C'est fou, je sais!* But exciting, too, *n'est-ce pas?* You'd better all still be able to come. We're sending out invitations, like, tomorrow, but I wanted to let you all know." She finally stops talking and bouncing and bows her head. I feel like we should clap or something.

"A pregnant bride. How totally *Kill Bill* of you," Chester finally says, and he and Steve take turns patting her back while she giggles and squeals. An eerie sense of déjà vu creeps up over me.

"Well, uh, back to work!" Steve says. "We've got an issue to put to bed, and, Jacquie, you're interviewing Luke Benton in two days at the Maritime. He'll be in town doing long-lead press for the movie, so you don't have to go to L.A. [Translation: Thank

God we don't have to come up with the cash to fly you there.] Get on the phone with Arjay to see if he's available to shoot him. If not, call that British chick who shot Penélope Cruz for us."

"I'm on it," I tell him, fired up again. I check my e-mail, hoping that Clancy has gotten back to me. I filed my commitment-phobia piece yesterday and haven't heard a peep. I think it turned out great. Our "love expert," this kooky and very witty shrink appropriately named Joanne Love, psychoanalyzed people like Jack Nicholson in *Carnal Knowledge* and Michael Caine (and Jude Law) in *Alfie*. It was classic: She said that the character in Wong Kar-Wai's movie *Days of Being Wild*, a ladies' man who throws out his lovers like yesterday's teabag, had probably been rejected by his mother. She hadn't even seen the movie, and that's exactly what happened. Anyway, I'm proud of the piece and eager to hear what Clancy thinks.

I e-mail Anthony, asking him to please fly in for the weekend of Sam's wedding. He'll still be shooting in Chicago—the shoot keeps getting longer—but I figure he can take one Saturday off, and I'm dying to see him.

After work, Alicia, who has been crashing with me a couple of nights a week since Anthony left, Lucy, and I hit the couch for a Luke Benton DVD marathon. Benton started out acting in a film based on a screenplay that he wrote himself, *Sick from the Start*, which was basically his life story, about a poor kid from the South working three jobs to support his ailing mother and two younger brothers. Years earlier, when Benton was seventeen, he'd been discovered in a diner by a scout who thought his ragged features put pretty boys to shame, and had been drawn into a world of money, drugs, and adulation that transformed him into a monster. He became one of those model brats the gossip pages adore, trashing hotel rooms, throwing very public hissy fits, and sleeping with and dumping every starlet and socialite from Madison Avenue to the Champs-Elysée. He crashed and burned by twenty-five, when he suddenly disappeared. It turned out that he had moved into the big beach house he'd famously bought for his mom in North Carolina, stopped drinking and started writing a screenplay, and, at twenty-eight, reemerged with *Sick from the Start*. And the world said, "Whoa, Luke Benton can act. And he can write." From then on, he's worked steadily. He got married (and divorced and married again), had a couple of kids, got divorced and married again (this is not a man who fears commitment), and has taken on about one film a year. My sister and I are watching the whole collection, or at least those we haven't seen before. Anthony calls during an intense moment in his first big-budget film, *Rage*, where Luke is confronting his father (played by Clint Eastwood) about how he wasn't there for him as a child and it's his fault that he has grown up to be a bitter, uncaring man just like him. When the phone rings, my throat is tight and sore and ready for the unlocking of the floodgates.

"Hey, baby," Anthony says. He sounds like he's in a hurry.

"What's up?" I ask, distracted. I motion to Alicia to pause the film. I grasp my hands together at my chest, pleading. She shakes her head, but hits Pause anyway.

"Babe, gotta run. Mikey stole a car and we're in hot pursuit, but I wanted to check in. Probably won't call later."

"Okay."

"Got your e-mail about the wedding. Can't do it. Things are too hectic."

"But it's just one night. Literally take the red-eye after work on Friday and go back on Sunday morning. It will be so easy. I miss you."

"Me too, beautiful, but I can't do it. This shoot is insane. Imagine if I missed this stuff."

"That's why you have a second camera."

"It's not like that, babe. I'm the producer, too. I can't just leave. Look, gotta talk to you about this later. Shit, gotta go." He hangs up and my lip starts to quiver. Alicia's looking at me and I wish she'd go away.

"Wanna go to Sam's wedding with me?" I ask her.

We're shooting Luke Benton at the Maritime Hotel's swanky outdoor bar, which is decorated with potted trees and Chinese lanterns. I get there early with my photographer, Arjay, to check out the place. While he and his assistant run around looking for the best spot to set up, the hotel manager escorts me up to Luke's empty suite. I sit down in the sleek, understated living room and look through the doors at the massive bed, where the movie star I'm going to interview spent last night. It looks as if it's been swallowed by its fluffy white duvet and matching pillows. Above the bed hangs a tasteful painting of a woman's bare derriere.

Luke Benton does not look like your typical handsome actor. He's forty-one and has an odd face that for some reason you can't stop looking at—more Owen Wilson than Jude Law. I don't find him attractive, but I like watching him on screen. When he flings open the door, though, and strides through it in a black T-shirt with a Ziggy Stardust decal and ripped jeans, I feel his entrance like a wave that rips me suddenly off my feet. In person his deep-set, sloping gray eyes and unusually large, toothy mouth are sensual, his towering height impressive, his presence magnetic. I guess this is what they call star quality. He is extremely attractive: striking, comfortable in his skin, the kind of guy you'd have really good sex with, then throw on clothes and run out tousled for beers and Chinese food.

"You must be Jacquie," he says, with a musical, slight Southern drawl, holding out his hand as he makes his way toward me. "Please excuse me for being late." He takes my hand and it tingles.

"No problem at all," I say, wishing myself out of my stupor. I've met hundreds of actors. Why am I acting like an ass? He throws himself down on the couch, right next to the spot where I'd been sitting, and pats the place where my butt should be. I sit. Someone knocks on the door.

"Come in!" Luke hollers, and a room service waiter wheels in a tray with a bottle of water and a plate of fries on it.

"I ordered fries," he tells me as the waiter places them on the coffee table in front of us. "My last vice, and I cling to it with relish. Want some?" He picks one up off the plate and places it between my lips. My cheeks become very hot as I chew. Luke bursts into a grin. "Mmmm," he says. "So good."

"Yeah, I'm a sucker for greasy food myself," I say, taking another. "And salty food. And sweets . . . Should we talk about your movie?" Luke eloquently analyzes *Bad Rap* and the politics that led him to take the part in a no-budget independent film by a first-time director. His passion is contagious, and forty-five minutes fly by, both of us animated and laughing often. I only have fifteen minutes until we have to go downstairs to the photo shoot, so I throw out some quick questions about earlier projects, his writing, his three-year disappearing act, and even a couple of more personal inquiries about his relationship with his two daughters and his very public recent marriage to a French actress half his age. He doesn't hold back at all and seems happy to share an intimate side of himself with me.

At one o'clock on the dot, Luke's publicist bursts in and asks us to wrap things up; we've got to get shooting. Behind him, in sweeps Luke's wife, Celine Devereaux, as stunning in person as on screen but much thinner. Her waist is about as big as my ankle. "Baby, baby, baby, I *meeessed* you!" she howls, launching herself feverishly at Luke, who's still seated next to me, wrapping her legs around his waist and shoving her tongue down his throat with complete disregard for me and the other onlookers in the room. I hastily snatch up my digital recorder and purse and rush out the door.

The bar downstairs is buzzing. The makeup artist has set up her table and is perched in a director's chair, impatiently wiggling her foot. Arjay has placed white Chinese lanterns artfully above a table and is taking Polaroids of his assistant in various positions around it. Smith, the publicist hired by the studio to promote the movie, is there chatting up Steve, who has turned up for the occasion, and the love of Smith's life, Foofy, is hobbling around looking for scraps of designer bar food.

"Foofy, come here!" Smith shouts, digging a treat out of his pocket. "We're about to get this party started." He throws his arms up when he sees me and rushes over to plant kisses on the air next to each of my cheeks. "Hey, doll, you look gorgeous! How was it?" I assure him that the interview went exceptionally well. We squeeze each other tight, in silent acknowledgment of the triumph we've managed to pull off together.

During the photo shoot, Celine has a hard time staying more than three feet away from Luke. At one point he's leaning against a photogenic wall posing for close-ups and she's crouched on the floor at his feet with her arms wrapped around his legs, gazing up at him rapturously and whispering the mantra *je t'aime je t'aime je t'aime je t'aime* into his kneecaps. While the makeup artist is refreshing Luke's face, his publicist approaches the besotted ingenue and whispers something into her ear and she's whisked off, only after she's jumped onto Luke's lap and buried her face in his neck and cooed, "I weell meeess you so mooosh, mon bebé. Ce n'est qu'un *fitting*. I weell be back by four o'clock. I loooooove you."

"Love you, too, angel," he tells her, as she scampers off to the limo waiting to escort her.

When the shoot is done and we're packing up, Luke's publicist approaches me and says, "Jacquie, Luke would like some more time with you."

"What do you mean?"

"He said you were rushed out of the interview earlier and he'd like to give you more time." I'm surprised: I considered the interview fairly indulgent, but I'm also touched and tell him I'd be happy to continue our conversation. I let Steve know I'll be staying, and Luke and I say our goodbyes. We stand silently side by side in the elevator as it rises slowly toward the fifth floor, where we get out and make our way back to Luke's room.

We take our places on the couch and I pull out my recorder and turn it on. "All right, so tell me more about this movie. What was it about a guy leaving prison that hooked you?" I say, not really knowing how much is left to be said.

"You know, it's a project I'm very proud of. The idea of starting over, of leaving behind destructive patterns and trying to be a better person, strikes something very deep inside of me. I've reinvented myself so many times." He's sitting about a foot from me on the couch and staring right into my eyes. I wonder if he thinks I'm pretty.

"You are known as much for your many lives as you are for your talent as an actor. Are there any surprises around the bend that you want to warn me about?" I think I detect a glint in his eye. He definitely raises his eyebrows mischievously.

"Hey," Luke says, reaching over and turning off my recorder, "let's talk about you now."

"What about me?" I ask, shivering slightly.

"How long have you been doing this?"

"About six years."

"Do you love it?"

"I used to say I loved my job so much I'd do it for free, but now sometimes I think I'd like to do other things as well."

"Like what?"

"Well, I've started writing relationship stories for a women's magazine. It's a lot of fun."

"I see you being a great writer, Jacquie, someone people will notice," he says, continuing to look straight into my eyes. I nod, wondering if he thinks my stomach looks fat in this skirt.

"I like you," he says and touches my cheek. It warms under his fingers. Is this actually happening?

"I like you, too."

Over his shoulder I see the bedroom with its fluffy duvet. The ass of the woman in the painting is bigger than mine, but next to Celine I'm gargantuan. If Luke and I had sex, he'd probably think I was a cow. What am I thinking? Luke and I are not going to have sex. Or are we? *Oh my God*, I think. And then: *Wait. I have a boyfriend.* Having one still feels new. It's been a long time since I've been with a man who trusts me and counts on me to be faithful, and even longer since I've gotten into a situation like this while I was in a relationship. Usually I only have to contend with myself, a guy (in this case, a rich, famous, astonishingly attractive and charismatic one), and the angel and the devil on my shoulders, who are bickering about how slutty I am and whether that's a good thing. Now there's all that plus a man with whom I might spend the rest of my life. Oh yeah, and one of the most beautiful women in the world, who happens to be married to the man whose thigh is now pressed up against mine. If I sleep with this guy, I'll become another notch in a movie star's bedpost and I'll freak out the whole time about how fat my butt is and whether I'm as good in bed as Celine Devereaux. But I will also have a great story to tell my friends. What's really standing in my way is the fact that I would be cheating on Anthony, and I don't cheat. Never have, never will. I just don't do it.

"You know," Luke says, running a finger lightly along the length of my jawline. "There was a time in my life when I would have taken your hand and guided you into that room over there without a care in the world."

My cheeks flush again. Oh my God. "You're married," I say.

"Well, that's the problem, isn't it?" he says, his thumb and forefinger lingering at the tip of my chin. "There was a time when that wouldn't make much of a difference to me either, but I'm trying to be a better person."

"I have a boyfriend," I say, relieved to have said it.

"He's probably a pretty special guy." I nod. He leans forward, puts his hands on my shoulders, and lightly brushes my lips with his. It sends a jolt through me, and I close my eyes to savor the sensation for a second before pulling away and gently encircling his wrist with my hand and shaking my head: no.

"Let's do it anyway," he snarls, running the back of his hand down my throat and tantalizingly along the edge of my breast. This guy knows exactly what he's doing: It feels so good, I have to squeeze my thighs together to stop myself from floating away—or into his bedroom. Luke looks into my eyes with hard determination. He is trying to hypnotize me.

"I can't," I say.

"All right, let's get out of here," he says, and jumps up from the couch.

"That's a good idea."

As we wait for the elevator, both of us start laughing, quietly at first and then like hyenas. "I can't believe I just had that conversation with Luke Benton," I say.

"For a minute there, I was just a man."

I nod.

In the elevator, he looks over at me. "What are you thinking?"

"Just wondering if I have any regrets," I say.

"Want to go back?" he asks, his mouth widening into a lecherous grin. I push him with my hip and shake my head in mock disapproval.

"Goodbye, Luke," I say, now in the lobby, and give him a forceful hug. Everyone at the reservations and concierge desks pretends not to be watching and wondering did we or didn't we?

Alone outside on Sixteenth Street in front of the hotel, I throw back my head and scream. An old lady holds her purse more tightly against herself. I take out my cell and call Courtney.

"Oh my God, Court! You're not gonna believe what just happened! Luke Benton hit on me! He, like, made the moves. I could have slept with him. I didn't, but I could have. He wanted to. Wow, we had this amazing connection. It's very *Celebrity*, don't you think? You know the Woody Allen movie? All alone in the movie star's bedroom and he starts making the moves. Woody did it again when Scarlett Johansson slept with that sleazy director in *Scoop*. But no, it was a real connection, more Diane Lane and that babe Olivier Martinez in *Unfaithful*, you know, wrong but impossible to ignore. I thought it was just me at first, but then it was totally mutual. Oh. My. God!"

"Jacquie!" she says. "This isn't a movie you're talking about. It's your life. And Luke Benton is married."

"I know that, Courtney. Obviously."

"Well, then, what are you so excited about? I don't find it interesting or sexy. I find it disgusting."

"That's all you have to say when this gorgeous movie star just hit on me in his hotel room? Yeah, this gorgeous, *married* movie star no less. Come on, even you have to admit that's pretty friggin' cool."

"I'm sorry, I really just don't think so. A famous actor with a reputation as an incorrigible womanizer almost cheats on his wife and you almost let him. Why? So you could tell everyone how great he is in bed? So you can say you slept with a movie star? You got him to cheat on his beautiful wife? All I can say is I'm glad you used whatever restraint you were able to muster, or I'd be sick. Jesus Christ, Jacquie, what about Anthony? What about the supposed love of your life?"

"I didn't do anything, Court. Jesus Christ, it was just kind of cool that we had this connection."

"Well, congratulations," she says. "You know, you are so fond of saying you're pathologically faithful, oh yes, and honest to a fault. But I'm not so sure. Sometimes I think you'd lie and cheat all the time if you knew you wouldn't get caught."

"That's a mean thing to say."

"Well, I'm in a bad mood and that's how it seems to me," she says.

"I'm hanging up," I say, and I do.

As I'm creeping along Seventh Avenue, agitated about the conversation, Clancy calls.

"Been meaning to call you," she says. "I was out with a twenty-four-hour flu."

"Are you okay?" I say, relieved that she wasn't blowing me off.

"Completely healed. But listen, Jacquie, I am thrilled with your piece. Not changing a word. You've got the *Luscious* voice down. It's smart, funny. I want you to do another for the next issue."

In the back of my mind, I remember that there's something I was upset about, but the thought is easily evicted from my brain.

"I thought of another idea: how to deal with a boyfriend who's married to his work. I'll give examples from workaholic movies like *His Girl Friday, Wall Street, Kramer vs. Kramer,* stuff like that. I'll have to think of one where the husband's workaholic tendencies drive the neglected wife to cheat. Duh, *Heat* with Pacino, remember that awful scene when he walks in on her with the new guy?"

"Painful."

"Hey, Clancy, do you think I might be able to write these regularly? I think there's an endless number of stories here."

"Shouldn't say anything, but I am going to propose it to the editor in chief. So fresh, unlike what I've seen in the other mags. Jacquie, I think we're onto something."

I'm bursting with excitement and want to call Anthony and tell him, but then I remember that he doesn't even know that I write for this magazine. God, the lies upon lies have become so convoluted, I can't even share this news with him any more than I can tell him I almost slept with Luke Benton. I guess I could just tell him about the workaholic assignment but he probably wouldn't be thrilled about the subject matter, and what if he started buying the magazine? I'd be screwed. Then again, he never reads my articles that he *does* know about. In any case, it's time I told him the whole story, but not while he's out of town. I have to do it in person. I have to be there to make sure he doesn't keep hating me when he starts hating me. Suddenly exhausted, I call Alicia and tell her to invite a friend to the premiere party for a Spanish film we were supposed to attend together. I can't do it.

I'm fast asleep at eleven-thirty when Anthony calls and says he can talk only for a minute because he has to head out again.

"You're obsessed with your job," I tell him sleepily.

"What?" he asks. He sounds angry.

"You are. You're obsessed with your work."

"Yeah, maybe I am, and what's wrong with that? I like what I do. I like to do it well. So, what's the big deal?"

"I just wish you had more time for me. I haven't seen you in such a long time and I have to take my sister to my friend's wedding." I roll over in bed and lean on my elbow, feeling more alert now. "Even when you are in town we only see each other for five minutes before bed. I don't know when the last time was that we've even spoken about something going on in my life. Have you ever read anything I've written? It just bums me out. That's all."

"Jacquie, I can't deal with this right now. I think I'm going to hang up before you really start pissing me off. Me and my crew are out here working our asses off and I really don't need this from you. Jesus Christ, Jacquie! You expect me to dump everything to come home for some wedding of some chick I don't even know? Show a little respect for what I do."

"Fine," I say. "I'm sorry."

"Good. I gotta go."

When he hangs up, I experience a sensation I've felt before, of grabbing aimlessly, trying to find something to hold on to before I fall. My arms and body feel heavy, as if I could sink right through the mattress. What is it with me that I always love men who are somehow out of reach? Anthony has handed me his love, his company, and his home, but he still isn't really here. He's still off somewhere without me, while I'm lying in bed alone. Yet, I was drawn to him before I knew what our life together would be like, back when he appeared only generous and loving. It's as if I subconsciously seek men who will leave me wanting more.

At some point later, I get up to pee and notice my phone flashing with a message. "Hey, baby, it's me," the message from Anthony says. "Was that our first fight? I don't think I liked it." He swallows hard and continues, "Hey, I was thinking maybe you could come down here for a weekend. I can take some time for myself, just as long as I'm here and on call. I think you'd have fun running around with us, too. It's a trip." He chuckles. "Baby, it's hard for me to be away from you, too, but I'm so tired. I sorta snapped back there. All right, baby, sleep tight. Um, later. Love you."

I hit 9 to save. It will be a good one to play when I'm feeling blue. It always cheers me up to be reminded that somebody loves me.

I fall asleep thinking about what to bring to Chicago: sneakers and cargo pants for roaming around with the crew, the black, lightly transparent halter dress Anthony loves, and my favorite slinky red Cosabella nightgown, which he hasn't seen yet—it's the perfect opportunity. I picture us rushing through the streets of Chicago on the heels of these wild, cocky teenagers whose jokes make us laugh. I imagine Anthony throwing his arm around me as dusk falls over a dank alley, where Mikey has slunk off to smooch with his skinny, bare-legged girlfriend with bewitching brown eyes. Anthony pulls me close and presses his warm lips to my forehead. "I'm so happy you were able to come down here, baby," he says. "So happy you're seeing all this for yourself."

Seeking large apartment in East Village or beyond. Overdue yet unexpected breakup has left me homeless. I have lived in the EV all my life, but might consider the right place in Brooklyn, Long Island City, open to suggestions. Ideal would be a large, raw space that can use some work. Could even go in on a building with someone if the right property comes up. Any leads, please call Zach.

11

I spend a good chunk of my weekend perfecting my Luke Benton piece, which reads like a tongue-in-cheek love letter—or is there such a thing as a lust letter? I'm proud of its humor, honesty, and sexual insinuation that never crosses the line of propriety. I know that Luke and his peeps will love it. I also devote some time to procrastinating. While I'm on Travelocity shopping for tickets to Chicago, Serena calls to let me know she's going out of town for a week, so Saturday I decide to run by to pick up my mail and take advantage of the trip to the city to do a yoga class. My body is crying for it, but once I'm actually in the studio on my Bubble Yum–pink sticky mat, my muscles resist nearly every pose except those that require total relaxation.

While we melt into an easy seated pose at the beginning

of class, Gwin gives us the usual dose of her personal philosophy. Today she describes a documentary she saw about a group of Tibetan Buddhist monks who created elaborately decorated mandalas out of sand only to destroy them afterward. She said that at first it was shocking to witness the destruction of breathtaking works of art that had taken many weeks to create, so contrary to our society, which believes in treasuring every artifact, every child's crayon drawing. But after watching for a while, she became hypnotized, acutely aware of the value of their actions, how in a larger sense they symbolized the Buddhist principle of nonattachment. "Challenge yourself to let go of your thoughts, your judgments, your need for people and things," she said as we sat cross-legged in the darkened room. "What do we gain from clinging to our possessions and ideas? Is there anything we get through chasing or grasping or hoarding that's worth holding on to? See if during the next hour and a half you can move through these poses without attachment. Break a habit today. Maybe find something different in these familiar movements than you ever have before. You might discover a shift, a sparkle, just by letting go of your usual routine."

She ends class as usual, telling us to put our hands together in front of our hearts and take a moment to think of something for which we are thankful. The first thing that comes to mind is my apartment, which is strange since I don't live there anymore, and then the faces of my mom, my dad, and my sister float through my head.

On the way to my apartment, inspired by the yoga class, I take a different route than my normal one and enjoy glancing into unfamiliar storefronts. In a fancy furniture store, a burly, black French bulldog stands in the middle of a display, gazing past me into the street. I follow his eye line and, for the life of me, can't figure out what has him transfixed. Wandering up Second Avenue, I notice a simple, hand-painted statue of Ganesh in the window of a crowded Tibetan shop. The elephant god is one of the most popular Hindu deities, and I've learned in yoga class—where we often chant to Ganesh—that he's the remover of obstacles and his presence in a living space brings good fortune. I buy the statue for my sister, who could use some good fortune. The salesman tells me to place the statue facing the front door so that Ganesh can invite in great riches and luck. He wraps it up in red tissue paper and I stow it in my bag.

I turn up First Avenue and across the street see Buster the wondermutt lounging in the sunny doorway of the hardware store. I cross to say hi to him. "Hey, crazy face," I say, ruffling his scruffy white fur. I squat down in the doorway for some lovin' and notice Buster's cute owner also squatting a few feet away through the open door, arranging ceramic flowerpots. I shamelessly watch his hard calf muscles flex as he reaches to grab something that's fallen behind a crate. "Hey," I call out. He's listening to his iPod, so I wave my hand to get his attention. When he finally sees me, the strangest look crosses his face, like he's been caught doing something illegal, and he hastily pulls off his earphones and stands up.

"Stashing pot plants in the merchandise again?" I ask.

His pale cheeks turn pink and he says, "No, hi, you just startled me. You haven't been here for a while."

"I actually moved out of the neighborhood," I tell him. "I, uh, moved in with my boyfriend." I feel awkward saying it, like I don't want him to know that I have a boyfriend. It's disturbing to me that a part of me still wants attractive guys to think I'm single.

"How's that going?" he asks, rubbing dust off his knees.

"Okay," I say. "Great. Well, you know, living with someone is hard work." Am I sounding too negative? I add, "It's totally worth it, though. It's great."

"Cool."

"What were you listening to?" I ask. "You seemed really into it."

"The sound track to this movie *In the Mood for Love*, a Wong Kar-Wai movie." He blushes again. "You probably know it."

"I love that movie," I say.

"Want to hear it?"

He walks over and places one of the earphones into my ear. After a second, he puts the other one in his own ear. It's a love song with a Latin beat, rhythmic, swooning, old-school romance. It's what I would want to listen to if I worked in a hardware store all day. I'm suddenly aware that the cute hardware-store guy is so close to me that I can feel the blond hairs on his bare arm touching mine. When I look up, his pale lashes flutter and his blue eyes catch mine for a second, and we pull away in unison, jerking the earphones out of our ears, so they dangle at his side. He takes a step back and clears his throat, and I fix my bag on my shoulder.

"Um, I've been meaning to ask you something," I sputter. "I mean, I could use your expertise. Do you know of a nontoxic alternative to Drano? The sink in my, uh, my boyfriend's bathroom, my bathroom, the sink keeps filling up with water."

"No problem. Just mix baking soda with a can of Coke and pour it down," he says.

"Really? God, thanks. How much baking soda?"

"About half a cup," he says.

"Cool, thanks," I tell him, noticing a penny on the floor between us and glancing to see if it's heads up. "I love that song. I'd forgotten how much I liked it," I say. "Well, I gotta go. Gotta check the mail at my apartment—my old apartment, really. I'm subletting it. Anyway, bye."

He waves, smiling slightly without opening his mouth, and turns away. I give Buster a last hug. As he lazily wags his tail, I reach over to pick up the penny and dust it off before sticking it into my pocket. I notice that the hardware-store guy is still watching me and my face flushes hot.

"I still pick up lucky pennies," I say, embarrassed. "Not like it does any good."

"Oh it does," he says. "You should see what life is like for people who don't pick them up."

When I get to my apartment, I unlock the bolt like a pro and just inside the front door find an addition to the household: a coatrack, one of those old wood and brass ones often spotted in Irish pubs. On it is a hot-pink raincoat and the jean jacket with the lamb's wool lining: There's still a man in the house. I run my finger down a soft sleeve and dump my bag onto the floor before turning into my bedroom. I catch my breath when my eyes fall on a simple, white blind up over the window; the dirty, green towel that was tacked up there for months is nowhere to be seen. I hop over to it and look up. It's been expertly installed and has a silver chain hanging down the right side to raise and lower it, an action I practice a few times.

"Serena! Your boyfriend is a genius!" I say, excited to snoop further. I notice that the simple, white curtains I bought on sale at West Elm months ago are finally hanging up in the living room, and on the coffee table that I painted orange stands a pot of red mini-roses, my favorite. They remind me of one springtime in Paris when I was angry at Philippe because the flowers suddenly appeared in all the florist shops, easily becoming the object of my deepest passion, and he never got me any, despite my constant hints that our apartment needed some greenery and color. Eventually I bought myself a pot and planted them in a big Moroccan bowl that I placed by my window. When Philippe got home, he went on and on about how beautiful they were. He honestly had no clue that he was supposed to have gotten them for me. Yet another illustration of two relationship basics: (1) Don't assume that a guy gets it. He is clueless and needs to be told explicitly, with a loudspeaker to the ear if possible, at a time of day when he is especially alert. (2) Never wait for him to do it. If at all possible, do it yourself.

Next to this particular mini-rosebush is a note that says, "S— Thanks for letting me crash. The light here is incredible. Hope it cheers you up. x." I assume that this is from Rory and think he's doing an awfully good job of winning her back. Inspired, I call Anthony and leave him a message suggesting that we fix up the apartment—repaint the bathroom, hang all those pictures that are stacked on the floor, clean up a bit. I feel impelled to renewed domesticity. On a whim, I go into my front closet and find the pile of flowerpots I lugged home on my birthday and select a small one that's stained a shiny cobalt blue. I take it into the kitchen, dig out a bag of soil I bought months ago but never opened, and set to work repotting the rosebush. *It looks beautiful*, I think, placing it back on the little orange table next to the note. Serena will like it better this way.

There's nothing but a couple of *Entertainment Weeklie*s and *New Yorker*s and a stack of bills in my pile of mail—plus a check for sixteen hundred dollars for the commitment-phobia piece.

I skip all the way over to the fridge, which is fully stocked with fruits and vegetables, milk, yogurt, salsa, hummus, cold cuts, jarred sauces, butter, jam, a six-pack of Sam Adams, Tupperwares full of leftover stir-fry and marinara sauce, plus chicken cutlets, fish, veggie burgers, and ice cream in the freezer. The cupboards, too, are packed with pasta, tortilla chips, pretzels, cereal, rice, couscous. There are even cans of soup and beans and bags of lentils. It feels like my parents' kitchen or something. I wander around a bit more and find guy products in the bathroom, a razor, an extra toothbrush, and Right Guard deodorant. I have no desire to leave yet, even though I feel like a jerk for making myself comfortable in what is essentially Serena's apartment, which she appears to be sharing with a man. It still feels like home to me, though. I pick up the most recent copy of *The New Yorker* and lie down on the couch to read it. My cell rings and I run to my bag by the front door, hoping it's Court, whom I haven't spoken to since our argument, but no, it's Jake. I miss the call but check his message.

"Yo," he says. "Checking in. Wanna get a drink? How's it going with your dude? I'm doing really good. The art is going good. Did you check out my show?" Shit, I forgot. "I got some interest from it, so effin' cool. Really. We should have a drink. I'll tell you more. Anyway, pretty lady, call me sometime. Late."

What is up with these guys? I call my sister to find out and she says, "As soon as they sense that you've moved on, they come running. It's like a law of physics or something. When you gravitate toward them, they pull away. Then when you start to recede, they rush up against you, try to suck you in like a drain."

"Can you still meet for food?" I ask her.

"Yeah, I'll be at that Italian place on B in half an hour."

"Cool, I'll head over soon. Call Jeremy." I know I should invite Courtney, too, but I'm not really in the mood to see her. With a little time to kill, I stick my head into the café to say hi to my cute boy there. He's busy, but runs over to see if I need anything.

"No, just wanted to say hi," I tell him.

"It's sad that you're not in the neighborhood anymore," he says, handing me a biscotti for the road.

"I know, I'll try to stop by more often." He squeezes my hand and rests his hazelnut eyes on mine for a moment. My stomach lurches. As I wander to the dog run, the park is crawling with good-looking men. Is it possible that there are more out today than usual? My eyes flicker from a blond in thick glasses and a plaid shirt reading on a bench to a shirtless redhead napping on the lawn. Am I being tested? A guy tossing a Frisbee to a cute friend looks over at me through the longest lashes I've ever seen. It's okay to notice male beauty when it's being shoved in my face, isn't it? I arrive at the dog run and stick my finger through the fence to let a baby Bichon lick it. In the middle of this wet, gooey greeting, Anthony calls.

"Hey you, what are you doing?" he asks.

"At the moment having my finger licked."

"Sounds sexy," he says.

"Not really. A moving cotton ball is doing the licking."

"Ah."

"So I was thinking I would come down this weekend. I wanted to check with you before I book the ticket, but this weekend probably makes the most sense."

"What?" he asks, sort of shouting into the phone.

"Where are you?"

"On the street, it's kinda windy," he says.

"You get my message about fixing up the place?"

"Yeah, got it. Awesome."

"Cool, I'm glad you're into it. So, does this weekend work?"

"What do you mean?" he asks.

"What do you mean, 'What do you mean'?" I ask. "We were talking about my coming down." The little dog had run away but now he comes back and stares up at me, mouth open and panting happily. I bend back down to pet him again.

"We were?" Anthony asks.

My abdomen tightens. "Well, you mentioned it," I say.

"You know, baby, I don't know if it's such a good idea. We're crazed, and I'd barely get to spend any time with you."

"Oh," I say, my fantasy of us holding each other in the dank alleyways of Chicago getting violently vacuum-sucked into the world of wonderful, would-be events that never were.

"I'll be home so soon, it doesn't make sense."

"I don't care, I miss you. I want to see you even if it's just a couple of days sooner."

"Why don't we plan something when I get back? A weekend somewhere, the Hamptons or my parents' place in the Catskills, go hiking. It's starting to get warm up there; I can take you to this se-cret lake where we swim. It will be so much better, just you and I. Or we could fly somewhere, Florida, the Caribbean, we'll think of something. Also, we'll put some time aside for fixing up our place. I know that's important to you."

"Uh-huh."

"You don't want to be around while I'm working, Jacquie."

"It's just that you said—"

"Well, I shouldn't have," he says abruptly. "I wasn't thinking. It wouldn't be cool for you down here. You'd be hanging out in a hotel room while I shoot sixteen hours a day. It would suck for you. And for me, 'cause I'd feel bad."

"You said I could come along," I say, under my breath.

"What did you say?"

"Nothing. Look, I'd better go. I'm late to meet Alicia."

"All right, baby. I'll call you tonight."

"Yeah, okay," I say.

"Love you," he says.

"Uh-huh."

I walk over to Avenue B wistfully replaying Anthony's message in which he invited me to come watch him play big, important producer in the mean streets of Chicago.

On the back porch of a groovy brick-oven pizza place on Avenue B, seated at a table littered with seven empty martini glasses, Jeremy is having none of my complaints.

"Look, I don't want to hear your bitching!" he slurs while grabbing his phone off the table.

I grab his wrist and say, "Jeremy, put it on vibrate and stick it in your pocket. Please."

Alicia's off asking the waitress where the hell our food is.

Jeremy shakes me off and sticks his phone into his pocket. "Jacquie, you're always moaning! Oh, my life sucks!" he says, feigning a girl's voice, or more specifically, mine. "My gorgeous, perfect boyfriend doesn't want to fly me to Chicago for the weekend! He wants to take me to an island in the Caribbean instead. He's so mean!"

"Come on, Jeremy, you know that's not what I mean," I say. "I wouldn't care if he didn't invite me. It's that he did invite me and then uninvited me or forgot he invited me, or I don't know what he did. I just don't like to be disappointed."

"Oh waaaaaaaaa!" he says. He holds out his hand in front of his face and starts counting on his fingers. "He's hot, although I wouldn't know firsthand because I've never met him. Alicia, is he hot?"

"Who?" she asks, coming back to the table.

"Duh, Anthony," he says.

"He's cute," she says, turning to face a busboy who arrives at our table with our fourth basket of bread, but still no dinner. "Basta with the bread!" she says to the busboy and turns back to Jeremy. "Yeah, Anthony: tall, dark, scruffy, nice eyes, five o'clock shadow. Very Calvin Klein model in the eighties before they started employing fourteen-year-old girlie boys."

"Okay," Jeremy says, continuing to count fingers. "He's hot. He asked you to move in with him. He told you he loved you after what? Two weeks?"

197

"Something like that." I smile, feeling ashamed.

"His apartment looks like it's been through a major earthquake," Alicia chimes in, Miss Tidier-than-thou herself.

"Unimportant. That's what cleaning ladies are for. Even the most anal among us needs a cleaning lady," Jeremy says. "He calls you every night before bed while he's out of town and promises to take you on a romantic trip as soon as he gets home. He thinks you're a total goddess and tells you all the time."

"Actually," I say, pulling in close and keeping my voice down, "he was pretty secretive the other day about going to get something in Chicago."

"Maybe he's getting you an engagement ring!" Jeremy says.

"Maybe he was getting a colonic," my sister says.

"Wouldn't that be amazing?" Jeremy says. "Our little Jacquie married!"

"I don't know about that," I say. "But the other day he said I gave him the best blowjob of his life."

"Whoa, whoa, whoa, you didn't mention that before, that changes everything," Jeremy proclaims. "Now we have definitive proof that he will never, ever leave you." He pauses for effect, then adds, "And he's gorgeous and loves you and is probably asking you to marry him. And you're still bitching, because why? Because he doesn't want you sitting bored in his hotel room while he's shooting? He'd rather you be happy and drunk at home with your friends? Jesus, Jacq, repeat after me: I am a lucky bitch."

"I am a lucky bitch," I say.

"I am the luckiest bitch," he says.

"I am the luckiest bitch," I repeat, laughing.

"I want you to repeat that to yourself every day eight hundred times, okay? Say it when you wake up in the morning. Say it before you go to bed at night. Because you are getting much too spoiled, missy."

Duran Duran's "Rio" comes on, and Jeremy starts bobbing his head and singing and the food finally arrives, an enormous thin-crust pizza with proscuitto and mushrooms and a family-size spinach salad. We attack.

On a perfect Saturday afternoon in June, Alicia and I go to Sam's wedding at a country-quaint restaurant with a garden around the corner from the beautiful three-bedroom brownstone with a garden that she and Charlie are in the process of buying in Brooklyn Heights. About seventy-five people squeeze in and crowd around the happy couple for the brief, moving ceremony, in which Sam and Charlie drink from the same wineglass and promise to love, honor, and cherish each other forever. Sam is even more beautiful than usual in a simple, flowing white gown, her golden hair tied back with an ivory ribbon. The occasion is so solemn and heart-felt, I find myself choked up and almost liking her. All the *Flicks* folks and our guests sit at one table, drinking bottle after bottle of Cabernet, making progressively sillier toasts—beginning with "Here's to Sam and Charlie's happiness" and degenerating into "Here's to always having a condom available when the moment strikes" and "Here's to Belmondo making one more decent flick before he croaks." We get sloshed and then walk over the Brooklyn Bridge together. It's a warm, breezy summer day, the kind that lures the masses out of hiding to walk their dogs and ride their bikes, while the music of birds and voices fills the air and children chime in with their babble and tears. Chester and I hold hands for a while, and I rest my head on his shoulder. My sister saunters dreamily along in a chic, brown-and-beige–striped strapless dress. We walk silently and float on the smells and sounds of the afternoon toward the skyscrapers of downtown Manhattan, which glimmer ahead of us picturesque as a postcard. I wish Anthony were here.

Serena left me a message the other day saying that she didn't think she'd mind all the boxes of books everywhere, but now they've begun to bother her. I've dragged my heels because I didn't know what to do with them. Obviously I can't bring them over to Anthony's. He'd wonder where the hell they came from and why I would suddenly need them. I have a small storage space in the basement and dread lugging them down there, but I guess I don't have a choice. I bribed Alicia with sushi tonight to come over and go through them with me. We'll sell anything I'm willing to part with to the used-book counter at the Strand and store the rest in my basement. It will be a pain in the butt, but I don't have much time. Serena gets back to town tomorrow afternoon, so I called her this morning and said I'd get them all out today.

Making our way up Avenue A, Alicia drawls, "When did the East Village become so retarded? Look at all the dorks and losers. Where did all the cool people go?"

"They all fled to Williamsburg when they heard you were moving there," I say.

When we finally make it to my building after the hour-and-a-half-long walk home from Brooklyn, it's five o'clock, and my red-wine buzz has turned into a hangover. Two buildings over, an entire family—mom, dad, grandma, grandpa, a bunch of kids—is hanging out in a beat-up van parked in front of their apartment, spilling out onto beach chairs parked on the sidewalk, either listening to or ignoring the aggressively lyrical tones of gospel floating through the closed windows and door of the nondescript Baptist church squeezed between their building and the old-folks' home on the corner. It always amazes me that there are two churches, three bars, an old-folks' home, and a Bible lady all on one block, an intriguing balance of conscience and debauchery. The neighbors' Yorkie, happy to be free from his usual post at the window, is running around barking as his humans sit quietly enjoying the evening air. No one seems to notice us except the woofer, who licks my heel as we pass. "Hey, little bear," I say, bending over to rub his furry back. Alicia starts whistling a tune I recognize.

"Is that the ice-cream-man song?"

"Yeah, so?" she asks. "That's my next career move. I'm going to get an ice cream truck." I laugh, imagining my sister becoming the ice cream man. I want to tell her how funny it would be to tell our parents' friends that my smart, hypereducated sister is the new ice cream man in town, but I'm laughing too hard to get the words out.

Two lanky Latin guys half our age pass us and one of them says to my sister, "Hey, you look like someone I want to hang out with."

"I have a terrible personality," she says. "You don't want to hang out with me." The guys walk on, perplexed.

"I hate your stairs," Alicia moans, like she does every time we climb them. When we push open the front door, though, our fatigue disintegrates magically: Along the wall running from the kitchen to the back windows is a beautiful, wooden bookcase that runs almost all the way up to my nine-foot ceilings. My books have been unpacked and neatly stacked on the shelves and the cardboard boxes have vanished. Alicia and I stand gaping.

"What the hell?" I ask, breaking the spell.

"Who got these?" Alicia asks, walking toward the shelves. A blue Post-it is stuck to my copy of *The Portrait of a Lady*. "These are amazing books! Now they have a nice home," it reads. There's a dustpan full of sawdust on the floor placed neatly next to a toolbox, an electric saw, and a bucket of wood stain.

"Nobody," I say. "He built them."

"Who?"

"Serena's boyfriend, I guess. Maybe to surprise her while she's gone?"

" I thought you said they broke up."

"Well, I guess they're back together," I say, noticing another note on the counter.

"Hey S," it says. "Took care of your book problem while you were gone. Now slow down and relax into this beautiful place, okay? Remember what Oscar Wilde said (Chrissie Hynde quoted him): 'We are all in the gutter, but some of us are looking at the stars.' Chin up, lovely!—Z."

" 'Z?' " I ask. "Who the hell is Z? Serena's boyfriend's name is Rory."

"Maybe they play some Zorro sex game?" Alicia suggests.

"Or maybe she has a new boyfriend."

"A really cool one," Alicia says. "I bet Anthony doesn't know how to build bookshelves."

"He doesn't even know how to use them. The cleaning lady he pays to pick up after him twice a month is the only person who ever puts a book on a shelf, let alone dust them."

As Alicia watches *Arsenic and Old Lace* for the fourteenth time on TV, I unpack a box of tchotchkes that I didn't know where to put before. I unwrap my treasures—an assortment of candles, a tiny statuette of a cat I bought in Madrid, a Day of the Dead doll my sister brought me from a shoot she did in Mexico, my grandma's ceramic angels that I got when she died, a bobbing-head Chihuahua that was a gift from Jeremy and Napoleon, stones and shells I've collected through the years, miniature Chinese lanterns, a Rubik's Cube my dad gave me for my fifteenth birthday, small framed photographs of my family and friends— and place them in front of books, on top of them, around them. I'm pleased with my creation—or rather mine and Serena's lover-boy's creation.

Anthony is arriving home on the Fourth of July and I'm so excited I could scream. In the end he wound up being gone almost six weeks and I don't think I can go another minute without him. He's coming home around eight, so I blow off the rooftop party in my neighborhood that everyone I know is attending and stay home and roast a chicken and open a bottle of wine. It's the first real meal I've ever cooked for Anthony, I realize as I'm mincing garlic and chopping a red onion. We always go out or order in. I'm too antsy to focus on the slow Chinese movie I have to watch for work—I look at my hands and realize over the past few weeks I've bitten off all my nails—and instead stick in *Sliding Doors*, the Gwyneth Paltrow movie where she gets to live two alternative lives with two different men. The door finally squeaks open at around ten, right at the end of the movie when Gwyneth is falling down a flight of stairs after learning that her boyfriend's mistress is having his baby. Suddenly there in front of me is Anthony, my boyfriend, whom I haven't seen in a month and a half.

"Baby!" I say, leaping off the couch.

"What are you watching?" he asks.

"Chick flick," I say, pulling away and stopping the DVD.

"Why do you watch that crap?" he asks, flinging his bag to the floor. "Such a load of bullshit they feed you. When will someone make a movie that shows the truth about love?"

"They exist," I say. "*Sid and Nancy, Annie Hall, Scenes from a Marriage*, God, tons. Someone usually winds up dead—or at least alone—but they do exist. I've got to say I love a good, corny romantic comedy, as long as the writing is smart. . . ." I could babble on, but he's not listening. He's squatting on the floor, playing with the loose skin around his faithful dog's face. "Did you miss me, baby? Did you miss me? I missed you, baby girl," he says. Lucy licks his face giddily. He looks up at me and grins irresistibly. "Did you miss me, baby girl? Did you miss me?"

"More than you can imagine," I say, meaning it. I fantasized about jumping on him immediately, but I feel timid after not having seen him for such a long time. I ruffle his hair and he straightens up to put his arms around me. He reeks of BO, but I don't care. He squeezes me tightly.

"I made dinner," I say. "Want some?"

"I'll pick at it," he says. "I'm exhausted." I put some chicken, salad, and roasted potatoes on a plate for him and pour him a glass of Syrah and sit on a stool to watch him wolf it down.

"I was hungrier than I thought," he says. He reaches over and grabs my waist and pulls me toward him. "Let's go to bed."

After we roll around for a while, I think he's fallen asleep, but he crawls out of bed and walks naked into the living room and calls out, "I got you something." He comes back with a shopping bag from the airport. In it is a girlie T-shirt that says, SOMEONE WHO ♡ ME WENT TO CHICAGO AND ALL I GOT IS THIS LOUSY T-SHIRT.

"Thanks, baby," I say. "Thanks so much." He reaches into the bag again and grins up at me mischievously.

"And another special treat." My heart pounds. "He pulls out an iPod in a bright pink case."

I bounce on the bed and hug him and cover him in kisses.

"Honestly, honey, you were the last person in the world who didn't have one. It was a mercy purchase."

"I love you," I say. "Thanks."

When I wake up at around nine the next day, Anthony isn't in bed with me. I figure he's making coffee or has run out for bagels. I wander into the living room and find a note on the counter: "Run to the editing rm, have to get tapes to editor. Back soon. Sushi tonite? I'll call. xo." I make a cup of mint green tea and watch the last few minutes of *Sliding Doors* in my underwear, with Lucy snoring at my feet. Then I call Alicia.

"So, he gave me an iPod," I tell her.

"That's way better than an engagement ring."

I spend the rest of my day finishing up my workaholic piece, which I like even more than the first one. I've dug up all sorts of obscure movies old and new about men who love their work so much that they end up alienating the women in their lives. Sometimes workaholism, I find, is indicative of a deeper rift in the relationship, like in *Far from Heaven*, in which Julianne Moore's husband, played by Dennis Quaid, spends all his time at the office but also happens to be having an affair with a man. Joanne Love, my new best friend, has hilarious things to say about these screen jerks. She thinks most of them need psychoanalysis, but some are just in the wrong relationship. "A man having a love affair with his work will probably be happier with a woman who doesn't demand much of his time. Conversely, a woman who requires solid pampering and a daily orgasm should seek a man who makes her needs a priority."

By the time I've put the final touches on the piece and e-mailed it off, gone grocery shopping just to get out of the house, and i-chatted with my sister for half an hour about how neurotic our mother is—she's flipping out that Alicia hasn't found a job and offered to pay for her to see a therapist—it's seven o'clock and I still haven't heard from Anthony. I call his cell.

"Whoa, is it that late?" he asks. "I'm sorry, baby. You wouldn't believe the footage we got. It's outstanding."

"Do you still want to get sushi?"

"I'm not quite done here, but . . ."

"I could come over there and we could order in," I suggest.

"Would you mind? You could watch what we've done so far. I think you'll love it."

"Yeah, that sounds good."

"What are we ordering tonight, guys?" I ask.

It's Saturday night and I'm in the editing suite with Anthony and his editor, Will, a natural-born funny guy who's extremely enthusiastic about the show. I've been there almost every night for the past two weeks. It's the only way I get to spend time with Anthony, so I've stopped fighting it. A couple of times I've even spent the night on the leather couch. We hauled in some old sweats and a down comforter for my personal use. They should probably give me an associate-producer credit at this point, considering how involved in the intricacies of telling this story I have become. I think the guys appreciate my perspective as a woman and an objective viewer, although the first few nights Anthony resisted.

"Thai," says Anthony.

"No more Thai!" Will protests. "Anything but Thai. Or sushi. Italian, the place with the lobster ravioli and garlic rolls, or the awesome salad place."

"Awesome salads," is my vote. "I love the one with cranberries and blue cheese."

"Lord help me, the one with tuna and olives and parmesan is *delizioso*," Will says.

"Ooh, there's also that really fattening one with shrimp," I say. "I can't decide!"

"Whatever, you guys. Salads," Anthony says. He can't understand Will's and my obsession with food. I persuade the delivery guy to stop by the deli and pick up a six-pack and chocolate chip cookies for us.

"And a pint of strawberry-cheesecake ice cream," Will adds at the last minute.

At this point, Anthony and Will have a rough cut of the first episode, in which the three main characters, Mikey, Delores, and a manic-depressive kid named Stu, are introduced. Anthony was right about how gripping the material is. Per the reality-show formula, we're given just enough backstory to make these three likable, so the audience can't resist suffering along with them. They shot four stories but are keeping only the best three. I feel bad for Bernie, a pale fourteen-year-old with a lisp who got caught shoplifting seven times before the cops hauled him in. Anthony's crew shot over fifty hours of him and none of it will be included, except for some early moments when he appears in court alongside Mikey. While I know my storytelling instincts are right on and my input helpful, I also know I'd be terrible at Anthony's job, because cutting out someone's story would kill me. I'd be so attached to the footage, my version would be twenty hours long.

Plus, I'd want to save all the kids. I'd want to hug them and give them money and invite them over to my house for lunch. I'd want to help them study and make sure they get into good colleges. I'd want to adopt them. I'm a completely useless distanced observer of real life. Better stick to celebrities.

"Hey, watch this," Will says, freezing a shot of Mikey giving his friend the finger. He proceeds to manipulate the Avid so that Mikey's doing a "fuck off" rap, flipping his friend off over and over again, going, "Fuck off, man, fuck off, man, f-f-f-f-fuck off!" Anthony and Will laugh until tears stream down their unshaven faces. I get depressed.

I wake up when Anthony lifts me off the couch at three A.M.

"Hey, pretty," he says.

"Hey back," I murmur, wiping drool from my cheek.

"We're getting you home to bed tonight, baby. Let's try to spend a whole Sunday together, okay?"

"You sure?" I ask skeptically.

"Yeah, the cut is getting good. We're taking a day off."

He half carries me into the elevator and then a cab, where I fall back to sleep until he carries me out of the cab and up the stairs to the apartment.

"Yay, we can have clean-house day," I tell him. "I weigh a ton, don't I?"

"Shhh, sleep," he says. "My little wisp of a girlfriend."

I laugh as he strains on each step under my weight, then wriggle out of his arms and walk up the rest of the way.

"Did you see the issue?" I ask him. "I left an advance copy in the editing room. I want you to read my Luke Benton article. It's good."

"Tomorrow, baby. Let's go to sleep."

In a hazy space between wakefulness and dreams, I imagine myself walking up our street and turning onto Bedford, deserted in the night, asphalt bare and glistening as if wiped clean by a recent downpour. I wonder at the absence of the usual night owls and grimy old men clutching brown paper bags as I float past eerily lit empty storefronts. My feet lift off the ground and a gust of wind carries me down N. Fifth Street past Driggs and Metropolitan and onto Havemeyer, where my bare feet touch familiar ground. I lie down on the warm threshold of Jake's loft and wrap my arms rapturously around sleep.

The next morning, when I get up, Anthony is already dressed and reading the paper at the kitchen table.

"You're up," I say.

"I'm heading in to work. Barrett wants to see a cut, so we're gonna get some beers and watch it. He always helps me with my stuff."

"God, Anthony," I say. "I thought we were gonna 'have a weekend.'"

His eyes turn hard for a second and then soften. "Editing is intense right now, I can't stop thinking about it, but it will let up. Once we get the first episode done, we'll settle into the rhythm of the show, and it will be quicker." I nod, wondering if I'll ever get used to this lifestyle. "Look, I'll leave early tonight, so we can have dinner."

"Okay," I say, pulling on the hem of his big T-shirt that I'm wearing, although I don't really feel okay.

"What?" he asks, getting out of his chair and dropping his coffee cup loudly into the sink. "Jacquie, don't give me this guilt shit. I can't feel bad about doing my job. This is my life. If you can't live with it, fine, but don't give me those fucking looks, like I'm hurting your feelings."

"I know. I just wish we could spend more time together—without Will and Delores and Mikey," I say, ripping off a fingernail so it bleeds. I zap myself with the rubber band and wince at the pain as he quietly rinses out his cup and puts it on the dish rack. I know I shouldn't, but I say, "This kind of thing happens a lot. I'm just sick of you letting me down. You know, we haven't made any plans to go out of town like you said we would, I still haven't met your parents, and you never really apologized about Chicago."

"Apologized?" he says. "For what? What the hell was I supposed to apologize for?"

"You invited me down there and then uninvited me and then said we'd go somewhere else, but we haven't, and I just want to know, you know, what the hell we're—"

"Oh no, we're not even going there, Jacquie. Oh no. You knew the deal when you moved in here. This wasn't some marriage, some kind of fucking lifelong commitment. This was, you know, what it was." He shoves a bowl on the counter and it falls into the sink and breaks. "Oh, fucking great," he says, looking around, flustered, before grabbing a sweatshirt and strutting out of the apartment. He slams the door behind him.

Lucy, who's been watching our fight like a tennis match, burrows her head under a couch cushion.

"Sorry, Lucy," I say.

I spend an hour moping about, feeling sorry for myself and wanting to call him, but suddenly a flash of inspiration kicks in and I throw on clothes and run out to the hardware store to get a new mop, terra-cotta flowerpots, lightbulbs, and paint swatches. I've always liked hardware stores because they offer tangible solutions to your problems, whatever they may be. You trip on an electrical cord on your way to the bathroom in the middle of the night—they recommend special tape to attach it to the wall. You keep misplacing a pot holder or dropping it into the filthy sink—they sell you a hook. You spill paint on the floor—they suggest Goof Off (who knew such a thing existed?) to get it off. Whatever urgent domestic matter befalls you, the guys at the hardware store know how to fix it. They sell screwdrivers, spackle, hammers, nails, dustpans, plant food, lightbulbs, water filters, key rings, potting soil, duct tape, and Brillo pads, all the little things that make life easier. The owner of the place up the block from Anthony's makes me ache for my old hardware store. He's a cranky old bald man who sits at the register and grunts and points, without ever taking his eyes off the sports section of the *New York Post*. I pay for my wares and joylessly depart for the corner deli, where I order a bacon, egg, and cheese sandwich, a gallon of OJ, and an enormous latte, which I down on the way back to the apartment and arrive bouncing off walls.

I spend hours scrubbing the floors, bundling old newspapers, gathering copies of Anthony's production reel that I find lurking in corners and putting them neatly into boxes, which I stack in the spare room that still isn't an office. I change burned-out bulbs, repot a pathetic basil plant that's been dying a slow death on the windowsill ever since I moved in, tape color swatches to the bathroom wall, which someone, presumably Anthony, painted with streaks of potential colors ages ago but never followed up on. I think we should go with a warm tone: pink, peach, salmon. Screw all his test strokes; as trendy as it is, green in the bathroom makes you look sickly.

At about three o'clock, ABBA blasting, soil scattered across the kitchen counter, the rest of the place in a state of chaos, I decide to confront a pile of framed photos stacked on the floor. While I'm pounding a nail to hook the first one (foggy beach scene, possibly Montauk), I slam my thumb with the hammer so hard that blackness crowds my vision. As I sit down to regain my balance, the phone rings. It's my mother.

"Hey, honey, what are you doing?" she asks.

"Cleaning up the place. Hanging pictures, repotting plants."

"I wish you'd do that at your own apartment," she says, her voice still deceptively sugary. "You own it, after all. It's very disturbing to your father and me that you're not living there."

"Well, you'll be happy to hear that my subletter is quite the little homemaker and the place looks better than ever."

"Oh." She pauses. "That's nice. Where's Anthony?"

"Working," I say. "Actually, I'm a little pissed because we were supposed to be doing all this together. Now the place looks like a hurricane hit and my thumb is pounding where I banged it with a hammer. I could use his help."

"Well, he has to earn a living," she says.

"I understand that. I just wish he were around here some of the time. He treats the place like a hotel. And he's always flaking on me, making plans and then breaking them."

"You know, Jacqueline, a man has to feel like he can work to take care of his family and not feel criticized. Honestly, you should be more supportive."

I stomp over to the stereo and turn down "Dancing Queen," which is giving me a worse headache than my mother. "You know," I say, "are you saying he's supposed to earn a living while I'm home slaving away?"

"You are exaggerating," she says.

"Yeah, well, you don't even know Anthony and here you are taking his side. It would be nice if you could see my side for once. Anthony is always working and I'm always alone and now I'm getting all this work done and it feels great, but I do wish he were doing it with me. What is so wrong with that?" I hold up a bouquet of split ends and bite them off one by one. I really need a haircut.

"You are so cranky today," she says. "I will talk to you later. Goodbye." And she hangs up. I blast "S.O.S.," ABBA's masterpiece, and take out my rage on the apartment, which I clean like a demon until I'm so exhausted that I tumble into bed and fall asleep immediately.

When I wake up the next morning, Anthony isn't there, as usual. I don't even get angry, I'm so used to it. I shower, feed the dog, take her out for her morning poop, and head off to face the evil subway crowd.

"I feel like shit," I tell Sam first thing in the door at work.

"How like shit?" she asks.

"Oh, I don't know, queasy, listless, no energy."

"Could you be pregnant?" she asks.

"Just because you're pregnant doesn't mean everyone is," I snap. "Sorry. No, I'm not pregnant."

When I sit down at my desk, I'm suddenly not so sure. I look at my calendar and realize that thirty-four days have gone by since my last period began and I usually get it every twenty-eight. *Wow,* I think, *what if I am?* My skin is sallow. I feel fat. Oh my God, what would I do? I picture lying in bed with Anthony and telling him that I'm pregnant, his sleepy face blissful with anticipation. I suddenly feel elated, imagining myself with a big, swollen belly under a totally stylish, bright red babydoll dress. I picture Anthony awed as he feels our baby practicing kickboxing maneuvers inside me, sitting nervously by my side in the hospital as I wait for another round of contractions to attack, falling asleep with our baby girl on his chest in front of a boxing match, throwing a football to a skinny little doll in shorts and a tie-dyed shirt with pink Popsicle on her face, zinc on her nose, and pale, freckled skin just like mine.

I decide that if I were pregnant, I would have the baby. I would marry Anthony and have a baby. We could hold the ceremony at his parents' place in the country (which I still haven't seen, even though he keeps promising), just a small wedding for our closest friends and family in the lush garden I imagine with gently swaying oak trees and multicolored poppies everywhere, and then we could have a big party in the city, maybe on Jeremy's fabulous roof deck, so that everyone we know could celebrate with us.

I call Courtney, with whom I've been playing a cautious game of phone tag, and tell her that I'm worried I might be pregnant and that if I am, I think I would keep the baby. "Are you sure Anthony feels the same?" she asks.

"Oh yeah," I say. "Totally." But I'm not, really. He does care about me, but he sure doesn't like to talk about the future. The serial-monogamist conversation springs to mind for the first time in a few weeks. In my mind, I tell him that I'm pregnant, and this time his face darkens with anxiety and suspicion.

"Hmm, I don't know, actually. I think so."

"Well, let me tell you something, Jacquie," Courtney says. "Never believe you can read a man's mind. You might think you're in sync and your energy and desires mesh, but you never really know. Men are another species and it's as different from ours as a monkey or a mule."

"I don't buy that whole Venus and Mars thing. We're all peo-

ple."

"Well, I'm starting to think it makes some sense."

"Court, this doesn't sound like you at all. Are you okay? Is everything all right with Brad?"

"Yeah, I'm fine," she says. "We're fine. We've had some hard conversations lately, but I don't really want to get into it. It's a big mess that I don't want to lay on you."

"Courtney, if you can't lay it on me, who can you lay it on?"

"I don't know. I don't feel like I have anyone but Brad to talk to about my life, and he's not around right now, so I guess I've been feeling pretty lonely."

"Well, why wouldn't you tell me about it?"

"You're on another planet. You're always looking over my shoulder at someone more interesting walking past or dragging the conversation back to Anthony or your job and I just don't know how to compete with those things. And lately you haven't even been around at all." I'm floored. "Jacquie, I'm sorting through some difficult issues that I've got to sort through alone. I should really go."

"Court, come on. I'm sorry I've been preoccupied, but I really want to talk to you. Please tell me what's going on."

"I will, Jacq, but another time, okay? I'm angry and busy and I should really go."

"But, Court," I say, and realize she's already hung up.

On my way home on the subway, there's an adorable little black boy in a Yankees cap eating M&Ms on the seat across from me. His animated face moves into bold shades of ecstasy when he's sucking on chocolate, then horror when his mother, a young pregnant woman, asks him to give his grandma an M&M. He refuses, then reluctantly acquiesces only after his mom calls him selfish and orders him to hand one over. When he catches my eye, I hold out my hand for a piece of candy, and he looks perplexed, then grins and thrusts a handful in my direction. I shake my hand to let him know I was only joking. He grins at me again and I grin back. Then he frowns dramatically and I frown back. A woman gets on at the next stop and starts singing a hymn so loudly that it resonates through the entire car. As she repeatedly belts out the words, "I'm going to see the Lord, my Lord, oh Lord, the Lord," the volume increases to an acidic shriek and people drop their heads to hide their laughter. The little boy smiles at me and once again holds out an M&M in my direction. I shake my head, as his mother hustles him off the train.

213

Before bed, I call Anthony in the editing room. "Hey, baby, I wanted to ask you something," I say. "Totally hypothetically, what would you do if I got pregnant?"

"Throw you down a flight of stairs," he says, without missing a beat. He laughs. "I'm kidding!" he says. "Jesus, I'm kidding. How cute would little Jacquie babies be?"

I get out of bed and write a quick e-mail to Clancy proposing my next story: Are men really dogs—simple creatures who live to be fed and have their tummies rubbed—and women purring pussycats that will scratch your eyes out if they don't get what they want? Are we two different species entirely? Let's see what the movies have to say about people who love each other but just can't get along.

When I wake up, I have my period.

have been dreading the day my apartment article comes out. The excitement I know I should experience never comes, because I know that when Anthony inevitably finds out, I'm going to have some serious explaining (and ass kissing) to do. I wake up on Monday morning to a feeling of doom.

Our weekend was glorious, like the early days of our relationship. Anthony came home late Friday night, nudged me awake, and said, "Guess what? I'm taking the weekend off." He put a red rose, the kind you buy from vendors on the streets of Williamsburg on weekend nights, into my hands so I could feel its smooth petals and snuggled up to me. "Let's just do nothing all weekend, okay?"

Apparently he told Will to get the show as close to perfect as possible by Monday, when Anthony would be in to give him the thumbs-up. He said he was confident that Will could do final tweaks without him. We spent most of Saturday and Sunday in bed, leaving only to walk the dog, answer the door when food deliveries arrived, and once sprint to the deli to satisfy a rabid craving for strawberry lemonade on my part and Oreos on his. We ignored the phones, watched movies on cable, slept for God knows how many hours in a row, blasted tunes and danced on the furniture, and had lots of slow, stupid sex, as day blended into night blended into day again.

And then it was Monday and I awoke with eleven pounds of steaming hot dread piled menacingly on my chest and preventing me from breathing right. As is usually the case with bouts of dread, this one turns out to be justified.

My phone rings just as I'm getting out of the shower. It's Clancy, shedding her clipped monotone for the first time since I've known her to shriek with delight.

"Your piece is on the stands!" she says. "I put three copies in the mail to you, but you can go grab one at any newsstand. It looks incredible."

"That's so exciting," I tell her, trying to work myself into some semblance of gratitude.

"And that's not all!" she says, and pauses to let me wonder for a minute what she could be referring to. "You, my dear, are going to have a column, a regular, monthly sex-and-the-movies column. Sorry we're going with sex over love or romance, but you know how salacious sells. We're calling it 'Reel Sex,' R-E-E-L Sex."

"No way," I say, plunking down on the edge of the bed and letting my wet towel fall around me.

"Yeah way. Brought it up to the editor in chief weeks ago, but, as with everything else, she took her time. Got back to me this morning. She's into it. One an issue. Eight hundred words, each at thirty-two hundred dollars. I'm putting a contract into the mail today."

"Wait, that's more than two dollars a word."

"It's four. You're a columnist now. We're very good to our columnists."

"Oh my God!" I say, jumping off the bed and doing a goofy naked dance. I must look like such a geek, I'm happy that Anthony isn't there to see me. "Clancy, you're the best. Wow!"

"When you have some time, can you get me ideas for your next, say, six pieces? I'll want to submit them for approval, and we'd like for you to start hooking your lead to an upcoming release. You know, find a sex-oriented theme among films about to hit theaters and flesh the idea out using your extensive knowledge of films past. That okay?"

"Yeah, no problem. It's a good idea."

She hangs up and I can't decide who to call first. This is the kind of news my mom will eat up, but it's only six A.M. in California, so I'll wait. I dial Alicia, who wants to take me out for a celebratory drink tonight. While we're on, my phone beeps.

"Jacqueline Stuart?" a woman's voice asks.

"Yes."

"My name is Hildy Baker. I'm a producer for *Between the Sheets of America*."

"Hildy like Rosalind Russell in *His Girl Friday*?"

"Named for her, actually. I used to want to kick my parents' butts for it, but now I think it's kinda different, kinda cool. Anyway, you familiar with the show?"

"Of course, the talk show with that funny guy in the bow tie."

"Yes, Conrad Watts, covering love, romance, and everything sultry in this great nation of ours."

"Sounds good," I say, putting on my bra and underwear. I'm verging on late for work.

"Well, we read your article about pretending to look for a roommate and thought it was sharp and sexy, the kind of story we're always looking for."

"Thanks," I tell her. "How'd you get my number?"

"I called four Jacqueline Stuarts in the phone book before an answering machine at the fifth's gave me this number."

"Nice job."

"We have a last-minute opening in our schedule tomorrow and were hoping you'd be able to come on the show to talk about your experience," she says. "We'd tape tomorrow and it would run the next day."

"You mean I'll be interviewed on TV?"

"Exactly, by Conrad and his cohost, Christine." She tells me not to wear white and gives me the address of the studio. I agree to be there at nine A.M. Now I can't avoid calling my mom, who sounds very groggy.

"You're not gonna believe this. You ready?"

She hums the affirmative.

"Okay, my *Luscious* article came out today."

"Um-hm."

"Go pick it up, okay? I'm really excited about it. It's my first article in a major national magazine. And here's the best part—I was offered a column! A monthly column where I give relationship advice based on the movies."

She squeals. It's a squeal as ecstatically shrill as that of Benjamin Braddock's mother when he announces he's getting married in *The Graduate*. I pull the phone away from my ear. "That's great, honey." She's always gushing about the accomplishments of her friends' kids and giving me advice that makes no sense about how I should go about getting a column, which she views as the ultimate sign of success for a journalist. Her moment has finally arrived.

"I get paid thirty-two hundred per piece!"

"Is that a lot? Hold on one second." I hear her saying, "Richard, Richard, wake up. Jacquie got a column at that women's magazine. Every month. Three thousand dollars for each article!" I hear my dad murmuring, "A column? What?"

"Oh, you are so clueless, Richard. Jacquie! She has a column!" she says. "You know, a regular column, a regular article that she writes for them every month. It's what I've been telling her to get for years now and she's finally doing it."

"Good, good, tell her good," I hear him saying, still half asleep. I smile, imagining him in his red pajamas and salt-and-pepper bedhead trying to work up some enthusiasm through his stupor.

"But listen," I say. "I'm going on TV tomorrow to talk about the piece on this talk show."

"Which one?"

"It's called *Between the Sheets of America*."

"Is it about sex?" She sounds as aghast as she can at six A.M.

"Sort of, sex and love and romance, anything like that."

"Can we watch it?"

"Yeah. I think it's on at nine Wednesday night. Check the *TV Guide*."

"I'm proud of you," she says.

On the way to work, I stop at the deli on my corner to buy the magazine and immediately page through it to find my piece. The title of the piece is "Room for Love: One Writer's Deviously Sexy Search for the Perfect Guy," and the first thing I see is a picture of myself that I completely forgot they'd taken. The one they chose is cheesy: me standing on the stoop of a perfect New York brownstone holding a rolled-up real estate section of the newspaper with one hand and crossing my fingers with the other. At least I look skinny. Shit, I hope no one Anthony knows gets to the magazine before I have a chance to sit him down and tell him the whole truth and nothing but. Luckily, none of his good friends is likely to read the magazine, except, of course, in the therapist's office or hair salon or manicure-pedicure place or gym, and his sister and girl friends could subscribe to it for all I know. God, I've got to tell him tonight. I skim through most of the story and it looks good. They've cleaned up my text, but basically it's what I expected.

All day long I get calls and e-mails from friends saying how much they liked the piece and congratulating me for becoming the downtown Candace Bushnell. Who knew how many people read this damn magazine? I love the flattery, but each pat on the back makes me more and more fearful that Anthony will find out, too.

After work, Alicia comes over to go through my closet. She brings a bottle of champagne to toast my success, and I drunkenly try on seventy-five outfits before settling on a straight charcoal-gray skirt with a pink Nanette Lepore top that gives me cleavage without making me look slutty and black strappy sandals for the show. When she leaves at eleven, I begin to prepare for the inevitable showdown with Anthony. I wash my face, brush my teeth, and sit down on the edge of the bed to rehearse. On second thought, I jump up and slug some Jack Daniels from the bottle on top of the fridge and brush my teeth again. I put on some mood music, hoping mellow tunes will subliminally make Anthony more likely to forgive me. I close my eyes and repeat "sut nam," which I remember means "truth is my identity."

Feeling soothed, I begin my speech. "Anthony, there's something I have to talk to you about." I begin to pace around the living room, picturing him in the armchair in front of the TV. "First of all, I want to tell you that I love you very much and am so happy that I met you and that we've had this time together." No good; it sounds like I'm going to break up with him. "First of all, I just want you to know how much I love you." I sit down on the couch and stare at Lucy's big fat adoring face smiling at me through her ridiculously cute underbite. "Lucy, you tell him."

I start again: "Okay, Anthony, I love you and I have to tell you something. You're going to be mad at me, but please hear me out. You know when I came here that day, the first day that we met? You know when I came to look at your extra room? Well, the truth is I wasn't looking for an apartment." I imagine him bewildered, that little furrow between his brows deepening as he strives to comprehend what I'm saying. "See, I was actually researching an article for *Luscious* magazine, about a great new way to meet men: through the roommate-wanted ads." I laugh, like *Ha! Isn't that clever?* and go on, "You see, I was pretending to look for a room so that I could meet guys, and then I wrote a story about it. The story came out today. It looks great, and in fact, I'm going to be on *Between the Sheets of America*. It's broadcasting in a couple of days, we can watch it together. Oh, Anthony, this is all pretty funny actually, isn't it?"

I stand up and pace again until I'm standing in front of the full-length mirror that leans against the wall behind the kitchen table. I stare at myself. "So, baby, I know I haven't been entirely truthful with you." Tears slide down my cheeks and I brush them away. "I haven't been entirely truthful, but I will be from now on. I promise. I know my promises must not mean much to you at this point, but I will prove to you that I am actually an honest person. Really I am, I swear." I sit down on a chair, still looking in the mirror and whimpering at my pathetic, pleading face. "God, before this whole thing, I couldn't tell a lie to save my life. That's why this has been killing me, your not knowing. It wasn't even my idea. It was my sister's idea and then my editor loved it and she said I had to go undercover. It's really good for my career. God, I'm getting a column in the magazine. It's so amazing. And then at some point I realized that maybe I actually would meet someone, and then I did. And it seemed like fate. It seemed magical, except for the lie." My face is red and puffy. "Anthony, it doesn't really matter how we met, does it? What matters is that we did. How crazy that we met in this bizarre way and fell in love! It's a great story, isn't it? A great story to tell our grandkids." I stare at myself for another second before moving slowly to the couch to lie down.

I guess he never makes it home, because I wake up on the couch in the morning, with Jack Daniels practicing karate chops on the inside of my skull. I only have an hour to get to the *Between the Sheets* studio, so I rinse off in the shower, put on the chosen outfit, and jump into a cab. On the way, I call a couple of the guys whose apartments I saw, only the ones I liked, and tell them about the magazine article. I would feel awful if they stumbled upon it. On the way out of the apartment, I grabbed the original notepad where I'd jotted down phone numbers and notes like, "big 2bd, Dumbo, med school, sounds like a dork, def. in the closet." And, "foreign, Israeli?, sounds cute, Long Island City, ugh, big loft, shit, GIRLFRIEND." I call Stanley the divorcé, who takes it well.

When I fess up to Claus the German, he says, "I did think something was strange."

"I know you did," I tell him. "I thought you had busted me."

He laughs. "Jacquie, I thank you for telling me this, and I wish you very good luck."

I leave a message for handsome Timothy and sheepishly leave another for John the musician I never met, thinking he'll be amused. A frisson runs down my spine when I hear his voice on his machine.

Screw Javier, that dog-bashing gourmet, I think, but then change my mind and call his home number, since I know he'll be working the breakfast shift. As I arrive at the nondescript building on West Thirty-ninth Street, Stanley calls me back.

"I saw it," he says. "I had to run out and buy it when you told me. I guess I didn't mind. It's funny. You have an interesting life, Jacquie."

"Thanks."

"I didn't ask you out." Yes he did! Inviting me to lunch definitely counts. "But I wouldn't mind. Are you still with Anthony?"

"Yes, I am."

"Oh good; I guess he didn't take it too hard when you told him about all this."

"Um, he doesn't know yet."

"Oh," he says. "Oh."

"Hey, Stanley, I'm late for a meeting. I've got to run."

I arrive at the television studio in Midtown a nervous wreck. Hildy approves my outfit and leads me into the Green Room, where I meet the host, Conrad, who immediately calms me down. He's short with glasses and a bow tie and he talks like he's swallowed a frog.

"You are going to look terrific on television," he tells me. "And you've got a charming yarn to tell. So, don't you worry now!" He grins at me and asks me briefly about my dating game so that he'll know which questions to ask once we're on air. The pre-interview goes smoothly and makes me feel more comfortable about the real thing. On the white vinyl couch in the Green Room, I eat cookies and drink tea with a girl whose third chick-lit novel hits stores on Friday and the lead singer of an eighties boys' band who's coming out with his first solo album. They've both done this kind of thing before and seem bored.

Just before I go on, Anthony calls. I'm about to pick up and then wonder what the hell I would say to him. That I'm at work? That I'm on my way? Or that I'm shooting the shit with a onetime pop star while waiting to go on TV to be interviewed about an article I never told him about that describes this funny scheme I invented for meeting guys by pretending to look for a roommate? "Oh yeah, baby, it's the one that tells the story of how you and I met," I would say. "I know, honey, I failed to mention it. You thought I was looking for an apartment, but that was a big, fat, fucking lie. It wasn't fate or destiny or our two worlds colliding through a beautiful, serendipitous act. It was a dating game that I created to try to trap a guy, further my career, make a buck." I turn my phone off and jiggle my heel madly as the chick-lit author laughs riotously on a big overhead monitor about a scene in her book where the heroine trips over a cocker spaniel and lands splat at the feet of the dog's handsome millionaire owner, whom I assume she marries in the end.

When the boy singer gets called into the studio, a makeup

artist with spiky bleached blond hair and too much black eyeliner enters to give me a once-over. I follow her into a brightly lit room where she sits me in front of a mirror and dabs concealer under my eyes.

"So, you pretended you were looking for a room so you could meet guys?" she asks in a thick Jersey accent. Guess I'm the talk of the town.

"Yeah."

"How'd it turn out?" she asks, powdering my face and blending the area around my eyes with her finger.

"I met a guy. We're living together."

"Cool. Maybe I'll try it," she says, and applies a soft burgundy color to my lips. "You like that?"

"Not a color I usually go for, but it works," I say.

"I think you're good," she says.

She's right. Gazing back at me from the mirror is a woman who should be on television.

"Hey," I say, "don't do the apartment thing. Do Internet dating or keep doing whatever you've always done. It's not really a very, uh, honest way to meet a man."

"Huh," she says, baffled.

"But that's not what I'm going to say on TV," I say. "Shit, I don't know what I'm going to say on TV." She gives my shoulders a quick, supportive squeeze.

I'm seated in a comfortable, gray leather chair facing Conrad and his cohost, Christine, a slim blonde in a cream-colored suit whose hair turns up pertly at her shoulders. She smiles warmly at me. As the cameraman announces that he's rolling, I breathe deeply a few times, hoping not to have an anxiety attack. I only get one shot at this; they interview me one time through and then cut out any disastrous moments.

Conrad introduces me and my article, explaining that I was single and depressed and got inspired by my sister, who was having great luck meeting guys while looking for an apartment.

"Why is looking at apartments a good way to meet men?" Conrad asks me.

"Well, you get right into these men's apartments," I say. "If you meet a man in a bar or at a party, for example, you might not see where he lives until the third or fourth date. You might really like him and then discover he has a pet boa constrictor in the bathtub or a whole wall of his bedroom devoted to 'N Sync. You learn an awful lot about someone by the state of their home."

"What was the most horrifying thing you encountered?" Christine asks.

"Hmm." I say. "It would have to be this one apartment in the East Village. The guy was attractive, but his place looked like something out of *Bachelor Party*. Remember that movie with Tom Hanks? There were pizza boxes and beer cans and stray clothes everywhere and it smelled like the garbage hadn't been taken out in a month."

"What did you do?" Conrad asks, laughing.

"Got the hell out!" I say. "I think I told him I was late for an appointment and would call him later."

"But you didn't," Conrad says.

"Well, I actually did call him back. It was early in the process, and guys weren't asking me out. A friend suggested that no one would ask a woman out if they actually thought she was going to be their roommate, so I called a few people back and told them I wasn't able to take the room, to see if it would change anything."

"Did it?" Christine asks.

"Actually, it did. That guy asked me if I wanted to get a beer with him. Of course I told him I was busy for the rest of my life!"

They both laugh.

"And you had some more interesting dates," says Conrad. "I guess a few of those got pretty hot and heavy?"

I blush. "Well, yeah, I guess there were some, uh, interesting dates, and maybe one that got a little hot and heavy, as you put it."

The audience laughs along with Conrad and Christine, who always love to get a little raunch on the show.

"So, Jacquie, would you say this was a successful experiment?" Conrad asks, winding it up.

"Extremely successful," I tell him. "I set out to meet men, and I met loads of them. I met artists, lawyers, professors. I met a designer, a chef, a reporter. And, most important, I met the man of my life, Anthony, a handsome, smart, talented TV producer."

"What did he think about this whole thing?" Conrad asks, even though I requested that he not ask me that question.

I feel my face redden on national TV. "Well, Anthony actually doesn't know about the article yet," I say, ashamed. "He still thinks I was interested in renting his spare room. I guess I'll have to tell him now, though, if he doesn't see it on this show first."

"So, you've been lying to him for a while and you live together?"

"Well, lying is a pretty strong word, I think. I mean, I've been keeping a couple of small facts from him, that's true, but who doesn't in a relationship? And isn't the important thing that we met, not *how* we met?"

"Well, I'm not so sure Anthony's going to feel that way," Conrad says.

Christine butts in. "Conrad, come on, you're being a bit harsh. Jacquie was going about her business, doing research for an article. She didn't know she was going to fall in love, right? Sure, she hoped she might, but she didn't realize that ethical complications would arise. How could she?"

"Right," Conrad says. "But now that they have? Jacquie, don't you feel like you should take responsibility for what you've done? Or let me phrase it another way. You went undercover for this article and met this wonderful man, but you've had to lie to him. Given your current situation, would you still recommend this dating scheme to other women?"

"I don't know, Conrad," I say, rattled. "I did this for two reasons: to research an article and to try to meet a nice guy. And while I did achieve what I'd set out to, I'm not proud of the white lies I've had to tell in the process. Dishonesty is not something I would ever advocate, especially when you're looking for love. I hope Anthony forgives me for my deception, and I intend to be honest with him from here on out. One thing I've learned through this experience is that honesty is the most important ingredient in a relationship."

"Words to live by, Jacquie," Conrad says, nodding gravely and looking, I think, pretty damn proud of himself. "Thank you for sharing with us your adventures between the sheets. I wish you the best of luck."

When I leave the studio, there's a message on my voice mail from Serena saying that she's out of town and needs to talk to me about something. When I call her back, it goes directly into her voice mail.

That afternoon after work, on our way to my favorite bar, Alicia and I run by my place to get my mail. We pass a homeless woman with long gray hair hunched on the sidewalk by a heap of garbage bags full of her belongings. She shifts and fiddles with her bra, hoisting her huge breasts into a cup and grumbles in a cigarette-burnt voice, "This is what I call hell," before putting her head down on a stuffed panda and falling asleep.

"That'll be me in ten years," Alicia says.

"That's not funny," I say.

When we enter my apartment, I am stunned to discover that Serena's squeeze has tiled my kitchen. My millions of metallic mosaic tiles that have been sitting on the floor in a bag with the word *backsplash* scribbled on it are arranged above my counter into the most beautiful backsplash I've ever seen.

"Jesus Christ, whoever this guy is, she'd better marry him," I say.

"Um, I think she is," my sister says, holding up the latest in

Z's epistolary oeuvre: "Hey, lovely. It feels great to be in this apartment for good, and even better that you are ready to move on with your life. I can't wait to walk you down the aisle! I love you, Z."

"What? She's getting married?" I lean against the counter, clutching the note I grab from my sister, suddenly short of breath. I don't know why this news should upset me, but it does. It seems unfair somehow that my subletter can break up with her fiancé and find a new one in three seconds flat, while I'm having so many problems with my boyfriend. The buzzer buzzes and I walk over to the intercom.

"It could be from the old dude," my sister says. "We don't really know."

"Well, that's probably why she keeps calling me, to let me know she's moving out. What will I do? But why the hell is he fixing the place up then?" I say, realizing that none of it makes sense. "Hello?" I say into the intercom.

"Serena?" says a male voice that sounds eerily familiar.

"Uh, no," I say.

"Hey, can I come up? It's an old friend, Anthony. I'm dropping off my directing reel."

My heart seems to stop beating. My sister runs over to the intercom and stutters, "Uh, God, I just got out of the shower, she's not home."

"I have a DVD for her," he says.

"Can you leave it by the mailbox?" Alicia says. "I'll make sure she gets it."

"Uh, yeah, sure." She buzzes him into the building.

I push the Talk button again and say, "I'm sorry. Really. Sorry."

"No problem," he says. I sit down on a stool, put my elbows on the kitchen counter, and start to cry.

Seeking a big apt in the East Village. As luck would have it, the great place I thought I'd found went up in smoke, so Buster the wonderdog and I are on the prowl again, and we have to move ASAP. The EV is our first choice but we're open to suggestions. Ideal would be a large, raw space that can use some work. There is no structural or aesthetic impediment we can't handle. Zach.

13

When I get off the subway at Astor Place in the East Village, there's a message on my voice mail from Serena, saying, "This phone tag is out of control. I really need to talk to you about the apartment. Nothing to worry about, but I do need to talk to you ASAP." I call her back and get her voice mail.

I'm meeting Anthony for dinner at a trendy bistro on Avenue C that he loves. He called me at work to say he had a couple of hours to spare and would love to grab a quick bite, just the two of us. He sounded rushed and distracted, making me wonder if he'd somehow found out about the article and was planning to confront me. Two days have passed since the article hit the stands, after all, and I still haven't told him, mainly because I literally haven't seen him. But now the situation is dire. My only hope is to preempt his confrontation with a confession. I plan to land it on him as soon as I see him, even get down on my knees and beg for his forgiveness if necessary.

My episode of *Between the Sheets* is on tonight, so not telling Anthony right away could be deadly. Before he called, I'd been planning to go to the bar to watch with everybody. Maybe I'll still go. Maybe when Anthony recognizes the humor in all this, he'll want to go with me. I picture him perched on a bar stool next to mine, holding my hand, chuckling as my TV self recounts my apartment-search antics, surrounded by Alicia, Court, and Jeremy, whom I can't believe Anthony hasn't met yet. I manage a smile, imagining Jeremy checking Anthony out and making lewd gestures at me behind his back. It's probably a dumb fantasy, but I'm clinging to it, terrified of the alternative. I'm actually shivering in anticipation and trying to bite my fingernails, but there's nothing left to bite. Maybe I'm just worried about the show. I think I did all right, but I suppose I could come off like an idiot, and I hope I look pretty. You never know how the camera is going to treat you. My bartending friend Johnny is so excited that one of his local girls has become a minor celebrity that he's christened the occasion Jacquie's Big Night and is offering free shots of Jack in my honor. Maybe I should stop by and get one before going to meet Anthony, I think, but I don't get the chance. While I'm waiting for the light to turn green at the intersection of First Avenue and Tenth Street, someone sneaks up behind me and pinches my waist, making me yelp. Anthony nuzzles my neck and says, "Hi, beautiful girl."

He definitely doesn't know about my article.

"So, back in your old 'hood," he says, laying his right arm across my shoulders. "Do you ever miss it?"

"I spend a lot of time here," I say, as we approach the building I lived in when I first moved to New York, a beat-up tenement that should be condemned and that happens to have an enormous rat running across its threshold. I scream and Anthony squeezes me more tightly, laughing at my girliness.

"That's my old apartment," I tell him, babbling nervously. "Lived there for years. I loved it so much, your typical East Village hole with the tin ceilings and slanted floors that had been painted a million times. I put on a coat of really pale green when I moved in, but they got so scuffed, a couple of years later I covered it with bright peach. Thought it warmed up the place. I heard when they booted me, they pulled out all the old detailing, turned it into a generic box, started calling it a one-bedroom, and cranked the rent up to sixteen hundred dollars."

As we stop to wait for the light to change at Avenue A, two wailing fire engines hurtle past us in rapid succession and turn swiftly onto Twelfth Street, one block beyond my own.

"What's going on? I've seen more fire engines go by," Anthony says.

I'm suddenly aware of a steady scream of sirens that I hadn't noticed before from my preoccupied bubble. We cross and rush up Avenue A. My heart pounds as we look to our right at my block and find total chaos: A cop car is blocking entry to the street. Four fire engines and an ambulance are parked right in front of my building, red and amber lights flashing. A crowd is gathered on the sidewalk and teeming onto the street. Firemen are rushing through the front door of my building. People are shouting, staring, looking frenzied, hot, frantic. There's smoke and electricity in the air as I run toward the commotion.

"Oh my God," I whisper. "It's my apartment."

"What?" Anthony asks me.

"It's my apartment," I say, looking at his face pleadingly. "Anthony. I'm, um, I've been meaning to tell you, my apartment, I have one, I'm renting it out right now." The heat emanating from the building feels like it's cooking my face and my bare throat and shoulders and I can't breathe very well. I crane my neck to look up. A tall ladder leads all the way up to the top floor.

"I don't understand," Anthony says. "Doesn't Serena live here?"

I turn to face him. "She's my subletter," I say. "Anthony, I am so sorry. I wanted to tell you." *This is it*, I tell myself. "When I came to look at your apartment, I wasn't really looking for a room. I was doing research for an article about looking for love in the apartment ads."

"What?" he demands, his face contorted into a mask of confusion and vulnerability that I've never seen him wear before. He's not angry yet—he doesn't understand what's going on—but with the red reflection of the flashing lights on his skin, I'm momentarily afraid: I wonder if Anthony would ever do anything to hurt me, I mean, if I wounded him deeply enough.

"I wrote an article," I say, and reach into my bag to pull out the magazine and hand it to him. "Anthony, I'm so sorry." I shake my head and wish I could take the time to explain this to him. I desperately want to cradle him in my arms and tell him I love him and explain why I'm not the awful person he must be thinking I am, but my head is swimming, my apartment might be burning, I have to go. Does that make me a terrible girlfriend? A terrible person? Oh God, I don't know. "Anthony, I need to talk to you about this. I'm so sorry, but I really have to go find out what's going on." I wave my arm around, indicating the disaster that I have to attend to, and turn toward the crowd to look for faces I know.

Lured by a familiar barking through the crowd, I push by a man holding a little girl who's pointing up at my building starry-eyed, to make my way to Larry, who is running around free of his leash, barking gleefully, clearly over the initial shock of the fire. The sweetness of his furry, white snout makes tears spring to my eyes.

"Hi, sweet face," I say weakly, afraid I'll cry, and he sprints over to me and starts squealing, happy to see me. Lucinda, his owner and the head of my co-op board, follows. I crouch down to cuddle Larry.

"You know this all started in your apartment, right?" Lucinda says, jutting her skinny hip out.

"What?"

"Someone, probably one of the people you've been subletting

to"—she says this as if describing an obscene sex act I'd performed on them—"lit a fire in your apartment. Or rather blew the place up. Karim from across the hall from you said he heard what sounded like an explosion."

"Oh my God," I say. "I hope they're okay."

"I guess no one was home when it happened," she says. "The guy found the fire and started yelling bloody murder. No one was hurt, thank God, but our building is pretty much wrecked thanks to you."

"I'm so sorry, Lucinda. I don't know what to say. I just got here. I don't know what's going on."

A fresh fire truck arrives with a fresh group of firemen aboard and they descend shouting and serious to dash into the building. I watch them as one at a time they risk their lives to save our homes. When I look up, my throat goes dry and I feel woozy, with so many people and sounds around me and the heat of the fire and the summer night stifling. There is smoke in the air and soot floating gracefully downward. A fireman hollers to clear the streets, but no one is listening. As I sway, I look up and see the face of the cute hardware-store boy gliding above me. He's all scruffy, like he hasn't shaved in days, with his choppy strawberry-blond hair in serious disarray. He's dressed like a lumberjack as usual, green and blue plaid flannel framing his boyish face.

How weird, I think as the ground rushes toward me and cute hardware-store boy reaches out his big hands to catch me.

"Are you all right?" he says, I don't know how many seconds later.

"Uh, yeah, I think." My head feels fuzzy, my eyes sting, and I'm leaning against the cute hardware-store boy, who looks distressed. He's holding my shoulders firmly in his hands as dozens of people mill about, some looking over their shoulders at me with quizzical expressions on their faces. Through the swarm, I think I see Courtney, but then realize it's someone else, as the cute hardware-store boy lets go of me with one hand to reach into his backpack and pull out a bottle of water. I hold my hand out toward the woman who's not Courtney, but immediately lose focus.

Still holding on to me with one hand, cute hardware-store boy puts the bottle under his arm and unscrews the top and hands it to me.

"My apartment is burning down," I say between sips.

"I know," he says. "I, uh, oh God, where do I start? Jacquie, I'm Zach. We've never officially met. I've been staying at your place."

"You're the guy who's been staying there? You're Z?"

"Yeah."

Although I'm fascinated by the fact that Serena's sleeping with my cute hardware-store boy and wonder how they managed to find each other, I suddenly remember that Anthony is somewhere here reading my article. "Oh my God, Zach, I have to go. Can I talk to you later?"

"But, Jacquie, please find me. We have to talk," he calls after me as I'm pushing west, looking for Anthony. I find him sitting on a curb with the magazine curled up in his fist.

"Anthony, I was going to tell you." The words spill out of my mouth and land in a puddle in the gutter in front of him. "I've tried so many times, but I didn't know how or you weren't around, and I was afraid you'd hate me. God, I was going to tell you the other night and fell asleep waiting for you to come home and we didn't see each other all yesterday and then tonight I was going to and this—" I look around me. "There were other times, God, that first day I was so close, but we got along so well and I didn't want to ruin it and then it just got harder and harder."

"Stop, Jacquie. Stop it."

I do, then I turn and let the weight of my body pull me to the curb beside him. He's sitting to my left, but I'm afraid to look at him. I stare instead at my hands trembling on my bare thighs, which are covered in a layer of sweat. It's so hot.

"Jacquie, I just don't know what to say."

"I know."

"You're so flippant about us in here."

He holds out the article, which I scan, finally reaching the last paragraph and reading the final sentence in horror: "Anthony, my wonderful new live-in boyfriend, still doesn't know the real reason why I turned up at his door that day, and I expect when he learns the truth he'll blow his top. But the good news is that if he kicks me out of his elegant Brooklyn loft, at least I know how to meet the next guy."

The blood drains out of me and I feel as though I will disintegrate onto the hot pavement. "Oh my God, Anthony, that's not what I wrote. I swear, oh my God," I say while I stare at my purple flip-flops resting pigeon-toed in the filthy gutter below me. "In my version, I was really contrite and prayed that you would forgive me, but they must have changed it."

We sit silently for a minute until he says, "Jacquie, I feel like everything is different."

Tears creep into my eyes. I've never heard his voice quaver like this before. He's always seemed so strong.

"What do you mean?" I ask.

"You know, when you showed up at my door, it seemed like a miracle." He pauses. "That's our love story. And it's false."

"I still showed up at your door," I say, barely able to speak or I'm going to start crying. "We still fell in love."

"Yeah, but it wasn't fate," he says. "You were trying to meet a guy."

"But I met you," I say, my voice cracking.

"I don't know. It's different." He stands and looks down at me. "Can you stay with a friend for a few days? I need to think about this."

I nod, trying not to cry. I look back at my building, relieved that the facade looks okay. I'm terrified to talk to someone about the state of my apartment, though. I stand up off the curb and brush dust off my butt.

"Anthony, I have to see what's going on. Will you please come with me? I'm so freaked out."

He shakes his head and turns his back to me. I hear him mumble, "I need a drink," and watch his handsome back enter the pub across the street from my building. I can't believe how physically attracted I am to this man who might be walking out of my life for good. When I can't see him anymore, I run for the nearest fireman, who must be about twenty-four.

"Hi, that's my apartment up there," I say, pointing. "The one where it started. Can you tell me anything?"

"It's bad," he says. "I don't know a lot, but we think something exploded, maybe in the bathroom. We put it out and everything will be okay, but there's a lot of water damage. Are you okay? Do you have a place to stay?"

I draw a blank. Anthony just kicked me out. But then I remember Courtney and Alicia. One of them will take me in.

"Yeah, I have a place to stay."

"Well, the marshal will come by to check everything out tomorrow. You should call the station to set up an appointment. Here's the number." As he's handing me a piece of paper, like a tornado Anthony reappears in front of me, rushing out of the bar and toward me as if he's ready to ram his fist—or me—into the first solid object in his tracks.

"Fucking shit!" he says, grabbing my shoulder and shoving me away from the fireman, to whom I make an "it's okay, I know him" motion with my hand. "You went on fucking TV?" he shouts at me, when we're out of earshot of the fireman. I guess I'm on TV in the pub. I guess I'm missing myself. "You went on fucking *Between the Sheets*? Fuck! Everyone I know in the world is probably watching and everyone is gonna know that you did this to me. Goddamm it!" He actually stomps his foot and gnashes his teeth. "What the hell were you thinking? What am I going to tell my friends? Jesus, I can't believe you'd be so deceitful and duplicitous and inconsiderate of me. You were, like, living a double life or something. Me and you were like a joke for you."

"No, Anthony, never—"

He shuts me up fast. "Can't you think for a minute about how your actions might affect someone else? Someone you supposedly love? Fuck! 'Hot and heavy,' you said. You got 'hot and heavy' with some other guy you met writing this thing? What? Was I just some other guy, the happy ending for your article? You waltz into my life, pretending to be my fucking soul mate or something, all pretty and nice, and you become this, like, perfect girlfriend, and then—this? You know, something always happens, every single time. I really thought we were great together, but the whole time you've been lying to me, scheming. You know how much honesty means to me. God, Jacquie, you know."

"I do know, Anthony, that's why it's been so hard. I was so afraid to tell you. God, Anthony, I know I lied, or kept the truth from you, but God, it was because I fell for you. You have no idea. I've been so broke and then my mortgage and my shitty salary and this editor of a major magazine offered me this story, it just seemed like a good story idea and, yeah, an opportunity, a good paycheck—and God, what if I actually met someone I liked? I wanted to fall in love and it seemed possible, to meet a nice guy, to meet you. Jesus, is that so wrong? I only lied so I could be with you. You have no idea how hard it's been. I had to find a subletter, then they burned down my apartment. Shit, my apartment! And it was all because I wanted it to work out with you." I hold my breath, thinking for a minute that maybe for once I said the right thing.

"No way, Jacquie, don't even try to make me feel sorry for you now. You fucking manipulative— Your apartment? Like I give a shit about your apartment that I didn't even know you had? I could give two shits about your apartment."

"Couldn't give two shits," I say, correcting his grammar under my breath, and wish I could take it back.

"What!" he yells.

"Nothing."

"I have to get the hell out of here," he says, and this time turns and runs, fast. Within seconds he's hit Avenue A, turned the corner, and vanished.

When someone lays a hand on my shoulder, I pounce. "What?"

It's the cute hardware-store boy, I mean Zach. "Hey, sorry," I say. I notice that his shaggy dog, Buster, is at his feet. I squat down to pet him—he smiles, shakes his butt, licks my hand.

"Hi, precious," I say, standing up again to face Zach.

"So, Jacquie, you know I was staying at your apartment."

"I do now."

Before he can explain, Serena appears and jumps into his arms crying fairly hysterically. "Are you okay?"

"Yeah, I'm fine, honey. I'm fine." He squeezes her and pulls away and holds her face in his hands so that she has to look at him. "Look at me. Look at me, baby, I'm fine, I got out. I'm fine." She keeps crying into his chest like a little girl, taking in quick sucks of air.

"You were in there when this happened?" I ask, my heart quickening.

"Yeah." He looks down at his feet. "I guess it was my fault."

"What do you mean?" I demand, suddenly pissed.

"I'm not sure what happened," he says, his lower lip quivering a bit, "but I painted your bathroom yesterday, so maybe there was stuff around, I don't know. I don't know what could have caused it. I was at the shop today and came back here after work, luckily it was early, and the bathroom was burning. I don't know how the hell—I thought I cleaned up well, but maybe I didn't throw everything away. I'm lucky I got back—"

"What the hell?" I ask.

"I don't know. I'm usually so careful," he says. His eyes are pleading with me. "The light was on, maybe something was plugged in, I don't know. I feel awful. I called the fire department and tried to smother it, but it was too big already. I yelled and banged on doors so everyone would get out of the building and then went back in to get out whatever I could before the whole place burned down."

"The whole place burned down?"

"Pretty much," Zach says in a voice no louder than a whisper. "I mean, I assume. It looked bad."

Serena looks like she's going to cry again. "God, Jacquie, I am so sorry about all this. I feel like it's all my fault." Next thing she's sobbing, and I feel like I should comfort her, even though her fucking boyfriend, who wasn't even supposed to be living here, burned down my apartment.

Zach leads her over to the curb and sits her down. He lets her rest her head on his shoulder, kisses her cheek, wipes a tear off her chin, and she looks up at him so lovingly, I suddenly remember being in an earthquake when my sister was a baby. My parents told me later they'd experienced tremors in L.A. before, but nothing this dramatic. It was the middle of the night and suddenly the whole house was rocking as if some giant creature were trying to rip it out of the ground like a turnip. My mother came into my room hysterical—screaming and swearing and running around erratically, unsure what she was supposed to do. When I saw her freaking out, I started crying. My dad picked me up out of bed and said, "Shhhh," and kissed me on the nose. I remember gasping, trying to stop crying, trying to settle my breath as it struggled for space in my little chest. Together we approached my mom. He put his arm around her, and suddenly she was fine. She stopped shouting and her eyes became wide. Then we all walked over to my sister's crib and stood around it silently until the rumbling stopped. The whole time I gazed up at my dad as if he were a god.

Zach lets go of Serena's tiny, shaky hand and walks back to me and says, "Jacquie, I am so sorry."

"Goddamm it! All anyone's doing is apologizing tonight. I can't handle it anymore. Will you just leave me alone? Please."

"But I want to help. Whatever I can do, really."

Suddenly I see red. I want to beat the shit out of this big blond guy who works at the hardware store and looks totally exhausted and pathetic and like he'd do anything to stop me from hating him.

"I think you've done enough, Zach. Jesus, I can't believe you were like living in my apartment and doing all this stuff—who the hell do you think you are doing all this stuff to my apartment? I mean, bookshelves and curtains, you put up a backsplash! What the hell?"

I glance down at my bag and see the light flashing on my cell phone. I wave Zach away and pull out my phone. Seeing my sister's name on my Caller ID causes my throat to constrict again. She says she's at the bar and no one knew where I was, she's called me fifteen times, the show just ended. I put my hand over the phone and tell Zach, who's still standing there, to please go away.

"But I need to—" he says as I shake my head and turn my back on him.

"Alicia," I say, gasping for breath. "My apartment burned down!"

"Oh my God, where are you? Are you over there?" she asks.

"Yeah, I'm here," I say. "Zach did it, you know Zach, Serena's—"

"Who?" she asks. "Not Z! Did Z burn your house down?" I start bawling. "Shit, I'm coming over there."

While I'm waiting, I call my parents to let them know. After initial hysterics on the part of my mother, I hear my dad telling her to calm down, and she gets back on the extension to tell me she'll set up a meeting first thing tomorrow at my apartment with the fire marshal and my insurance agent and another with the lawyer who helped me buy the apartment.

"Thank you so much for dealing with all this, Mom," I say. "I'm pretty frazzled." She assures me it will all be all right. Meanwhile, Zach has gone off, I guess to check on Serena, and he comes back with this enormous garbage bag full of stuff and places it on the curb next to me. I put my hand over the phone.

"This is the stuff I got out of your place," he says and hands me a piece of paper with his phone number on it. "If you need to reach me," he says quietly.

I nod at him. He stands there for a second and then lowers his head, all hangdog-like, and turns and slinks off. He looks back over his shoulder at me and blushes lightly when he sees me catching him, which almost makes me laugh, in spite of the circumstances. My sister turns up, wearing a flame-red dress and flip-flops.

"God, this sucks," she says, absorbing the chaos. "We were all wondering where you were and you didn't pick up your phone."

"I've been right here the whole time," I say. She grabs my hand and pulls me up off the ground. I lift the garbage bag, which is really heavy, and she helps me haul it as we walk the three blocks to the bar. We don't talk much.

"I think Anthony and I broke up. He found out about the article."

"That sucks."

"Yeah." I continue to follow her through the shadowy streets.

When we step through the front door of the bar, everybody applauds. I wipe sweat and ash off my forehead and put on a happy face.

Johnny hands me a shot of Jack Daniels, which I swallow in one gulp. "Can I have the next one with ginger ale?" I say, thinking, *It will be okay, it will be okay, it will be okay. Drink whiskey with ginger ale and it will all be okay.*

"Anything for you, beauty queen. You are a star!" He leans over the bar and plants a big wet one on my mouth.

"I wasn't too horrible?" I squeak, actually starting to cheer up a bit.

"You were fantastic," he says, "gorgeous."

"You didn't tape it, did you?" I say, embarrassed by how badly I want to see the show, in spite of everything.

He holds up a videotape. "I was going to take it home and let you lull me to sleep with your sordid tales, but I guess I can let you borrow it."

"Pervert," I tell him and push through the crowd until I find Jeremy and Courtney, who jumps up and throws her arms around me. She pulls away and looks directly into my eyes. "Oh, honey, sweetie, are you all right?"

"I'm okay, okay as you can be when your house has just burned down," I tell her. "I'll find out more tomorrow. Can I stay with you tonight? Anthony and I had a huge fight when he found out about the article, and I think we broke up."

"Oh, honey, of course you can."

"Come sit with us," Jeremy says, patting the seat next to him, which Napoleon reluctantly relinquishes and jumps on his daddy's lap. I keep standing. "You can cry on my shoulder. It might seem like small consolation, but I must tell you that you looked fabulous on TV. A real bombshell."

"Thanks," I say. "It does actually make me feel better."

"I like this look. Terrific new accessory, bag-lady inspired, I presume?" I look down at the garbage bag I've been lugging around. "Which would be appropriate for your new living situation. Sorry. Really bad joke."

"I have no idea what's in it. The guy who's been staying at my place rescued some stuff."

I scoot into their booth and open the bag. When I reach inside it, the first thing I find is a thick photo album containing pictures of the trip Courtney and I took to Europe after college graduation. She ended up coming home after three months, purportedly because she ran out of money, but really because she missed Brad too much to stay away. But I wound up getting a job teaching English in Paris, the city I'd loved since I first visited it with my family at thirteen, meeting Philippe, and staying for two years until I moved to New York to go to grad school.

"Check this out," I say, pushing the album toward Courtney.

Jeremy scoots up next to her to look at the pictures, holding Napoleon in his arms so he can see, too. I cut out all sorts of magazine pictures and words and pasted in postcards to create a book-long collage of our trip and my subsequent life in France. "I'm so glad he saved it."

"So fortunate," Court says and holds it up to show me a spread of us, young and tan and grinning and topless on the beach in Mykonos. "We were so happy and carefree. Sometimes I do miss those days," she says, and I notice that her face is drawn. I've never seen her so skinny.

"Hot stuff," Jeremy says. As they continue ogling our bare boobs, I dig around in the treasure chest, which seems to contain another album, one of my jewelry boxes that happens to have my most valuable pieces, including the few I got when my grandmother died, my *Sex and the City* DVDs, five of my favorite books—*Eloise, The Passion, Franny and Zooey, Writing Down the Bones, The Unbearable Lightness of Being*—and all of my thirty-seven journals of various shapes and sizes, which I wrote in religiously from the time I was ten until the last few years, when I became a busy, flaky grown-up with less time to devote to pouring out the contents of my soul. I hold up my first one ever, a little Hallmark diary with a picture of two angels in an apple tree and a lock on it, and start to cry.

"What up with the blubbering," says my sister, arriving on the scene.

"He saved all my journals. That was so nice," I say. "God, I've been leaking from the eyeballs ever since I got here tonight. It's pathetic. I'm an emotional wreck."

"You've just lost all your possessions," Courtney says, reaching across the table to hold my hand. "Honey, it's completely normal."

"All your CDs, books, furniture—oh, that amazing Persian rug," Alicia says.

I picture my apartment and all the things in it that I'll never see again. I can't quite grasp the enormity of my loss. "I found it at a flea market for nothing," I say, missing the rug intensely. "And that amazing red velvet armchair I lugged up from the street."

"All your clothes," says Jeremy. "You took that fabulous vintage coat over to Anthony's, right?"

"Oh, Jeremy, not my favorite coat."

"You left it?" he says, flabbergasted. "What were you thinking?"

"It's summer. I left all my winter stuff. Oh God, my pink parka, my agnès b. trench coat, all my cashmere."

I'm about to get really depressed, until my sister cuts in. "I wonder what vibrators do when they burn. You have the Bunny, don't you? Poor barbecued Bunny Foofoo."

"Luckily I put that personal stuff in a box in the basement when Serena moved in. Wish I'd done the same with my clothes."

I look into the bag and pull out a couple of framed photographs that used to be on my bedroom wall, one of my mother as a little girl sandwiched between my grandparents. My sister squishes into the booth next to me, puts her arm around my shoulders, and squeezes. Then she takes the photo slowly out of my hand and kisses it. We turn our heads to face each other and when our eyes meet we look quickly away.

I reach back into the almost-empty bag and find a black, squishy thing at the bottom. "Oh my God," I say. "He saved Chubby."

"Another one of your sex toys?" Jeremy asks.

"No," I say, whimpering again as I pull out the squished, pitiful-looking teddy bear who's helped me fall asleep since college. Napoleon growls at him.

"That was a lovely thing to do," Courtney says. "Really thoughtful. Who is this man who collected these things?"

"Zach," Alicia says. "Serena's perfect boyfriend."

"Yeah, who burned down my apartment."

14

Courtney and I take a cab back to her place in Park
Slope. I'm so tired, I barely make it up her stairs
without falling asleep on the banister. She graciously offers to carry the garbage bag containing my worldly possessions.

"Oh, sweetheart," Courtney says while unlocking her
front door. "It's not all lost. Remember, you do have quite
a lot of things at Anthony's. We can arrange to pick them
up later this week."

"Where would I put them?"

"Here for now. We'll figure it out."

"I don't know, getting my stuff from his place makes it
all seem so final."

"You're right," she says, turning on the light and dropping the bag in a corner of the living room. "Let's not

worry about any of that yet. You can borrow clothes from me, I have an extra toothbrush, use anything you need."

"Thanks, Court."

She goes into the kitchen to make a pot of chamomile tea, which she says will calm my nerves, and I plunk myself down on the couch next to Chaz, who purrs and rubs up against me. I pick him up and hold him against my chest and he gazes into my eyes soulfully.

Courtney returns with two steaming cups of tea and sits down next to us. Chaz glances over at her as if to say, "Sorry, Mom, Jacquie's needing some feline therapy tonight, I'll catch you later," and then shifts around and rests his chin on my belly.

"Oh, sweetheart, are you going to be okay?" Courtney asks.

"Of course I am," I tell her, not so sure myself.

"Jacquie, when I'm feeling down, it often helps me to remember all the things I do have. You weren't harmed. You have your health and your family and friends who love you and work that you're passionate about." I nod my head. "Homes can be rebuilt and furniture and clothes are nothing but flimsy pieces of fabric and wood and metal. But the most valuable things remain."

I have the sensation of being in a Lifetime movie-of-the-week where the girl's house burns down. I think I might have even seen that one. Or maybe I'm confusing it with an International House of Coffees commercial, the kind that actually sometimes makes Courtney dab at her eyes. "Apparently the Red Cross will give me a debit card for two hundred dollars for toilet paper and pajamas and prescriptions that burned," I say.

"See, that's a start," she says, all earnest. Courtney sips her tea and says, "How are you doing about Anthony?"

I shift around on the couch and Chaz shoots me a disgruntled look. I wonder if he'll abandon me for his more reliable, less squirmy mom. "Not so hot," I tell her. " I feel like we were so great together, like he was the guy I'd been looking for all my life, and I somehow managed to screw it up anyway."

"Jacquie, you know there are two people in every relationship."

"Yeah, but this was my fault. This was a horrible betrayal on my part," I say, choking up. "I always end up chasing them away."

"Jacquie, maybe he's not the right man for you."

"Come on, Court, he's gorgeous and smart and he makes me laugh. Remember all those things we talked about, my perfect divine romantic partner? He's interesting and loves film and the sex is good."

"But what about kind and generous?" she asks. "What about openhearted? I don't know how generous he is with himself or his time, for example. He hasn't made much of an effort to get to know the people that matter to you. And, more important, you're not happy. You've been so anxious and you've told me several times you were fighting."

"It leads to great sex," I say, forcing a smile.

"That's not good enough," she says.

Maybe she's right, I think, but I'm still not willing to let go of Anthony, whom I picture walking away sad and hurt tonight, looking so gorgeous in his baggy cargo shorts.

"It was so amazing in the beginning," I say.

"If you'd gotten to know him before you moved in with him, this all might have gone differently," Courtney says. "It's Jake all over again, really, only in disguise. Anthony made your heart dance, so you dove in before you even knew if he was the kind of guy who would hold you if you were bleeding to death. Would he?"

"Of course he would," I say, then crack a smile. "I mean, if he wasn't on deadline."

Courtney smiles at me weakly. "Anthony's a lot of fun, but he might just call 911 and get back to chasing bad guys around with his camera."

I grab a piece of my hair to search for split ends, then go for my wrist, but I'm not wearing the rubber band. I wonder what happened to it. I'm not sure if Court is right about Anthony, but it occurs to me that I don't really know him that well.

"You know, Jacquie," Courtney says, "if you were to let a man get to know you, really get to know you, before starting some mad, passionate affair, he'd still be smitten. You are a wonderful person. You don't have to sleep with a guy or stir up some great drama to make him like you. He'll like you when he gets to know you, too, if he's the right guy."

I look into her green eyes, mystified.

"Sometimes I think you don't realize that," she says, taking my empty teacup from my hands and carrying it into the kitchen.

When we're lying in bed a few minutes later, I feel uncomfortable. It's not just the big lump of Chaz draped over my ankles or even his claws randomly digging into my shins through the blankets. I know I haven't been a very good friend to Courtney lately and here she is being so nice to me, taking care of me and patiently listening to my woes like she always has.

"Court, I'm so sorry that I haven't been around lately," I tell her. I'm shivering lightly, knowing that I have to proceed. "I got so caught up in Anthony, I think I just neglected a lot of things in my own life and unfortunately you were one of them. I'm really sorry."

"Thank you, Jacquie," she says. "I have been feeling like you've checked out on me lately. I needed to hear you say that."

"How's everything with Brad?" I ask. I can hear her breathing, but she doesn't say anything.

"We're—" She pauses. "Jacquie, I don't know how to say this. I'm, I'm thinking I might leave him."

"WHAT?!" I sit up, scaring Chaz off the bed.

Court sits up, too. "It's been really hard with him touring," she says. "At first, we talked every day and I tried to be supportive and we still felt like the old us. But lately it has shifted. Brad feels like a different person to me. He's so high on the excitement and the crowds and maybe even the female attention and I can't say I blame him, but it's begun to affect us."

"How?" I croak.

"Well, for one thing, you know we've been trying to have a baby."

"Uh-huh," I say, acknowledging my least favorite topic of conversation.

Court pulls the blanket off her and pushes it to the end of the bed with her feet. She's wearing an enormous white men's T-shirt over plaid boxer shorts.

"Well, Brad let me know recently that he doesn't want to have a child. He doesn't think it fits into his schedule, his 'vision' of how his life should be."

"That doesn't sound like Brad," I say.

"I know," she says, tears creeping into her voice. "He's different. He can be so cold and distant, in ways I've never seen before. It's made me feel like maybe we've only gotten along so well because we've never been tested, like we were fine when everything was coasting along smoothly, but maybe we're not equipped to deal with discord or we just don't know how to disagree. It is possible that we want different things out of life. Maybe we were always going to falter as soon as life tested us, and this has been our test. Brad's getting what he's always wanted, a career as a musician, and it is in direct conflict with the things I want: a quiet life in brownstone Brooklyn with my husband and a child. I've felt so alone, like I don't know him anymore, now that he's out there leading the glamorous life he's always been meant to lead and I'm here, completely alone."

My throat feels as if enormous, frozen hands are squeezing it tightly. If I open my mouth to speak, I might let out a scream that would never stop. Poor Court. I can't believe she has been going through all this and hasn't felt like she could talk to me about it or that she's been going through it at all. I don't know how I'd survive if Courtney and Brad got divorced. Their relationship has been the one sure sign of hope for me. To imagine it crumbling is to imagine life as barren, cold, and loveless, desolate like a postapocalyptic landscape out of *Mad Max*, so much more devastating than my own breakup with Anthony. The guilt I feel at being unaware of Courtney's pain is unbearable.

"But, Courtney, Brad loves you," I say.

"I know he does. I just fear we want different things."

"No, no, that's not true," I say, digging for the words I think Courtney needs to hear. "That's never been true. You've always been happy together, for almost fourteen years. This is only temporary, Court. This is nothing when you think about sixty more years together. It'll be a mere blip. Think about it. You'll be ninety and going, 'Didn't you go on tour when we were in our thirties, honey? I barely remember that.' But you'll still have each other and your kids and your love. You'll still be reading him his horoscope and bugging him to take his herbal remedies and he'll be rolling his eyes, then thanking God for his wonderful, loving wife. Please, Court, you are so lucky to have each other. Don't risk losing that, please talk to him. Please go see him and talk it out and see what you need to do to work through this. Go tomorrow. Call in sick. Please, please, Court, will you go call him right now and tell him you're coming?"

"Okay," she says weakly, as if she's only doing it to make me happy, and I'm so pathetic right now that she'd better do whatever it takes to cheer me up. She slowly pulls herself out from under the covers and puts her feet on the floor. As she walks unhurriedly out the door, I pat the covers to get Chaz's attention.

"Come here, baby," I call. He jumps back onto the bed and I pull him over to me. I fall asleep spooning the big furry white beast.

When I wake up, I'm alone in bed. Chaz and Courtney are nowhere to be found. I pad out into the kitchen and find a note on the counter from Courtney saying she went to work and to give her a call. She says there's muesli and tea in the cupboard next to the fridge. I glance at the clock on the stove and am shocked to see that it's ten-fifteen. I must have really needed to sleep. I pick up the phone and dial *Flicks*. Steve answers.

"Hey, you," I say.

"Hey, where are you?" he asks.

I tell him about my apartment and ask for the day off. He tells me to take as much time as I need.

"Though don't forget we're closing next Friday," he says. "Your glance back at the work of Rock Hudson looks good, but your 'best movies to get your man in the mood' piece is due. Do you want to have Sam write it?"

"No, no, I'll get it done," I assure him and then reconsider. "Actually, yeah, would you mind?" It's the first time I've ever turned down work, but I feel incapable of writing an article right now, especially a lite & snarky one.

"Hey, don't forget the Movies Matter party tomorrow. I understand if you can't, but I would really like it if you could make an appearance."

I'd forgotten all about this event that the magazine is sponsoring, an enormous multimedia exhibit in a warehouse in Chelsea with political video installations and performance art and a DJ. Some band is playing at midnight.

"Oh God," I say. "I completely forgot. Yeah, I'll be there." It's my managing-editorly duty, even if my whole life did just get blown to bits. "Oh shit, I have a meeting at the burnt-out shell that used to be my apartment. I have to run," I tell him. "I'll see you tomorrow."

My mom left a message last night to meet the marshal at noon and she was going to try to get an insurance agent there at the same time. I persuaded Jeremy and Alicia to join us. They always manage to make me laugh even at life's cruelest moments, a talent I thought could come in handy around now. I call Courtney and she tells me she had a productive conversation with Brad last night that lasted two hours. He's in transit today, but suggested that she fly up to Toronto over the weekend, because they'll be there for three days and have a light schedule. He said he loves her and wants to work everything out. My heart feels as though it's going to bust out through my rib cage.

When I hang up, I call and order flowers sent to Courtney's office, with an apologetic haiku on the card:

> *Sorry I checked out*
> *Love you more than Häagen-Dazs*
> *Now go fetch your man.*
> *xo, Jacquie*

I arrive at my building and take deep breaths before opening the front door and entering the lobby, where the curmudgeon who lives on the first floor is checking his mail. A horrible, toxic smell assaults my nostrils. I can only imagine what it's like upstairs. My neighbor's eyes light up at the sight of me. "How are you, miss?" he says, the first words we've exchanged since I moved in. "Horrible tragedy, horrible. Do you have a place to stay?"

"Yes, I'm staying with a friend. Thanks for asking."

"Good, good," he says.

"Do you know if everyone else in the building is okay?" I ask. "Was there any damage to other apartments?"

"Several have minor water damage, I believe, but only Lucinda's was seriously damaged," he says. "She's directly below you. I think she'll have to stay away for a month or so as they work on her apartment."

"Poor Lucinda," I say. "I feel terrible." I make a mental note to find out where she's staying and bring her flowers and a treat for Larry.

"Have a good day, miss," my neighbor says, closing his door behind him. Maybe he's not such a curmudgeon after all. I slowly climb the stairs to my doom.

My apartment is black and wet and dark, the gaping cave of a man's mouth who has had all his teeth bashed out with a hammer. For some reason I think of *Saving Private Ryan*, Omaha Beach after the storm. All I can do is stare, blinking. The windows have been boarded over, so only pinpricks of sunlight enter around the edges, sending thin, diagonal shafts onto the floor. I have to step up a good foot and a half to enter, and my shoe lands not on the floor but on something mushy and soft. I'm standing on a mound of sludge, some combination of plaster, ash, water, and what I imagine is the remainder of my stuff. My eyes take a while adjusting to the absence of light. There isn't much left of my bedroom walls to my left. Most of the drywall has burned through the bottom half, leaving the wooden skeleton standing there like charred Popsicle sticks. The entryway closet is another stump. I can see right through it to the washer/dryer in the kitchen, black with soot. I might hyperventilate. It looks like there's still a tub, toilet, and sink in my bathroom, hooray, but they're cracked and battered. I guess the heat of a fire busts porcelain right up. Random wires hang from the ceiling.

I tiptoe over the mountain range of muck on the floor to make my way in. My eyes are starting to acclimate to the dark. It's cold here. I wonder for a minute if I'm hallucinating, if this isn't really my amazing apartment that I only bought a few months ago. I remember sitting on the floor with Courtney, lighting candles, making wishes. Was that right here? For a moment, I am stupefied that my life has changed so drastically since then, that I had a boyfriend who has since left me, an apartment that burned down, a life I barely recognize. There are certain things I've always been sure of: that I'm a good person, an honest person, a good sister and friend, that I'm able to acknowledge and laugh at my flaws before working to reverse them. But lately I'm not so sure. I've been lying to Anthony ever since I met him. Lies roll naturally off my tongue. I have become one of those people who frantically justifies her behavior rather than takes responsibility for it, one of those people I've always disdained. I don't recognize myself any more than my apartment. And I can't blame Anthony for the shift. He never asked me to change. I wanted him so badly; I wanted to be immersed in his world so much that I sacrificed my own.

My buzzer buzzes—nice to know it still functions—and I let

everyone in. In a minute, Jeremy and Alicia are standing at the door with the fire marshal and a woman I take to be the insurance agent. Jeremy and I look at each other for a second—and then burst out laughing. My sister joins in, until the three of us have to hold on to one another for support as tears of laughter cover our faces. The fire marshal and insurance agent smile at us politely, mystified.

One word at a time, I spit out, "Nice. Apartment. Huh?"

The spell is broken, and I put out my hand to shake those of Bob the fire marshal, a strapping guy in the expected attire, and Ms. Stelling from my insurance company, who is appropriately dressed in jeans and galoshes. Guess she knew to expect a swamp instead of a floor. "Hi, I'm Jacquie. This is my apartment." We walk around together as Bob describes what happened.

"Smoke rises," he explains, pointing at the walls of the living room, which are progressively blacker as we look up toward the ceiling. Some furniture is standing, but it's disgusting and soggy from the massive amount of water the firemen sprayed on it. My two wicker and pine bar stools are lying crumpled halfway across the room from where they used to sit. I imagine the big strong firemen flinging them there, breaking the legs right off. Burnt books are scattered all over. Of the ones still on the shelves, the higher I look, the blacker the spines. I wonder what can be saved. I probably have too many books anyway. Certain spots of the floor are visible through the muck, the floorboards no longer flat, but each curled into a C shape from the heat. It's pretty in a bizarre way. I tell myself to bring a camera next time.

"Here's my rug," I say to my sister, indicating a solid, black ball of damp fabric the size of one of those exercise balls at the gym that is scrunched up in the corner. I pick it up and pry apart the tightly wound, drenched fabric. "Maybe a good cleaner can save it?" I say.

"You're dreaming, *hermana*," Alicia responds.

The kitchen got hit harder than the living room, I guess because it shares a wall with the bathroom, which is where the fire started. The stove and fridge are covered in thick black dust. The granite countertop is there, but it's lying on top of a heap of soggy, charred bits of plaster, ash, pots, pans, other remnants of my cabinets, which were swallowed whole by the fire. The backsplash is still there, leading all the way up to the only two pitch-black cabinets still hanging. I run my finger along Zach's handiwork, making a clean trail in the soot to reveal beautiful, unscathed metallic tiles still clinging to the bare walls. I rub the black dust between my thumb and forefinger in a daze. Nothing remains of my desk or anything on it. It seems to have dissolved completely into the mountain of debris covering the floor.

The fire marshal tells me they've determined that the fire was accidental, the result of a spark coming into contact with polyurethane that had recently been put down on the bathroom floor. Apparently the walls had also been painted, creating additional fumes. The spark most likely came from ancient wiring in the light above the bathroom sink. I freeze. I cringe. My breath stops flowing into my lungs. This was my fault. Or not exactly my fault, but I should have had that fixed months ago.

I take deep breaths and continue to follow the marshal around, into my bedroom, which has also been decimated. My bed frame melted onto the floor, the way a record used to warp if you left it sitting by a window in the days of vinyl. The insurance agent announces that she has everything she needs and asks me to e-mail her a list of my possessions, indicating everything that was damaged or destroyed, and says a lot of it will be covered. I say a silent prayer that I took my parents' advice for once and got homeowners' insurance. She says she will be in touch and takes my cell phone number.

"Hey, Lucinda downstairs has insurance, doesn't she?" To my relief, she says that she does and that she's handling her case, too. Bob announces that he's taking off as well and tells me to call if I have any questions. I borrow a flashlight and promise to drop it off at the station on my way out.

Once they're gone, Jeremy, Alicia, and I start chuckling again, but it's sad laughter this time.

"Let's go find your coat," Jeremy says. I make my way into my bedroom closet. The door, well, half of it, which now has the consistency of burnt firewood, is still dangling from its hinges, but the mirror that was affixed to it is nowhere to be found. I shine light inside the somber cave and notice that most of its contents are bundled in a big colorless ball on the floor jammed up against the back wall, which I approach. I pry off a layer and examine it: a crispy, hard, shapeless board that on further inspection becomes the red polka-dotted dress I wore to my birthday party. I try to flatten it in my hands and it rips in half. Alicia giggles.

"It's not funny. I love that dress," I say.

"Well, maybe you can use that emergency debit card to go shopping. Two hundred bucks can get you six items from H&M," Jeremy says.

"I don't think that's what the Red Cross has in mind," I tell him.

"Why not? You lost clothes in the fire," he says.

"Shut up," Alicia says. "You'll get bucks from insurance and we'll buy you a whole new wardrobe. I always thought that dress was a little 2002 myself." I hit her on the head with the left half of my crispified former favorite dress. It breaks. "That stinks," she says. I flick some ashes out of her hair.

"Let's get out of here. I can't deal with it," I announce, and we all go get coffee at my corner café. I tell the cute waiter what happened and he says my latte and croissant are on him. I can't remember the last time I actually paid for anything there.

"So, guess what?" Alicia says. "With all the drama, I haven't had a chance to tell you, but I got a cool gig." She tells me that she's going to be doing pro bono commercials for the animal shelter where she's been walking dogs. "No money, obviously, but it's finally something I'm excited about. I called a copywriter and art director I know and they're in for free. I'm producing, and we're doing three spots.

"Oh shit," she says. "I've got to go. I'm supposed to walk Sporty and Jeannette today, my two chubby Labradoodles."

"Excuse me?" Jeremy asks.

"Designer urban hybrids, half Lab, half poodle, Labs that don't shed, poodles with no issues. Tell me you don't have any in the dog run." Jeremy shakes his head. "They're all the rage in Brooklyn, along with Puggles, half pug, half beagle, friendly, loyal hounds with squished faces."

"We have at least six of those in the dog run," Jeremy says.

"The breeders can't mate their dogs fast enough to keep up with the demand. But I think you should get Nappie a little baby Chi-poo brother, half poodle, half Chihuahua. And my sister should get a schnoodle, half poodle, half schnauzer. They are painfully cute."

"I need a home first," I say.

They both take off and I decide to stay and write. I take out my computer and start putting down thoughts about the fire and losing my possessions. Next thing I know I'm just writing. And writing and writing, about life and priorities and how badly I want a home that feels like a home. I have not written just to write, just for me, for so long that I almost forget what it feels like to put words down that are not about a movie or what twenty-something girls should do to hold on to their boyfriends, but just my thoughts—about life, about what is going on in my head, about Anthony and why it didn't work out between us. It feels so good, it's almost like sex, which is convenient, since I'll probably never have any again. I'm perched in my seat, back arched, sort of swaying back and forth. An observant bystander might think I'm masturbating.

Gradually my narcissistic ramblings begin to take shape. It's not just, "Woe is me, my apartment burned down and my boyfriend left me, where did Anthony and I go wrong?" It's more about the destruction of my home and my relationship in a larger context, against a backdrop of men and women loving each other enough to construct a life together, to stop playing house long enough to build a home. To cut the bullshit and be honest and real, the way we are with our friends and families. The way Courtney and Brad have always been with each other, even when the truth is so painful that it risks ripping them apart. What makes a relationship real, I realize, is caring enough to eliminate the masks and the defenses and really talk to each other—and agree to help do the dishes and pick up a quart of milk on the way home, if that's what it takes to make one's lover happy. Have I ever felt that way? Certainly not since Philippe, and I left him, maybe because I was too young to handle that kind of openness, or maybe because I knew in my gut that my future didn't lie with him. I needed to build my own home here in New York.

My outpouring becomes the beginning of a sort of essay, I think, about the importance of honesty in relationships and the small, unexciting, yet intimate moments that make those relationships solid. For a second I wonder if it is any good at all and then realize that I don't care. I take a deep breath, thinking *sut*, and let it out slowly, thinking *nam*.

I consider going back to the apartment to start digging through muck, but I feel exhausted and would rather go back to Courtney's and take a nap. I drop off the flashlight at the fire station on Thirteenth Street and say hi to all the cute firemen I recognize from the other night. I'm like a celebrity over there now. They take a break from lathering up the trucks to flash matinee-idol grins at me and ask how I'm holding up. I smile pretty, but don't have the energy for proper flirting. I don't even go by my favorite hardware store to buy a flashlight, but stop by the generic one around the corner from the fire station instead. I don't have the energy to see Zach yet. That's going to be one weird encounter. Maybe I'll have the fortitude to face him when the dust settles.

15

As I turn the corner onto Courtney's street, I spot Anthony on her stoop, his long, bare legs punctuated by
rust-colored Adidas stretched lazily out over the stairs. He
doesn't see me immediately, since he's staring intently at
an article in *The New York Times*, which is spread out in
front of him. Spots of sunlight that have squeezed through
the gently swaying branches overhead play on his handsome arms and shoulders. Little wings flutter around my
heart.

"Hey," I say, approaching the stairs. He looks up with a
sad smile.

"Hey. How are things?"

"Good," I say. "Courtney's taking care of me." I sit
down next to him, with enough space between us that I
don't seem presumptuous.

"I want to talk to you," he says, scooting around to face me and squinting against the sun. "I don't want to break up. I know I've been a dick for the past couple of days, but I want to be with you."

He reaches into his jacket pocket and looks into my eyes with an expression that says, "Never doubt me again. I'm your knight in shining armor."

"I've been thinking and I realized how important you are to me," he says, looking down at his hands, which appear to be holding something. "I got you, um, it's not some kind of big engagement ring or anything like that. It's this ring of my mom's that I have, but I want you to wear it." In the palm of his hand sits a gold band with a thin cluster of diamonds on one side. He picks it up and slips it onto my finger. It's so perfect, I could burst.

"I saw the rest of the show, the *Between the Sheets* you were on," he says. "Will taped it. It was nice how you were so concerned about me and how I'd react. I felt like a jerk." He stands up and looks down at me, opening and closing one of his hands rhythmically. "Do you think we can try again, Jacquie?"

My heart is banging around like a tiny puppy's as I jump up and throw my arms around his neck and he buries his face in my hair—it's so easy to fall back into him.

I imagine our wedding right here on Courtney's stoop in Park Slope on a fall day with red and yellow leaves whipping around us and so many of our loved ones crowding the street, they have to close it off to traffic. I hear the taxis honking at the disturbance and see my sister's grin on the stairs next to me, my mom brushing tears of relief off a sculpted cheekbone, my dad's proud expression on the sidewalk at her side.

"Oh, baby, yes! Of course I want to be back together, of course I do," I say, squeezing him and looking up into his beaming face. A nervousness nips at the back of my mind but I swat it away, along with the mental image of Courtney's skeptical, frozen, faux smile as she stands on the stoop in a burgundy bridesmaid's dress clutching my sister's arm so hard she'll leave fingerprints. I imagine pushing her over the railing of the stoop, her limbs flailing wildly as she lands in a bush. I want so badly to savor this happiness.

I leave a message for Courtney saying I won't be sleeping over tonight, and Anthony and I hop a cab back to his place—our place. Anthony has bought flowers, two dozen pink roses, which he's arranged in an orange juice bottle on the coffee table, and he runs around like a fussy housewife lighting candles, picking up a sweatshirt from the floor and tossing it into the bedroom. He's straightened up since I left: The piles of newspapers are gone, photos are stacked neatly by the living room wall, and even the spare room looks a little less cluttered when I poke my head in.

"I started clearing out some of that junk," he says with a shy smile. "Brought a load out to the Dumpster. I'm determined to turn that room into an office if it kills me."

We order Chinese and eat it while staring at a movie about a fat talking cat. Anthony falls asleep immediately after swift, sleepy reunion sex, even though it's only ten o'clock—I guess he worked through the night again—but I'm completely wired, my mind chattering endlessly. Our fight clearly got Anthony thinking about what he wants from our relationship and I annoyingly find myself obsessing about what I want. I wish I could just be happy, but my anxiety is too ominous to ignore. When I told my old therapist that I was never sure about Philippe, she said that maybe I was the kind of person who would never be sure about anything, whose nature it was to analyze, question, and doubt. At the time, I was grappling with what I wanted to do professionally. I had also agonized about whether I should move to New York or California from Paris and finally chose New York simply because I got into grad school here. Deciding between the fish, the steak, or the vegetarian couscous on a menu can be traumatic for me, let alone the chocolate-mousse-v.-crème-brûlée question. So, settling on a life partner? Maybe my therapist was right. Maybe I have to hold my nose and jump. I mean, I think I could be happy with Anthony. I suspect I could have been happy with Philippe, too, for that matter, had I just been willing to commit to him. He and I had dinner at a dimly lit Vietnamese restaurant on our block in Paris the night we decided to break up. At one point during the mostly silent meal, I asked him why he loved me. "What gives me the greatest pleasure in life is looking at you, talking to you, and making love with you," he said, and I began to cry, for a moment sure that I was doing the wrong thing, letting this wonderful, devoted man slip away because I was scared shitless. Why should I do that again?

I'm about to cuddle up to that thought when another one hits me in the head: Maybe I am totally retarded when it comes to menus, but what if when something really matters, I do know what I want? Once I started writing, for example, even when I was just doing movie reviews at fifty bucks a pop and waiting tables to supplement my income, I never considered any other job ever again. Once my feet touched New York City pavement, I knew it was home. And what if there's a man out there who would make me shout "Eureka!" from the rooftops? Someone who would stir a certainty deep in my gut that says, *Go ahead and tattoo his name on your tummy, girlfriend, because this is The Guy.*

Eventually I kick off, probably late, because I don't wake up until eleven the next day, drenched in sweat. I wander dazed through the apartment, which again looks as if a bar brawl passed through. Anthony has disappeared, leaving a mass of destruction in his wake. The clues—scripts, contracts, open film-reference books, tapes, and CDs strewn on the coffee table, floor, and kitchen counter, couch cushions jutting at odd angles—suggest the loss of a necessary object. Something has even managed to collide with my roses and a spray of pink petals and disembodied buds are miserably scattered. I turn my back, pretending I didn't just see the mayhem, and instead shower, leave swiftly, and head over to the East Village to start cleaning up my own mess.

It's a scorcher out, the first really hot, muggy day, and it's not even August yet. People hate steamy New York summers, but I love them. The city belongs to the few of us who choose to sweat it out rather than flee to the beach and dare leave our air-conditioned apartments to wander the deserted, still streets. I love that girls run around with no makeup, braless, in the flimsiest of garments. It's as if we shed our inhibitions along with our clothes and suddenly find ourselves permitted to bare our skin, drink more booze, laugh harder, dance or play tag or grope our boyfriends with abandon right in the middle of the street. The balmy air is so heavy, I can feel it weighing me down, luring sweat out of every one of my pores, slowing down my usually brisk, New Yorker–paced steps to a crawl. It feels sultry, thick, as if the air itself has a personality. The East Village sidewalks are practically empty, with those doing the slo-mo crawl down them pushing tired limbs through air as thick as pudding. I make my way to Avenue A via Sixth Street—a detour, but my dripping body is hungry for something cold and sweet—and almost knock over a screeching little boy in his underwear hopping blissfully under the water spraying out of a fire hydrant. His big sister is watching from a stoop, hesitant, judgmental, envious, while their young mother in Daisy Duke shorts smiles and shakes her head at her happy boy. I step into the air-conditioned soda fountain on Avenue A and order a chocolate-vanilla-swirled frozen yogurt on a sugar cone from the modelesque Polish girl who works there, before again braving the steaming street.

"Where'd ja get that?" asks a grungy twenty-something guy with stringy dyed black hair and a dragon tattooed across his shirtless chest. As I point at the soda fountain behind me, liquid drips onto my forehead. I gasp and snap my head back to squint at an air conditioner looming above that has perspired onto me— it still surprises me every time. In front of a dingy corner bar, a preteen girl whose breasts are spilling out of the front of her mi-nuscule green dress is flirting with a preteen boy in a baseball cap who's playing it cool. As I pass, he says, "So, do you have any plans tonight?" She devours the poor pup with heavy-lidded eyes, taking her lower lip between her teeth for a moment. Her answer will clearly be his salvation. I'm remembering that age fondly when a leathered man with butt-length dreadlocks stops dead in his tracks in front of me and points at my feet.

"You have the most ravishing feet I've ever seen. I have to paint them."

I look down at my weathered pink flip-flops in wonderment.

"No, really, man, they're mind-blowing," he says. "This isn't a pickup, seriously, bring a friend with you, whatever, to my studio, but I must paint your feet. It's my duty, man, never seen anything like them."

"It's not a good time right now," I tell him, but take his phone number and promise to call when my schedule opens up. As I move past, his eyes never leave my skinny, pale ankles.

A big, bushy Irish wolfhound limps past me and I say, "Hi, baby face, I'm sorry about your leg." It's an illness really, my compulsion to talk to every dog I see. I think I'm afraid they'll recognize a kindred spirit in me and feel hurt if I don't acknowledge them. I tell myself I'll dump the rest of my frozen yogurt on the next street corner, since it's loaded with sugar and calories and dripping all over my hand, but when I get there, it's too good to part with. I finish it all the way to my corner, where I nod at the family hanging out in their van while wiping yogurt on my old cutoff khakis, and blow kisses at their yappy Yorkie, who barks as I pass.

The door to my apartment isn't locked. It pushes right open, and I immediately sense that something is different. The windows are still boarded over and the space is still dark, but the toxic smell has grown less pungent and the muck in front of the door has been cleared away. A waist-high pile of full garbage bags sits in the middle of the dank cave that used to be my bedroom.

"Hello?" I say, entering cautiously.

"Oh, hey." Zach the hardware-store boy's head pops out from

behind the washer/dryer. He's wearing a dust mask that he pulls down around his neck when he sees me. Then he blushes, as usual, so deeply that I can see it in the dark. He walks out of the kitchen wiping his hands on the bottom of the Smokey the Bear T-shirt he's wearing over a pair of filthy jeans.

"Hey," he says. "I've been cleaning up the place."

"You've made major headway," I say, my eyes adjusting to the darkness. There's another pile of garbage bags in the living room, which must contain all the ash and plaster that was covering the floor, because there's very little of it left. A portable fan hums in the corner, its metal face turning slowly left then right, doing its best to dry up the dampness. The exposed floor is a sight: the damp floorboards curling cutely, yet disturbingly, upon themselves. A pile of cleaning supplies covers the kitchen floor: mop, broom, dustpan, various bottles, rags, sponges. There's a shovel leaning up against the washing machine.

"You didn't have to do all this," I tell him.

"Well, yeah, I kind of did," he says, walking over to the bookshelves he built. He turns away from me and starts to sand the wood down with a block and says over his shoulder, "Grab one of those sponges over by the fridge. They're good for getting the soot off."

I pick one up—it's dry, not like a normal sponge—and start wiping off the refrigerator. "You think you can save those?" I ask.

"Definitely," he says. "Sand 'em down and stain 'em and they'll be as good as new."

I look around, trying to get used to my burnt-out home. "Hey, where's my couch?" I ask.

"I put it up on the roof," Zach says. "Had to carry it up on my head. It was soaked. I think if we leave it in the sun, it might be okay. The cushions are crunchy and I don't know if you'll be able to get the smell of smoke out, but they can be reupholstered. I put that red chair up there, too, and the rug that was bunched up in the corner."

"Thanks," I say, peeking into the refrigerator, which Zach has emptied. "Hey, you haven't found any of my stuff buried in here anywhere, have you? I'm wondering about jewelry."

"You got that one box?"

"Yeah. God, I never did thank you for that. That was so nice. I don't know how you did it, but you managed to get almost everything I have of my grandmother's."

"Were you close?"

"Yeah, she was around a lot when I was a kid," I say, dropping my bag to the floor and leaning against the exposed washing machine. An image of my grandmother comes to mind, rubbing lotion on my legs after a bath. "Soft as velvet," she would say, tears gathering in her brown eyes. "Please God, let me live to see you married. I so want to see you a bride."

"She died a few years ago and my grandfather later that year," I say. "I was inconsolable. I think I wondered if anyone would ever love me that much again. Sorry, that must sound pretty stupid."

"Not at all," Zach says.

"I don't know what the hell I'm talking about," I say, suddenly embarrassed. "How do you recommend finding my valuables?"

"I've bagged up a lot of debris," he says. "But I left most of the bedroom for you. Maybe you'll be able to find something. I did some Internet research, though, and I guess it's hard to find objects in the parts that get hit the worst. They get pulverized."

"My bedroom did suffer," I say.

"Some of the books that were closer to the floor are all right," Zach says. "Soggy but legible."

I approach the stack he's made on the floor: a motley assortment of plays, a Yeats anthology, movie guides, Toni Morrison, the Proust I never read, Tim Robbins, a stack of romance novels. I run my fingers along the damp pages of a doozy called *One Steamy Summer* before making my way past the countertop, which Zach has leaned against the kitchen wall, past the pile of garbage bags and the flame-broiled wooden stakes that used to be my bedroom walls, and sit down on the floor to start digging though the rubble to search for anything that might belong to me.

"I laughed when I saw all those romantic books," Zach says. "I got into your books when I was staying here. It was a workout, all those writers you like who make you work for it—Woolf, Faulkner, Nabokov. I read a lot, kept discovering new stuff, like Italo Calvino, awesome, and then I found that hidden stash." He chuckles.

"I was trying to write one," I say, refusing to give in to his mockery. "I heard there was a formula to romance novels, so I got the guidelines from one of the major publishers, thought maybe I'd take a stab at it."

"Oh, tell me you didn't like reading them. You didn't have to get thirty-eight of them."

"I bought about twenty for a buck at a stoop sale, but fine, I admit I did like them a little." I laugh. "I even started writing this essay about my guilty addiction, you know, the English-major geek who gets hooked on Harlequin. Never finished it."

"You could still," he says. "You're a great writer."

"Oh really."

"I've been reading you for years," he says. "Your film stuff."

"You read *Flicks*?" I'm incredulous. Only directors, movie fanatics, and the indie community read my rag.

"I have a subscription," he says.

"That's hilarious," I say, refocusing on the rubble, but I'm sure his face is crimson.

The first thing I locate is a huge chunk of blue ceramic with dirt still clinging to it. It's a piece of the flowerpot I planted Zach's mini-roses in. The flowers themselves were collateral damage. I look up at him and remember how sweet I thought it was when he brought that plant to Serena, back when he was a mystery to me. How funny that I knew the guy fixing up my apartment all along. It's comforting to know it was Zach, someone who's always been so kind and generous. Digging my fingers farther into the muck, I touch something hard and bore a little tunnel around a smooth object, which turns out to be a Day of the Dead skeleton my sister brought me from Mexico. Its bones are charbroiled. I wonder how it got all the way over here from its shelf.

"Look at this," I say to Zach, holding it up.

He walks over and peers at the tiny, black and white doll. "Only a dead guy could survive the flames," he says. "Check out his expression."

I look down into my palm at the spooky grin on its face. The particles around the doll have dried out a lot. They feel soft and dusty on my hands. I fill my left hand and with my right push away gray and black dust, liberating solid chunks with my fingers to see if they might be anything valuable.

"Hey, you know the books that you saved during the fire, why those?"

"I don't know, really. I didn't have time to think, I just grabbed, but I guess they seemed worn, like you paid attention to them," he says. "I guess they were the ones I would have rescued if it was my fire."

We spend the next hour there, Zach sanding while I dig and chuck hunks of gloop. I don't find much except a couple of shattered nail polish bottles amid the unidentifiable slabs. I'm acknowledging the surreal humor in my situation and feeling calm, my mind quiet for the first time in a while.

"You know, Zach, I have good news for you," I say. "Once the place is fixed up, you can go on staying here if you want."

He spins around, wiping his hands on his jeans. I don't know why it's hard for me to tell him.

"My boyfriend and I were breaking up, but now it looks like we're staying together," I say. "I'm going to keep living at his place."

"Oh," he says, turning toward the shelves for a second and

then facing me again. "I never understood why you would live somewhere else when you have this great apartment."

"Well, I just told you, I'm staying at my boyfriend's. His apartment is bigger, so it makes sense. I guess we'll see what happens in the future."

"Yeah," he says.

"I love Anthony and I'm gonna try to make it work and if that means not living at my apartment, so be it," I say, feeling as if I have to defend myself. "He gave me a ring."

"You're engaged?"

"Well, not *engaged* engaged," I say. "It's more like a promise, you know, to get married eventually."

"Right," he says and turns around to keep sanding the bookshelves.

I keep picking through shards, pissed off and irritated that Anthony didn't ask me to marry him. What the hell is a promise ring anyway? Did he even say it was a promise ring?

"You know," I say, staring into the mountain of dust at my feet, "things are going really great for me right now, you know? My job, the column, did you know I got a column at that magazine *Luscious*?" I look up at him and he nods. I wonder how he knows. "I guess I'm not busier than anyone else in New York, but lately I feel like I'm on some kind of spinning ride at an amusement park that's going faster and faster and I'm glued to the walls and the floor's dropping and I'm waiting to tumble when it comes to a halt, and it's starting to make me dizzy and a little nauseous, even though it's exhilarating and fast, and I don't know how to get off. And now there's all this." I thrust my hands out, indicating the pitiful remains of my life. "I don't even know where to start with it and I have nowhere to go. Then this guy that I really do care about tells me he wants to make this relationship work and maybe it's what I'm supposed to do."

Zach walks slowly toward me. I lift my chin up toward him from where I'm sitting Indian-style on the damp, blackened floor.

"I always wanted to live a simpler life," I say, "to find a small, quiet space where I could have some peace, maybe even get a dog. This apartment felt like a start, and I don't know what to do now." My shoulders slump as I start to cry into my hands.

"Shhhh," Zach says, crouching down and putting his arm around me.

He's so big, I feel safe and warm and don't want him to go away. When I stop crying he pulls away from me and lightly places his hand on the back of my neck. My whole body tingles.

"This place can be rebuilt, Jacquie," he says, scooting around to sit on the floor in front of me, the bottoms of his knees hitting the tops of mine. "I know it seems bad right now, but when you get the insurance money, all you'll need is time, energy, a little vision. It should take six months. With focus and determination, I give it three."

"Where is Buster?" I ask.

"With Serena," he says. "I didn't think I should bring him here. Who knows what he'd get into? You know, Jacquie, there's nothing to be afraid of. Here's an idea: get excited instead. This is a clean slate, anything can happen. I mean—" He bites his lip. I feel like this is when he's supposed to reach out and kiss me before the sexual tension suffocates both of us, but that's not a possibility, is it?

"I should really go," I say, jumping up and away from him. "I have this party thing."

"Yeah, I have to go pretty soon, too," he says. "Gotta meet Serena to taste wedding cake."

Now it's my turn to blush and move quickly to the door.

As I'm swinging it open, Zach says, "Jacquie, I have to apologize." I turn around to face him. "I knew about the light in the bathroom. I'd seen it spark before, and in my line of work, I never should have let that slide. I kept meaning to fix it, but never got to it. You just never think this could happen."

"I should have fixed it, too, Zach."

"Yeah, probably."

When I leave, I don't feel like going back to Anthony's, so I take the F train to Brooklyn and tumble into Courtney's inviting, king-size bed, where I fall dead asleep in minutes.

Three month sublet: Beautiful, sunny 2-bedroom with vibrant, warm energy available on quiet, tree-lined block in Park Slope. Fully furnished with lovely, eclectic pieces, luscious plants, homey details, hardwood floors, fireplace, terrace, dishwasher, high-speed Internet. Additional perk: subletter will have the fortunate opportunity to spend time with our big, fat, gorgeous feline whom we will be missing like mad. Call Courtney.

16

I wake up from my nap to Chaz complaining about how desperately and immediately he needs to be fed. When I pry my eyes reluctantly open, he is seated on top of Courtney's pillow directly in front of my face, iridescent eyes unblinking, obviously irked.

"Fine," I say, "fine," and sleepwalk into the kitchen to fetch him a scrumptious health-food brand Turkey and Giblets Feast. It stinks up the whole room as I spoon it into his crusty dish. I open the refrigerator and pull out the Brita pitcher, pour myself a tumbler of water, and guzzle the whole thing. The clock over the stove says eight-twenty when I make my way back to the bedroom and crawl back under the covers. "Shit!" I jump up again, more awake now. The *Flicks* party started at eight way on the West Side, and I'm in Brooklyn. Can I never be on time? I drag myself into the bathroom to examine myself in the mirror and am alarmed to see puffy eyes and big, frizzy hair that resembles Carole King's circa 1973. "Shit," I say again, realizing that I can't avoid taking a shower and at least wetting my hair. I turn on the hot water and run a brush through the bird's nest on my head. "Your hair is like a broom," I remember my grandma saying in her Yiddish accent. I miss my grandma. While the shower's heating up, I grab an open bottle of white wine from the fridge, pour a glass, and place it on the edge of the tub to sip while I'm washing off my nap.

I end my shower with a blast of cold water in an attempt to de-puff my eyes and retrieve some of my usual bounciness. Even a girl mid-existential crisis whose apartment burned down can muster up enough pep to face a minor New York cultural event, right? I take a handful of hair product out of the medicine cabinet, glob it onto my wet mop, wrap it all up in a towel, finish off my glass of wine, refill it in the kitchen, and race into the bedroom. It's a quarter to nine when I call a car service (ETA: in five minutes), throw open Courtney's closet door, and, without having to think, pull out a totally un-Courtney emerald-green, silk, sexpot cocktail dress that she never wears and I've always coveted and the black strappy sandals that accompany her to weddings only. How lucky am I that both my best friend and my sister wear size 8 shoes and size 6 dresses just like me? I toss the towel from my head onto the edge of the bathtub, slather lotion all over (even though it will slide right off me in the heat of the night), and when my car honks, I scrunch my wet hair, down my wine, grab my purse, and jet out the door. I'll put on makeup in the car, which will cost me twenty bucks—that's what I get for sleeping for three and a half hours in the middle of the afternoon.

When I reach the party, at a monstrous warehouse in Chelsea, I see a throng of people crowding the front door, trying to persuade the pack of perky publicists to let them in. Luckily for me, big boss Steve happens to be out there chatting up one of the bouncers, and he grabs my hand and pulls me past the red rope.

"Hey, how are you feeling?" he asks, wearing a look of fatherly concern.

"I'm great," I tell him, tipsy. "Stoked to be out." Stoked? I must be drunk.

Steve pats my back and nudges me into the industrial elevator, which subsequently lurches up and ejects us on the second floor, which is so packed with people that I have to squeeze past sweaty limbs, chests, and backs to find the bar and order a two-dollar beer in a plastic cup. Techno music blasts and videos play on most of the walls towering twenty feet overhead. My eyes are drawn from one projection to the next, unable to focus on anything specific. I swerve toward the corner farthest from the bar, where the crowd thins a bit, and become hypnotized by images of women of different shapes and sizes on the wall in front of me. They're all dressed in the uniform preferred by twenty-something inhabitants of Williamsburg: some variation of stretchy, blousy, vintage, eye catching, low slung, bleak. The cuts quicken until the women are slamming against the makeshift screen one upon another in rapid succession. They should blur into some vague generalization about womanhood, but they don't; each maintains her individual beauty and distinctness. There's something poignant, mesmerizing about the piece.

"Like it?" a familiar male voice asks over my shoulder.

I swing around to find Jake standing next to me in baggy jeans and a tight orange Frosted Flakes T-shirt, and grab his shoulder to steady myself.

"I do, so much," I say. "Is it yours?"

"Yeah," he says proudly, a wide grin on his pretty face. "I'm doing video and photography stuff these days, installations, you know."

"Congratulations," I tell him, taking a sip of his strong cocktail.

"There's a gallery interested in me," he brags. "Maybe two. One place bought two of my paintings."

"That's great, Jake," I shout over the music. "Hey, you didn't sleep with all those chicks, did you?"

He laughs a low, devilish laugh. "Not all of them," he says. "None of them while we were together. I promise." I realize I'm not jealous of those girls or annoyed that he's been slutting around since we broke up. Jake is not someone who can get to me anymore and it feels great.

"Hey, I want to hang out, Jacquie," he says, feeding me another swig of his drink. As I bite my lip, about to tell him why we shouldn't hop back into bed, which is of course what he means, he says, "Can we, like—? It's weird, you know? It was crazy when we were hanging out, but I feel like you inspired me or something, like this work is a lot because of you or something." He looks down and futzes with a hole in his shirt that reveals a circle of tanned, flat stomach. "That's probably kinda lame, huh? But you believed in me, you know, maybe we should try to see if we could, I don't know."

He stares at me with hard eyes that soften as they land on mine and reaches out to run a single finger down my bare shoulder. His touch makes me want to pull him toward me, crash against the wall, wrap my legs hard around his small waist, grind myself up against the seam of his jeans as he grabs my ass, as he would, bites my lip, mauls me in a room full of my friends and acquaintances. But I stop myself.

"Jake, this wasn't me. It was you," I say, recovering from my raunchy reverie. "You just needed to find your medium, you know what I mean? It's about confidence and getting into yourself and finding out what your strengths are, you know? It was bound to come once you let yourself go." Damn, I sound like a barfly perched on a stool, pontificating for whoever will listen. "I don't think you really want me back in your life, Jake. Remember how insane we made each other?"

"We fucked great," he says, making me laugh way too loudly.

"Yeah, we did," I say, savoring the ache he can still ignite between my thighs just by saying the f-word. "But that's not everything." I reach out for him and he leans into my arms.

"Jake." I feel so much tenderness for him, I almost tell him I love him, but I know he'll take it the wrong way. "I really care about you. I'll always be your friend."

He straightens up and runs his hand coolly through his shaggy hair.

"Yeah, me too," he says, his eyes beginning to dart around the room, eventually landing on an older man in really expensive jeans, whom I take to be one of his professional suitors.

"Hey," he says, pushing his chin out in the man's direction, "I should bolt." He nods at me and scampers off, leaving me alone with an endless loop of beautiful New York women that my ex-boytoy had sex with. There are so many of them. I watch for a while until my sister pokes me in the waist with a skinny finger.

"Hipsters are so over," she snarls over the music, "there are way too many asymmetrical haircuts here," and drags me back to the bar for a refill and then onto the dance floor, where Steve and Jeremy are bumping and grinding all over each other. I wonder why I never thought of setting them up; they're so obvious. Jeremy's cradling a bottle of tequila, which he dangles in my face.

"Where'd you get that?" I shout, taking a swig.

"Blew the bartender," he says.

I take another sip and shake my head, hoping it will make it go down easier. "I was just drinking wine at Courtney's," I say.

"Wine, then liquor—never been sicker, thicker, bicker, dicker," he slurs, wagging a finger at me and offering the bottle to Steve, who's gazing amorously into his eyes.

"You are wasted, mister," I say. "And in vino veritas."

"In tequila, vomit and stupidity," he says, winding his arms more tightly around my boss's waist.

My sister and I dance with them to a trippy mash-up of "Superfreak" and "Sweet Home Alabama," and I wave at Jake's bland, cute roommate who is DJing. Jeremy doesn't check his cell phone once during the entire song. From out of nowhere, Chester spills a beer on my arm and I shake it off flamboyantly, rolling my eyes in mock disgust. He sticks his tongue lecherously between two fingers in homage to the scumbag whose truck Thelma and Louise

blew up, before shuffling off to harass Spencer and his wife, who are swaying on the edge of the dance floor, trying to decide if they should join us. The music transitions smoothly into Robert Palmer's "Addicted to Love" and we all abandon our cool, swirling our sweaty manes around shouting, "You're gonna have to face it, you're addicted to love." Jeremy and Steve are pointing at each other and singing, "Might as well face it, you're addicted to love. Might as well face it, you're addicted to love," when I feel a sudden urge to throw up and run. Steadying myself, I spot Courtney making her way out of the elevator. As I push through the crowd, Sam slams into me, apologizes without even looking to see whose bones she might have broken, and continues yelling at Charlie, flailing her arms around like a diva pissed off that her agent isn't earning her enough money. If the music weren't so loud, I'm sure Sam and Charlie would be making quite a scene. I wonder with a sick thrill what they're fighting about and kick myself for falling prey to the worst type of schadenfreude—at the expense of my friends. I scold myself and grab Court by the bony shoulder.

"You're here!" I say.

"Not just me!" she says with an ethereal grin.

I follow her eyes toward the bar and see Brad's familiar poofy head making its way toward us. "Oh my God!" I scream.

Brad hands two beers to Courtney and picks me up and twirls me around. "Nice dress," he says.

"You can have it," says Courtney.

"Really?"

"I never wear it," she says. I hug her and ask Brad what the hell he's doing here.

"I missed my girls," he says with a grin. "I couldn't wait for Court to come to me. I had to prove my love with a grand gesture."

"Guess what!" Courtney says, bouncing. "I'm going on tour with Brad!"

I squint at her quizzically.

"Court's going to look into getting someone to cover her summer school class so she can come on tour with me. I've only got another couple months, so it shouldn't be hard."

"Shut up!" I squeal, relieved that they've decided to stay together.

"This being-apart thing clearly isn't working for us," Brad says, putting his arm around her shoulder. "I'm a miserable wretch without her." Court smiles and leans into his chest. "I start to lose touch with the things that are important to me. In a perfect world, Court will get knocked up immediately—" I drop my jaw and throw Court an expression of "Wait a sec—you said he didn't want kids," and she smiles back at me in an expression of "Of course he did, he just needed me to remind him."

"I'll be the fattest groupie in the history of groupies!" she says.

"Woo-hoo!" I say, swaying my hips drunkenly to the music.

"You know, Jacquie, my wife is a very silly lady," Brad says. "Doesn't she realize that's what love is? You come with me, I go with you. We're in it together. Know what I'm sayin'? Even the things I do for me are really about you, baby. We're in it."

"Oh God, I feel a song coming on," I say.

Brad hits me on the head. I spin around and notice Steve and Jeremy making out on the dance floor and Alicia flirting with DJ No Personality. It all makes me dizzy.

"My sister is so not ready to settle down," I shout.

"She's finding herself," Courtney says. "She's going to be fine, Jacquie. You just have to accept that your little sister is on a different schedule than you are."

"You're right," I say. Alicia is never going to wash my dishes. She's never going to call to let me know she's alive after a night of urban escapades. And she probably won't choose one man, one job, one city until she's forty-two. And that's fine for her. I guess I need to stop playing worried big sister and let her be.

I jump when someone grabs me from behind and swing around to see Anthony, all smiles. I'm surprised that he's here; he told me he had a meeting tonight. He hands me a beer and kisses me on the mouth.

"Oh God, don't know if I need another one," I say. "Feeling a bit woozy. Anthony, you remember Courtney, and this is Brad, Courtney's husband. Brad, Anthony, my boyfriend." Brad winks at me and they shake hands. I down my beer.

"Great to meet you, man," Anthony says. "Love your stuff."

"Thanks, thanks a lot."

As Anthony babbles to Courtney and Brad about how excited he is that we're back together, while checking his blinking phone to see who's calling him and scoping out the room to see who he knows, I can no longer hear what he's saying. Through a boozy haze, I watch his ridiculously sexy lips moving over his adorably crooked teeth as his words become a rumbling, a foreign language, static. He reaches over and takes my hand in his and raises it to his mouth to kiss my knuckle. I swell at his affection, as I always swell at his affection, so infrequent, so unexpected, like finding a twenty-dollar bill in my coat pocket when it's raining and my wallet's empty and I need cab fare home. If he were always this loving, always around, would I still want him? The party blurs as I ask myself whether Anthony loves me. How can he? He doesn't even really know me, yet he is making an effort. He's here, talking to my friends, blowing off a meeting, being the boyfriend I've wanted him to be. So what is my problem? It's as if I am sitting here waiting for him to mess up.

"Anthony?" I interrupt. When he doesn't respond, I raise my voice. "Anthony! I have to talk to you." The three of them turn toward me. I wave at the happy couple as I steer Anthony through the crowd. I don't want to talk here, so I lead him by the hand out of the building, down the block. We dodge traffic and race across the highway until we are looking out onto the Hudson River, where he nuzzles my neck and inches his hand up under my dress. We fool around for a while, him fondling my thigh, me sitting on the railing, tugging him toward me with my legs.

"Anthony," I whisper, grabbing his hand. "Anthony, do you love me?"

"Of course I do," he says, kissing my fingers one by one.

"You don't really know me very well," I say. "I know that's my fault, I mean, there are things I kept from you, but sometimes it's like you don't want to know more."

"That's crazy," he says.

"Since we've been together, I never see my friends or go out for work or do yoga."

"You do yoga?"

"Obsessively."

"Oh shit." He laughs. "Well, yeah, I guess you're right, but I'm looking forward to getting to know you better."

"So why do you love me then?" I ask, jumping down from the railing.

"Because you're hot," he says. "Kidding! We have fun together and you're smart and sexy and you get my work and love my dog and make me laugh."

"I don't know," I say, looking off into the night, trying to figure out what the hell I'm trying to express to him. "I just think sometimes that I've been trying to turn you into someone you're not. I mean, I love so many things about you, but I haven't really been happy, which is weird because you are exactly what I want in a man." I look down, suddenly ashamed, and add quietly, "Or what I thought I wanted." I look up at him. "My fear is that I liked you so much I didn't take the time to really look at you or us and figure out if we were right for each other. It's like we're both in love with love and were so happy to find this person who fit the fantasy."

I don't know where these words are coming from. I've certainly never thought them, not consciously at least. "You let me down a lot," I say. "You love your work and don't really care that much about mine, and some people don't need a boyfriend who wants to read their articles or ask how their day was or get excited about fixing up a house so it looks like a place where both people live, but I guess I'm somebody who needs a lot of attention, who needs to be adored."

"I adore you," he says softly, with such a sad expression that I think I might dissolve into a puddle, like Amélie did after letting the man of her dreams walk out of her world without telling him that she loved him. "Look, Jacquie, I thought a lot over the last couple of days. I know I'm gone a lot and it's been hard and we fight and stuff, but I'm aware of that and I want it to be different. I'm really trying. I love you, I want to get to know you better, I want us to get to know each other better. Shit, I'm putting myself on the line here." His cell phone rings and he takes it out of his pocket, flips it open, looks to see who's calling, opens his mouth as if to apologize for taking the call, then apparently changes his mind, silences the phone, closes it, and puts it back into his pocket.

He really is making an effort.

So what is wrong with me? I start to cry and Anthony reaches out to comfort me.

"What's wrong, Jacquie?"

"Anthony, I think I fell in love with a version of you that I thought I could turn you into, the one who would take me into consideration and be interested in my life and include me in his, some future Anthony I thought I could force you to become. But that's not fair, it's not who you are." Who the hell am I? This isn't me talking. This couldn't be thirty-two-year-old, unmarried Jacqueline Stuart. Anthony isn't a guy you dump. Anthony is a guy you walk off into the sunset with, happily ever after, fade to black, cue generic classic love song covered by nineteen-year-old pop star. Who am I channeling? Courtney, who just two days ago told me that Anthony might not be The Guy? Joanne Love, advising strong women nationwide to hold out for the man with whom you can "truly be the version of you that you love the best"? Certainly not my mother, who, if she were here, would bang me over the head with a wrought-iron frying pan she just happens to have in her purse and apologize to this tall, handsome, potential son-in-law for my brief lapse in sanity. I just can't fathom where these strange, unrehearsed words are coming from.

Here is Anthony, beautiful Anthony, saying he loves me, saying he wants to make it work, promising that it will be different. And I am making all kinds of excuses, telling him all the things that are wrong with us. Fighting him as if I know some secret. What's going on? Am I the commitment-phobe that Alicia accuses me of being? Am I so scared of love that I'm willing to let another wonderful man out of my life just to avoid having to commit? I start crying harder, my chest racked with sobs.

The truth is simple. I am a simple creature, an Aries woman, baby of the zodiac, wide-eyed, trusting, basic in my desires, transparent of emotion, with the rudimentary needs of a child. I do know what I want. I know what I need. And no matter how often I choose to doubt it when it serves my purposes, my gut never fails me.

"Anthony, I'm so sorry," I sputter through my tears. I take a moment to breathe regularly again. "I . . ." I look into his sad, blue eyes, wanting so desperately not to hurt him. But I don't have any choice. "I don't love you."

He looks down at his hands.

"You're a confused girl, Jacquie," he says, hitting the railing hard with his fist.

"No," I say. "I'm not confused. I am sorry and so sad, but I am pretty clear about this."

"Fuck," he says, pounding the railing with his fist. I put my hand on top of his, and he tugs it away before turning to walk silently down the dark, empty path toward the highway to hail a cab.

I look into the water at the glimmer of the city reflected in its blackness as hot tears spill down my cheeks, for Anthony's pain and for mine, for yet another love lost. As I get older, breaking up becomes more and more terrifying. I know that every time I leave someone, I'm upping the ante, announcing to myself and the world that I am confident that someone better for me exists out there. But I am not confident at all. I am throwing myself into the abyss.

Suddenly all I want is to be in my apartment. I know it's a cold, black, dank hole these days, but it's still my home. The home I should never have left. I wonder if I can sleep there, find a dry corner. I know it won't be very comfortable, but I really just want to go home.

I start walking back to the party. After dragging myself for a minute, I begin to run—like a bandit with the heat on my tracks, which is not easy to do in three-inch heels. By the time I collide with the crowd spilling onto the sidewalk and see Steve and Jeremy getting into the only cab on the block together, I'm done with the shoes and pull them off. I keep running, but have to glue my eyes to the ground to avoid broken glass and rusty nails, and I smash into Sam, who's stomping angrily down the street with Charlie limping after her. I wonder if she kicked him in the shin— or the balls. She glares at me and keeps stomping. My sister is passionately kissing DJ Boring against the door of a gallery across the street. I imagine she'll crash at Jake's place tonight. I stand in the middle of the street, cushioned by the balmy air, for a moment before taking off sprinting again.

When I reach Fourteenth Street, I admit to myself that I cannot run any longer. Craning my neck for a cab, I see a crosstown bus coming. I jump on, greeted by a frigid air-conditioned gust, and collapse, winded, into a solo seat on the left side of the bus, jiggling my left leg over my right into the aisle as the city drifts past—fast food, dive bars, the all-night bustle of the Meatpacking District. I look at my reflection in the window, my hair pulled up on top of my head, makeup long gone, face calm, even the little wrinkle usually visible between my brows at peace. I rub my goose-pimpled arms for warmth and wipe smudged mascara off the skin under my bottom lashes and focus again on the passing city. I love New York so much, I could make out with it. I look at the front of the bus, suddenly aware that we've been immobile for a while, impatient that we're only at Seventh Avenue. When an insistent clanging indicates that the driver will be lowering the front steps to allow a disabled person to board, I lose it.

"Oh my God!" I announce too loudly, shoving through the standing passengers and banging out the back door, swooning into the caress of hot air that catches me as I burst from the icy bus. Now I run as fast as I can again, waving my arms around, hoping to catch a cab. They're all full of passengers, their extinguished call lights taunting me. I'm contemplating hitching when I miraculously spy a taxi spitting a raucous foursome into the street. A man in a steel-gray suit and I leap at the back door at the exact same time, but I am a woman with a mission and he sees "don't even consider it, buddy" all over me and demurs, stepping backward and bowing his head.

"Eleventh Street and Avenue A, please," I tell the driver, now zipping past Urban Outfitters, cheap shoe shops, discount lighting emporiums, gyms, 99-cent stores, Diesel, Whole Foods, Union Square, Virgin Megastore, Trader Joe's. I'm bouncing up and down on the cheap vinyl seat. We can't get there fast enough. I hide my face in my arms as we screech to a halt behind a tow truck making a left turn onto Third Avenue, telling myself to breathe, dammit, breathe, breathe, breathe. Finally we're whizzing down Avenue A, by the cigarette-smoking crowd outside a chic Asian place on my left, a woman talking and gesticulating wildly to herself on the right. For a minute I think she's crazy, despite her slender hips and good haircut. I stare at her over my shoulder, mystified as she shrinks behind me, until it hits me that she's deep in conversation with another person on the other end of her phone. I had forgotten cell phones existed for a second. It occurs to me that I know exactly which charming two-bedroom in Park Slope I'll be sleeping in while my apartment's in rehab and start to laugh, feeling a bit crazy myself, hopping out onto the crowded street nearly hysterical.

I run toward my apartment, fast, hard, till I'm out of breath and sweating and feeling like Bridget Jones racing to catch Colin Firth in my underwear or any number of starlets running breathlessly through airports and train stations to stop the love of their lives from zooming off to a new life on the opposite coast. But I am alone, racing only to get home. The air around me warms my damp skin like a furnace as I unlock the front door to my building and jet up my stairs. When I push the door open, my apartment is completely black and it smells bad. I feel completely let down. I stand in the doorway and wonder what the hell I expected anyway. A surprise party?

I drop my bag in the hallway outside the front door and slowly enter my apartment, the door clicking shut behind me. By the time I'm halfway through the dark hallway, I'm deflated and acutely aware of the fact that I have nothing—no boyfriend, no apartment, no life. As I'm standing there paralyzed by self-pity, a rustling on the other side of the room startles me and I scream.

"Jacquie?"

I hear the scratch of a match, the whir of a flame, and a candle is lit, illuminating Zach, the cute hardware-store boy. I never noticed he was a leftie before. He looks disheveled, bundled in his faded jean jacket that's lined in lamb's wool. He lights another candle. He hasn't shaved in days and the stubble on his face is the amber color of maple syrup with sunlight shining through the bottle. His eyes are sleepy, a very pale blue like the sky when wispy white clouds are floating past. I'm ashamed of myself for thinking in such mushy metaphors. Steve would never stand for that crap in the magazine.

"Hey," Zach says.

I slowly approach as he pushes himself up to a seated position. "Zach," I say, breathing in sharply. "You're still here."

"I fell asleep."

I look around at the candlelit furniture he's dragged back in from the roof, the garbage bags, the beautifully sanded bookshelves standing incongruously in the middle of the hollow shell of the home I loved so much. I can't think of one thing to do to start making it better.

"What can I do?" I ask him. "Give me a project."

"It's the middle of the night," he says.

I look at him in a way that says, "What's your point?"

"You could rub my hand," he says. "It's sore from all the sanding."

"Okay," I say shyly and lower myself in front of him to sit on my heels. My knees hit the cold, dusty floor. Zach stretches out his left hand toward me. I turn it over and rub his palm firmly with my thumbs, working the flesh between the small bones of the front of his hand with my other fingers. The skin there is surprisingly soft, so different from his rough, calloused palms. I feel my face flush and glance up at him to see if he noticed. He smiles. I'm thankful for the fan sending cool air at me from the corner.

"You're good at that," he says. My heart pounds on my rib cage, reminding me of its existence. He gives me his other hand, which is bloodied and scraped across two knuckles.

"Oh my God," I say.

"I forgot about that."

I grab one of the candles and make my way into the bathroom, where I manage to find a tin first-aid kit, with Band-Aids and a bottle of alcohol inside. I grab a paper towel from the kitchen on my way back and look at Zach sitting patiently Indian-style watching me. With his hair sticking up he looks about twelve.

"You're an Aries, aren't you?" I ask.

He nods. "How did you know?" I shake my head and kneel down to clean up his hand.

"Hey, what are you doing here?" Zach asks once I'm done putting alcohol on the wound.

"I broke up with my boyfriend," I say, feeling like I might cry again.

Zach reaches out to touch my shoulder and I pull away from him, pushing myself up and moving to the other side of the room.

"I'm sorry," Zach says, standing up to take the Band-Aid that I hold out in his direction. We're silent for a minute as he puts it on his cut. Then he says, "I guess he was that guy you were fighting with in the street the other day at the fire, huh? He wasn't good enough for you anyway."

"What?" I snap. "Who the hell are you, Zach, to judge me or Anthony? You don't know him. You don't even know me. You're just some guy who's fucking Serena."

"What?" he says, rushing over, inches from me, his cheeks flushed. "Serena's my sister."

"Your sister?" I choke, my face and chest getting hot. His sister? Serena and Zach brother and sister? I feel totally thrown.

"What the hell?" I say. "Oh my God, I can't believe you . . . Why didn't anyone tell me?"

"I assumed you knew," he says. "Wow. God. I figured you knew."

I look around me at the bookshelves, the backsplash, the books he so carefully stacked. "Why did you do all this? I mean, I thought you were a couple, I thought you were doing this to impress Serena."

Zach shifts from leg to leg and then turns to his left so I'm looking at his profile. It's delicate, like a child's. He stares at the little window in my kitchen as if thinking very seriously about what I just asked.

"Shit, Jacquie, I did it for you. Isn't that obvious?" He turns and looks at me, then glances down at the ground in front of me. "I mean, I still remember the first time you came into the store. It was, like, seven or eight years ago. You'd just moved into your first apartment in the neighborhood and you needed a screwdriver. I got you our best-seller, eleven in one for sixteen ninety-five. You were so excited. I wasn't working there yet. It was before my dad died and I was still in school, studying to become an architect, but I'd help out on weekends. My dad came over and put together this whole toolbox for you, and you were . . ." He clears his throat and glances at me for a second. "I don't know, you were just . . . you did this thing where you'd, like, bounce and get all your hair in your hands and put it on top of your head, and then you'd take it back down. I couldn't stop watching you—you were, I don't know, pretty, alive, and I liked how you treated Buster." He laughs nervously. "I'm surprised you didn't notice all these years."

He's standing very straight now, with his arms running awk-wardly down his sides, looking at his feet again.

"Oh my God," I say.

"I've pretty much always had a girlfriend," he says. "I was with one girl I lived with for almost five years."

"Serial monogamy," I say.

"I guess some people would call it that. I think my ex called it that, but whatever, it never felt right." He's silent for a moment, but I don't say anything.

"When my sister sublet this apartment and it turned out to be yours," he says, "I thought maybe it was fate. This will sound stu-pid, but I thought maybe on some level I had been waiting for you. And now look . . ."

I force my eyes away from him and scan the destruction around us. My throat tightens. I lean against the refrigerator and slowly let my body glide down until I'm sitting on the cold floor. I don't know what to do with this information. Zach sits next to me. He's wearing his soft jacket that smells like leather and grass.

"Where are you staying?" I ask him.

"With my sister."

"When is she getting married?"

"Next weekend."

"Who is she marrying?" I ask.

"Rory," we both say at the same time.

"Of course," I say. "I'm so happy for her."

"Me too," he says. "I always liked Rory, and he really loves her."

"You know, I never got to see my bathroom painted pink."

"I was skeptical, but it looked great," he says.

And with that the handsome love interest—the soft-spoken, sweet guy in the wings whom the audience has been rooting for all along—leans over and kisses me, softly, as if he's been waiting to kiss me all his life.

"What are we doing?" I ask after a moment's sweet kissing. "You're the guy who burned down my apartment."

"I'm the guy who's helping you rebuild it."

"Have you ever seen *Grease 2*?" I ask.

"Tell me you don't like *Grease 2*," he says.

"I love *Grease 2*," I say defensively.

"First *One Steamy Summer* and now *Grease 2*? And here I had you figured for an intellectual snob," he says, shaking his head.

"I am totally an intellectual snob!" I say. "*Grease 2* is a cult classic, so bad it's brilliant. It launched Michelle Pfeiffer's career." Zach smiles at me and I smile back at him. "I was just thinking this is kind of a *Grease 2* moment. You know, you're the sweet, shy guy who was always nice to me at the hardware store and then I find out you're also the cool, hunky fixing-up-my-apartment guy I've secretly had a crush on for months." I blush wantonly. "You have no idea what I'm talking about."

" 'You were the one who went in my dreams and I never knew it?' " he says, quoting *Grease 2* lyrics, blushing back at me.

"Oh wow, a closet fan."

"I've watched it too many times with my sister," he says.

"'I wanted to tell you time and again but I couldn't do it,'" I sing quietly.

"Don't get me started," he says. "I do a mean 'Cool Rider.'"

I hold an imaginary mike to my mouth and continue to sing, more loudly now. "'All that you are is all that I need, no more pretending. Now I can be me and you can be you and we're never-ending, whooooaah....'" I'm embarrassed—it sounds like a declaration of love. There's no way I can sing the next line: "'We'll be together, always together/Like birds of a feather, for ever and ever/We'll be together.'"

I don't know if it's too brazen or just too bad.

Zach laughs, because he's hearing the lines playing in his head, too, and puts his hands on either side of my face. "It's much more a Clark Kent/Superman moment than *Grease 2*."

I'm so happy he's not sleeping with Serena. Ew, he's her brother.

When he pulls me tightly against him and kisses me again, I feel high. I have an urge to scream, to sing cheesy love songs at the top of my lungs. It's this amazing kiss that makes my head spin. I'm going with it and not thinking, allowing my hands to take their own initiative, wandering through his baby-soft hair, over his broad shoulders and back. I can't believe I'm kissing Zach the cute hardware-store boy, who burned down my apartment, and getting soot all over my dress. I almost start laughing as I imagine our clothes starting to fly off, Courtney's pretty green dress that's now mine landing in an elegant heap on my lumpy, damp floor. That is what's going to happen, right? I mean, it is time to lose the clothes. Right? That's what usually happens in my life anyway. In the movie version. But suddenly my mind kicks in and I abruptly stop kissing Zach.

I pull away and hold him at arm's length, breathing quickly. His face is flushed. His eyes are gentle. He softly lets his hands drop and says, "Jacquie, I'm right here."

He looks right into my eyes as he says it and I know that he's telling the truth. For some reason, I think about dropping my bag on the floor by the door when I come home at night. It's my bag and my door and my floor and I know it will still be there in the morning.

I used to have this thing in college. I thought if I could only sleep with a guy, it would all be okay. Then I thought if I could only sleep with him more than once, two times, three times, then for sure it would mean something to him and he'd stay. But to make him stay, I would become this desperate girl doing everything in my power to get him to sleep with me, calling in the middle of the night, pleading, running my fingers suggestively along his forearm when we ran into each other on campus, reminding him how much he should love me. But I wouldn't be me anymore, just this well of desperation, and that would be just the thing to send him looking for the next girl.

In the movie version, Zach would gently remove my clothes and we would make perfect love. In real life, when he kisses me again, it occurs to me that we've got tomorrow to kiss and the next day and the one after that. I purr, a sort of sexpot moan that lets him know I love the feeling of his lips on mine, his tongue in my mouth, his soft stubble rubbing against my cheeks and chin, his arms around my waist, his pelvis, thighs, chest pressed against mine. I take his bottom lip between my teeth and let it go again, before pushing his chest lightly away from me with one hand.

"Zach, do you want to get something to eat?" I say. "I need something in my stomach to soak up all this tequila."

"Yeah," he says, with a shy laugh. "I haven't eaten since lunch. I'm starving."

He touches his lips to mine again lightly, letting the tip of his tongue linger for just a second, sending a jolt of electricity through me that lands squarely between my thighs. I am such a slut. I ignore an impulse to rip his clothes from his body and wrestle him to the floor, and instead stand up and smooth my brand-new green dress, as cheesy *Grease 2* lyrics dance through my head. Zach crosses the whole room in three wide, handsome strides and kneels down to blow out the candles on the floor, smiling up at me before the room goes black. Then he stands again and finds me with his hands in the dark.

Wrapping his arms around me, he says, "Welcome home, Jacquie."

Outside, I hear the sounds of the East Village: the laughter of the smokers huddled outside the bar across the street, sirens wailing in the distance, a motorcycle showing off on Avenue A. Somewhere a girl cries out with unadulterated joy. Somewhere a car alarm shrieks its irritation into the night. Somewhere a dog barks, maybe Larry, and another, maybe the neighbors' ferocious Yorkie, joins in his serenade. Enveloped in complete darkness, Zach takes my hand and we find our way through my damaged apartment that we are going to repair. I push the door open, and we stand facing my bright hallway, blinking side by side, fingers entwined, dazzled by the light.